A COLLECTION OF FAVORITE STORIES

from *Light Magazine*

Published by
RABBI YEHOSHUA LEIMAN z"l

Copyright © 2015 by Israel Bookshop Publications

ISBN 978-1-60091-401-0

All rights reserved. No part of this book may be reproduced or transmitted in any form or by any means (electronic, photocopying, recording or otherwise) without prior permission of the publisher.

Book design by: Rivkah Lewis

Published by:
Israel Bookshop Publications
501 Prospect Street
Lakewood, NJ 08701

Tel: (732) 901-3009
Fax: (732) 901-4012
www.israelbookshoppublications.com
info@israelbookshoppublications.com

Printed in the United States of America

Distributed in **Israel** by:
Shanky's
Petach Tikva 16
Jerusalem
972-2-538-6936

Distributed in **Australia** by:
Gold's Book and Gift Company
3-13 William Street
Balaclava 3183
613-9527-8775

Distributed in **Europe** by:
Lehmanns
Unit E Viking Industrial Park
Rolling Mill Road,
Jarrow, Tyne & Wear NE32 3DP
44-191-406-0842

Distributed in **South Africa** by:
Kollel Bookshop
Ivy Common
107 William Road, Norwood
Johannesburg 2192
27-11-728-1822

מעט מן האור דוחה הרבה מן החושך

*A little of the **LIGHT** dispels much of the darkness.*

*T*HE STORIES IN this volume all appeared in *Light Magazine*. *Light Magazine* was an independent, groundbreaking, English-language, *frum* magazine that delighted and informed readers from 1970 to 1982.

Light Magazine was conceived and published by Yehoshua Leiman, *z"l*, a master editor and translator. The magazine contained not only stories but also translations of many important *hashkafic* articles by such *gedolim* as Rav Aharon Kotler *zt"l*, Rav Shimshon R. Hirsch *zt"l*, and Rav Shraga Feivel Mendlowitz *zt"l*. In its pages could also be found eye-opening accounts of Jewish history and current events of the time.

To obtain available back issues of Light Magazine, please contact the Leiman Family at mitemar99@gmail.com.

Contents

How Rav Chaim Brisker Saved Georgian Jewry 1
Dance in the Dark 7
"Leizer! Remember!" 11
The Grand Inquisitor of Madrid 16
The Count's Purse 22
Fiesta at Aranjuez 29
Zman Simchaseinu in Death's Shadow 38
Reverie 44
The Search 49
Unexpected Evidence 53
Only One Way to Go 61
The Demonstration 69
Evolution of a Theory 74
The Telltale Bribes 84
The Great Cold 92
Treasure Hunt 97
Boris Ivanov's Seder 104
The Genuine Article 112
Mordechai's "Religious" Education 117
A Pinch of Snuff 124
Yetzer Hara to Retire? 130
The Winning Loser 134

Three Broken Legs 142
In Her Husband's Place 147
Payoff in Padua 152
"Anyone Can Make a Match" 164
A Pogrom in Lodz 176
To Ask the Chafetz Chaim 186
Six Magic Words 191
The Price of a Mitzvah 198
Never Despair! 206
The Angel 226
The Benefit and the Doubt 232
Rain 243
Specialist 251
A Political Lecture 255
One Moment 260
A Little Bird Told Me 288
Forgery 297
The Blind Fiddler 304
The Price 307
Audit 313
The Stranger 325
Two Disguises 338
Rush Hour 342

SHEINDEL WEINBACH

*Is truth stranger than fiction? You're not sure?
Then read this fantastic but true story.*

How Rav Chaim Brisker Saved Georgian Jewry

"You've got to drop everything, Ilana. I've got a *ma'aseh* to tell you."

I look at the clock. He's half an hour late already, the rice is about to burn, the soup is boiling over, Laibi has one foot over the high chair, and Yehudis, her nose running away with her, is tugging at my skirt trying to tell me something; probably that her nose is running. And I'm supposed to drop everything and listen to a *ma'aseh*. Not that I don't like *ma'aselach*; don't get me wrong, *chas v'shalom*. I was put to bed on *ma'aselach* for a good quarter of my life.

"*Nu, vos far a ma'aseh?* A story about the Kedushas Levi, maybe?"

"No, Ilana. Sit down a minute. I want you to hear this."

"About Reb Velvel?" I ask, still absentmindedly. "Reb Chaim?"

"No, no, Ilana. Sit down now and listen to this. It's a true story."

"And the others are fairy tales, maybe?"

"Forget the wisecracks. This one is really *moiradig*. You'll flip when you hear it. It happened just this morning in the *beis medrash*."

Well, I can't resist a *moiradige ma'aseh* for too long. Guess it goes back to my childhood. And I'd better sit down if I'm going to flip. I'll turn the fires off and let the food get cold. It won't catch pneumonia.

"Okay, Moishe. I'm just *chalishing* to hear your *moiradige ma'aseh* already."

"Well, it started off in the morning. When I get to the *beis medrash* there sits an old man with a long beard. He's in a corner, all by himself, looking into a Gemara."

"*Nu*, what's so unusual about that? Like you never saw an old man in a white beard looking into a *sefer* before? What do you do in the *beis medrash* yourself every day, anyway?"

"I know, I know, but you don't see. He was the only old man in the *beis medrash*. The rest of us are *yungeleit*. Have a little patience, for goodness sake, and let me get on with the story. Well, I settled down with my *chavrusa* and started *seder*. About an hour later, we got stuck on a *sugya*. I had to look something up in a Rambam and there I see the same Yid in the same corner. He hadn't budged. Comes eleven thirty, there he is still, sitting and learning. When one o'clock rolls around we're all closing shop and there he sits, just like before. I couldn't help staring. Just then he looks up and beckons. I was sort of waiting to get a chance to *chap* a shmooze with him, so I hurried over.

"'*Ich hub a kasheh oif di Gemara*,' he tells me. That's as good an introduction as any Yid can desire.

"I listen and give him a *terutz*.

"Then my *chavrusa* interrupts. Well, before you could say Bava Kamma, the old man was firing out *sevaros* and quoting a Gemara here and another there. And we took him up and argued back and forth, amazed at how much he knew. The *beis medrash* was empty and our voices got louder and louder. You know how it is."

"Uh huh, I know. I know how many suppers have gotten cold over *shvera sugyos*. Not that I mind, really."

"Finally the dust settles. The old man closes his Gemara and gets up.

"'*Mistom* this is the Chevroner *beis medrash*,' he remarks casually."

"Very funny, Moishe. Why, any *cheder yingel* can tell the difference between a Chevroner and a Brisker. Who was this old guy kidding?"

"You can say that again. It hit us like a bombshell. We just stared at him blankly for a long while. Who was he kidding? And who was he anyway?

"'*Fun vannet kumt a Yid?*' one of us finally asked. He just made with his hand. You know. We asked again and he said he lived in Givat Mordechai. No one had to tell us he hadn't been born there! We asked him whatever made him think that this was Chevron.

"'I know Chevron is building a new *beis medrash* near where I live. I just figured this was the old one. Everyone's heard about the Chevroner Yeshivah in Yerushalayim!' He looked around helplessly at our unbelieving faces.

"'But Reb Yid, there is more than one *beis medrash* in Yerushalayim!'

"'Yes?' His eyes lit up. '*Baruch Hashem*. This is the first chance I had since I came here to take a walk and find me a place to learn,' he explained apologetically. 'You know how it is,' he looked from face to face for reassurance, 'coming from another country, settling down, fixing up a household…'"

"*Ribono shel Olam*, where was he from?"

"'*Fun vannet kumt a Yid?*' I asked again.

"Again he made an impatient motion with his arm and parried with a question of his own, 'Well, which *beis medrash* is this if it isn't the Chevroner Yeshivah?'

"'*Dos iz der Brisker beis medrash, Reb Yid.*'

"'*Der Brisker beis medrash!!!*'

"The old man's face paled to match his beard. He swayed but we quickly supported him. He sat down slowly, all shaken. What had shocked him so suddenly? Our thoughts of lunch disappeared with the buses we had missed. We crowded around the old man, hoping to discover some clue to the mystery.

"'*Der Brisker beis medrash!*' he exclaimed again. '*In Yerushalayim! Zogt mir shnell, Reb Chaim lebt noch?*'

"We were astonished. 'No, Reb Chaim left us many years ago. In Europe still.'

"'*Reb Velvel…Reb Velvel lebt?*'

"'No,' again we informed him. 'Reb Velvel was *niftar* twelve years ago.'

"We just couldn't figure it out. Here was a Yid who obviously knew how to learn, who had heard about — had probably known — Reb Chaim and Reb Velvel. Yet he took it for granted that there was only one yeshivah in *Yerushalayim Ir Hakodesh*. *Ribono shel Olam!* Where had he been the last fifty years? Asleep in a cave?

"The old man continued breathlessly, 'Reb Velvel left children behind?'

"'Yes.'

"'Do they live here?'

"'Yes, Reb Dovid lives not far away!'

"'Take me to him! Take me there quick. I must see Reb Chaim's *einikel*.' He got up and grabbed my arm. That's how I got elected to take him to Reb Dovid. When we got there I told the *rebbetzin* that I had brought an old Yid who desperately wanted to see Reb Dovid.

"She looked doubtful at first. Reb Dovid usually rests after lunch.

"'Tell him the Gruzhiner Yid is here,' the old man announced emotionally.

"She shrugged her shoulders slightly but dutifully went to call Reb Dovid.

"'Dovid,' she knocked softly, 'The Gruzhiner Yid is here.'

"'The Gruzhiner Yid? Which Gruzhiner Yid?'

"Well, he came out anyway and the old man ran forward to kiss his hands. 'Do you know who I am?' he exclaimed. He made it sound like Mashiach's right-hand man. '*Ich bin Der Gruzhiner Yid.*'

"Well, it seems this announcement had no significance for Reb Dovid. At best he wondered how *a*, or pardon, *the* Gruzhiner Yid knew Yiddish, Georgia being separated from Brisk by thousands of miles of mountains, deserts, rivers and maybe even a sea or two, for all he knew.

"'I'll tell you who I am,' the old man began. 'I came to Brisk when I was fourteen years old. That was over seventy-three years ago. Reb Chaim saw me then and said that I must stay in his home and study with him. He said that I was the salvation of Georgian Jewry. No one knew then what he was talking about, much less myself, but I stayed by him for almost twenty years. He gave me *chinuch* like a son and I will never forget him. He arranged for me to have *shimush* in *hora'ah* by the Brisker *dayan*, Rav Simcha Zelig Riger.

"'When World War I came along I went back home to Georgia. Then came the Russian Revolution. We had no contact with the outside world, we didn't hear of Brisk anymore, or of Reb Chaim, or of his son, Reb Velvel. We dared not imagine what had happened to them during the two World Wars.

"'During this time I became the chief rabbi of the capital city of Georgia while my brother was appointed chief rabbi of all the Georgian Jews. The years I had spent by Reb Chaim gave me strength to survive the difficult periods after the Revolution and during the strict regime of Stalin. I kept *Yiddishkeit* burning in the families of my *kehillah*, and gave them the courage to stick together in the face of Russian atheism. But now, thank G-d, we were *zocheh* to bring our *kehillah* to *Artzeinu Hakedoshah*. Here, I hope, my brother and I will continue to serve the *Ribono shel Olam*. But it is all thanks to your grandfather.' Here, as he kissed Reb Dovid's hand again feelingly, his tears fell and glistened like jewels. 'Only thanks to him were we able to survive at all. How can I ever repay you? Do you know now who I am? My name is Moshe Debrashvili, and my brother is Yaakov Debrashvili.'"

Editor's Note: Rabbi Yaakov Debrashvili was the chief rabbi of the Georgian Jews in Eretz Yisrael.

S.M. LIEDER

Jewry, half-asleep in galus, *rouses itself on Pesach to make our Father in Heaven happy with a*

Dance in the Dark

His preparations for the Seder complete, the Shpoler Zeide looked up. That was the signal for his youngest son. "*Kadesh*," he piped. "When Tatte comes home from shul on Pesach night, he must make Kiddush immediately."

The Shpoler's mellow gaze held the child's eyes patiently, expectantly. But the boy clearly had nothing to add.

"Why don't you finish?"

"What do you mean?" the child was perplexed.

"Don't you know the rest of *Kadesh*?"

"For *Kadesh*? There isn't any more."

"You mean your *rebbi* didn't tell you any more? Or did you forget?"

"No, Tatte, I didn't forget. The *rebbi* didn't tell us any more."

"Then I'll teach you the whole thing: *Kadesh* — When the father comes home from shul on Pesach night, he must make

Kiddush immediately so that the children shouldn't fall asleep and should ask *Mah Nishtanah*."

The child repeated the words with the same melody his father had used, and the Seder at the Shpoler's had begun.

ଓଧ୍ୟ

Duvid'l Melamed knew that the Zeide would have something to say to him sooner or later about the missing piece from *Kadesh*. But he wasn't expecting it late that same Pesach afternoon at the *tish*. He started when the rebbe's gentle voice came clearly through. "Duvid'l! Why didn't you teach the *yingelach* the complete traditional reason for *Kadesh*?"

"I felt it was too long for such little ones to memorize. Besides, the *din* applies to every Jew even if he has no children in the house. So the reason is not accurate."

"How can you say the reason is not accurate?!" The closest tone to fury the Shpoler was capable of sent a tingle up the spines of all the chassidim. "Are you wiser than all the *melamdim* for generations back? You have no idea why our forefathers instituted this custom, those exact words. So how do you make a change? Don't ever again change a *minhag kadmonim* for some reason of your own. I'll explain the words to you this time, and you will all realize the folly of tampering with *minhagim*."

ଓଧ୍ୟ

"Rabbi Chiya introduced the *parshah* of Pesach in *Emor*," says the *Zohar* to *Emor*, "with the *passuk* from *Shir Hashirim, I am asleep but my heart is awake*. Jewry says, 'I am asleep in *galus*.'"

We see that the Jews' exile is considered a lower level of living akin to sleeping, for they are constantly in trouble, oppressed, and suffering.

Our forefathers based the introduction used by the children for the Seder on Rabbi Chiya's introduction. "When the father comes home from shul on Pesach night" is an allusion to our Father in Heaven returning to the heights of heaven after Ma'ariv in shul with impoverished Jews suffering from the turbulence of *galus*, with bone-weary Jews exhausted from the toil of preparing for Pesach — all these Jews, He witnessed, came to shul despite their troubles, to *daven*, to sing Hallel to Him enthusiastically, to pour out their hearts before Him. "He must make Kiddush immediately" — He must renew our *kiddushin* to Him (*I betroth you to Me forever — Hoshea* 2:22) and redeem us from *galus* immediately "so that the children should not fall asleep" — so that the Jewish children should not fall deeper into the sleep of *galus* and *chas v'shalom* lose hope of ever being redeemed — "and should ask *Mah Nishtanah*" — in order to be able to ask their Father in Heaven why this *galus* is so much longer and nightmarish than any previous one.

CR80

He burst into tears. Raising his hands heavenward, he implored, "Tatte, Tatte! Redeem us now from this *galus* while our hearts are still awake. Don't let us fall asleep entirely!"

All the chassidim burst into *teshuvah* tears. Long minutes passed while, heads cradled on arms, the entire *olam* wailed like children.

At last the Shpoler lifted his head. "Enough! Now we must make our Tatte happy. Let us show Him that His children can dance in the dark!"

A *niggun* was begun. Voice joined voice. Soon the Shpoler had them all on their feet in an ecstatic, never-ending circle.

YEHUDA L. GIRSHT

"Leizer, Remember!"

His mother's legacy revives a labor camp inmate.

ADAPTED BY SOSY APPEL

THE WIND HOWLED, slapping snow brutally across the courtyard of the Bavarian labor camp. Shouts of "Attention! Stand still!" reverberated in the hollowness of the night.

Straight rows of haggard prisoners leaned close to each other as if for protection and warmth. Their pale faces told of long days spent digging bunkers between iron rails and snow-covered trees. Their bodies, nearly lifeless and numb, spoke of hunger and of destitution as they stood at attention on S.S.-man Hindschell's orders.

Night after night, upon returning tired and hungry, when they trod breathing heavily to their dark and dingy shacks, Hindschell would "amuse" himself for an hour or two. Hindschell, tall, erect, and splendidly dressed, stood composed, his eyes smiling with the manic grace of the cultivated German. He would require the haggard prisoners to move in accordance with his fanatic precision. He always spoke fluently, distinctly, all his movements precise. The prisoners who failed to please him were taken out of line and beaten mercilessly, blood trickling from their wounds till their bodies succumbed. Then Hindschell's eyes would light up, and his smile would widen. The prisoners would return to their shacks to put their wretched bodies to sleep.

Tonight, as the snow fell furiously on the camp, Hindschell kept the prisoners for an hour of his regular amusement.

"Attention! Stand still!" was heard in the stillness of the night. Hindschell's eyes noticed the smallest imprecision in movement, the slightest imperfection in manner.

The prisoners, their feet frozen, tried — oh, how they tried — to stand erect under his gaze. For the first time, Hindschell noticed a wan, sickly youth named Leizer. The hollow-cheeked lad looked lost, staring into the distance as his hands nervously felt for something in his pockets.

The commanding voice was heard distinctly, "What's there?" The boy's face, already pale, turned as white as the snow beneath him. He tried to utter something but could not. "Come out of the line!" the same harsh voice cried again. With tottering knees, Leizer tried to walk, but his shoes got stuck in the snow some distance from Hindschell. He looked from side to side in bewildered hope of a means of escape, and then, at last, faced Hindschell's preying eyes.

"Empty your pockets!" But Leizer's hands could not move. Two S.S. men violently ripped the boy's pocket open and a tiny siddur fell to the ground. The siddur's pages were soiled from much use, and its covers were falling apart.

Hindschell's steel gray eyes blinked in disappointment at the collection of old pages. He had been sure the boy's pocket contained some morsel of rotten food, and had been relishing the prospect of giving a lecture on the magnitude of the crime of theft. Disappointed, Hindschell bit his lower lip. One of the S.S. men handed him the siddur and he looked at the pages filled with Hebrew script. The letters aroused his wrath, and his eyes glittered with sadistic pleasure. "What is this?" he questioned.

Leizer's face had frozen in utter confusion, and his lips could find no answer. He raised his shaking hand to his mouth to indicate prayer. Hindschell's hand suddenly and violently thrust itself upon Leizer's face. A trembling "*Oy vey*" escaped Leizer's lips, and the kick that followed threw him down. A shudder passed through the prisoners standing in silence. Against the background of this silence, a fluent German voice spoke, "This will be your punishment if you continue to bring cursed Jewish books into our German camp."

As Hindschell departed, he ripped out the pages of the siddur and threw them victoriously into the air. The thin bits of paper rose in the wind and scattered in all directions. The moon looked down at them mercifully and gave them its blessing as they flew heavenward. The prisoners returned to their barren shacks.

Leizer was forced to stand at the barbed-wire fence with hands up. He stood bitterly alone in the biting cold of the night. His thin hands held on to the fence, and his mind turned to memories of the past to warm him. Successive pictures of his mother passed through Leizer's mind — as she lit the Shabbos candles, her eyes filled with mercy and kindness, her face lit up with purity and warmth. How his mother had cried when they last parted! He remembered the last day in the ghetto before they were torn apart, and his eyes blurred. His mind was overcome by dizziness.

He recalled that early dawn when all the prisoners were herded into the main street. Men, women, and children pressed against each other with bitter cries of anguish. Mothers held on to their children in despair. Some looked for a last way of escape, but the Germans had planned well and the whole ghetto was surrounded. His father had tried to utter a farewell, but his lips had not obeyed. His mother, with her deep, penetrating eyes, had said something as she placed the small siddur into his hand, "Remember, my son, your mother's last wish. Wherever you go do not forget to say the Shema I once taught you."

He could still see the Germans as they tore his mother away from him, and he could hear once more her last cry, "Leizer! Remember!" Now even that last hope was to be taken from him. He resolved to collect the scattered pages at midnight when everyone would be asleep. He could never forget his mother's last wish.

"Attention!" two S.S. men commanded. Leizer awakened to the reality of ice beneath his shoes and the bitterness of his loss. He faced the two S.S. men and returned upon their command to his room. The prisoners were already sleeping. Leizer turned again to his memories, to the past when he had prayed daily from the little siddur that was so dear to him and which he had kept hidden from the S.S. men beneath his shirt. Why he had forgotten to do so this time he could not remember, nor could he understand. He tried to rest, but his soul gave him no peace. Outside, a silence spread across the camp, and Leizer knew the S.S. men had left.

Beneath the ebony sky, the ground was white with snow. Leizer silently picked up the few torn pages that were yet left. He nearly lost hope when he saw he could not read them. Then, two words clearly imprinted on one of the pages stuck out clearly in the moonlight, "*Shema Yisrael…*"

He now had hope. He would remember. Silently he returned to his shack, and lay upon his board repeating Shema with a softness and purity that angels bore heavenward.

Outside the moon shone brightly.

ISHAYAH MOULENE

The Grand Inquisitor of Madrid

ADAPTED FROM A STORY BY RAV MEIR LEHMANN

IN 5252 (1492), when Isabella the Catholic decreed the cruel expulsion of all the Jews from Spain, that beautiful, fruitful land had a population of half a million Jews. The Jews had been living there well over one thousand years as laborers, farmers, artisans, and doctors. They had established great *yeshivos* that had produced giants of the spirit. And many Jewish families were included in the Spanish nobility.

When the decree of expulsion was promulgated, most of Spain's Jews left the land where their forefathers were buried, their homes and their lands — which no one offered to buy — and set out upon their wanderings in the great world, to suffer sorrow and pain.

Yet there were many Spanish Jews who could not bring themselves to exchange their homes and wealth for the wanderer's staff. They preferred to accept Christianity — or at least so it seemed to everyone. But in secret, in underground hideaways, they maintained their Jewish faith.

These *anusim* lived in constant fear. Often, the wealth of one of these Jews would serve as excuse enough for the Inquisition to have him arrested and burned at the stake. Sometimes even the unfounded report of an enemy was enough to have him sentenced to death.

ଔଃଚ

Peretz Matteira lived in Toledo in 1570. His great-grandfather had been converted to Christianity against his will, but had continued to keep the mitzvos in secret. Peretz was an orphan, an only son, and had inherited a beautiful home with a large vineyard. When Peretz's neighbor desired the vineyard and Peretz refused to sell it, the man had informed the Inquisition that Peretz was a secret Jew. Peretz had good friends inside the Inquisition who warned him in time of the danger ahead, and he escaped a few days before Pesach with all the cash he had in the house.

He decided to go to Madrid, where he hoped to find a place to hide with one of the *anusim* until after Pesach, when he would try to leave the country. But he faced a dangerous problem: He couldn't just walk into any house and ask for hospitality. Such a request might cost him his life.

He walked around the streets early on the morning of his arrival in Madrid — the thirteenth of Nissan — worried. He noticed many farmers' carts bringing produce to market, and he unthinkingly followed them to the marketplace. There he noticed a well-dressed gentleman, accompanied by his servant, going from display to display, buying first lettuce, then horseradish, then celery, and then other vegetables. It struck Peretz that the man might just be a hidden Jew buying the vegetables he needed for Pesach. Then he realized that it might be a coincidence, and the man a devout Catholic who would consider it a sacred obligation to hand a Jew over to the Inquisition.

Though puzzled, Peretz felt he had no choice. He followed the two men to their coach parked a few yards beyond the marketplace and, when they began to ride off, he leaped onto the back of the coach and held on for dear life as the horses raced through the streets and alleyways of Madrid till they pulled up in front of a beautiful estate.

Peretz jumped down and greeted the gentleman as he alighted. "Sir, I have very important information for you. May I speak with you alone?"

The man nodded, and Peretz followed him into the house, up the carpeted marble steps through the art-filled corridor into the gentleman's private study. "What do you want?" he asked.

Tremulously, Peretz declared, "Sir, I saw you buying *maror* for tomorrow night's Seder."

The man turned pale. "Eh?" he retorted angrily. "Are you trying to blackmail me? Or are you planning to inform on me to the Inquisition —"

Peretz burst into tears. "*Chas v'shalom*! I came to find a haven in your house. I'm a homeless *anus*."

At once, the gentleman's face underwent a complete change. He stepped over to Peretz and hugged him. "Welcome, my brother! *Kol dichfin yetei v'yechol*. Join us at our Seder in safety and security."

ଓଽଠ

In a spacious, well-furnished underground chamber, Don Antonio del Banca, his wife Miriam, his daughter Esperanza, and their loyal butler, Alonso, sat down to the Seder table with their guest, Peretz Matteira.

Saddened by their personal helplessness, yet happy that they could at least keep Hashem's mitzvos in secret, they proceeded to fulfill all the mitzvos of the Seder. Don Antonio and Peretz were students of Torah so they livened up their Haggadah recital with a variety of explanations and commentaries. They sang *Nishmas kol chai* and Hallel in which they expressed the unity of the Creator and praised Him. When they had drunk the fourth *kos* and completed the Seder, del Banca was reluctant to terminate the festiveness and kept singing more songs of praise to Hashem.

Abruptly, the singing died. The women screeched and passed out. The men stared ahead of them, shocked, paralyzed with fear. A black-cloaked priest had entered the secret door to the hidden cellar, and stood there, holding a great, golden cross in his right hand: the Grand Inquisitor of Madrid in person.

Don Antonio was the first to regain his speech. He groaned, "Woe! *Ribono shel Olam!* We are the victims of informers!"

"Very true," said the inquisitor in a slow, festive tone. "You unfortunates have been informed upon. Your old nursemaid, Antonio. She died a short while ago, after confessing and revealing the location of the secret cellar in which you practice Judaism. Do you know what penalty awaits you?"

The women began to stir as Don Antonio dully replied, "Death."

"*Death at the stake,*" the priest emphasized each word.

Don Antonio fell at the priest's feet and entreated him, "Your attire identifies you as the Grand Inquisitor of Madrid. Kind sir, have mercy on all these innocent souls. Bring only me before the Inquisition Tribunal. I shall give you my entire fortune. I am extremely wealthy, and have hidden my fortune where no one but I can find it. Have mercy and burn only me."

"No! Never!" cried Dona Miriam. "If you won't have mercy on my husband, take me with him!"

Peretz walked up to the priest. "Generous sir, if you must take a sacrifice, take only me. I am alone in this world. No one will mourn me. I shall be happy to die to save this wonderful family."

Esperanza, too, fell at the priest's feet and begged him to take her instead of her parents.

The old servant, Alonso, too upset to be able to speak, stared entreatingly at the inquisitor, pointing at his own chest to indicate his readiness to die if the priest would only spare the others.

Tears welled up in the Grand Inquisitor's eyes, and he was unable to suppress them. The hand that had been holding the cross dropped to his side, and in a tear-choked voice, he said, "My friends, I shall save you all from death! Sleep in peace tonight. I'll clear you of all suspicion, and placate the Inquisition Tribunal. Tomorrow night, wait for me here after nightfall."

He left as silently and as swiftly as he had come.

꙰

Despite the tension of the long day, Don Antonio began the preparations for the second Seder immediately after Ma'ariv. "If we must die," he said, "let it come while we are fulfilling Hashem's mitzvos."

An hour after sunset, a tall man entered the well-lit secret basement. The Grand Inquisitor removed his cloak to display festive civilian garb, and joined the others at the table.

"My brethren," he addressed the nervous del Bancas and their guest, "I wish you the best of everything. As far as the Inquisition is concerned, I found you all sound asleep last night and, although I did find the secret basement your old nanny described in her confession, you use it as a storeroom for merchandise. I ask no thanks of you other than that you grant my wish to participate in your Seder. I am also an *anus*, a Jew like you — in secret."

Don Antonio was astonished. "Sir!? Are you joking?"

"I'm not in a joking mood tonight. Let me tell you my story in brief: My grandfather, the son of the great *gaon*, Rabbi Moshe del Medigo, was compelled to convert, but in secret remained a determined Jew. When I turned thirteen, he began to teach me Torah. When he was certain that I was strong-minded and strong-willed enough, he asked me to undertake an arduous task — to study for the priesthood in order to infiltrate the Inquisition where I would be in a position to help fellow Jews. 'If you save even one Jew,' he told me, 'your efforts will not have been in vain.' Yesterday I finally achieved my goal — five times over. Now please begin the Seder. It is many years now since I was last able to participate in a Seder."

Don Diego del Medigo turned out to be a very knowledgeable Jew. He, Antonio, and Peretz exchanged *divrei Torah* on the Haggadah. When they reached *Nishmas* they all together recited with tremendous joy and deep *kavanah*, "The soul of every live being will praise Your Name, Hashem, our G-d; and the spirit in every body… Other than You, we have no King Who redeems and rescues…"

AHUVA COHEN

Can you figure out what will happen when the rav *agrees to help in the case of*

The Count's Purse

"Rebbi, Rebbi," cried a frantic voice, accompanied by a loud knocking on the door.

Rav Eliyahu Chaim Meisel of Lodz abruptly stopped his Gemara *niggun* and rushed to the door. He threw it wide open. The man who had been leaning forward to pound the heavy wooden door once more, stumbled forward precipitately and fell into the *rav's* arms.

"Rebbi," demanded the man after he had disentangled himself, "do you always answer the door yourself? Where's your *shamash*?"

"I sent my *shamash* out on an errand. Besides, Moshe Leib," Rav Elya Chaim continued, a smile lurking in the eyes shadowed by thick, graying brows, "did you have to raise such a ruckus just to ask me why my *shamash* didn't come to the door?"

Moshe Leib stared at the *rav* in bewilderment for a moment, then he threw back his head and laughed heartily. "I have to hand it to you, Rebbi," he said. "You always manage somehow to make a Yid forget his troubles, even if it's only for a second. But," his face grew sober, "you are right, of course. I came to you for help. I am involved in some bad trouble, and I thought to myself: who can help me out of this mess? Naturally, I thought of you."

Naturally. No Jew in Lodz thought of anyone else. No matter how small the problem or how immense, Rav Eliyahu Chaim Meisel was the one to go to — for material assistance, for advice, for encouragement. He was as brilliant as he was generous, as fierce of spirit as he was soft of heart. He was a man of action, a great man who matched the city whose *rav* he was from 5633 (1873) to 5672 (1912), the developing and prosperous Polish industrial city of Lodz. For Jews from cities outside of Lodz, too, he became renowned as a last resort for problems that no one else could solve.

Rav Elya Chaim led the man to a seat and asked gently, "Reb Moshe Leib, I'm glad you thought of me and came here. I hope, *b'ezras Hashem*, that I'll be able to help you. But first tell me. When you asked yourself whom you could turn to for help, shouldn't you have thought first of the *Ribono shel Olam*? I am only one of His many *shlichim*, you know."

Moshe Leib tugged his beard nervously and looked uncomfortable. For three full minutes, while the *rav* waited patiently, silence reigned.

Finally he burst out, "Rebbi, I know this is a terrible thing for me to be saying, but after what happened to me, I just felt so, so — well, resentful against the *Ribono shel Olam*. You see, it was a mitzvah that got me into this whole mess in the first place."

"Impossible!" Rav Elya Chaim exclaimed, his beard bristling

angrily. "*Shlichei mitzvah einan nizokin*. But suppose you tell me more about it," he added in a softer voice.

"Well, Rebbi, as you know, I'm a *pashute* Yid, a large-family man, and I work hard in my butcher shop all day to earn enough to feed my tribe. But I have no complaints, *baruch Hashem*. Like I always say, if you have good health and a *shtikl parnassah*, why gripe? Well, anyway, you remember what a beautiful day it was last Sunday? No rain, no snow, clear and sunny — 'a day right out of Sivan,' Reizele says to me. I think that's a good expression, don't you, Rebbi? My Reizele has a way with words.

"Well, I was on my way to Reb Leizer the *shochet's* house. I wanted to speak to him about a certain cow that he was supposed to *shecht* for me. I was taking my time, just strolling along, not thinking about anything in particular. How could I, on a day like that? And then," and here Moshe Leib paused dramatically, "I saw it!"

"Saw what?"

"The purse. It was a green velvet purse, the kind that all the nobility carry. Quite indistinctive in that respect, if you know what I mean. I saw first off, from the look of the thing, that it belonged to someone quite wealthy. And the contents convinced me even more." Moshe Leib lowered his voice. "Rebbi, the purse contained one thousand rubles."

He looked quizzically at the *rav* to see if his words had had the proper effect, but Rav Elya Chaim seemed singularly unimpressed.

"So?" he prodded.

"So," sighed Moshe Leib, "I took the purse home and the next day I searched the newspaper to see if someone had advertised the loss. That was where I made my mistake. I should have just kept the thousand rubles and been done with it."

"Why, Moshe Leib, what a thing to say!"

"I know," returned Moshe Leib with an even bigger sigh, "but just wait until you hear the end of my story and then see if you don't agree with me. Well, as I was saying, I looked in the newspaper and there, sure enough, was a large advertisement stating that a purse containing a large sum of money had been lost and the owner would pay a reward of one hundred rubles to whoever would return the purse to him. Rebbi, one hundred rubles is no small sum, especially when you have as many mouths to feed as I do. You can just imagine how happily I sped to the address given in the paper, one of the mansions on the outskirts of town belonging to a young Polish count named Poliaczewski. I was soon admitted to his presence and, after handing over the purse, I stood expectantly, waiting for the reward.

"Reward," Moshe Leib repeated with a bitter laugh. "Rebbi, instead of giving me one hundred rubles, the liar accused me of having stolen a thousand rubles from his purse and of returning only one thousand. 'Dog!' he shouted at me. 'Thief! My purse contained two thousand rubles!' His curses fell about me as thick as rain. I begged him, I pleaded with him. 'Forget about the reward,' I said, 'you don't have to give me anything if you don't want to. But if I returned your purse and your money why are you raising such a senseless accusation against me?' But my words fell on deaf ears. With kicks and blows to hasten me along, he threw me from his house. Now he has brought his accusation before the police and I have been summoned to trial. What am I to do? What hope is there for me? It's my word against his. He is a *goy* and the judges are *goyim*. Rebbi, you must help me!"

"Calm yourself, Reb Moshe Leib, I will help you," Rav Elya Chaim reassured him. "But how did you have the audacity to blame your troubles on the mitzvah of *hashavas aveidah*? It is not the mitzvah that is at fault; you are at fault. Your only concern was to collect the reward. Had you been a little more concerned with fulfilling the mitzvah, all of this might have been avoided." Noting the crestfallen look on Moshe Leib's face, Rav Elya Chaim hastened to comfort him.

"Be that as it may, you've surely learned your lesson. And now you're not to worry. It will work out for the best. When is your trial?"

"Next Tuesday."

"Do you have a lawyer?"

When Moshe Leib nodded affirmatively, Rav Elya Chaim said, "Send him to me sometime before the trial. *B'ezras Hashem*, everything will turn out fine."

The next day the lawyer arrived, and he and the *rav* stepped into an inner room where they conferred for half an hour. When they emerged, both were smiling.

Well, thought Moshe Leib, who had been waiting impatiently in the outer room, *I don't see what there is to smile about. I'm the one who's awaiting trial next week, not they.* But somehow, he couldn't help feeling confident. If anyone could get a Yid out of a tight spot, Rav Elya Chaim was the one.

○‿○

Moshe Leib had never been in a courthouse before, and he was scared — there was no other word for it — plain scared. Everything contrived to give him that feeling. The judges with their great black robes, the uniformed policemen, the magnificent courtroom. And the people! It seemed to Moshe Leib that half of Lodz was present.

They probably all came to see me get sent off to prison, he thought morosely.

He spotted his lawyer in the crowd and rushed up to him.

"Hey, Moritz," hissed Moshe Leib into the lawyer's ear, "what did Rav Elya Chaim tell you? Come on, be a sport."

But Moritz Kalmanson only shook his head smugly. "He just told me how to handle your defense," he returned maddeningly.

And with that Moshe Leib had to be content, for the hubbub around them suddenly ceased, and they just had time to hurry to their places before the judge pounded his gavel for the case of the People versus Moshe Leib Berger. His trial was beginning!

First Poliaczewski was called to take the stand, and he repeated his accusation. The purse had contained two thousand rubles and the Jew had returned to him only a thousand.

At this point, Moritz Kalmanson arose and was granted permission to question the prosecution's witness.

"Your Excellency," he began, addressing Poliaczewski, "are you willing to swear that the purse that you lost contained two thousand rubles?"

Without thinking twice, Poliaczewski put his right hand on the Bible and swore that the purse he lost had contained exactly two thousand rubles.

"Honored judges," Kalmanson addressed himself to that august body, "I have no doubt regarding the oath of this young count. If he is so positive that his lost purse contained two thousand rubles that he is willing to swear to it, then unquestionably it is so. On the other hand, my client, Mr. Berger, would not have returned the purse he found at all if he had had dishonest intentions. He could just as easily have kept it, and no one would have found out. The fact that he *did* return the purse is proof of his honesty. Let us then look at the facts. Moshe Leib Berger claims that the purse he found contained one thousand rubles. Count Poliaczewski swears that the purse he lost contained two thousand rubles. One conclusion is clear. The purse Mr. Berger found is not the one Count Poliaczewski lost. The purse my client found clearly belongs to some unknown owner who lost one thousand rubles, and who hasn't claimed it as yet. Whereas the purse that Count Poliaczewski lost is still missing. I suggest that the purse my client found be returned to him until such time as someone claims it."

Poliaczewski immediately turned as white as a sheet, and the judges barely repressed their smiles. The judges bent their heads together and consulted with one another in low tones while the spectators brought out the fruit and cookies that they had taken from home for just such an exigency. As they munched, the full meaning of what they had just seen and heard dawned upon them. They chattered and called to one another across the seats.

"Hey, what do you think the judges will do now?"

"Pretty smart of that lawyer, huh? Those Jews sure know how to stay out of trouble. Accuse everybody and accuse nobody, that's their way."

"I bet that rabbi of theirs had a hand in this. I'll say this much for him. He's got a really keen mind."

The judges, sensing the truth, but not wishing to embarrass the nobleman, did exactly as Kalmanson — at the *rav's* suggestion — had proposed. And Moshe Leib returned home a thousand rubles richer for his pains.

HERSHEL WOLF

Fiesta at Aranjuez

You know, of course, that the power of a son is greater than that of a father — a father can only help his son get through this world. Even if he is an Avraham Avinu, he cannot help his son on the Yom Hadin. But the mitzvos of a son can earn Gan Eden even for a wicked father, and the *aveiros* of a son can give a dose of Gehinnom even to a tzaddik. That's why a father has to make sure that his children stay on the straight and narrow.

But that wasn't the problem facing Hernandez and his son José. Well, on the one hand, Hernandez was dead — he'd been dead a long time. But on the other hand, there he was, alive as can be. Well, sort of…

Oh dear, that always happens whenever I tell a story. I start in the middle and get all mixed up. So I'll rest a bit and have a few sips of ginger ale, and start again from the beginning.

Ah! That's better. Now, where was I? My full name is Estrelita Carla del Monte y da Costa, or at least that's what it probably would have been if my ancestors had never been expelled from Spain. Presently, though, my name is Esther Kayla Bergmann. I have spent the last sixteen years researching the history of the Jews in Spain, and I'll let you guess why. This story is mentioned by Rabbi Eliyahu Hakohen in his *sefer*, *Shevet Mussar*, but I have filled in many more details. It took place in Spain just before the Jews were expelled and the *goyim* started that horrible Inquisition. What a time that was! What *gedolim* lived then! Rav Yitzchak Abuhav, Rav Yaakov Konpanton, Rav Yitzchak de Leon, Rav Yosef Caro, and others whose names are even less familiar to you. José himself wasn't much of a scholar. Nowadays he'd probably be reckoned a great *talmid chacham*, but for his time he was just another ex-*yeshivah bachur* who'd left yeshivah because his father had sent him to college for a secular education — the old story.

Oh, yes, they had universities in those days. Hernandez da Costa was a very wealthy businessman and he wanted to prepare his son to deal with the *goyim* and, eventually, when the time would come, to take over the business. So he sent his *ben yachid* north to the great University of Salamanca in Old Castile. There, the *goyim* did a good job and taught him their customs, graces, modes, and fashions.

And so José Manuel da Costa learned to enjoy himself like the rest of the *goyim*. He liked to run, not to get to shul for *davening*, but just to see if he could run faster than anyone else. And he liked to watch the bullfight. If you were to watch bullfights, you'd see cruelty, *tza'ar ba'alei chaim*, perhaps an occasional murder, plenty of *middos ra'os*; you might even realize, if nothing else, that it's a bad waste of time. But when a *goy* watches a bullfight, he sees two animals fighting for their lives. The one, of tremendous strength and ferocity. The other, weak, but agile and clever. And the spectators project themselves into the fight and fight with them. If their animal wins, they are happy; if their animal loses, they are sad. So the crowd fights together, shouts together, and becomes like one huge animal. The individual is caught up by the mass exhilaration; he forgets himself and his troubles. All he sees is the illusion of himself battling in the arena. Is he different from a drug addict in his world of fantasy?

You're laughing, I see. Well, we are just as foolish as they were. They shouted "*Olé!*" and we shout "Hooray!" Whether it's two people trying to batter each other to a pulp or twenty people chasing a ball, the same crowd is watching the same people or animals fighting it out in front of them. But don't get the wrong idea! José was still very *frum*, and never missed putting on *tefillin* or *davening* on time with a *minyan*. So when he came home from Salamanca, he came as a fine, eligible young man.

The town of Aranjuez, high up on the plains of New Castile, stands astride the banks of the River Tagus. Boats sail downstream, westward to Toledo and then onward to Lisbon on the Portuguese coast. The main highway from Madrid crosses the river there and then continues south to Cordoba and on to Cadiz on the Mediterranean coast. The people of Aranjuez thought highly of themselves and their town. After all, the town was famous for its beauty and, more important, their bullring was bigger than the one in Toledo and second only to the one in Madrid.

So José went into business, was successful, married, and had a family. When his father passed on, he took over the family concern. As a man of considerable wealth, he became a leader of the Jewish community and busied himself with the affairs of the town as well. Naturally, he could never have become one of the city fathers — that was only for Catholics — but he was well respected and helped out where he could. You can well understand that such an important person couldn't run or jump like he used to — but he could go to a bullfight. Sure it says in *Shulchan Aruch* that you're not allowed to. Even though the *Shulchan Aruch* hadn't been written then, José knew the halachah from the Gemara and from Rambam. But he also must have known a *heter*. Because José was a real *frum* Jew, and if he hadn't found a *heter* for it, he would have died rather than put a foot in the place. What kind of *heter* did he dredge up? For a start, a man in his position had to keep friendly with the *goyim*, and the bullfight was the only social occasion that did not involve religion. And if that wasn't enough, he was enough of a *lamdan* to dig something up to satisfy his conscience. But, let's be honest, when the *toreador* did a neat turn or when the bull got really mad, José was up on his feet with the rest of them, shouting for all his worth.

The town used to buy their bulls at the market in Madrid. They had an agent who kept an eye out for animals with spirit. Whenever he saw one that was suitable he would jump in ahead of the agents from other towns and buy, regardless of cost. When he had purchased enough bulls for a tournament, he would send them the thirty miles south to Aranjuez, and the mayor would declare a holiday and everyone would go to the bullfight.

One day, the agent saw a bull the likes of which he'd never seen before. So huge, such strength, and what a temper! He bid and bid, and finally bought it at a fantastic price. But who cared? To get such a bull was worth any money. The agent quickly sent a message to the town to prepare themselves for the chance of a lifetime. They were to build an especially strong pen because the old one wouldn't last ten minutes with this bull.

Eventually, the bull arrived, breathing fire and roaring like thunder. The whole town turned out to see it, and the city fathers fixed the tournament for two days later. José, of course, was as excited as anyone else. He canceled a business trip and made sure nothing would keep him from the bullfight. "Made sure!" Huh! Who can make sure of anything in this world? All of José's plans were sent flying by his dream that night. Some dreams are *shtusim*, but others cannot be ignored.

○§○

José could not ignore his dream that night at all. His father, the late Hernandez da Costa, appeared to him.

"Yosef, my son!"

"Yes, Father!"

"Know, my son, there are many methods of punishment in the other world, and they are as different as the number and quality of one's sins. Some of my sins made it mandatory that my *neshamah* return to the world you are in as a *gilgul* in the bull that has been prepared for the tournament the day after tomorrow. The only way for my *neshamah* to have its proper *tikkun* is for you to *shecht* the bull so that it is kosher and feed it to poor *bnei Torah*. This is what the Heavenly Court decided, and they gave me permission to tell you. Through that *tikkun*, my *neshamah* will be able to progress from being a *gilgul* in an animal to become a *gilgul* in a person and thus be worthy of serving Hashem again. Don't forget, Yosef! Don't spare money or effort. Help me! Help your father! Do you hear, Yosef?" Hernandez da Costa disappeared and José awoke a very worried person.

Nowadays we don't read much about *gilgulim* and *tikkunim* and things like that. But in those days they were on a pretty high *madreigah* — José wouldn't have gotten *semichah* without knowing the whole of *Shas* by heart! And José knew a little bit about Kabbalah, too, so he understood what his father had gone through. He realized that it could have been much worse. After all, the bull is at least a *tahor* animal — if his father had had to start lower down on the scale, as a *tamei* animal, or as a fish, or as an insect, or even as a vegetable, it would have been much worse for his father. Additionally, here José was being given a chance to rescue his father's *neshamah* and give it the *tikkun* it needed.

But how?

The next morning, before José could get bogged down by serious worrying, he went to the *chacham* of the *kehillah* and told him the whole story. The *chacham* agreed that José had to try his hardest to save his father but he also agreed that it would be very hard indeed. How could he do it? To buy the bull from the town was impossible — they'd never sell it at any price. Steal it? Even if he could find a *heter*, it was too well guarded to steal. Nor could he put the bull out of action by "accidentally" wounding it, because he might make it a *treifah*, after which *shechitah* would be useless. They finally worked out a plan that stood a chance of success.

José went straight to the head of the town council, Don Pedro de Valencia. Try and imagine a city in the middle of the night — but with the sun blazing down like a furnace — shops shut, shutters and windows closed tight, not a soul to be seen. For three hours, heat and silence have the town all to themselves. Everyone sleeps. Including Don Pedro and Don Pedro's servants. José had to bang at the front door for a good ten minutes before a bedraggled servant opened the door and he had to wait another ten minutes before a sleepy-eyed Don Pedro came to receive his guest.

"My dear Señor José, what a pleasure to see you." The two gentlemen bowed to each other and they got down to business. José explained his wonderful idea, which could not have waited another few hours until after the siesta, because of the time required for its preparation.

In view of the exceptional quality of the bull, José proposed to make a general town festival, a fiesta. He offered to buy, out of his own pocket, ten cows and have them slaughtered and roasted for all the townspeople to enjoy after the tournament. Furthermore, he proposed to have the cows slaughtered and prepared according to the Jewish custom so that everyone, irrespective of religion, could enjoy the food. Naturally, the idea of a free meal, plus the chance to socially integrate the Jews with the rest of the community — all paid for by the Jews! — appealed to Don Pedro. He gladly gave his consent. José left and Don Pedro went back to sleep.

José got down to work. First, he ordered ten cows for immediate delivery. Then he sent a fast messenger to Toledo, thirty miles north, for an extra *shochet* and a *bodek*. By nightfall, the cows were in the stall of the *kehillah's* slaughterhouse, the two Toledans were on their way, and the whole town was united at the double expectation of the bullfight and the grand fiesta.

In the middle of the night, an uproar broke out in the cows' stalls. A mad dog had gotten in and the cows went berserk. Well, the stalls were old and normally only had to handle one or two cows. So it didn't take long for the maddened cows to break down the walls and go on a rampage in the middle of the town. You can imagine the tumult. José was soon on the scene with a few of his servants, and they managed to round up the herd.

Then José had a request to make of Don Pedro — could they house the loose cows overnight in the stalls of the bullring? Well, what could Don Pedro say? The alternative was for the cows to wander around town all night. He agreed as long as José took his chances with the bull, and disposed of the cows as soon as possible. José led the cows into the stalls. Surprisingly, the bull received them hospitably. Then, when the Jews from Toledo had arrived and had rested up from their journey, they got down to work.

When dawn broke, the bullring attendants were not at all surprised to discover ten butchered carcasses, carved up for the fiesta. But they were absolutely dumbfounded to discover a cow in the stalls! Now, anyone can tell the difference between a cow and a bull — even a Jew. What could José say? What a disastrous mistake! Perhaps it was the strange lighting from the flares. And then, everyone had been so tired… José made excuse after excuse but it helped little. The town went into mourning — shocked at the loss of the bull. No tournament.

Those stupid Jews! That José!

José nevertheless went ahead with the scheduled fiesta. The meat was koshered and then roasted on spits until the aroma had wafted across the whole town. The people came, one by one, two by two, ate their fill, and felt a little better. Someone José had hired pulled out a violin and things began to get lively. People began to feel that the Jews weren't so bad. After all, if they're so silly that they can't tell the difference between a cow and a bull, it's not their fault. They were born like that! The Jews, of course, kept completely clear — who could tell what might happen if the crowd turned nasty. José, as host, simply had to be around, but he kept as much in the background as possible.

He told no one how the bull had become quiet when the *shochtim* came. How the bull had licked his and the *chacham's* hands. Or how the bull had kneeled and then rolled over onto its back to be *shechted*. Who would have believed him anyway? The meat of the bull was koshered and salted and sent downriver to Toledo to the big yeshivah. The hide was kept to be made into *batim* for *tefillin* and parchment for *sefarim*.

So Hernandez da Costa had his *tikkun*.

José had his own *tikkun* about nine years later: After the expulsion from Spain, he stayed behind to sell off his business. The Inquisition caught him and decided he'd make an excellent example. When a Jew is killed by *goyim* because he is a Jew, and he accepts his fate, his *neshamah* has a perfect *tikkun*. So, while the *goyim* were dancing and cheering with delight, José was preparing himself for the ultimate sacrifice. And, as they fell lower than the lowest animals, José delivered up his *neshamah* with the purest *mesirus nefesh*.

MOSHE PRAGER

Zman Simchaseinu in Death's Shadow

Meet some of the true heroes of the Holocaust.

DESPITE THE CONSPIRATORIAL atmosphere of the chassidic rebel movement, the word of its existence spread like wildfire, and the tales of its heroism served as solace for the oppressed.

Cracow served as the nerve center of the chassidic underground. Cracow's noble, ages-old Jewish community was crushed under the burden of the cruel decrees it was compelled to bear. For Cracow had been turned into the Capital of Wickedness by the German occupation forces. Cracow became the base of operations for the S.S. and Gestapo beasts. And thus Cracow was first in oppression and first in horrors. Little wonder that the spirits of Cracow's Jews fell, and fear and terror found room in their hearts.

Moshe Goldstein of the Cracow suburb Podgorze, who now lives in New York City, tells how he met the underground chassidic clique:

"It was during Sukkos of 1942. The Jews still alive in the ghetto were dispirited; they had given up hope. I was living in a room on Nadwiszlanska Street, across from the city slaughterhouse. In middle of the night, I was aroused by a noise in the courtyard. What had happened? The Gerrer chassidim had crept out of their hideout in a nearby cellar and had 'taken over' the little sukkah standing in our yard. They were emaciated, weak, and starved. I took pity on them and brought every bit of food I owned out into the sukkah for them. There were about ten of them. One, I recall, was Shmelka Lipschitz. Another lad was named Noach Zinz. Koppel Liebowicz's brother-in-law, whose name I don't recall, was also there. So was the son of Rav Shabsi Rapaport, one of Cracow's *rabbanim*.

"Their joy knew no bounds. They recited the *Leishev Basukkah* and *Shehecheyanu brachos* with great emotion. And then they broke into an enthusiastic dance. They danced for a long while, fearless. I stared, amazed, at the circle of dancers. Until that moment only death had danced in this ghetto. Anyone still alive in the ghetto was an amputated limb — lacking parents, lacking family. We were aware that we had been granted a momentary reprieve before the rest of the ghetto would finally be liquidated. Everyone bent every effort to obtain a special S.S. work card. Whoever could obtain the red seal of the Gestapo on his work card held onto it as if it were a life rope. But these dancing lads cared not at all for the regime of murderers. They cared nothing for the murderers' gift of life. They cared nothing for the entire, horrible reality."

⊂≈⊃

Mendel Brachfeld, a respected chassid of the rebbe of Bobov, is a scholar and a clear thinker. Every word, every expression he uses is carefully chosen. He describes his experiences with deep, unmasked emotion: "For over two months, my younger brother Moshe and I hid in the rubble of Cracow's ghetto. We set up a hideout within a hideout so that even the Gestapo bloodhounds — both the four-legged kind and the two-legged variety — could not track us down. It was a hideout worthy of the name. We hid in an attic within which we fixed up a sleeping-perch on a roof beam. We lay there by day without moving a muscle, and at night we would descend to seek edible matter in every nook and cranny of the wasted ghetto. We were sure all along that we two were the only ones flitting about the ghetto ruins like two lost souls. Who would have imagined that the last of the Gerrer rebels were still alive — and in the same fearful condition as ourselves?

"Where did we discover one another? In Plaszow Camp's Section Eight, a special division in the German prison camp — after we were caught. When we were brought before one of the ghetto executioners, he was astounded and burst out laughing, 'Aha, my foxes! How did you manage to stay out of our sight so long?'

"He turned to his men and ordered, 'Take these foxes to the labor camp! First, though, question them! But very politely. That's my order!'

"Well, orders are orders. We were questioned and searched. My pockets yielded a *gartel*, which tickled the butchers' funny bones, 'Are you planning to hang yourself, Jew?'

"A Jewish *kapo* who was present, explained to them that chassidim wear such belts at prayer. This time the butchers cackled shrilly, 'Aha. So you're Talmudists, too?!'

"That brought on the order to put my brother and me in Section Eight.

"To our great surprise and joy, we found several members of the chassidic underground there — we had never expected to see any of them alive. There was Getzel of Slupca, Moshe Eisenberg and his father, Reb Pinchas. There was Simcha Rothstein, Refael Horowitz, and someone else whose name I forgot.

"How can I ever forget the days we spent together in prison with those Gerrer lads? They plainly sanctified G-d's Name even in prison. Everyone, prisoners and wardens alike, regarded them with great respect. They maintained exemplary cleanliness in their cell: the floor was always clean and everything in place. Whoever came in contact with them was impressed by their honesty, their decency, and their simplicity.

"Why did the cruel murderers keep us so long in Section Eight just like that, without any 'investigations' and without any torture 'games'? That's something we didn't and still don't ask any questions about. Each of us felt *hashgachah pratis* in our every step and in every action. Every portion of suffering was rationed out to each of us with minute precision. And every one of the daily miracles took place at the very time and the very place it was needed. For next to the name of each of us was plainly written down and signed and sealed in G-d's Book of Life — 'who will die at the time originally set for him, and who will die before his time.' Thus it came to pass that in the very days that mass murders took place daily in Plaszow, we sat in prison as if we had been entirely forgotten. Until the day came that the commander of the 'Death Brigade' suddenly reminded himself of his 'foxes.' My brother and I were transferred to the smithy of Plaszow's *Julag* (*Judenlager*: Jews' Camp), whereas the Gerrer lads were sent off elsewhere. Where? I don't know. But one thing is beyond doubt:

wherever they were, no matter the circumstances, they surely sanctified *Shem Shamayim*!

"I just recalled an interesting fact. Something I heard told about them. It was the last Simchas Torah of the Cracow ghetto. In the ghetto proper, confusion reigned, for the Satan's devils, according to their custom of disrupting a Jewish Yom Tov, had announced that an exile 'quota' would have to be met that day. Simultaneously, they staged a roundup in the streets and in the houses to prepare a death camp shipment. On such a day of turmoil and grief, who could pay attention to Simchas Torah? Only the brave fighters of the chassidic bunker. They were not satisfied with the achievement of celebrating Yom Tov with a festive 'meal' in the darkness of their bunker; they had to have *hakafos* in accordance with the *din*. How did they manage that? In the Cracow suburb called Postakow, there was an empty, abandoned, little *beis medrash*. The boys stole out there in the middle of Simchas Torah eve. They brought along the tiny *sefer Torah* in their possession, and they danced all that night in honor of Hashem's Torah.

"That's what those fellows were like!"

∞

The only lad in Cracow's chassidic underground who survived — through G-d's mercy — was Shmelka Lipschitz. He 'lived' in Plaszow. Whoever saw him knew immediately who he was and to which clique he belonged.

Now it's Shmelka Lipschitz's turn to speak.

"What can I tell you? All the Jews were holy and pure! Here. Take what happened on the first night of the Sukkos holiday in 1943. That month had been turned into the biggest month of butchery in our camp. The enemy demanded sacrifices for every

Yom Tov. On Rosh Hashanah, two hundred Jews were taken to the slaughter; in mid-Yom Kippur, ninety souls; and the day before Sukkos, another one hundred and fifty sacrifices. Despite all that — what do you think the remaining Jews were worrying about and working for? They were looking for ways to fulfill the mitzvah of sukkah, and to recite *Shehecheyanu* upon the occasion of *Zman Simchaseinu*!

"On that first night of Sukkos, a silent march took place at one end of the camp: Where were the marchers going? Into the truly temporary sukkah that had been put up in the camp lumberyard. The laborers who worked in that part of the camp had that very day built a shed as a 'storeroom' for their tools. The 'storeroom' naturally had no roof, but had been 'temporarily' covered with remnants of lumber which provided perfectly kosher *s'chach* for a perfectly kosher sukkah. The news spread from mouth to ear, and the prisoners risked their lives by leaving their sheds and marching to the secret sukkah. I was among them. In the sukkah I stopped for a moment, recited *Shehecheyanu*, and stepped out on the other end. There was no time for any more; the march was far from over."

Condensed from Those Who Never Yielded, *the story of the death-defying chassidic underground, translated from Hebrew by Yehoshua Leiman. Published by Lightbooks, 1980, re-printed by Israel Bookshop Publications, 2013.*

AHUVA COHEN

Reverie

Relive a chapter in the history of the Yeshivah of Volozhin.

WHITE BEARD FLECKED with gray nested in cupped hand, gnarled hand and streaked beard testifying to the years of their possessor. Certainly the cheeks stretched taut above the beard did not; nor did the eyes, still expressive and penetrating despite the hint of bewilderment they tended to show during the last year.

Rav Naftali Tzvi Yehuda Berlin raised his head and shifted unhappily in his chair. "Reb Chaim," he murmured brokenly. "Reb Chaim."

Even as he spoke the name, he felt himself caught up in its never-failing magic. It seemed that only yesterday a pale boy of eleven whose heart sounded loudly in his ears — he, Hirsh Leib Berlin — had stood on the threshold of the Yeshivah of Volozhin.

Although only a quarter of a century old at the time, the Yeshivah of Volozhin had already drawn considerable attention to itself, and with good reason. Prior to the 1800s (5550s), *yeshivos* as we know them today were nonexistent in Eastern Europe. Instead, most small towns and villages throughout Russia and Poland maintained their own groups of students who learned in the local *beis medrash* and were taught and guided by the town *rav*. These young men and boys ate at the homes of the townspeople by a rotation system popularly termed "*essen teg*." The yeshivah as a whole was financially dependent upon the local residents. Under the *teg* system, the students conveyed the voice of Torah out of the *beis medrash* into the homes of the *ba'alei batim* where it was joyously welcomed. The integration of the students with the townspeople was brought to completion by the local *posek* in his dual role of *rav* and *rosh yeshivah*.

As early as the 1600s (5400s), however, the drawbacks of the village-supported yeshivah began to be apparent. Many of the towns refused to maintain students, and those *yeshivos* that did exist were often in dire financial straits. In the mid-1700s (5500s), the foreshadowing of the Haskalah movement signaled new danger. Far-seeing *gedolei Torah* of the age were quick to grasp the shattering effects that the yet unborn movement would have on the traditional religious pattern of Lithuanian village life. They realized, too, that any spiritual disintegration taking place in the villages would have a devastating effect on the *yeshivos*, dependent as they were on the towns for their spiritual and material survival.

A new type of yeshivah was needed: one that would function independently of the local community and thus be immune to the powerful currents that threatened to sweep over Eastern

European Jewry. The answer to the problem came in 1802 in Russia, in the form of the first of the great modern Lithuanian *yeshivos* — Yeshivas Volozhin.

The new yeshivah corresponded exactly to what the leaders of the generation had envisioned. Its founder, *rosh yeshivah*, and patron, Rav Chaim, the *rav* of Volozhin, dispensed with the *teg* system and alone supported the ten *talmidim* who gathered around him. When the yeshivah had grown to the point where Rav Chaim's personal wealth was no longer sufficient to maintain it, he appealed to the Jewish communities throughout Lithuania and to the Jewish nation as a whole. The communities responded with enthusiasm, and from then on each Volozhiner student received a stipend which he used to purchase meals and lodging wherever he wished. The institution of the stipend system was an important innovation; it raised the dignity of the *talmid* in his own eyes and in the eyes of others by transforming him from an object of charity into a self-supporting member of society.

Rav Chaim's momentous accomplishment in creating the Yeshivah of Volozhin induced others to follow his example, and it was not long before the great Lithuanian *yeshivos* began springing up all over Eastern Europe. Mir, Kovno, Kelm, Novardok, Slabodka, Slonim, Radin, Telshe, and Ponevezh followed one another, in rapid succession, patterning themselves on Volozhin.

In addition to originating the pattern that the Yeshivah of Volozhin would follow in providing for material needs, Rav Chaim also set forth the principles for the yeshivah's spiritual direction, based on the approach of his *rebbi*, the Vilna Gaon. *Bekius* (comprehensive knowledge) as opposed to *charifus* (acuity) remained the guiding principle of the yeshivah throughout the entire ninety years of its existence, despite the fact that the *roshei yeshivah* and students alike excelled in both. In his concern with clarity, simplicity, and truthfulness in the study of Torah, he paved the way for the advent of the *Mussar* movement, whose leading figure, Rav Yisrael Lipkin of Salant, was a *talmid* of Rav Zundel of Salant, a *talmid* of Rav Chaim.

Finally, Volozhin created a new and more powerful concept of the role of the *rosh yeshivah* as distinct from the communal *rav*.

ೂಲ

The impressionable eleven-year-old standing in awe in the middle of the great *beis medrash*, and excitedly surveying his surroundings, was unaware how closely his own fate would be tied up with that of the yeshivah in the years ahead. How could he know that he was destined to marry Rav Chaim's granddaughter and eventually take over the leadership of the yeshivah? Or that he would be the one to steer Volozhin through its years of glory and subsequent decline, and would finally stand, a broken and played-out witness, at its funeral?

The eleven-year-old boy could not have known any of this, any more than that same boy over half a century later could have foreseen the rebirth of the yeshivah years after his death. All he knew, as he stood in the doorway that wintry morning, was the pounding in his ears and the quickening of his heartbeat when he said the name "Reb Chaim" to himself.

ೂಲ

The old man sighed. No, he had had no inkling then of what was in store for him, he mused. If he had, would he have done it anyway? Had it been worth it?

A picture came into the Netziv's mind and he pressed the back of his hand against his eyes in an effort to shut it out. It was the same nightmarish picture that he had lived with in every one of his waking moments since the closing of the yeshivah a year and a half ago…

The uniformed guards had encircled the old building and were loudly ordering everyone to leave. They were coming out reluctantly, the *talmidim* and the *rabbeim* with tears streaming down their faces, all carrying the worn *Gemaros* and the precious *sifrei Torah*. But not he. He was standing at the small window of the *beis medrash* and looking out at the familiar faces until his heart could no longer contain the pain. Finally, he too was carried out by his students. Unconscious, he mercifully did not hear the door of the yeshivah being locked securely behind him…

The picture faded and was replaced by another one. It was a typical weekday morning in the great yeshivah, and the sunlit *beis medrash* was rapidly filling with *talmidim*, some already swaying over their *shtenders*, others gesticulating warmly in heated defense of an idea. Even now he could see them, some of them not much older than children, others with full-grown beards, yet all the eyes burning with the same intense enthusiasm. He knew them all, had taught them all, loved them all. They were his children.

A half-smile lit up the old man's face and he knew that had the eleven-year-old boy been aware of everything that would happen to him, he would have put up his hand, lovingly kissed the *mezuzah*, and with the same firm step entered the drama of Volozhin.

SALLY LOVE

That night, bedikas chametz *was preceded by*

The Search

"WELL, BOYS," BEGAN Chaim, "this *ma'aseh* occurred a number of years before your Momma and I were *zocheh* to each other. My father took me to the Maggid of Mezeritch to witness the Maggid's *hislahavus* during *bedikas chametz*.

"After we had finished *Shemoneh Esrei*, we waited for the Maggid to finish. We impatiently waited an hour. Finally my father remarked, 'This is strange. Usually the rebbe rushes through Ma'ariv on this night in order to rush to the mitzvah.'

"I watched, fascinated, the fervor with which the rebbe '*shukkled.*'

"'*Sha! Sha!* The rebbe is finished,' cried some chassidim expectantly. But the rebbe didn't acknowledge his congregation. Instead, after *Aleinu*, he entered his chamber.

"We watched the door tensely. Minutes, then hours, dragged by. We were all tense and impatient.

"'*Vey! Vey!*' cried one elderly chassid. 'Some evil has *chas v'shalom* been decreed against the Jews, and the rebbe is contending with the Heavenly Courts!'

"A murmur of apprehension followed.

"'Look,' cried one young boy as he peered through a crack in the door. 'The rebbe is just sitting there. He's not moving a muscle.'

"'Listen, friends,' I pointed out, 'perhaps the rebbe has forgotten that tonight is *bedikas chametz*. Let's knock on his door and remind him.'

"Two important chassidim led the way and we entered the rebbe's chamber.

"'Ah-ah-ahem, Rebbe, ah…it is midnight already, and we have not yet searched for *chametz*.'

"The Maggid raised his eyes, '*Oy*, my dear ones, the heavens prevent us. It is very bad…'

"The rebbe bowed his head in despair. 'We will not proceed until we have provided for the Jew who has no matzos for Pesach.'

"'Is that possible?' the chassidim whispered to one another. 'Such an oversight!?'

"My father took command of the situation.

"'Quickly, Chaim, take Yossel and Shmuel and go to Moshe Tzvi's bakery. Search every house at that end of town. Reb Yosef and I will start at the other end of town.'

"The other chassidim were dispatched with equal alacrity.

"We searched and searched. At first with enthusiasm. Soon, however, our spirits flagged, for we could find no one who lacked matzos for Pesach.

"'Rebbe,' we cried, half-happy, half-worried, on our return, 'the whole town is provided for.'

"'No, my children, I hear a pitiful *neshamah*. He is in despair, for he has nothing with which to greet the Yom Tov. Go to the farms. Bring him to me.'

"Again we dispersed. We awakened people from their sleep. We investigated. We questioned everyone; to no avail.

"Well, my father and I undertook to search all the way to the next town. An hour before dawn my father cried, 'Look! See that hut?'

"'No. Where? Oh, that? It doesn't seem fit to live in.'

"'Come, let's look!'

"We knocked and were greeted by an old Jew. We told him of our mission.

"'Welcome, my friends. You've found the right place. That is, I hope I'm the only one,' said the old man. 'I am a tailor. For years I've made a living from my trade — enough to go to the holy Maggid every year before Pesach and give him money for *ma'os chittim*. I was even able to disburse money with my own hands to a few destitute people whom I knew personally. Those were good years. But this past year I've been ill, bedridden. I couldn't work. My savings are gone, and I have nothing with which to greet the festival of freedom.'

"Tears of pain and anguish ran down the old tailor's face. But we were jubilant.

"'Where is your compassion?' asked the puzzled tailor. In reply we led him to the rebbe.

"As we entered the rebbe's room, we saw his eyes light up with a holy fire. When the other chassidim saw that, they were ready to jump for joy.

"He gave the old tailor a goodly sum of money. 'Buy whatever you need for Yom Tov. What remains, distribute to the poor as you are used to doing.'

"Only then did the rebbe proceed with *bedikas chametz*, and never was he as suffused with heavenly joy."

AHUVA COHEN

With a little siyata d'Shmaya, *the rav of Lodz turns up*

Unexpected Evidence

AHRELE WAS DAYDREAMING again as usual. He stared moodily at the discolored yellow wall of the classroom but he did not see it. In Ahrele's imagination the faded yellow wall had been replaced by a gleaming white one, the eastern wall of Lodz's largest shul.

But who was this handsome young man, cloaked in a long black *kapote*, *gartel* wound around his waist, a sleek fur *shtreimel* atop his head? Why, it was none other than Ahrele himself. Ahrele with the addition of a full black beard and minus his freckles. Ahrele grown up, a *talmid chacham* and a respected *rav* in his community.

Slowly Ahrele ascended the steps to the *bimah* and began to speak. "*Rabbosai*," he cried, clenching his fist and flinging his arm forward in an emphatic gesture. "*Rabbosai*…"

"Ow!" yelled Shmulik, who occupied the seat in front of Ahrele's and whom Ahrele's fist had caught squarely on the back of his head. "What's the big idea?"

Ahrele snickered. He honestly didn't mean to laugh; Shmulik was his best friend and not for all the world would he hurt his feelings. But so engrossed had Ahrele been in his daydream that he hadn't until that very moment realized what was happening, and it struck him as being enormously funny.

Ahrele snickered again, and before he knew it he was snorting with laughter.

All at once Ahrele noticed that it had become very quiet, too quiet. His classmates' grinning faces were bent studiously over their *Gemaros* while Shmulik was regarding him with a look of sad bewilderment which hurt Ahrele more than words.

"Ahrele," Reb Mendel's voice broke the stillness. "I want to speak to you after class."

The classroom immediately hummed once more with activity as the pupils bent their heads over their *Gemaros*, this time in earnest. Ahrele tried to concentrate but he felt too dispirited to think properly. No matter how hard he tried he always wound up in hot water with his *rebbi*. Reb Mendel would be sure to ask for an explanation and he would be equally sure to say when Ahrele had finished talking, "If you want to become a *rav*, Ahrele, and give *drashos* in a shul, you won't get there very fast by daydreaming about it. Better learn your Gemara instead."

And the worst part of it was that deep down in his heart Ahrele knew that his *rebbi* was right. Ahrele had been through many such after-school sessions before, and Reb Mendel was always right.

The trouble was that Ahrele got into and out of scrapes as easily and as naturally as one would expect of a lanky, tow-headed, freckled, eleven-year-old boy who was bursting with pep and mischief. And since Ahrele's best friend, Shmulik, though of a more studious bent, was blessed with the same gifts, the pair was always in trouble.

The day dragged by endlessly, but finally it was over. As the last of his classmates filed out of the room, Ahrele's eyes met those of his *rebbi* and he glanced quickly down at the worn top of his desk.

"*Nu*, Ahrele?" Reb Mendel prodded. Ahrele opened his mouth to speak, but the words died on his tongue. Following Ahrele's frightened gaze, Reb Mendel saw a uniformed policeman standing stiffly in the doorway. "I have come to inspect the classrooms of this school as part of a routine government inspection of schools," he announced. "You are the teacher?"

"Yes."

"Why is the boy here?"

"He misbehaved in class and was told to stay after school."

"Stay where you are," the policeman ordered. Then to Ahrele, "Get out of here, kid! Beat it!"

Barely had the man spoken than Ahrele was out of the door. But once on safer territory his curiosity got the better of him and he hid himself in a little supply room right off the classroom, from which vantage point he could both see and hear everything that was taking place.

The inspection was a long one, but at last it ended. Ahrele watched the officer march out. Then Reb Mendel, after a last look around the room, gently closed the door and left.

All was still and Ahrele was about to leave his hiding place to run home, when the sound of footsteps made him freeze. Peeping around the wall, Ahrele saw that the policeman had returned.

Now what does he want? Ahrele wondered. *And why isn't Rebbi with him? Could he have forgotten something and come back for it?*

Ahrele did not have long to wait to find out, for at that moment the policeman pushed open the door of the classroom and, going over to the closet where the *sefarim* were kept, grabbed a siddur and began to rip out the pages.

Ahrele's eyes filled with tears, and a murderous rage swept him. *I'll show this policeman, this rasha…this…I'll show him. Why, I'll… What will I do? What can I do?*

And abruptly Ahrele's fury was gone, quenched by the tiny, defeated, and oh-so-sensible voice at the back of his head. *There is nothing I can do. Nothing. There is no one around to hear me shout for help. To attack the man is out of the question. He is three times my size and, besides, he has a gun. Rebbi must surely be home already, but by the time we'd get back the policeman would have completed the damage and made his escape. No, I need someone who lives close by.*

Suddenly, Ahrele remembered that the *rav* lived on the next block. Ahrele knew the exact house because he had been there on an errand for his father the week before. Ahrele crept stealthily out of his hiding place, and noted with relief that the policeman was facing away from the window.

If only the rav *will be home. If only the fellow doesn't run away before we can return*, Ahrele thought fervently as he raced up the street. Rav Elya Chaim himself answered Ahrele's knock and, as they ran back to the school, Ahrele stammered out his story.

Only eight minutes had elapsed from the time that the policeman had re-entered the classroom, but to Ahrele it seemed like hours, and he was amazed to find that the officer was still there.

As they paused outside the classroom door, Rav Elya Chaim gently pushed Ahrele into the small room where he had originally hidden, ordering him not to leave it under any circumstances until he gave his permission to do so. He then entered the classroom alone.

The youthful policeman had just torn apart a Gemara and was trampling on the pieces when the *rav* entered. He looked up startled and the pieces of paper dropped slowly from his hands as the blood drained from his face.

The officer, whose name was Paul Olesmo, had never expected to be caught in the act and certainly not by the famous Jewish "detective rabbi" whose skirmishes with Polish anti-Semites always ended in his favor.

Olesmo considered making a break for it. It was easy enough. The *rav* could see that he was armed and he wouldn't dare try to stop him. Olesmo patted his gun, and Ahrele, who was watching from his hiding place, shivered, *Will he shoot the* rav?

On the other hand, Olesmo's thoughts raced on, an escape might not be such a good idea after all. If it came to fighting — and it might — one could never tell; it might look bad for him. An armed man attacking an unarmed one... *No! Better to play along*, he decided. Besides, he was sure that he would get off easy. He was a favorite with the higher-ups in the police force and they would use their influence to see that he got off free. He wasn't likely to get much of a sentence anyway. A few Jewish books more or less. What did anyone care? The judges wouldn't care either.

The policeman's facial muscles relaxed and the blood flowed back into his cheeks.

And so, when Rav Elya Chaim asked the policeman for his name and identification number, Olesmo gave them readily. Ahrele was puzzled. He was sure that Rav Elya Chaim had said something mysterious to the policeman to bring him around so quickly.

But Rav Elya Chaim was far from puzzled. He had understood the Pole's willingness to accommodate him only too well. He knew what the man had been thinking and he could not help admitting to himself with a flash of anger that it was only too true. Olesmo indeed had nothing to fear.

The policeman left.

"It must not be so," Rav Elya Chaim resolved. "This man must not go off scot free. *Ribono shel Olam!* How much longer will these *goyim* tear up *sefarim* with impunity? It must not be."

But how to avoid it? "Ahrele?" he called, remembering the boy in the supply room. The boy came out as Rav Elya Chaim bent down and began to collect the scattered fragments of *sheimos*, kissing each torn page tenderly as he deposited it in a pile on one of the desks.

Ahrele joined him. They worked together until they had finished, and then Rav Elya Chaim straightened up and looked at Ahrele as if seeing him for the first time.

"Would you like to be present at the trial?" he asked, his eyes twinkling.

Would he like? Ahrele glanced up speechless with delight, but then a dreadful thought struck him, "I'll be missing class. Will Rebbi —?"

"I'll explain everything to your *rebbi*."

Rav Elya Chaim took the pile of *sheimos* and, accompanied by Ahrele, made his way to the police station to file charges. The preliminary hearing was set for the next day at 10:30 a.m.

When the *rebbetzin* entered the *rav's* study an hour later to inform him that supper was ready, she found him sifting rapidly through a pile of torn papers, *sheimos*, they looked like to her. He seemed to be searching for something as he methodically set page after page aside, the worried crease on his forehead deepening with each page set aside. Not understanding, but not wanting to bother him, the *rebbetzin* quietly closed the door and went out.

☙❧

Ahrele perched excitedly on the edge of his chair. He saw Rav Elya Chaim and tried to catch his eye but the *rav* was immersed in a *sefer*. Ahrele saw the policeman standing calmly with some of his buddies.

The judge rapped for order, read the charges, and asked Rav Elya Chaim if he had anything to add.

"Your honor," Rav Elya Chaim began, "I have here one piece of the evidence of the crime with which Officer Olesmo is being charged. This page, which was torn in half and trampled upon by the accused, is a page from the Jewish prayer book. The prayer upon this page is called *Hanosein Teshuah*, and it is a prayer that Jews offer up for the welfare of the Czar. I contest that the action of the accused in desecrating this page is not only an insult to G-d and to the Jews but is an insult to the Czar as well, and as such deserves a heavy penalty. The Czar's honor demands that the perpetrator of this crime be severely punished. I rest my case."

There was a gasp from Olesmo as he fell back into his chair. The judge took the tattered page which Rav Elya Chaim held out, and ordered a recess while a translator was brought. After the expert had testified, the judge passed sentence. "We sentence the defendant to four years of hard labor in prison for his crime against the name of our gracious majesty. The court is dismissed."

As Ahrele stood outside waiting for Rav Elya Chaim to come out, he overheard snatches of conversation about the hearing.

He could barely keep himself from jumping up and down with joy when Rav Elya Chaim finally emerged and came down the steps to join him.

"That was terrific," said Ahrele, his eyes shining. "I heard one of the men say you should have been a lawyer."

"I am, sort of," replied Rav Elya Chaim, laughing. "I'm glad you enjoyed the hearing, but there's one question I've been meaning to ask you. What were you doing in the classroom after school yesterday when the policeman came? How did you happen to be there?"

The joy went out of Ahrele's face; he looked down at his toes.

"Never mind," Rav Elya Chaim went on. "You don't have to tell me if you don't want to. I know the answer anyway."

"You do?" Ahrele stammered.

"Yes," Rav Elya Chaim answered gravely. "There's only one reason I can think of for why a boy might still be in *cheder* after all his classmates have left. Do you know what reason I'm thinking of?"

"Yes," Ahrele whispered.

"Do you know, Ahrele, that you did a very brave and quick-thinking act. If it hadn't been for you, the policeman might never have been brought to justice. A boy with such a good mind and such outstanding *middos* could become a really great *talmid chacham*."

Ahrele grinned. *If the rav thinks I'm such a masmid, I'd better become one.*

SHLOMO BEN-DOVID

When you hit rock bottom there's

Only One Way to Go

ADAPTED BY SHEINDEL WEINBACH

WHEN REB TZEMACH arrived on *aliyah*, his were not the problems of clearing half a dozen lifts through customs with a minimum of damage. All of Reb Tzemach's earthly possessions were packed in one battered trunk. The rest of his assets, five of them, stood hand in hand behind him while the immigration official directed him to the camp that would be their first home in Eretz Yisrael.

Back in Europe Reb Tzemach had had a successful pharmacy, but that was all but forgotten in the nightmare of the ghetto. Left behind, but not forgotten — ever — was Reb Tzemach's wife, *aleha hashalom*.

It was her spirit in the form of a deathbed request that kept the family together as a unit. For Reb Tzemach, like thousands of others, might easily have been swayed or tricked into relinquishing his children to one of the political parties whose agents worked relentlessly in the immigrant camps, buying, bartering, or snatching children away from their "green" parents. Children who were separated from their parents during the first crucial weeks of their stay were brought up independently and many never saw their parents again. Nor did they express a desire to do so after the thorough indoctrination they received in their new homes.

While Reb Tzemach's family was saved from a fate worse than death, the fate that stretched bleakly ahead looked none too rosy. After the absorption authorities became convinced of Reb Tzemach's determination to keep his family united, they left him alone and were more than glad to allow him to go to Yerushalayim. No job was provided for him, no living quarters, just a few crumpled *lirot* too creased to even rustle in his pockets.

Fending for himself, Reb Tzemach discovered an abandoned stone ruin in the Musrara section, a few yards from the border. It wasn't much more than a roof over their heads, but it was enough for a beginning. Besides, it was theirs, a four-cubit plot in Yerushalayim that no one was likely to take away from them.

The first thing Reb Tzemach did after laying claim to his home was to register his children in religious schools. While they were away, he shopped and cooked and did what cleaning there was to do. It was out of the question for him to set up shop again. He did not have the means for it. And so, when his meager savings ran out, he turned to begging. It was not an easy thing to stretch out a hand and be dependent upon the good will of an occasional passerby. But when one passerby turned out to be a *landsman* of his who recognized him, Reb Tzemach resolved to end his degradation and stay home, even at the price of his only source of income.

Having hit rock bottom, there was only one direction for his fortunes to go — up. A merciful Father in Heaven did not ignore the cries of five orphans and their widowed father.

A few days later, as Reb Tzemach was busying himself about the house, he heard cries of alarm and rushed outside to find where they were coming from. A neighbor had severely injured himself with an ax while chopping firewood. Reb Tzemach rushed back to get his black bag of pharmaceuticals, a relic from better days, and was soon at his neighbor's side, stopping the bleeding and dressing the wound. He carried the man inside just as a doctor arrived. Reb Tzemach stood quietly by while the doctor examined the dressing.

"It's quite a professional job," he admitted with a note of admiration. "There is nothing left here for me to do."

This incident won Reb Tzemach a reputation as a healer, a reputation that grew as more and more people began to avail themselves of his services, always with satisfactory results. They grew to have confidence in his deft fingers and his knack for prescribing the right medicine. And above all, they respected him for his patience in dealing with human ills that do not always stem from physical ailments. Whoever knocked at Reb Tzemach's door was welcomed in and left soothed.

As his practice grew, Reb Tzemach began to stock up on medical supplies. He kept everything locked up in a pantry, not out of fear of robbers but simply because he kept rat poison beside his regular medical supplies. The poison was much in demand in the poor, ramshackle neighborhood.

The money began to trickle into the household, but the good days did not last for long. A sharp knock at the door one day proved to be a summons for Reb Tzemach to appear before a health inspector.

"Where is your license?" the inspector asked Reb Tzemach. "What right do you have to practice medicine without a proper license?"

Reb Tzemach smiled wryly. "Sir, I came to this country straight from the ghetto with barely a penny to my name. I was a licensed pharmacist but if you don't take my word for it..." he shrugged his shoulders helplessly and let the answer trail into thin air.

The inspector's manner was kind and sympathetic, but it didn't help much when Reb Tzemach heard the verdict that he must pass a test in pharmacy within the next three months and that, of course, he must stop practicing without a license.

The next morning Reb Tzemach went dutifully to the university to find out the details of the test he needed to take to qualify to practice pharmacy. He discovered that things were not so easy. He would first have to study Hebrew properly in an Ulpan course. Only then would he be eligible to register for the compulsory half-year refresher course in pharmacy, for which he would have to pay a five hundred-*lira* registration fee. And only then could he take the licensing examination!

Five hundred *lira*! Reb Tzemach had never seen that much in all his days in Israel. Five hundred *lira*! To begin with, how and where was he going to scrape it up? And how would his family subsist while he spent his time "educating" himself at the university? The man behind the information desk had no answer to those questions.

Reb Tzemach returned home in despair. To fulfill such impossible requirements was out of the question. And even though he was a law-abiding citizen at heart, he had no recourse but to ignore his three-month ultimatum and to continue his practice as before.

All he succeeded in doing was gaining those three months, during which he practiced undisturbed. But when they were up he was summoned once more to the inspector's office.

Once again Reb Tzemach faced the future with all the chips down. But even in the blackness, hope glimmered. That glimmer of hope lay wrapped up carefully in some rags at the bottom of his old trunk. Reb Tzemach bent over and carefully unwound some layers of the past to uncover a Chanukah menorah. A survivor of the cruel ghetto, stripped of all earthly possessions, Reb Tzemach did not now cherish the menorah for its sentimental value. Here and now Reb Tzemach could not afford sentimentality. He took the menorah into trembling, loving hands and caressed its silver branches for the last time. Then he put emotion aside and started polishing the menorah briskly, revealing all its hidden facets and highlighting its visual assets until he was satisfied.

Reb Tzemach stepped out of the house. The five children would miss the menorah that they cherished almost as strongly as he. But they were in their *chadarim* now. He walked hurriedly to the silversmith's, weighing the question in his mind for the final time. Was there another way out? Could he possibly move his family away and start all over again? Where would they go and where would they find another roof over their unfortunate heads? How could they leave the shelter they gratefully called home, the house from whose roof he could see the Har Habayis framed by a sky so blue it seemed to reflect the Heavenly throne itself! Should they stay — without any source of income — and starve? Certainly not. With a firm step, Reb Tzemach made the rounds from shop to shop until he got the price he asked. This was by no means the true worth of the silver, jewel-studded menorah, but Reb Tzemach was realistic. He pocketed the bills, twenty fifty-*lira* notes, and turned to leave.

He never knew what tempted him to turn back to the shopkeeper and ask, "How long will you hold it for me if I decide to buy it back?" Reb Tzemach did not notice the worldly-wise smile that the silversmith gave the threadbare indigent. All he registered was the "Two months" that soothed his ulcerated heart.

With a jaunty step, Reb Tzemach turned to the market to enjoy the luxury of spending money freely. It was Erev Shabbos and five hundred *lira* was all he required for the registration fee. The rest was his to spend as he wished. Reb Tzemach felt that his children deserved meat, wine, and sweets for at least this one Shabbos. He bought generously. If G-d had provided for them until now, He would surely continue to do so.

It was afternoon by the time Reb Tzemach had finished his Friday shopping. His spending spree had so infected him that he had put aside caution and removed the entire roll of bills from his pocket while paying the vendors. This had not gone unnoticed and, when he passed an empty lot near his home, he was accosted by a rough character armed with a gun.

"Let's have it," the man snarled from the side of his mouth.

Reb Tzemach pretended ignorance. "What do you mean? All I have are these bags of food."

The *gazlan* was in no mood for petty arguments. Covering him with the hand that held his gun, the man thrust his left hand into Reb Tzemach's pocket, drew out the roll of bills, and ran. Reb Tzemach was left there, in the middle of a dirty, deserted lot, without money and without his menorah.

It took a while until he shook himself out of his daze. "It's Erev Shabbos," he suddenly reminded himself. "If I have no money and no menorah, at least I do have these sacks full of food to prepare."

When he reached home, he resolved that at least during

Shabbos he would not worry or show any sign of his great loss. He greeted his children happily. They joyously unpacked the cornucopia of goodies that had cost their father all of one thousand *lira*.

The house sparkled that Friday afternoon. The bubbling cholent tickled hungry noses with its promise of a belly-filling feast. Everyone scrubbed up extra special to greet their weekly royal guest, Queen Shabbos.

Reb Tzemach washed and changed to his other clothes, bravely sharing his children's joy. Just as he was about to step out of the house to go to shul, he was quickly summoned to the aid of a neighbor who had suffered some accident. Reb Tzemach sent his boys off to shul and took his black bag of medicines and headed toward the injured man's home. For nearly an hour, he applied all his knowledge, experience, and skill to pulling his patient back from the brink of death. When he was able to rise and leave, he felt deep inner satisfaction that he had saved a human life.

Isn't it worth more than all the money in the world? he thought happily.

As he approached his house, Reb Tzemach was met by his children who had already returned from shul. "Don't go home," they whispered in his ear. "Four men are seated at the table, and they have eaten our food."

Reb Tzemach was beyond the point where he could feel further pain. Had he not suffered enough today? Wearily but carefully he approached a window and looked into his own house. It was true. Strangers had partaken of his meal and had made themselves unwelcome tenants in his own home. Another longer look told him that they were Arab terrorists. But wait! What were they doing? Their dirty heads were lolling on his white tablecloth — were they sleeping? Without emitting a sound? Without moving?

Reb Tzemach quickly dispatched a child to summon the police. When they arrived, the Arabs had still not awakened, and the police were able to enter the house boldly.

The capture of the four terrorists was an anticlimax. They were already dead. Having slipped across the border, the men had been sidetracked by the light in the empty house and then by the aromatic smell of good food. They had helped themselves generously from the cholent pot, but the seasoning was not spicy enough for their Oriental palates. They had broken into the medicine cabinet and extracted a likely looking gray powder which they mistook for pepper. It wasn't. They never lived to find out that they had generously seasoned the cholent with rat poison.

The real climax to the day's events was the police notification that Reb Tzemach was entitled to half the contents of the dead men's pockets. When Motza'ei Shabbos rolled around, Reb Tzemach stopped in at the Russian Compound, and found that not only could he afford to pay the registration fee, but that he would also have enough to buy back his precious menorah and support his children while he prepared for his license exam.

R. HERSHOWITZ

One Jew's bitachon *caused Hashem Himself to make*

The Demonstration

IT IS LIKE a magnet — Yerushalayim radiating mysterious holiness, drawing its people from the length and breadth of the country. The roads to Yerushalayim are filled with the songs of the Jews who have left their homes and fields to come and celebrate Yom Tov at the Beis Hamikdash.

The *rabbanim*, the *chachamim*, and the dignitaries of the city have left their seats of learning to stand by the gates and personally welcome each incoming group of weary but joyous pilgrims. Among them is Buni, one of the wealthiest men in Yerushalayim. On his face you see a trace of the anxiety that fills his heart. He looks at the impassive sky. It is months since the land has known rain — the streams have dried up and the city reservoirs are almost empty. Very soon the joy and the devotion will die in every heart: how can hundreds of thousands of people celebrate Yom Tov gathered in a single city beneath the blazing sun with scarcely a drop of water for each?

Wistfully, Buni thinks of the twelve fountains on the outskirts of the city, the possession of the Roman governor stationed in Yerushalayim. The fountains have their source in slow springs. But the adjoining cisterns are brimful. It will still be many days before their supplies are exhausted.

The crowds are continually swarming into the city in ever-increasing numbers. They are hot and tired from the lengthy journey.

If only those fountains were mine, thinks Buni, *how good it would be for my people.* An idea blazes into his mind. *They can be mine, of course they can be mine!* His anxiety dissolved, his eyes are bright with determination. *These officers are greedy for money. I have the bait to satisfy them.*

Beckoning to the two servants who are with him, Buni hurriedly leaves the scene. Every path and turning of his beloved Yerushalayim is known to him. He leads the way down the narrow, winding streets to the large, imposing mansion which stands apart, isolated from the rest of the city. Its fat, self-indulgent owner is standing in the spacious grounds. He gives a greasy smile of anticipation to his wealthy visitor.

Buni is forthright. "My people have come from throughout the country to celebrate our festival in Yerushalayim. Yet there is no water for them to drink. Lend me your twelve fountains. I promise to return them full when my people have gone home."

"How can you promise to return them? The springs do not trickle quickly enough to refill the cisterns. With what will you fill them?"

"With rainwater."

"And if it doesn't rain?"

"Then I will pay you twelve *kikarim* of silver instead."

The governor rubs his hands in silent glee. How can the Jew be so certain that rain will fall? They fix a date by which the water must be returned or the money paid.

The bargain is completed.

Yom Tov passes in great joy. Water? There is enough for everyone's needs, leaving the hours free for devotion and exultation. The people return to their homes inspired by the spiritual experience of being in Yerushalayim and at the Beis Hamikdash, fortified to continue their work with faithfulness until the next Yom Tov.

ଔଞ୍

Much time has passed. The visitors have all gone home. Yerushalayim has long since resumed its daily routine. Yet the skies still remain blue and placid.

The appointed day arrives. Shacharis is hardly over when Buni sees the governor's servant standing outside his gates. "My master demands his water or his money."

The note of triumph can be detected even in the tone of the servant.

Buni looks at him in surprise. "Tell your master that the day has just begun."

The hours wear on. The noonday sun beats fiercely upon a parched earth.

The servant reappears. "My master demands his water or his money."

Buni eyes him calmly. "Tell your master that the day is still long."

The hours that seemed so many have slipped into the past.

The sun is slipping into the west. The *Minchah* offering is being brought in the Beis Hamikdash.

The servant comes back. His tone is demanding.

"My master is waiting: his water or his money?"

Buni looks into the distance at the descending sun.

"Tell your master that the day is not yet over."

The servant hurries to repeat the message to his master. The governor's greedy eyes flash his scorn. "Foolish Jew! For months we have seen no rain. Does he think it will fall for him now?"

The governor enters the bathhouse, followed closely by his servant bearing his most dignified robes. Is he preparing himself for the wealth almost in his grasp?

The heart of the governor is locked with a double seal of pride and greed. But Buni's heart is firm with faith. Humbly, he enters the *azarah* of the Beis Hamikdash. Enrobing himself in a *tallis*, he stands with head bowed in *tefillah*.

"*Ribono shel Olam*," his lips move in impassioned prayer. "You know that I did not act for my own glory, nor for the glory of my father's house, but only for Your Glory, that there should be water for the *olei regel*."

At that moment the skies darken with clouds, and rain begins to pour upon the earth, faster, heavier, until all the cisterns overflow.

His heart overflowing with gratitude, Buni leaves the Beis Hamikdash. Outside on the drenched streets, he meets the governor leaving the bathhouse.

Buni accosts him. "You must pay me for the surplus water."

"I know that your G-d has brought all this rain only because of you. But the water didn't fall until the sun had set — you still owe me the money."

In silence Buni turns away and re-enters the Beis Hamikdash.

Enrobing himself in his *tallis*, he stands once more in *tefillah*, "*Ribono shel Olam*, demonstrate that You have beloved ones in Your world."

At that moment the wind blew, the clouds dispersed, and a brilliant sun shone on the western horizon.

HERSHEL WOLF

Evolution of a Theory

DR. YAAKOV SCHEINER WINS NOBEL PRIZE!

Professor Scheiner Lectures Before Tremendous Audience at Carnegie Hall!

*Y*ANKY VISUALIZED THE headlines. It wasn't that Yanky didn't want to learn Torah — *chas v'shalom*! But he couldn't help daydreaming about achieving fame and fortune. *The famous Rabbi Doctor Y. Scheiner, dressed in a smart white coat and a big black yarmulke.* What *a* kiddush Hashem! Knowing that many of the greatest scientific discoveries had come from simple accidents or random observation, Yanky felt he had a good chance even without going to college. In fact, if he made a really good discovery now, all the colleges would rush to offer him honorary doctorates and he'd never need step inside a college — except to receive the awards. The only problem was, *How do you make such a discovery?* Suddenly, in the depth of his mind, Yanky had one of those flashes of inspiration experienced only by the elect — an *Idea!*

Yanky noted the types of vehicles on the roads and in houses — bicycles, carriages, scooters, little cars, big cars, trucks, buses, and so on; *how come there are so many different kinds?* Did such a question ever occur to you? Probably not. But then the chances are that you do not have the ever-questioning, ever-probing mind of a truly great scientist who, in his relentless search for the absolute truth, leaves no stone unturned — like Yanky.

The vehicles, concluded Yanky, *have evolved!* The theory was elegant. When Yanky got home, he went straight to his room to work on it. On large pieces of clean paper, Yanky made lists and diagrams classifying the different types of vehicles and arranging them in order of development. Everything fit perfectly: From the basic bicycle, two main directions of development took place — powered vehicles and unpowered vehicles. Unpowered vehicles remained primitive — simple bicycles, children's tricycles, carriages, strollers, etc. The powered vehicles, though, were much more successful; they multiplied and developed. At first the species were very primitive, like motorbikes and motor scooters but, at the tricycle stage, a wonderful improvement developed — the outside body which shielded the occupants from the weather's harshness. Thus did the little pop-pop motorized tricycle develop an extra wheel and become the small car, and so on.

Of course, Yanky was the first to admit that there were serious faults with the theory. How could inanimate objects develop and grow? Clearly there had to be some way, some process for such a growth, as yet undiscovered and waiting to be revealed to the world. Daddy's voice broke through his questions, "Yanky, Minchah! Come, it's late already!"

Through Minchah and Ma'ariv and supper the problem weighed heavily on Yanky's thoughts. Then, during the prunes and custard, the second bolt of inspiration struck. He hurriedly gulped down the rest of his food, dashed through *bentching*, and rushed upstairs. "Daddy, can I borrow your encyclopedia, please?"

"Okay, Yanky, but put it back when you've finished with it, and don't use sticky candy wrappers as bookmarks." Five times Yanky climbed the stairs, each time hauling four hefty volumes from the living room to his bedroom. "Good night, everyone!" Yanky closed his door for the night and settled down to work.

By the time the light of dawn cast its pale glow onto Yanky's desk, the main parts of the theory had taken shape. Wearily, Yanky put down his pen, turned off his little electronic calculator, and lay down on his bed to catch an hour of sleep before Shacharis.

This part of the theory had its roots in an incident which had occurred when Yanky was young. The wheels of a passing car had thrown up a screw which had hit Yanky in the face and embedded itself in his nose; he still bore the scar. Obviously there is a continual process in which the wheels of vehicles throw up bits and pieces, nuts, bolts, nails, screws, and all sorts of odds and ends from the road surface. Though most fall back onto the road, it is only a matter of time before a useful piece will hit a passing vehicle in a useful place so as to improve that vehicle in some way. However, the real objection was, *How could the piece attach itself to the vehicle?* The screw had embedded itself in Yanky's nose, but it couldn't embed itself in a piece of iron unless it was flying at a tremendous speed and it would be unrealistic to expect that. At that point, Yanky was blessed with another brilliant brainwave.

In dry weather, he had noticed, cars gathered a lot of static electricity. Sometimes, when you touched the door, you got an electric shock which packed a real punch. He knew that the voltages built up in this way were often very large — perhaps thousands of volts. Also, he had learned that pure metals are smelted out of their ores by mixing them with various cheap and common chemicals in a furnace. If those ores and chemicals were present in road dust and covered the surface of a vehicle as a layer of dust, a spark passing from one vehicle to another would resemble a miniature furnace and cause metal in the dust to be smelted out and deposited on the vehicle. And, in any case, the spots of metal would build up on the vehicle and perhaps a useful structure would eventually be formed. Yanky ruffled through his encyclopedia checking facts and figures. Everything fit perfectly. *Iron is found as iron oxide in rust and in rock dust. Aluminum is very common as alum in clays and as aluminum silicates in rocks, quartz, etc. Carbon dust, as from rubber, would mix with the fresh molten iron to make steel.* So, under suitable conditions of ambient temperature, relative humidity, and atmospheric pressure, it would only be a matter of time before a vehicle would be improved. Yanky had discovered the mechanism of growth!

However, all theories must be tested by experiment and proven in the harsh light of facts. But how could this theory be tested? Yanky had another brainwave.

Yanky visited the local junkyard. "I'm working on a scientific theory. Can I please inspect your junkyard?" he asked the owner.

"Okay, my lad," the owner replied, "but be careful. I can't take responsibility if anything falls on you."

Who cares about personal risk when one is on the brink of greatness? Yanky strode into the yard and began looking closely at the types of vehicles in the pile. Making statistical assessments, Yanky noted the occurrence of each type of vehicle at each level of the pile. It looked good. After supper, he analyzed the statistics. It worked out better than he had dared hope.

Right at the bottom of the junk heaps were loads of old bicycles, carriages, and children's tricycles. Then came a few motorized bicycles and scooters, and there was one covered tricycle. Then, higher up the heap, came small cars and then, bigger cars. And right on top was a huge bus!

Before disclosing his findings to the world, Yanky reckoned it would be best to discuss the matter first with an expert. Mr. Moss, who lived next door, had a big car and knew a lot about them, but he wouldn't be able to have a good chat with him until next Sunday afternoon. So Yanky made an appointment and waited impatiently till the appointed time.

Yanky strode next door with a big, fat file under his arm. Mr. Moss led him into his study, and Yanky explained the theory. He was able to elaborate and explain how the two-cylinder engine developed into the three-cylinder engine, and then into the four-cylinder, six- and then eight-cylinder engines; how the two-stroke cycle gave way to the four-stroke cycle; and how the air-cooled engine developed into the water-cooled engine. Mr. Moss was amazed at the technical details flowing from Yanky. When Yanky had finished, Mr. Moss sat back and thought for a long while before saying, "Well, it's certainly an unusual and original theory, but I think I can disprove it." Mr. Moss went to his bookcase, took out a book, and gave it to Yanky. "This is a book on the history of car manufacture. It tells quite clearly how cars developed. There was no accident and no chance weldings. The car was developed by inventors who knew what they wanted and used their intelligence to achieve their aim."

Yanky flicked through the book with a superior smile on his face: he'd seen books like this in the library. "I've noticed that none of these books is written by the supposed inventors themselves. They're always written by someone who either read the facts in another book or who was told about it by other people. The truth is that these so-called inventions evolved as I explained and the so-called inventors claim the credit for themselves."

Mr. Moss was taken aback by Yanky's swift reply. "How long do you reckon this evolutionary process of yours would take?"

"About three thousand years," he replied.

"But this book states that the first motor car was invented only about one hundred years ago. How do you explain that, Yanky?"

Yanky was not dismayed. "I told you, the so-called date of invention is really the year they found it. Actually, the car itself must have been a good few thousand years old."

That really knocked Mr. Moss for ten. It took him a good few moments to regain his composure. "Come, let's go for a drive and I'll show you something."

They went out to the car and got in. Yanky's eyes opened up wide as he gazed at the array of knobs and dials and lights on the dashboard. Mr. Moss slipped the car into gear, and they moved off smoothly. They didn't seem to be going anywhere in particular. "Enjoying the ride?" asked Mr. Moss. Yanky smiled, nodded, and sank deeper into the leather upholstery.

Suddenly, out of the corner of his eye, Yanky caught sight of a most monstrous vehicle. "Stop, Mr. Moss!"

The brakes squealed as the car came to a halt.

"Look at that!" Yanky pointed to the ugly sight: a weird and ghastly collection of pipes and knobs and bits and pieces. Obviously it was some sort of vehicle, for the engine and wheels could be discerned and there was even a steering wheel, but there was no bodywork and the whole thing was filthy black and covered with grime. "Look! So many useless vestiges."

Yanky got out for a closer look. "No outside bodywork, so it's obviously very primitive." He walked around it, humming and ha-ing.

"In my opinion," Yanky announced after a few circuits, "this is known as a living fossil. The line of development followed an original course but was hampered by too many useless vestiges to be successful."

They walked back to the car. Mr. Moss got in and fiddled with something under the dashboard, and the hood sprang open, revealing the engine in all its glory. "Well, Yanky, what do you think of this specimen?"

With a yelp of delight, Yanky sprang forward to feast his eyes on the gleaming interior. He'd never actually seen the inside of a car before, but having read all about the subject, his expert eye quickly picked out the main components. He saw the massive engine with the gleaming crankshaft and eight gleaming piston rods, the carburetor, the dynamo, and the fan — but wait — there seemed to be an extra carburetor and there were odds and ends and bits of wires all over the place that were clearly useless. "Very nice, Mr. Moss, very advanced, but there seems to be quite a few vestigial parts."

Mr. Moss smiled. "What do you mean by vestigial parts, Yanky? You've mentioned it a few times already."

Yanky was rather surprised that Mr. Moss didn't know the meaning of such a simple word. "A vestigial part is a carry-over from an earlier form but which has no purpose in the car now. According to my theory, cars have developed by themselves; the presence of a vestigial part is a clear proof because it is useless in its current existence, and can only be explained because it was at one time useful."

Mr. Moss gave a loud laugh. "Oh, Yanky, you're really getting yourself into a mess now. Just because you don't know what a part means you call it useless?"

Yanky blushed.

"Huh, I bet you even thought that the extra carburetor was a 'mistake.'"

Yanky's blush went a deeper shade of red. "I...I...I..." he stuttered.

"You didn't even know that some engines have two carburetors! Look!" Mr. Moss took Yanky on a guided tour of the engine compartment, and explained what each component and wire was used for.

"So you see, Yanky, each little part has a specific function and it is designed and manufactured specifically for that function. Just because you don't know what that function is doesn't mean it doesn't have one. Had you thought about it, you would have realized yourself that an intelligent design is proof of an intelligence behind the design. Just look at this car! How could it have come by itself? Each and every part is so beautifully designed and manufactured specifically for its purpose."

"But what about that monstrous vehicle on the road?" protested Yanky. "All those useless pipes and knobs and things."

Mr. Moss gave another laugh. "I thought that would throw you. I saw it on my way home before Shabbos. It happens to be a road-paving machine. It does the work of ten people in half their time. A machine like that costs about $100,000. I can guarantee that there isn't a single useless screw or inch of metal in that whole thing. Come, jump in. I can see you want to think a bit."

Yanky's face had fallen so low he nearly tripped over it as he got into the car. They drove silently for a while. "I really made a fool of myself, didn't I, Mr. Moss?"

"Yes, Yanky, but only to me. So you're still okay." Mr. Moss smiled.

"But how could I do such a thing? I can see now how right you are. How could I even begin to think of such a stupid idea? Cars make themselves!" Tears began to glisten in Yanky's eyes.

Evolution of a Theory

"I'll tell you why, Yanky. It's because you wanted to become famous, so you looked for an idea which would bring you fame. Fame was your goal, so you were not looking for truth and did not see it even when it was staring you in the face. Had you been looking for truth, and left fame to the *Eibershter's cheshbon* you would have seen things differently. Don't look so glum, Yanky! Some people go through their lives imagining that they're searching for the truth when really the ulterior motives at the back of their minds lead them way off. At least you've learned your lesson young. Ah, we're home now! Cheer up, your mother will get worried if she sees you with such a sad face."

Yanky forced a wan smile and climbed out of the car. Slowly he went indoors, excused himself from his usual afternoon snack, and went straight up to his room. There he sadly began tearing up his elaborate notes — the wasted fruits of many hours of hard labor. But there was still something nagging at the back of his mind. He couldn't put his finger on it, but he knew that there was still a proof left unsatisfied. Then he came to his junkyard analysis. That was it! The figures proved it. Once again the old thoughts began rushing through his mind. *Perhaps there is still something left to the theory; perhaps there is still a chance for fame and fortune. I'll have to check up again on my findings.*

Next day, Yanky's route home took him past the junkyard. Yanky looked and checked and double-checked. All his figures tallied. Suddenly he heard a gruff voice behind him. "You got a problem, boy?"

He spun around to see the owner standing there. "Yes," he replied, "I can't understand why at the bottom of the pile are old and rusty bicycles and carriages and little things, while at the top of the pile are fresh, large cars and trucks. Surely these things should be equally distributed throughout the pile?"

"Haw! Haw!" the man laughed raucously. "That's what's botherin' you, eh? Well, you see my crane over there?" Yanky followed the man's finger and saw a huge crane towering above them. "Well, it's got a big grab. When I pick things up and load them onto the truck for the metal work, the little things fall through and stay on the pile — then I just dump the new stuff on top of it. 'Nother reason is I could only afford to buy old bikes when I first started my business. Now it ain't worth my while and I don't bother with 'em. You happy now?"

Yanky nodded, thanked him for his kindness in answering his question, and went on his way home again. Simple! No? *Nobel Prizewinner! Professor! Honorary doctorate! Headlines! I could kick myself.*

He did.

AHUVA COHEN

Rav Elya Chaim's **chachmah** *convinces a hard-hearted judge in the case of*

The Telltale Bribes

Feivel rolled over and buried his head deeper in the pillow. "Go 'way," he mumbled sleepily.

"OPEN UP IN THE NAME OF THE CZAR!"

It had been a hard day at the office of the Lodz Jewish Orphanage where Feivel Aaronson worked as a clerk, bookkeeper, office manager, and treasurer all rolled into one. Not that Feivel minded having to work hard at his job. Not at all! A lot of work for Feivel was a sign that money was pouring into the institution's usually near-empty treasury, and good-hearted Feivel rejoiced at the orphanage's good fortune. Feivel was a bachelor and a confirmed one at that. Oh, there was a time many years ago when Feivel had wanted to marry, but then his father had been sick and he had had to work hard to support his mother and six younger brothers and sisters. Afterward, Feivel's father had passed away and his mother had remarried, but by then he was almost forty, and he'd gotten used to living alone.

Now, worn out from the day's work, Feivel slept soundly.

"OPEN UP IN THE NAME OF THE CZAR!"

This time Feivel did not stir. Even if the shouts had penetrated his deep sleep, it is doubtful whether he would have paid them much attention. Loud commotions in the dead of night, raised voices, the shattering of glass, bayonet handles beating against heavy wooden doors — none of these sounds were unusual in the streets of Lodz at the turn of the century. The seeds of revolution were sweeping Russia and Poland, and Lodz was not immune. The revolutionaries, mostly students, were advocating the overthrow of the Czar and an independent Poland. Clashes with the police were frequent and fierce. In fact, the general state of affairs had become so bad that it was unsafe to leave money in the banks. Feivel had gotten into the daily habit of emptying the orphanage's cashbox into a little brown sack which he carried for the purpose. He would pin this sack inside his shirt and, once home, he would transfer the little sack inside a bureau drawer. There, nestled among his underwear, shirts, and socks it would lie safely while Feivel dreamed untroubled dreams until the next morning when he would return it to the gray strongbox in the office. And so tonight the little sack in the bureau drawer contained the huge sum of six hundred rubles. And Feivel Aaronson, exhausted from his hard day's work, slept soundly on.

"OPEN UP IN THE NAME OF THE CZAR!"

A dim something penetrated Feivel's consciousness, causing him to stir ever so slightly.

"OPEN UP IN THE NAME OF THE CZAR!"

Feivel threw one arm out over the side of the bed and struggled to open his eyes.

A shot rang out, and Feivel, rubbing sleep from his eyes, tumbled out of bed and ran to the door.

"OPEN UP IN THE NAME OF THE — So! You've finally decided to open up, have you?" the largest of the three policemen boomed.

"We are under orders to search this house," the first policeman said loudly. "We are conducting routine nightly searches for holders of revolutionary material." Feivel sighed a heavy sigh of relief. Well, he certainly had nothing to fear then. Revolutionary papers? He hardly knew what it was all about. That was all fine and good for youths of nineteen, but for a respectable man of middle age…

Suddenly the peaceful expression on Feivel's face turned to one of dismay, for the three policemen were tearing through the rooms, wreaking havoc in every corner. With his saber point, one slashed the strawfilled mattress on which Feivel slept, another strewed the contents of his kitchen cupboard all over the room, the third…

Feivel's eyes bulged as he noticed the third man pulling drawers out of his bureau. Stealthily, Feivel began to edge his way forward to where the little brown sack lay, but he was too slow. The policeman was eagerly ripping the sack apart and calling at the same time to his two companions.

"Hey, comrades! Look at this!" The three crowded around the sack, eyes brightening with greed. Feivel saw the look that they exchanged and rapidly began to explain how he came to have such a sum of money in his house, stressing that it was charity money. But the policemen were too overjoyed with their good fortune to want to listen to explanations.

"Be quiet, Jew!" snapped one. "Don't expect us to believe your stories. All revolutionaries are liars."

"Revolutionary?" gasped Feivel. "I'm no revolutionary."

"Aren't you?" retorted the cop. "Then what are these?" He held out a batch of leaflets, and Feivel stared at them with a sinking heart. He had seen those leaflets before. They were printed by a group of students in one of the large Polish universities and they called for the overthrow of the Czar!

Nothing can be more incriminating than the discovery of those leaflets in my house, Feivel thought. But he was mistaken. For at that very moment, the same cop thrust something else under Feivel's nose.

"And what about this?" he demanded sarcastically. "Would you be so kind as to explain where this came from?"

It was a *rifle*.

Feivel did not answer. *What is the use of protesting?* he thought bitterly. *The cops know as well as I do that I'm innocent.* Oh, it was clear to him now. The policemen had somehow found out that he took the daily cash receipts home with him and they had purposely included his house in their daily search. But to protect themselves from ever being caught, they had turned around and accused him of revolutionary activities. After all, what better way to silence an innocent man and to effectively tie his hands than to put him on the defensive? Who would believe him? No one, you could be sure of that. And they had even planted the evidence so as to completely foolproof their story.

Still, perhaps these gendarmes are not completely heartless. Perhaps it is worth another try.

"Look," began Feivel pleadingly, "please don't take the money, I beg of you. It isn't mine, I told you it belongs to charity. But I have here fifty rubles of my own. Take that instead, if you must take something."

"Are you trying to bribe us, too?" sneered one of them. "A rifle, revolutionary pamphlets, and a fifty-ruble bribe. That will look quite impressive when your case comes up in court." His two companions burst into loud guffaws of laughter.

Feivel was too stunned and despondent to speak. They had purposely twisted his words against him. It was no use. *Who can I possibly turn to for help? Who can I convince that I'm telling the truth?* he thought frantically. But he did not have much time to ponder this question for he was suddenly grabbed by three pairs of hands and roughly hauled off to prison.

However, help was forthcoming and from an entirely unexpected direction.

Feivel's little house looked out on a tiny courtyard. Adjoining the courtyard on the other side was another little house in which there lived an elderly widow named Hinda. It so happened that on this particular night, it being quite hot, both Feivel and Hinda had left all their windows open. And so Hinda was able to observe the whole sequence of events and to hear everything that was being said as well. Now, as soon as the sun began to rise, she hurried as fast as her old legs could carry her to the home of Rav Elya Chaim Meisel, the *rav* of Lodz, where she poured out Feivel's story.

The *rav* asked Hinda a few questions and sent her home with his assurance that he would do all he could for the unfortunate man. Then he dispatched his *shamash* to the police station.

An hour later the *shamash* was back in the *rav's* study.

"I'm sorry, Rebbi, but they won't let you appear at the hearing. I've tried every way I could to get them to reconsider, but they remain adamant."

Rav Elya Chaim thought for a while. Then, in a low voice, he explained something to the *shamash* who listened earnestly. A few minutes later the *shamash* went out again, heading as before toward the police station.

⊙

Feivel slumped dejectedly in his chair and tried to shut out the grinning faces of the three policemen facing him. One thought stood out clearly from the confused jumble of thoughts that was Feivel's mind. *I must plead guilty to all these charges.*

"You are guilty," the *rav's shamash* had whispered to him through the bars of his stuffy cell only a half hour earlier. "Remember that you are guilty of all three crimes: the papers, the gun, and bribery. But you must insist that the gendarmes got their story wrong. You did not give all of them together one fifty-ruble bribe, you gave each of them fifty rubles. That makes 150 rubles altogether. Remember that!"

Feivel was remembering. *There are few people I trust as much as Rav Elya Chaim Meisel. He is famous for his around-the-clock readiness to help a fellow Jew. And he is a great* talmid chacham. *So if Rav Elya Chaim tells me, Feivel, to plead guilty, then there must be a good reason behind it.*

Still, Feivel was afraid. *To admit to three such terrible accusations is bad enough, but to admit to more than even they have accused me of — to confess having tried to bribe the policemen with 150 rubles instead of fifty — making my crime all the worse — that is too much.*

I won't do it! Feivel decided suddenly. *I'll declare my innocence. Surely the judge will listen to me!*

The judge rapped for order and the hearing opened. The self-appointed leader of the three policemen arose and testified that they had entered Feivel Aaronson's house on the night of

September 6th as part of a routine search and had found a pile of revolutionary leaflets as well as a rifle.

"The accused then tried to bribe us with the sum of fifty rubles, suggesting that we split it evenly among us," he concluded. "I have the money right in my pocket, and I'll turn it over to the court for the trial. The pamphlets and the gun are here, too."

"Lies, lies, it's all a pack of lies," burst out Feivel, unable to control himself any longer. "They planted the leaflets and the gun in my room to corroborate their story. As for the bribe, it's a lie, too. I tell you…"

Feivel saw that it was no use. "All right! All right!" he shouted angrily. "I'm guilty! I admit it! I plead guilty to all three charges."

The judge smiled happily. *Now we're getting somewhere.* He opened his mouth to say something but Feivel had not finished and this time he was allowed to speak.

"I'm guilty, do you hear?! I had the papers, I possessed the rifle, I gave the gendarmes 150 rubles."

The judge looked puzzled and the policemen stared at one another, bewildered.

"One hundred and fifty rubles?" the judge repeated thoughtfully. "Don't you mean fifty rubles?"

"No," Feivel repeated stubbornly. "One hundred and fifty rubles. There were three gendarmes and I gave fifty rubles to each of them. That makes 150."

The judge glanced over at the policemen who were whispering together.

"Stand up!" he barked. They jumped up from their seats. "Empty out your pockets."

"Your honor," began the spokesman, but the judge stopped him.

"Empty out your pockets. I want to see who is telling the truth."

The three policemen began to fish around in their pockets, pulling out coins one by one.

"I said empty them!" the judge roared. "Turn your pockets inside out immediately!"

Shamefacedly, the policemen complied, and six hundred rubles dropped out to the floor. The judge gazed down at the money and then up at the policemen, comprehension dawning on his face.

"May I inquire how you gentlemen come to be carrying such a large sum of money in your pockets?" he inquired icily. "Furthermore, it strikes me as slightly odd that all three of you should have exactly two hundred rubles apiece in your pockets on the same day."

The three policemen broke down and confessed their crime. They were tried and sentenced to several years in prison. Feivel Aaronson was released immediately. Naturally, his first stop was at the home of Rav Elya Chaim where he poured forth his thanks to the *rav*, vowing that never again would he doubt — even for a minute — that advice given by Rav Elya Chaim Meisel of Lodz was advice worth following.

SHEINDEL WEINBACH

Love of Torah makes one realize the insignificance of

The Great Cold

THE SOUND OF "Brrrr" and a heavy stamping of semi-frozen feet filled the shul on one of the coldest days that Slutzk had known for many winters. The small group of *mispallelim* was huddled around a blazing stove that offered its warmth only to the immediate vicinity. The great cold displaced the usual idle chatter about business, politics, and local news, as they waited for a *minyan* to assemble for Minchah. The shul slowly began to fill and, when the *yahrtzeit chiyuv* felt that only a few more stragglers might be expected, he went up to the *amud* and began to *daven*.

The bulk of the *mispallelim* bolstered their *hislahavus* by *davening* as close to the stove as possible. The poor *chazzan*, however, had to stand up front, where his breath almost froze in his face. Yet he seemed to be doing his best about shaking off the cold. In fact, he seemed almost unaware of it as his voice rang out in fervent prayer. Every once in a while a sigh would intertwine itself in the *nusach* or a tremor that bespoke a secret communion with vivid memories of a loving father who was now basking in the radiance of the *Shechinah* (Rav Yaakov Dovid was certain of *that*).

Was it his defiance of the cold that made the *tefillah* that day seem more meaningful? Or was it the wave of nostalgia which swept the group along with Rav Yaakov Dovid's emotional *tefillah*? Wave upon wave of feeling built up, crescendoed, until it reached a climax and broke. Rav Yaakov Dovid had burst into hot tears which condensed on his cheeks like crystal beads. His sobbing emitted cloudlets of steam which strained heavenward. And all around the group huddled round the stove, tears were evoked in empathy.

Rav Yaakov Dovid's cries seemed to fill an eternity.

Actually, the emotional interlude only lasted a minute or two. When the Kaddish had been said and the *davening* completed, he went to join the group around the reassuring stove and to revive them with *l'chaim* in memory of his departed father.

Many of the *ba'alei batim* from the group, comprised mainly of older men, had lost fathers and commemorated their *yahrtzeit* in the traditional Jewish way. Why was it, everyone seemed to wonder, that this particular occasion had moved them so much? It couldn't have been the memory of Reb Zev! He had been a good Jew. G-d forbid that anyone should say something against him. But he had been a simple bricklayer, no different from other bricklayers. Faces turned questioningly, expectantly, toward the *ba'al yahrtzeit*. What had been the reason of the outburst of tears during the *davening*, they demanded silently.

Rav Yaakov Dovid faced his silent questioners and began to speak.

"Yes," he sighed, "I have cherished memories of my father just as you all recall your own parents with love and sorrow. It is not only the calendar day, his *yahrtzeit*, which has brought him back to me so vividly today. It is the great cold. You see, cold played a big part in my childhood and if I suffered from it, my father surely suffered many times more.

"When I was young, a *cheder yingel*," he reminisced with a sad smile, "I was taken to a private *melamed*. My parents were not rich. They could not afford a private *rebbi* for their son. Whatever they paid for my education cost them dearly. My tuition was paid in money scrimped from food and clothing, not from denied luxuries. My father firmly felt that the money invested in his son's Torah education was worth every penny.

"I remember one particular winter. A heavy snow fell and isolated our town from the world. My father had no work and subsequently no wages. It made no difference, however, to my education. I kept up my private lessons faithfully, trudging through the snow each day to the house of my *melamed*. One day my *melamed* told me that if my father would not send the tuition he owed for the past two weeks, he would be forced to accept another boy in my place. He had to live, too, after all.

"When I relayed the message to my father I saw a desperate look flicker over his face. 'What!' he cried in anguish, 'not send my boy to study Torah? That would be the end of me!' Like a trapped animal he stalked about the room until reality broke through his dark thoughts and reminded him that it was time to *daven* Minchah.

"My father trudged through the cold streets to shul. The *davening* over, he turned to leave. Just then the president went up to the front of the room and pounded on the table for attention.

"'Who can build me an oven?' he asked. 'My daughter is getting married next week, and she needs a brick oven for her new home. I will pay well.' There were several bricklayers in our town, any of whom would have been glad for the job. There were, however, no bricks to be gotten since transportation was at a complete standstill. But the president couldn't wait. People were surprised to see my father approaching the president and offering his services. It was not the latter's business where the materials came from. His was to pay. He opened his purse and gave over the complete amount to my father who assured him that his daughter's oven would be built in time.

"When he returned home," Rav Yaakov Dovid continued, "he gave me the entire sum. 'Give this to the *melamed*,' he instructed me. 'Tell him that I am paying for the two weeks I owe him and for two weeks in advance. It is best to be safe. One never knows what will happen…' I could see how relieved he was now that the money had been entrusted to me and set aside for the specific purpose of paying my tutor. Now I saw his chin become firm and a calm, determined look enter his eyes.

"That night I lay awake, thinking, wondering, puzzling. Suddenly I heard a banging, not a chance sound of something falling but a studied sound of a man working with tools. I crept out of bed and saw my father bending over, his tools scattered about him, prying and banging at the bricks which made up our own oven. Working carefully so as not to crumble the materials, he was taking apart our oven, brick by brick! These were the materials he would use to build the president's daughter's oven!

"That was a cold winter. I'll never forget what we went through. I don't know where it was colder — outside or inside. Mercifully the wind did not penetrate our house, but the cold was our constant companion.

"I almost didn't come to Minchah today," Rav Yaakov Dovid admitted. "It was so cold outside. It brought memories of blue lips and frosty toes that never would warm up. But the cold also evoked the image of my father, legs braced and back bowed, hacking at our oven. How could I deny him a Kaddish on his *yahrtzeit* when he sacrificed so much for me, for my Torah?"

Rav Yaakov Dovid, the Ridbaz, got up, put on his overcoat, and wound a woolen shawl around his neck. He stepped out into the great cold.

TZVI ZOBIN

Have you grown enraptured by the music? Have you forgotten all about the jewels waiting for you to take in life's

Treasure Hunt

Uncle Silas leaned back in his armchair and glared over his cigar tip at Shloimy. "So you really think that your father, may he rest in peace, and I have both wasted our lives; that we have missed the point of life and that the million-dollar chain of stores that we have built up is an illusion created by the Devil to draw us away from the true path?"

Shloimy swallowed hard but he didn't flinch. "That does not seem to sum up the situation, Uncle."

"Thank you, Solomon," Uncle Silas growled sarcastically. *At least he's got guts, that boy — just like his father*, he thought to himself.

"The Midrash gives a *mashal*, a parable —"

"There's no need to translate the easy words, Solomon,"

interjected Uncle Silas. "I haven't forgotten everything I learned in yeshivah, even though it was nearly forty years ago."

"Sorry, Uncle. Anyway, the Midrash gives a parable — sorry, *mashal* — of a king who opened up his treasury to the public for one day. Anyone could take whatever he wanted. But at the entrance to the vaults, the king put his orchestra which played the most fantastically beautiful music. Everyone who came grew enraptured by the music, and forgot all about the money and jewels waiting to be taken. Finally, at the end of the day, the doors of the treasury were shut and the orchestra stopped playing. When the spell of music was broken, everyone realized that they had all lost their chance to become rich."

"And you, Solomon, think that people are as stupid as that nowadays?"

Shloimy nodded.

"Are you willing to put your money where your mouth is, Solomon?"

Shloimy's right eyebrow rose half an inch.

"I'll explain," continued Uncle Silas. "Before you got bitten by this religion bug, you majored in physics, right?"

Shloimy nodded.

"Okay. Let's do this scientifically. I suggest we try an experiment to test your theory. In three months' time, we're celebrating twenty-five years since your father and I opened our first shop. As a publicity stunt we'll run a sweepstake in aid of some charity and, as first prize, we'll let the winner have the run of our Madison Square branch for one hour. But we'll arrange the store like the king in the *mashal*. We'll start the winner off at the bottom of the store and put the jewelry department at the very top floor, and arrange the intermediate floors as attractively as possible. Now, anyone with any sense will go straight to the jewelry department. According to your theory, he'll be distracted by the other departments and waste his time on trivialities. So, Solomon, I suggest that you pay for everything taken from the jewelry department and I'll cover all other expenses. If you are correct, you won't lose a cent; if not —"

"I stand to lose a good few thousand dollars more than you do, Uncle," cut in Shloimy. "You'll have to raise your end of the bet in case I win to make it fair."

Uncle Silas toyed with the watch-chain spanning his ample assets. *Just like my brother — if only he'd get some sense and come into the business with me, we'd really go places. Perhaps this "experiment" will knock some sense into him.*

"Okay, Solomon," he said aloud, "if you win, I'll build an extension to your yeshivah in memory of your father."

"Done — let's shake on it!"

They shook hands and settled back to their coffee and cake.

"You know, Solomon," Uncle Silas broke the long silence, "I think we can refine our experiment a little more. I recall that one *pshat* about Gehinnom is that when a person stands before the Final Court, they play back to him a review of his entire life. Then he sees the chances he missed and what he lost, and realizes how he misspent his time. That itself is part of Gehinnom, correct?"

Shloimy nodded.

"So let's tell our sweepstake winner to mark with a special marker everything he wants in the store. Then we'll make a big twenty-fifth anniversary banquet where we'll present him with his selections. Hmm... We can give him a tape recorder and tell him to speak out all his thoughts during his treasure hunt. Then, when we play back the tape at the banquet and present him with what he's marked — well, if he used his time and kept his head, he'll be in heaven! If not, perhaps he'll learn the lesson you're trying to teach me!"

"Do you think people will appreciate the *mashal*, Uncle? Do you think people will recognize the *nimshal* and understand that we have to concentrate on stocking mitzvos instead of being distracted by the materialism around us?"

"Don't set your sights too high, Solomon. If you think it's worth your while spending a big chunk out of your *yerushah* on convincing me, okay. But if you want to convince the whole world, it'll cost you a lot more than that!"

☙❧

Good morning, ladies and gentlemen — or rather — good evening! When you'll be hearing this tape recording, we'll all be together at a fantastic banquet held in celebration of the centenary of the world-famous Fortnum and Lacey's Department Shop. As the highlight of this celebration, and to show their great generosity, they have given me, the winner of the grand "Help-the-poor" sweepstake the run of the entire building for one hour. I have a special marker, and everything which I mark will be presented to me after this tape has been played over to you. So now I'll be giving you a commentary of what I do, over the next hour.

I'm in the elevator on my way down to the basement for the start of the hour. It's rather cold as I've had to leave my suit jacket and coat at the entrance so that I can't take anything out when I leave. My plan is to go straight to the jewelry department and put my mark on as many valuable items I can find.

Here we are — basement — and it's exactly ten o'clock, so off I go. Wow! What a store! Look at all these counters and showcases full of the best; and what thick carpeting this is! Brr! It's chilly. This looks like the men's clothing department so I'll just put on a few bits and pieces and get myself warm. How about a smart suit? Hmm! What's my size? Ah! This looks okay for size but what a color! I can't wear that! Hmm! Ah, this looks okay and the fit is perfect. Oh! Look! Here's a Crombie overcoat — just what I've always wanted — and it's my size; good! I'll put it on, and then off I go to the jewelry department.

Puff! Puff! There seems to be miles of corridor here.

I think I'll go first to the sports department and get a pair of roller skates so that I can get about much quicker. That's on the next floor so I'll take the elevator.

Here we are! Now, where are the roller skates? Ha, got them. My goodness! These are rubbish; look how dangerous they could be, tut! tut! These are much better, and these others are very good indeed. This pair is guaranteed for one year but those are guaranteed for five years so I'll take them.

Ah. They're on now so I'll go straight to the jewelry department. Wait! Look — here's a guide to the store showing how all the departments are laid out. This is excellent — just what I need. I must study it properly so I'll take the elevator up to the next floor to the furniture department and get myself seated.

Here we are. Now, where's a nice comfortable chair?

This one looks okay and it rocks as well. Oh, *a mechayah*! Now let's take a good look at this guide. Hmm! Very interesting, it's got some very funny cartoons and a crossword puzzle. I'll just hop up to the stationery department on the next floor and get a pencil... Wow! How time flies! It's 10:15 and I'm still sitting here. I'd better get a move on, and go straight to the jewelry — top floor. Okay. Oh, but wait! (Mild rumble is heard.) I'm starving! First floor is the kosher delicatessen department. How can I think clearly and find the best jewels if my stomach is rumbling? I'll just drop in and snatch a few bites to eat — it'll only take a few seconds.

Here we are. I'll take this tin of gefilte fish, and a few of these salami slices — oh, and a bottle of wine and some cake to wash out my mouth between the fish and meat. Oh, dear! I need a can opener for the fish. I'll get one from the hardware and cutlery department and then go back to the furniture department so that I can sit down while I'm eating. A dog eats standing up!

Oy vey! That wine's gone straight to my head. I must take a short nap. I've still got over half an hour and that's plenty of time. But I can only allow myself ten minutes so I'll go up to the electronics department, get an alarm clock, come down here and rest on one of these beds and then, when I'm refreshed, I'll go straight to the jewelry depart —

BBBrrring!!! Oh — my head! What's making that noise! Oooh! I must sleep a bit more…

Help! It's 10:50 — only ten minutes left! *Oy vey!* I must be mad to have slept now! Where's the elevator?! Puff! Puff! Must look a sight, roller skating along with his smart suit and overcoat. Puff! Puff! But I don't care, as long as I put my mark on a few nice diamonds…

Wow! At last I'm here in the jewelry department. Now to work. Oh, dear, there are so many counters and showcases; I don't know where to start. Now, take it calmly and don't panic. I've got to be cool and methodical. I've got seven and a half minutes so I'll work out a plan to cover the whole department scientifically. I'll just run down to the stationery department, get paper and pen, and draw up a plan.

Right! This plan looks okay. Now all I need is a stopwatch and I'll be all set to go. Ah! Here we are. Now which one shall I take? This Omega or the Ingersoll? The Omega is more accurate but the Ingersoll is waterproof as well. I'll take it. Okay, here I go.

Oops, there's a man coming my way. I wonder what he wants? He's carrying a big clock.

"The clock says eleven o'clock! Your time is up!"

My time is up?!

It can't be — I haven't marked anything yet! No! No! Give me one more minute! Please! This is my big chance! Please just one minute more!!

When a natchalnik *invites himself to a Seder there must be a good reason for it.*

Boris Ivanov's Seder

SIXTY AND SOME years ago a wave of revolutionary activity across Russia preceded the actual Russian Revolution. When the people tried to unite against the Czar and his ministers, the government set about putting down the rebellion with an iron hand. An "iron Russian hand" is impossible to explain to anyone lucky enough not to have been caught in its grip. For those who happened to feel Mother Russia's iron hand, no explanation is necessary. As this pre-revolution happened unfortunately to have a small percentage of Jewish voices among its supporters, that iron hand crushed down the Jewish population with extra-loving care.

Our *shtetl* was no exception. We, too, had our little "circle" (a group of kids who never actually *did* anything, but just talked a lot). In order to root out and wipe out the enemies of the motherland, the government did some shuffling in the police force, bringing in a new chief of police from whom, it was said, we would "lick honey." The "good" policemen smiled when they beat us black and blue — what was going to be with the Haman from Hamanland who was coming with a special assignment to "teach" us *Yidden*?

The new chief (*natchalnik*) arrived. Our community leaders held emergency meetings while the rest of us prayed and fasted. Ideas were considered and rejected until it was at last decided to tread the well-worn path and smear his palm with a little something special (the way to an underpaid cop's heart is through his palm). This difficult and decidedly unpleasant task was laid upon the shoulders of Reb Wolf Korshel, our local Rothschild. Then, too, Reb Wolf had a special merit — his family was as clean as a whistle when it came to revolutionary activity: the secret files of the secret police never saw the name Korshel. Reb Wolf accepted his assignment with the blessings of the community.

On a certain day, Reb Wolf sent a message to the chief that he would like to come and welcome him in the name of the Jewish community. The chief greeted him enthusiastically, treated him to tea, and chatted about this and that, especially about the situation of the Jews — did they make a living? Did they get along with their Christian neighbors? And more. At the end of their little chat, the chief expressed his satisfaction with the visit and asked Reb Wolf to come again.

When Reb Wolf reported back to the community leaders, they were astounded to hear of his enormous success. After the initial shock had worn off, we tried to figure out what it all meant and we came to the conclusion that the new chief was a smarter than average *goy* who was pretending to be buddies with us in order to discover the inner secrets of our little community, and then he would rip off the mask and show his true colors. It was decided to play along with him on the one side while keeping a wary eye out on the other.

A few days later Reb Wolf paid another visit to our top cop. And they had another pleasant little chat. At the end of this visit, Reb Wolf removed a sealed envelope from his pocket and pressed it into the chief's hand saying, "Gospodin Natchalnik — I know the wages you get from the government are not enough to live comfortably. So here's a little loan, and when you have any extra money you can pay me back."

"Thank you very much," answered the chief, "but I really can't accept a loan from you. I don't need any extra money — my wages are enough. I'm a bachelor with no wife or children to support, and I don't drink at all."

Reb Wolf tried to persuade him — no success. As Reb Wolf left that time he had grave misgivings — the policeman was as clean as a whistle. A public official who can't be smeared is a sure sign of trouble.

A few weeks passed. Then the chief of police sent a message to Reb Wolf that he wished to see him right away. Reb Wolf hurried over with his heart churning in anticipation. The chief greeted him in his usual manner, offered him a seat, and announced gravely, "Somebody has been passing out pamphlets denouncing the Czar. I already arrested two Russian boys. But I know that two Jewish boys were also involved: Leibel D. and Avrom S. I want you to tell them I know all about it, and my advice to them is to stay out of what's none of their business. A Jew's got no business in Russian politics. If they don't take my advice now I'll be forced to take them in like their buddies. So far I haven't reported them to the police. You know how it is. Then the matter would be out of my hands, and those two kids would get blamed for everything while the two Russians would go off scot-free. That's why I don't want to turn them in. Don't force me to do what I don't want to."

Reb Wolf relayed the message, and two "heroes" were summoned with their fathers to the *rav*. The *rav* laced into them good and proper, and then turned them over to their fathers who lectured them out all over again, punctuating their *mussar shmuessen* with a few well-placed smacks until Leibel and Avrom promised not to have any more to do with unkosher activities.

After that little episode, the chief became a big mystery to all of us. It looked like he was a *mentch* after all, and maybe even a bit of an *ohev Yisrael*. So why didn't he want to accept the bribe? Or maybe the whole thing was just part of his act? We talked and knocked our brains together but couldn't solve the riddle.

Two days before Pesach, Reb Wolf was in such a hurry that he didn't notice the police chief coming the other way. He stopped Reb Wolf and, smiling blandly, reproached him in a hurt voice, "You don't recognize me? Don't you want to recognize me?"

Reb Wolf, disturbed by the reproach, mumbled something about being in a hurry because of preparations for Pesach. "That is a festival by the Jews," he explained to the *natchalnik*.

The chief listened with interest. "When is this Yom Tov Pesach?"

"The day after tomorrow," replied Reb Wolf. "That is, tomorrow night the Yom Tov begins."

"Oh, I know," he said. "At night the *yontif* begins with a big banquet. It has some special name. I once used to know what it was, but I forgot."

"The Seder."

"Yes, yes! The Seder night, the Seder." The *natchalnik* stood for a while deep in thought, and suddenly blurted out, "If I were to ask you to invite me to the Seder do you think you could let me come?"

Reb Wolf felt as if he had suddenly been struck by lightning. He didn't know what to answer. A *goy* at his Seder table he needed like a hole in the head. It would wreck the whole mood of the Yom Tov. And then what would he do if this Eisav put his hairy red hands all over the wine?

The police officer noticed that Reb Wolf was struck dumb by the request. He opened his mouth to say something but changed his mind about it and remained quiet until Reb Wolf came back to his senses.

After a while he remarked to Reb Wolf, "Well, if you want to invite me to your Seder, let me know by twelve o'clock tomorrow. But if not, there won't be any hard feelings, and we can still be good friends, all right?"

Reb Wolf finally found his voice. "On the contrary, I'd consider it a great honor to have the Gospodin Natchalnik at my Seder. But you have to understand that the Jewish ritual pertaining to food is very strict at this time, and you will have to conduct yourself accordingly."

"I hope I don't cause you any inconveniences," said the chief.

"Tomorrow night I'll send my son to call you," Reb Wolf told him, and with that their conversation was over.

The Seder was celebrated in grand style. Around the long table sat Reb Wolf's family: wife, sons and daughters-in-law, daughters and sons-in-law, and grandchildren, with Reb Wolf sitting at the head like a real king. Reb Wolf's guest, Boris Semyonovich Ivanov, was seated next to one of his sons-in-law who could speak Russian and explain to the *natchalnik* what the Seder was all about.

Reb Wolf recited the Haggadah in a sweet, soulful *niggun*, stopping from time to time to say a good *vort*, a *pshat*, a *drush*, or just a little thought. He almost forgot about his guest. But when he happened to catch a glimpse of the police chief, he noticed he was sitting there solemnly, sunk in thought, his face clouded. Reb Wolf thought, Nu, *what can a* goy *understand about the Seder? All he cares about is the* seudah.

He finished reciting the first part of the Haggadah, and everyone washed for the *seudah*. When the fish was served, Reb Wolf stole another glance at the police chief. He was still sitting just as seriously and thoughtfully as before, eating the fish with half a mouth as if something heavy was hanging on his mind.

"Don't you find the fish tasty?" asked the concerned host.

"Oh, the fish — it's very good, very tasty…but…"

And suddenly a very strange thing happened. The police chief suddenly burst into tears and let out a tortured sob. Reb Wolf and his household sat up stiffly and looked at each other in alarm. What was going on? The *natchalnik* continued to sob incoherently until Reb Wolf's son-in-law managed to calm him down sufficiently so that he was able to speak. And then he stammered four words in Yiddish: "*Ich…bin…a…Yid!*"

When he recovered his poise he told the whole story: As an eleven-year-old boy, he had been kidnapped from his mother, a widow, and carried off into the Russian army. He had been sent deep into Russia to work for a farmer, and had to live a long time on bread and water and raw potatoes until he came down with a fever. When he recovered he forgot everything and thought that he was really the farmer's son. He had been awarded a decoration for outstanding service in the army and been appointed to a high rank in the police. Then he became the chief of police of a big town and almost entirely forgot his Jewish heritage.

And then something happened to remind him. He found out that the peasants were planning a pogrom against the Jews in his town. He held it was his duty to prevent the pogrom from taking place. He was responsible for the welfare of everyone who lived in that town, including the Jews. On the day of the pogrom, he mobilized the police force and rounded up all the pogromists. A week later he was informed that, as a disciplinary measure, he was being demoted from his position and sent elsewhere. What had he done wrong? His superiors had explained, "You don't interrupt a pogrom! The police are not supposed to make their entrance until the pogrom is almost over and all the mischief has been done." That was the official policy. Why? Because first of all, everyone knows that the Jews are revolutionary troublemakers and a pogrom or two will keep them in their place. Secondly, if the peasants are busy knocking off Jewish heads they won't be tempted to knock off the Czar's.

That little lecture reminded Boris Semyonovich Ivanov who he really was, and from that time on he decided to counteract the anti-Semites and show the Jews how good he could be to them. But *Yiddishkeit* — that was so far removed from him, it was almost like something alien.

And then, two days before Pesach, he met Reb Wolf in the street. Reb Wolf reminded him that Pesach was coming, and suddenly there appeared before his eyes a faraway image of a Seder at his father's table when he was a little boy. He couldn't have been older than nine or ten. His father was still alive and celebrated the Seder exactly the way it was supposed to be. The image was not a very clear one — he saw it like through a foggy glass. So he badly wanted to be at another Seder once more…

And now here he was at Reb Wolf's Seder. What he saw and heard — he couldn't describe. The Russian explanations were no good. All he felt was a gnawing in his heart. It was as though he could see his mother standing next to him begging, "My baby, come home!" He remembered how his mother had followed the wagon which was carrying the Jewish children into the Czar's army, calling after him: "Baruch Chaim, when you get out of the *Yevanim's* hands go into a shul and say Kaddish for your mother, because by that time I'll surely be in my grave." Now he could at last fulfill his mother's request.

"Would someone please show me what to say and how to say it, and then tonight I will let my mother know that her last wish was fulfilled, because tonight I intend to put an end to my miserable life."

The women dabbed at the tears from their eyes. The men sat like stones and their eyes were soggy.

Reb Wolf was the first to break the spell as he said, "Yes, brother, tonight you will certainly put an end to the miserable life of the *natchalnik* Boris Semyonovich Ivanov. He's gone, dead and done for. From now on, in his place is a Jew with the name Baruch Chaim ben Shimon. Just as our fathers went out of Mitzrayim and began a new life, so will our dear returning brother begin a new life. You've been redeemed! And in honor of your redemption let's drink *l'chaim!*"

Reb Wolf's words poured a new spirit into Boris-Baruch. They shook hands, kissed, and embraced like long-lost brothers. After the Seder, Reb Wolf and Boris-Baruch spent many hours planning the future of Baruch Chaim.

Chol Hamoed Pesach our *natchalnik* disappeared.

Translated by Leah M. Berkowitz from Dos Yiddishe Licht, **with permission**

Who cares if the label correctly identifies

The Genuine Article

ISAAC FRIEDMAN QUICKLY descended the steps of his stoop to the snow-covered sidewalk below. As he walked along his block with its row of slum houses still sleeping in the early morning sunshine, the gusts of wind blew against him and he had to fight for every step he took. The cold air stung his face and made it red. It seemed to go straight through his coat and gloves, and pierced his flesh till it reached his very bones. It was with relief that Isaac finally reached the subway station.

The year was 1919, and Isaac Friedman was forty years old. His life had been a difficult one, and he looked older and somewhat broken. But Isaac was happy. He had a wonderful, hardworking wife and good children. His eldest, Moshe, was going to be a real *talmid chacham*. They had said the same thing about him, Isaac reflected, before he had had to leave yeshivah and go to work. That was a long time ago in Europe, and Isaac didn't like to think about that. Here in America he felt he was happy. He had a good job, didn't he? Here his family would never go hungry. Nor would they ever know the beauties he had known in Europe — at least not the children. They would never know what the great yeshivah was like, or the Jews of his town whose lives centered about it. They would never experience the *melaveh malkahs* with the holiness almost palpable and the Jews singing with such fervor from the depths of their hearts.

Isaac didn't really like America. It was too materialistic. The Jews in his neighborhood spoke Yiddish and kept the commandments — at least some of them — but he felt that they did it more out of habit than anything else. They were more interested in sending their sons to college to acquire prestige and prosperity than in sending them to yeshivah so they could be good Jews. In Isaac's town in Europe, a Jew would sacrifice anything for Torah.

No, here his children could never have the joy he had had in Europe, but they would never have the pain either.

ଔଛ

The train had reached his station, and Isaac got out and walked the block and a half to the shop where he worked. As he opened the door he felt a rush of warm air engulf him. Inside the shop it was dark, and Isaac's eyes were not yet accustomed to it, so he had to search through the gloom to find the figure that was speaking to him.

"You're late, Isaac," said the boss. Isaac didn't answer. He walked across the wooden planks to the back of the shop, and hung his overcoat on a hook. Then he got to work.

It was 5:30 p.m. and Isaac was busy unpacking a new shipment when the boss came over and tapped him on the shoulder. "Isaac, could you do something else?"

Isaac looked up.

"I'd like you to label the shipment of handbags that came in yesterday." The boss handed Isaac a box of labels. "I'll be in the back working on the books."

Isaac nodded.

He walked toward the shelf where yesterday's shipment of handbags was lying. Absentmindedly, he began to attach a label to one of the handbags. Suddenly, the writing on the label caught his eye: GENUINE LEATHER. His hand froze in midair. The handbags that had come in yesterday were imitations, every one of them. It was cheating, it was cheating the public. It was dishonest, it was wrong, it was a sin. Isaac began to walk toward the back of the shop to tell the boss that he would not put the labels on. But his steps faltered and finally came to a stop. If he refused to put the labels on, the boss would fire him. If the boss fired him he'd have a hard time finding another *shomer Shabbos* job. In the meanwhile, what would his family live on? It's not easy to find a job in a country where you can hardly speak the language and must miss a "workday" every week. If he didn't do it someone else would put the labels on anyway; the public would still be cheated. Besides, what difference did it make if those silly ladies got genuine leather or not? They couldn't even tell the difference. But it would make a difference to his wife if he didn't label the bags. She would have to suffer so some women could have genuine leather.

The boss came out from the back of the shop. "Forgot my pen," he said, smiling at Isaac. The boss looked around. "Hey, Isaac," he said, "how come you aren't putting the labels on the handbags?"

For a minute Isaac didn't answer. When he did, his voice was low but firm.

"Because they're false and dishonest labels. Those bags are not genuine leather."

"So. Who's going to know, the fancy ladies? They couldn't even tell if they were made of paper."

"No, they couldn't," answered Isaac. "That's why we have to label them. Correctly. Who will know? The same One Who will know if you desecrate the Sabbath, that is Who will know, and that's enough for me."

"Now hold on, Isaac, don't fly off the lid. I'm as religious as the next guy, but business is business. No one is getting hurt. It's not like we're putting poison in a bottle and labeling it medicine, G-d forbid."

"No, it isn't," answered Isaac, "but nevertheless, it is cheating."

"If you're going to get stubborn about this, Isaac, things can get very unpleasant. I can have another worker in here in five minutes. Laborers like you are a dime a dozen."

"Yes," answered Isaac.

"So put the labels on."

"No."

"I can be pushed only so far, Isaac. My patience is going to snap."

"And I too can be pushed only so far. No! Don't you understand? Money isn't everything. I will not sell one bit of Torah for money, not one bit."

It is a shame, thought the boss even through his anger, *that Isaac is such a greeny. If he had been in America a few years longer, this would never have had to happen.*

❦

As Isaac walked down his block the cold stung him as it had done that morning, and the wind was even greater. But the weather cooled down his spirits and he no longer felt angry or embarrassed, just sorry. He was sorry for his children, sorry for his wife, sorry for himself, and sorry for the society that was destroying itself and didn't even know it. He was even sorry for the boss.

By now Isaac had reached his house, and as he stood at the foot of the stoop he looked up at a light that was shining from a second-story window. It was his kitchen window, and he could almost see his wife behind it cooking supper. His wife was always happy when he came home. *Only tonight*, thought Isaac, *she will not be happy, not with the news I'm bringing.* After he had thought about it, though, he knew it was unfair. His wife would tell him he had done right; she would be happy he had done what he had. She would, in fact, be proud of him. *What a wonderful woman*, thought Isaac, *what a real* eishes chayil.

Once again he lifted his eyes toward the lighted window. The light seemed so warm, so comforting, so loving. It reminded him of — at first he couldn't remember what, and it disturbed him. With a smile and a sigh, it came to him. His light in Europe had looked the same way.

P'SACHYA ASHLAG

Mordechai's Religious Education

Based on a still-open case history in the P'eylim files, this story is not typical, for its hero was saved. Typical are the tens of thousands of children Youth Aliyah stole and robbed from Yiddishkeit *who were not returned to their parents' faith.*

MONDAY, 3 IYAR

THE CROWD, THE tumult at Lod Airport confused thirteen-year-old Mordechai Mordiyan. One of a planeload of boys Youth Aliyah brought to Israel in 5739 to escape what anti-Semitism there was in Iran, Mordechai stood with his luggage piled neatly, an island unto himself. His fellow travelers were greeted and embraced by waiting relatives. Mordechai's father had decided only at the last minute to send him along — when the

Youth Aliyah *shaliach* had promised that Mordechai would receive a religious education. The elder Mordiyan had had no time to write to his brother and brothers-in-law in Israel that his son would be arriving there.

A stocky, middle-aged man approached Mordechai. Looking at a list he held, he asked, "Are you Mordechai Mordiyan?"

"Yes."

"Shalom! I'm Chaim, a Youth Aliyah *madrich*. I'll be taking you to the traditional youth village of Ashlayot. That's our truck standing out there. Put your bags in and take a seat."

It was after nightfall when they arrived at Ashlayot. Mordechai's eyes felt heavy and his small body ached with fatigue. As soon as he was shown to the room he would share with two old-timers, Rachamim and Yosef, he fell asleep.

TUESDAY, 4 IYAR

MORDECHAI JOYFULLY SPRANG out of his bed, thrilled at his first morning in Eretz Yisrael. Yosef and Rachamim were gone. He washed up and ran out to find the shul. He had become a bar mitzvah only a few months before, and every morning felt a renewed thrill at the novelty of putting on *tefillin*. Looking for the shul, he wandered into the dining room, where he found the boys sitting at breakfast. The clock on the wall indicated seven o'clock. He wondered, *Could they have finished* tefillah *so early?* Spotting Chaim, the only face in the dining room familiar to him, he ran over and asked, "Did I miss *tefillah*?"

"Look, Mordechai, it's different here in Israel than in Iran. Here we don't put on *tefillin* or say *tefillah* every day. But of course we can make an exception for you if you insist."

Mordechai was almost in tears. "I don't understand, Chaim."

Chaim had played this scene before many, many times, and his lines rolled right off the tip of his tongue, "My dear fellow, don't worry. You'll gradually understand that the mitzvah of *yishuv ha'Aretz* overrides all other mitzvot. You go right ahead now. The *beit knesset* is the building behind the dormitory."

It was then that Mordechai realized that, except for some of the new arrivals, not a single one of the boys or the men had a yarmulke on his head. Mordechai wandered numbly out. It was some time before the words formed in his mind, *Is this what I came to Israel for?* He found his way back to his room, shut the door, and donned his *tefillin*. Tears streamed down his face when he reached the words, "*Hoshi'einu v'nivashei'ah*."

Yosef and Rachamim returned from breakfast to find a despondent Mordechai sitting on his bed. "Now, what's bothering you, old chap," Yosef teased.

"You wouldn't understand if I told you. After all, you don't come from a religious home."

"What do you mean?" Rachamim smiled. "My *peyot* were as long as yours when I arrived here — four months ago. My father is a *shochet* in Casablanca. He sent me here with Youth Aliyah after a long-bearded *shaliach* assured him that I'd get the best traditional training. I found it difficult to adjust to the Ashlayot environment at first. But it's lots of fun here. Don't worry. You'll get used to it soon."

FRIDAY, 7 IYAR

THE SPLISH-SPLASH of the water as the boys showered before Shabbos held out great promise to Mordechai. His face almost glowed with his credulous certainty that on Shabbos things would be different at the "traditional" youth village. He entered the shul building, and was soon joined by a few moths which fluttered frenziedly about the unshaded light bulb. The moths kept up their suicidal tilting at the bulb while Mordechai recited the saddest *Kabbalas Shabbos* and *davened* the loneliest Ma'ariv of his life. Then he headed for the dining room.

"*Shabbat shalom*, Mordechai," Rachamim greeted him as he entered. "Where have you been? We just finished *Kabbalat Shabbat*, and I was wondering what had happened to you."

Not knowing that the *Kabbalas Shabbos* prayers Rachamim was referring to came from a specially printed Youth Aliyah siddur that made no mention of the *geulah* or of Mashiach, Mordechai began to feel relief. His hopes rose higher when other children also greeted him with "*Shabbat shalom*," and he saw that the tables were festively set.

Then Chaim walked in, carrying silver candlesticks on a tray. He set them down on the head table, and lit the candles in them — without a *brachah*. Mordechai didn't even try to control himself, and shouted out, "What is this? It's an hour after sunset already! How can you light candles on Shabbat?"

Chaim had heard that question — and answered it — several hundred times. "You're right," he said placidly. "But how can we sit down to a Shabbat meal without the Shabbat candles?"

Mordechai ran to his room, sobbing bitter, angry tears.

TUESDAY, 8 TAMMUZ

"MORDECHAI, GO OVER to the office. You've got a visitor."

"A visitor?" *Who can that be?* he wondered as he walked toward the administrator's office. A heavy-set man who looked somewhat like Mordechai's mother greeted him, "Shalom, Mordechai. I'm your Uncle Nissim."

"Uncle Nissim!" Mordechai joyfully kissed the older man. "Will you be taking me home with you?"

"Don't you like it here?"

"I hate it here! There's no *tefillah* here, there's no Shabbat here, there's no kashrut here. If Hashem wasn't everywhere anyhow, they wouldn't even let Him in."

"Then why should you want to come to my house?"

"But Uncle Nissim, can't you arrange for me to be transferred to a religious institution?"

Nissim was not as experienced as Chaim in these matters. "Mordechai, forget all this business about religion. This place is an excellent home for you and its school is one of the country's best. When you've graduated, I'll see to it that you get the best high school education available and then on to university, if you wish."

"Uncle Nissim, I don't want a *chiloni* education. I want to attend a Jewish school and learn Torah. I want to be in a place where I can eat the cooked foods, where I can be *mitpallel* with a *minyan*, where I can keep Shabbat. Won't you help me, Uncle Nissim?"

"You're too young to understand what's good for you. Youth Aliyah will give you the foundation you need, and I'll help you move along in the right direction. I know what it takes to succeed in this country. Here's some money for you. Leave everything to your uncle."

WEDNESDAY, 9 TAMMUZ

The rising sun's rays announced five thirty through the half-closed shutters over Mordechai's bed. The reveille bell wouldn't be ringing for another hour. Mordechai rose, washed, packed a handbag, and tiptoed out of the room. He *davened* a fervent, final Shacharis in Ashlayot's abandoned shul, and headed for the bus stop down the road.

The faces in the crowd at the bus terminal in Yerushalayim lifted Mordechai's spirits. He exulted at the sight of covered heads and faces framed by beards and *peyos*. *Now I'm in Eretz Yisrael at last.* He showed a man his Uncle Yaakov's address, and the man told him which bus to take to get there.

Yaakov Mordiyan was eating lunch with his family when the doorbell rang.

"Shalom. I'm Mordechai. Are you my Uncle Yaakov?"

"Yes." They embraced.

"Where were you all this time?" Yaakov asked. "Your father wrote that you were here, and we expected you to come visit us."

"I've wanted to come to you for weeks, but I had no money till Uncle Nissim visited me yesterday."

"You mean that awful man gave you money to come visit us?" Aunt Naomi wondered.

"Not exactly." Mordechai told them about Nissim's plans for him.

"That's terrible. That my nephew should come to *Eretz Hakodesh* and be brought up like a *goy*?! Don't tell me you consented," Yaakov worried. "You still have your *peyot* and your *kippah* on your head, and I see your *arba kanfot*. That must be a fine religious school you're in!"

Mordechai proceeded to tell them all about the "religious" school he had left.

"If you didn't look so emaciated, I wouldn't believe a word of it," Aunt Naomi commented. "Now, you sit down to eat. Then you tell us the whole story again from beginning to end."

THURSDAY, 10 TAMMUZ

Yaakov Mordiyan had heard about an organization called P'eylim. That afternoon he used the telephone in his shop to ring their number. The young man on the line explained what sort of affidavit Yaakov would have to fill out in order to gain custody of Mordechai, and that evening he visited the Mordiyan home.

"You're a brave fellow, Mordechai. We're proud of you. We can't place you in a yeshivah now because it's almost *bein hazmanim*, but we can arrange for you to be in a summer camp that has a learning program. As for you, Mr. Mordiyan, to gain custody of the boy you'll have to…" He gave Yaakov all the procedural details.

By the time Yaakov Mordiyan had filled out all the necessary depositions and had finally taken the trip to Ashlayot to pick up the rest of Mordechai's belongings, he no longer doubted any part of Mordechai's story. With his mature perception, he noted that matters at Ashlayot were far worse than his innocent nephew could have imagined. On the following evening, he made a *seudas hoda'ah* to commemorate his nephew's providential escape from the "traditional" youth village.

AHUVA COHEN

Rav Elya Chaim Meisel teaches a thief a lesson. Tuition fee:

A Pinch of Snuff

MOSHE YAWNED AND stretched happily. He had completed the business transactions successfully and his profits were in his wallet, safely tucked under the mattress. And today he would be going home.

The thought made him jump out of bed. *Why, it must be late, and I have to catch a train!* He groped for his heavy gold watch, his most valued possession, but stopped abruptly as he recalled that the watch was hidden with his wallet under the mattress. No matter. He would dress and *daven* first and then, just before leaving, he would remove his valuables from their hiding place. No sooner had Moshe put away his siddur and packed the last of his clothing when there was a knock on the door. A man stood there.

"The innkeeper sent me, sir. You asked to be notified of the train schedule and he said to tell you that there is a train out in ten minutes. If you're all ready, we can just make it to the station."

Quickly, Moshe grabbed up his valise, capped his hat on his head, and followed the man, who was a sort of jack-of-all-work around the inn, down the stairs. A few minutes later Moshe was standing in the station, congratulating himself on the good timing. He even had a few minutes to spare before the train came. Moshe raised his hand to glance at his watch and froze… His wrist was bare!

With a start, he realized that in his haste to leave, he had left the watch and wallet under the mattress. Moshe sighed in exasperation. Now he would have to return to the inn, and when the next train would be leaving Lodz was anybody's guess. Still, there was no help for it, and so, his valise clutched tightly in one hand, Moshe started back for the inn.

"Well, well!" boomed the innkeeper. "So you've come back. A new business deal? Want your old room back?"

"No, no," Moshe replied hastily. "I forgot my watch and wallet in the room and came back for them."

"I'll take you up there," the innkeeper said. "Ordinarily I enter the room as soon as the guest leaves to make sure that nothing has been left behind, but this morning I was busy, and so no one has entered your room since you left."

The innkeeper unlocked the door as he spoke, and Moshe immediately made a beeline for the bed and searched under the mattress. His things were gone. Systematically, he began to search the room, but his search revealed nothing. The wallet and watch were nowhere in sight.

"I don't understand it," Moshe said. "They were right here and you just told me that you didn't enter the room. Perhaps one of the cleaning staff…"

A Pinch of Snuff

"No, no," the innkeeper insisted. "The keys were in my pocket the entire time. No one could have entered your room."

"But someone must have taken the things," Moshe said, beginning to grow angry.

The innkeeper began to grow angry, too.

"I tell you no one has been in here. Perhaps you lost them in the station. Or maybe a pickpocket took them. How can you be so sure that you left them here?"

But Moshe *was* sure. He knew that he had not left the inn with his valuables and so now his suspicion fell on the innkeeper. It was obvious that the latter, if guilty, had no intention of admitting anything.

Better play the game his way, Moshe thought, and so, forcing a smile to his lips, he said pleasantly, "You're probably right. I'll go back to the station now and ask around. Perhaps someone saw some sign of my things there."

The innkeeper grinned. *That takes care of that*, he thought to himself in grim satisfaction, as he started down the stairs. Once on the street, Moshe did not go to the train station, however; instead, he turned and headed toward the home of Rav Eliyahu Chaim Meisel, the *rav* of Lodz.

"*Shalom aleichem*, Reb Moshe!" Rav Elya Chaim greeted the ex-Lodzer warmly, as he stood in the doorway of the *rav's* home a short while later. "And what brings you to Lodz?"

"Oh, just some business," Moshe replied. "But perhaps you had better ask me what brings me to your house? That's a more crucial question."

"I see," Rav Elya Chaim replied quietly. Reaching out a hand, he drew his visitor into the study and closed the door.

"I didn't go to the police because I don't have a scrap of evidence," Moshe concluded, "but I know he did it. He's the only one who had a key to the room and, when I entered with him, I saw immediately that someone had been there in the interim. I had left the closet doors ajar, and when I came in they were tightly closed."

"Are you sure?" Rav Elya Chaim asked with a start.

"Absolutely," Moshe replied.

The *rav* thought. "I know!" he said finally. "The innkeeper has a *din Torah* about to come up in my *beis din*. I'll summon him here on the pretext of preparing for the *din Torah* and, in the meantime, I'll figure out a way to determine whether he's really guilty."

Early the next morning, the innkeeper was ushered into the *rav's* house. "I'm glad you sent for me, Rebbi. I've been meaning to drop by about this *din Torah*."

"Good, good," the *rav* replied. "Let's get started." They were deep in discussion of the impending *din Torah* when the *rav* noticed that the innkeeper had removed from his pocket a beautifully jeweled snuffbox, and was sampling a pinch.

The *rav* leaned forward and expressed his admiration for the snuffbox.

"Isn't it lovely?" the innkeeper agreed enthusiastically. "It was my father's, may he rest in peace, and I always carry it with me. I can't be without my *shmek tabik*."

"Such intricate workmanship," the *rav* exclaimed. "Could I see it more closely for a moment?"

"Of course, Rebbi," the innkeeper said, handing it to him. "And try a pinch of snuff while you're at it. I use only the best."

Rav Elya Chaim complied, and was just beginning to praise the innkeeper's tobacco, when he suddenly interrupted himself.

"Will you excuse me for just a moment?" he asked the innkeeper. And, before the latter could reply, he hurried out of the room, the snuffbox still in his hand.

The innkeeper waited, five minutes, ten, but still the *rav* did not return. *Where can he be?* he wondered. Deciding that some urgent business had probably arisen, he settled down to write up his plea for the *beis din*. He wrote rapidly for twenty minutes and then stopped. Half an hour had passed already, and still the *rav* had not returned.

ଔଽ

When Rav Elya Chaim had hurried out of the room, he had immediately called his *shamash*, who listened attentively to the *rav's* instructions and then nodded to show that he understood.

"But quickly," Rav Elya Chaim added, thrusting the innkeeper's snuffbox into his hands. The *shamash* hurried off.

Arriving at the innkeeper's house, he knocked at the door and found himself face to face with the innkeeper's wife.

"Yes?" she inquired.

"Your husband sent me here," the *shamash* explained. "He asks that you give me the watch and the wallet to turn over to him." The woman regarded him suspiciously.

"What watch? What wallet?"

"I really don't know," the *shamash* replied. "I am the *rav's shamash* and your husband is in conference with the *rav* at present concerning his forthcoming *din Torah*. In this connection, he sent me to you for the watch and the wallet."

Seeing that the woman continued to regard him with suspicion, the *shamash* took out the snuffbox, saying, "Your husband sent this with me so that you could trust that these are indeed his instructions."

The woman peered at the snuffbox, and relief flooded her features. "That's his, all right," she said. Hurrying into the house, she returned with the watch and the wallet and gave them to the *shamash*.

When the *shamash* arrived back at the *rav's* house, breathless, Rav Elya Chaim took the valuables from him and locked them into a desk drawer in his study. He then entered his bedroom where Moshe was waiting and asked him if he could provide *simanim* to identify his watch and his wallet. Moshe proceeded to identify them in such minute detail that there could be no doubt that what the *shamash* had retrieved from the inn was his. The *rav* went into his study, removed the articles from his drawer, and laid them in Moshe's hands. Promising to donate a large sum of money to the poor of Lodz, Moshe gratefully took his leave.

The *rav* then hurried into the room where he had left the innkeeper and apologized for the delay. "And here is your snuffbox," he added. "I ran out with it in my hands."

They spent a few more minutes discussing the innkeeper's *din Torah* and then the latter left.

When he arrived home, his wife met him at the door. "Why did you send for the watch and wallet?"

"What?" he replied. "What are you talking about?"

"Why, the *shamash's* visit. What did you think?"

The innkeeper listened in mystification as she began to explain, but shortly his bewilderment gave way to fury and humiliation. Tricked! And there was nothing he could say or do.

Scoop of the Century!

Yetzer Hara to Retire?

OUR TELETYPE FLASHED the following item early last month: (FIFTH HEAVEN NEWS SERVICE) — OUR SPECIAL GEHINNOM CORRESPONDENT REPORTS THAT THE *YETZER HARA* HAS FORMALLY REQUESTED THAT HE BE ALLOWED TO RETIRE. THE EXACT MOTIVATIONS OF THE ANCIENT ANGEL POPULARLY KNOWN AS "SAM" ARE UNKNOWN, AS NO REPORTER DARES COME WITHIN FOUR MILLION SQUARE CUBITS OF HIM. SPECULATION IN THE SIXTH HEAVEN IS THAT THE REQUEST WILL BE TURNED DOWN.

We immediately assigned the biggest tzaddikim on our staff to the story. Their report may well be the scoop of the century.

By means we cannot reveal, our reporters were able to obtain copies of the correspondence between the *yetzer hara* and the *Sar Hap'nim* (whose name we dare not mention for His Master's Name is within his — see *Rashi* on *Shemos* 23:21). Because of its obvious benefit to humanity, we are making the first of these letters public. It is dated Rosh Chodesh Adar II, 5730.

Text of *Yetzer Hara's* Letter

Most honored and revered _____,

Your Reverence is well aware of the manifold duties I have executed over the millennia. My efforts — successes and failures alike — filmed in HeavenVision, are in the archives. I have nothing to be ashamed of. Everything I did was for our Master's glory.

For the nearly six millennia since Creation, I have had to hold down three jobs: that of Satan — constantly showing the Master the faults of His people; that of *yetzer hara* — constantly keeping people at Full Temptation Level, never an iota above or below their Free Choice Level; and that of Angel of Death.

I submit that the role of *yetzer hara* is played out, and I'd like to be permitted to retire from that position. I'm not trying to shirk any of my duties; it's simply that the job doesn't require my abilities anymore, and I could use my talents elsewhere for the Master's glory, or devote more time to my two other roles.

It may sound like I'm saying the *yetzer hara* role is old-fashioned, so I'd like to qualify that. Neither the role itself nor I are anachronisms. But times have changed, and with them the people. The people in this fifty-eighth century have made great advances in communications and have simply put me out of business.

For example: I work hard on one fellow, and get him to deny the obvious and become an *apikores*. Then he goes on radio and saves me the trouble of pressuring thousands or even millions of people. Or he makes a movie that goes all around the world and graphically demonstrates the *apikorsus* and *kefirah* to millions at least as well as I would have done had I tackled each one's imagination individually. The same holds true for newspaper editors and reporters, and for heads of education departments and ministries throughout the world.

Allow me to cite two examples that will clarify my point. A little over one hundred years ago I had to sweat blood to get a full quorum of *maskilim*. Once I had them in my hands, I set them to work to prod Czar Nikolai to do some dirtier work that I couldn't rely on the *maskilim* for. Even when Nikolai's army forcibly converted thousands of Jewish children, it wasn't much good. The hue and cry in the civilized world and the natural Jewish resistance to *shmad* turned the whole business into a fiasco, and I had to pull Nikolai out of the frying pan into the fire (so to speak) to put an end to it. Today, though, the spiritual heirs of the *maskilim* have usurped the land and the name of the Jews, and are delivering millions of Jewish souls to *apikorsus* without formal *shmad*. And no Jew can shout "*Shmad!*" except at the relatively few *goyishe* missionaries. Nor can the world shout "Cruelty!" because this modern *shmad* is labeled "Jewish education." So it goes well: Mass production of *apikorsim* without any need for "holy" water.

Or take the matter of women's attire. Do you know how long it used to take me to get a Jewish girl to turn immodest? How much blood, sweat, tears, and money went into such an effort? And the return wasn't worth the investment. I needed a whole movement like Shabsai Tzvi's or Mendelssohn's in order to get any number of girls to give up their modesty. Today there's no problem. Of course I needed Herzl's twist on Mendelssohn's movement to get things moving. But now every single new style is caught up by the mass media, and the mass-miseducated Jewish girls are easy prey.

In brief, the intensive training I gave to one thousand Grade A *apikorsim* about forty years ago coupled with mass communication has removed any need for my personal services as *yetzer hara* in the foreseeable future. I therefore request that I be freed from the task of *yetzer hara*.

Very respectfully,
Samech-Mem

AHUVA COHEN

Rav Elya Chaim Meisel, the rav of Lodz, *creates*

The Winning Loser

NEVER PUT YOUR faith in a lottery ticket. How do I know? What makes me such an authority? Never mind how I know. I just know, that's all. Never put your faith in a lottery ticket.

There were few people who needed to hit the jackpot more than I did when I lived in Lodz forty years ago. I wasn't much of a breadwinner even before then, but Chava never complained. "You'll do better tomorrow," she used to say. "Tomorrow you'll have *mazel*."

Well, a whole succession of tomorrows didn't bring me any better luck, but somehow we struggled along. Pay back some money here, borrow some more there, settle one debt, incur another — that's how it went. Those were bad economic times in Lodz and most of my neighbors were in the same boat.

What did you say? You had heard that Lodz was such a thriving city and especially the Jewish community? Yes and no. The city as a unit was prosperous and there were plenty of wealthy industrialists. I guess you could say that the standard of living was fairly good. But there are masses of the poor in every city who suffer most during the hard times. And I was among them.

To get back to my story, after quite a few years of scraping, things finally seemed to be improving a bit. I found another job in a factory and, though we were still poor, it looked for the first time as if we almost might be better off someday.

It was then that the thunderbolt fell. I came home about a month after Yisrael had been born to find Chava standing in a corner of the kitchen, crying.

"Chavi, what's the matter?"

No reply.

"Chavi," I gasped, "is Yisrael…"

"No," she said, "the baby is fine, *baruch Hashem*."

"Then what is it?"

"When I went out to buy fish for Shabbos today I met the *almanah*. Do you know who I mean?"

"Yes." A fine woman, this *almanah*. I knew her husband *zichrono livrachah*. We went to *cheder* together when we were kids. He died very young, leaving a nineteen-year-old widow and a year-old orphan. She had never remarried, and she worked hard to raise the little boy.

"Not so little anymore, though," I thought aloud. "Must be in his early twenties."

"Twenty-three to be exact," Chava responded.

"His name is Shloima and he is apprenticed to a *sofer*," Chava went on. "Soon he will be able to work on his own. He is a fine young man from what I have heard, a *ba'al middos* and a *talmid chacham*."

"So?" I demanded, puzzled. What do the sterling qualities of Shloima, the *almanah's* son, have to do with my Chava standing in a corner of the kitchen and crying?

"So?" Chava echoed. "Sara suggested making a *shidduch* between her Shloima and our Shaindy."

I was speechless with astonishment. *Shaindy! Shaindy is too young to marry, a mere child. Why, I would as soon think of leading Shaindy under the* chuppah *as I would little Perela in her diapers!*

"She's so young —" I began.

"Yossi," Chava interrupted me, "Shaindy is almost twenty."

I could only gape. Shaindy had grown up before my eyes and I hadn't paid any notice.

"Well," I said slowly. "He's a fine boy and I certainly have no objections."

"Neither do I," said Chavi. "And neither does Shaindy."

Well, here was another astonishing thing! "Shaindy! You've spoken to Shaindy already!"

"No," she said simply. "But I can tell."

Women are an amazing people, I reflected. How *can she tell?*

"Okay," I said irritably. "So you can tell. Everything is perfect then. We all agree."

I could already feel the *chasunah* music in my bones and I hummed a little tune. But Chava didn't look happy in the least, and suddenly I remembered that a moment ago she had been crying.

"Yossi," she said, "have you forgotten the dowry?"

I had forgotten the dowry completely. How could I be so stupid?

"Well," I said bitterly. "There go all the fine plans. The *shidduch* is off."

"But Yossi, the girl must marry somebody. If it isn't Shloima the *almanah's* son, it will be someone else. And we must have a dowry for her."

The woman is right, I thought to myself. *A dowry must be had.*

"Chava, don't worry, don't cry. I'll think of a way to get the money. Hashem will help."

The next morning I was awakened by the clanging of pots in the kitchen and Chava greeted me with a happy smile.

"Good morning," she sang out. I stared at her suspiciously. What could have happened during the night to account for this change of mood?

She glanced around first to make sure that none of the children were within earshot and then she began. "Do you remember what we were talking about last night?"

Remember? I didn't sleep half the night for worrying and she asks me if I remember.

"I think I have the solution," she continued eagerly. Without waiting for my reaction, she rushed on, "We'll buy a lottery ticket."

"A what?"

"A lottery ticket. If we win, the prize money will be enough for Shaindy's dowry and there may be enough left over to buy all the children new shoes. They certainly need it."

My first reaction was to laugh, but I could not bear to spoil the triumphant happiness shining in Chava's eyes.

"Chavi," I said, "it's a nice dream, but that's all it is. A dream. There are thousands of numbers. Who's to say we'll win?"

"Who's to say we won't?" she countered illogically.

And so the battle was on. Back and forth we argued, neither side gaining and neither about to give in, when suddenly I realized that it was getting late.

"I'm leaving for work now," I announced. "I'll be home around three, and I am *not* bringing home any lottery tickets."

But once at work, all of Chava's arguments came back to me. And the more I thought about it, the better I liked the idea. If we *did* win, all our problems would be solved.

On the way home, I decided to take a little detour and stop by Chatzkel, the lottery vendor. Not to buy a ticket, of course! Just for a little chat — to pass the time of day.

"Hey, Yossel," he hailed me. "You're just in time."

"In time?" I stammered. "In time for what?"

"To buy a ticket. I have one ticket left from this particular lottery. Number 702. Interested?"

"Who, me? It was Chavi who —" I broke off, suddenly realizing what I was saying.

"Well, what's the difference?" he said practically. "It's one pocket, isn't it? Now listen, Yossel, your fortune is made. Why, you even look lucky. I see luck shining all over your face."

"You — you do?"

"Sure. And this ticket is a steal. Only twenty rubles."

"Twenty rubles!" I gasped. A small fortune. We had ten spare rubles which we keep on hand for an emergency and it was this that Chava had been nagging me to use for a lottery ticket. But where in the world would I get another ten rubles? Well, never mind. I would get it somehow. By now my mind was so fired up with the idea of the lottery ticket that I just had to have it.

I dashed back to the house and grabbed my silver pocketwatch, which I had *yarshened* from my father. I quickly made my way to the pawnshop. Our business was quickly transacted, and the ten rubles I received from the pawnbroker found their way as quickly into the hands of the lottery ticket seller. And I, minus my most valuable possession and twenty rubles, felt myself to be the richest man on earth.

"Hello, Reb Yosef. How are you?"

I looked up in surprise. It was the *rav*, Rav Elya Chaim Meisel!

"Rebbi." I took hold of his sleeve. "Do you see what I have in my hand?"

He took the lottery ticket from me and studied it a moment, turning it 'round and 'round in his hand.

"A twenty-ruble lottery ticket! Are you such a rich man, Reb Yosef, that you have twenty spare rubles to spend on a lottery ticket?"

"Me? Spare rubles?" I burst out laughing. "Rebbi, I never had a spare ruble in my life. But my wife thought we should try our luck in the lottery. So I took the ten rubles which we kept on hand for emergencies and I pawned my watch to get the other ten. Rebbi, do you think I'll be lucky?"

He regarded the ticket with amusement, but when he answered his voice was throbbing with excitement.

"Reb Yosef, this is a lucky ticket. Seven hundred and two — I can see that you'll be a rich man. Yes, I can see it."

"Can you, Rebbi? Do you really think so?"

"I'm positive. Seven hundred and two. How fortunate you are that you have this particular ticket. I'm glad that you showed it to me. I want to become your partner in the lottery." And he pulled out his wallet.

I could have danced for joy. *The* rav *himself thinks it's lucky, and he's so sure of it that he'll risk ten rubles to go in with me.*

But what's this? That's twenty rubles that he's handing me, not ten.

"Rebbi, the ticket cost twenty rubles. You only have to give me ten."

"Never mind, never mind," he said absently. "I want to give you the whole twenty rubles. Here, take the money and go redeem your watch from the pawnshop."

For the next two weeks, I could barely eat, barely sleep, barely keep my mind on my work. And then, finally, finally, the day of the drawing arrived. I bought the newspaper and scanned the list of winners.

But there must be some mistake. My number is nowhere on the list. I haven't won, not even the lowest prize. Broken, I made my way to Rav Elya Chaim's house and found him in his study.

"Rebbi, the ticket...didn't win."

He looked up from his *sefer* as calmly as if I had told him that it had stopped raining.

"So what else is new?" he said.

"Rebbi! Aren't you surprised?"

"Of course not."

"Rebbi! But you gave me the twenty rubles because you thought the ticket was so lucky."

"Do you think I believed for one minute that your number would win? I gave you the twenty rubles so that you could redeem your watch and so that you wouldn't be without extra cash in the event of an emergency. I only pretended that I wanted a share in the ticket so that you would accept the money. Next time don't do such a foolish thing."

What was there to say? I was silent.

"Reb Yosef!"

"Yes, Rebbi."

"Why did you buy a lottery ticket in the first place?"

So out came the whole story, about Chava crying in the corner of the kitchen and about Shaindy and the *almanah's* son.

"How much do you need to marry off your daughter?"

I calculated quickly. The *nadan*, the *chasunah*…

"Three hundred rubles," I answered.

Wordlessly, he went over to a drawer and took out a sealed envelope.

"Here. Take this," he said. It was no use to protest. I knew that I needed the money and Rav Elya Chaim knew it, too.

Once home, I ripped open the envelope. It contained 350 rubles, enough to marry off Shaindy and fifty rubles with which to buy the children new shoes.

I turned the envelope over and saw that it was addressed to Rav Elya Chaim Meisel and there in the left-hand corner was the stamp of the *kehillah*.

And then I remembered. Three hundred and fifty rubles was Rav Elya Chaim's monthly salary. I was present at the *kehillah* meeting when the decision was made.

Do you suppose that he handed over to me his entire month's salary, just like that, without even opening the envelope? No, it's impossible. It couldn't be. Then again…

I wonder…

CHANIE D. SHWEIBEL

Three Broken Legs

Reb Gershon the grain merchant entered the spacious Altneu Shul, shook the snow off his overcoat, and blew on his hands to warm them from the fierce cold he had just escaped. Then he walked over to the roaring stove to warm himself properly before he settled down to business. Business? Pleasure! Reb Gershon thoroughly enjoyed this early hour of daily study which brought back to him the inspiring years he had spent in yeshivah before his large family had forced him to seek a source of *parnassah*. But he took it very seriously as well: This hour of preparation before the *rav's shiur* and the hour of the *rav's shiur* after *davening* were inviolate to him.

Reb Dov Ber the *shochet* joined him at the warm stove. "That's strange! Reb Shmuel isn't here yet. How will we be able to prepare properly?"

"It's hard enough keeping up with the *rav* even after an hour of preparation — how will we ever understand the *inyan* today if Reb Shmuel isn't here?" Reb Gershon frowned. "Here's Reb Chaim the *shamash*. I'll ask him."

"Reb Chaim, what happened to Reb Shmuel this morning?" he asked, nodding to the empty seat. "Slipping up on the job?"

"It's not my fault," the *shamash* shrugged. "I woke him as usual. He's an old man after all. Maybe he just isn't feeling well."

The *shochet*, the *shamash,* and the merchant sat down at the table and were soon immersed in their study. The shul slowly filled up with *mispallelim* who joined the early birds.

The *rav's* entrance hushed all voices for it signaled the beginning of the *davening*, of which every minute and every word was precious. Rav Yechezkel Landau, the recently chosen *rav* of Prague, was in his early forties, world famous as *posek* and *gaon*, although he would not publish his *Teshuvos Noda B'Yehuda* until some twenty years later.

The *davening* over, the men returned to their *Gemaros* in anticipation of another experience in Torah revelation. For a *shiur* from their *rav*, the *gadol hador*, was a veritable taste of *Olam Haba*. Left behind were mundane cares as the men daily plunged into the refreshing waters of the Talmud, trying hard to keep up with the *rav's* energetic strokes, gasping in wonder at the depths he attained.

But the *olam* was in for a surprise that morning.

Standing at his *shtender* as usual, the *rav* did not open his Gemara. Instead he began a fire-and-brimstone *drashah* on *chessed* and *tzedakah*.

"A *drashah* is all fine and dandy," muttered Reb Gershon to himself, "but in the right place and at the right time." The "right places" to his mind were the tradesmen's *shtieblach*, and the "right time" — Shabbos afternoon. *And the right person, too,* he added mentally. *What in the world is the* rav *doing saying a* drashah *— Prague lacks no* darshanim.

By the confused looks clouding the faces around the table, it was apparent that similar thoughts had filled the heads behind those faces. A drashah *in the middle of the week!* It was unheard of! And delivered by the *rav* himself!

"Ah," exclaimed Reb Gershon to Reb Simcha the cloth merchant the next morning as they entered the *beis medrash* together. "I bet today's *shiur* will be twice as good as ever."

"As if that were possible. The *rav* always says his best, puts all of his *ko'ach* into the *shiur*. But I'm sure *we* will enjoy it twice as much after one day's loss. You can't imagine how disappointed I was yesterday. I was grouchy all day."

Little did they know. They were in for another *mussar shmuess* — on the same subject, no less. Were it not for the *rav's* world stature, the disappointed looks on the faces of the *olam* would have turned to murmurs. But the men sat through the *drashah* patiently, again unmoved.

It was after the *rav* had left that they voiced their dissatisfaction.

"Perhaps we should send someone to speak to him," was one suggestion.

"Maybe the *rav* needs a rest, a vacation," another man offered.

But it was Reb Itzik's suggestion that was finally followed. As a retired, well-to-do furrier who had known many *rabbanim* and *darshanim* over the decades, his advice seemed wisest. "A little patience, my young friends," he said. "Let us wait at least until tomorrow before we make any hasty judgments."

The morrow came, but the situation did not change. The *rav* again addressed them all on the subjects of *tzedakah* and *chessed.*

A committee was quickly formed after the *shiur* to deal with the matter. Reb Itzik, Reb Fishel, and Reb Gershon knocked on the *rav's* door. Sonya, the *goyishe* servant girl, answered their knock. "He went to the marketplace! Of all places! Just imagine — the *rav*, who never takes an unnecessary step, gone to that dirty place filled with coarse peddlers, screeching women, and chickens."

The three men set off for the marketplace. They could see many dozens of townspeople, all headed in the same direction.

"What's all the commotion about?" inquired a seamstress, poking her head out of a second-story window.

"Why, haven't you heard?" answered Chana Baila the butcher's wife.

"Yoo hoo, Yenta," shouted Chana the apple woman, pushing her cart ahead of her as fast as the cobblestones allowed. "Leave your laundry for another time. Come! See! *Oy*! That I should live to see the *rav* of Prague going to do business in the market!"

The marketplace was thronged by the time the three men arrived. Business traffic was at a complete standstill. All eyes — curious, worried, anxious, puzzled — focused upon the imposing, tall, bearded man who, even in the squalor of a public mart, commanded attention and respect.

"People of Prague," he began. He had no need to repeat himself, nor to raise his voice, for everyone was immediately hushed.

"Here I stand, holding this three-legged stool," and he lifted it. "As you can plainly see, one leg is broken. Can I still use the stool?"

"Sure!" and "Just prop it up!" could be heard from all sides.

The *rav* nodded. "Fine. But what happens if two legs break? Can I still use the stool?"

The crowd was puzzled: *First of all, since when does the* rav *of Prague* darshen *in the marketplace? Secondly, what is he driving at? And thirdly, what can you do with a stool when two of its legs are broken?*

Jews are still the cleverest of people. The first two questions they couldn't answer; so they would just have to wait. As to putting a broken-legged stool to use…

"Why, just break the third leg to even them all out," someone called out half-jokingly.

"You are very right, my friend," the *rav* smiled. "The only way to restore the stool's balance is to break the third leg. *Al shloshah devarim ha'olam omed*: The world stands on three legs. *Al haTorah v'al ha'avodah v'al gemilus chassadim*. The leg of *avodas hakorbanos* was broken when the second Beis Hamikdash was destroyed. *Chazal* propped it up with *tefillah* which is a substitute for *korbanos*, so that the world could continue to stand.

"But now that you have become penny pinchers and refuse to support the poor, whether by outright *tzedakah* or through loans, you have broken the leg of *gemilus chassadim*. You thus leave me no choice. In order to balance the world, I must break the leg of Torah by stopping my *shiurim* and going out into the marketplace."

The second leg was soon mended. And the "committee" had its *shiur* again.

SHEINDEL WEINBACH

Was he really Shimon, Freidel's long-lost husband, or was he an impostor? Will you be able to guess how the Noda B'Yehuda tested the man who came

In Her Husband's Place

"Hey, Velvel! If that isn't Reb Shimon walking down the street, I'll eat my hat!"

"I wouldn't be so hasty in my choice of a penalty, Shmuel. But I'd also wager that that's Reb Muttel Zaltzer's son-in-law."

Shmuel and Velvel, on their way to the *beis medrash*, could not help wondering what had caused Shimon to return to Prague after so many years of unexplained absence. And for that matter, what had caused him to disappear in the first place.

"Look — the exact same walk, that carefree stride of his. Remember, Velvel?"

"And the same way of tilting his head slightly to the side. There now, he's turned his face. His beard is much thicker now.

And his hair thinner. But I guess twelve years will perform changes in any man."

"Oh, I have no doubt that it's Reb Shimon. The question is, shall we approach him or not? What have we really got to say to a man who left his young wife an *agunah* for so many years? I know what Reb Muttel, her father, went through. He's a cousin of mine. Poor Freidel, though, has suffered immeasurably."

"Well, it's none of my business, at any rate. I never knew him more than to nod hello to. I don't intend to be late for the *shiur*. Oh, look. He's headed for his *shver's* house. We can offer our greetings later at Minchah."

"Right. But still, I wonder…"

The two men turned in to the *beis medrash* while Shimon continued for a block and finally paused in front of a large stone house. He adjusted his hat, straightened his vest and jacket, and briskly employed the brass lion knocker.

Reb Mordechai Zaltzer himself, master of the house, opened the door. Attired in his overcoat, he had been about to leave. Utterly taken aback, Reb Muttel just stood speechless in the doorway. Finally regaining his usual composure, he greeted his son-in-law.

"Shimon? Can it be you? After all these years? Well, come in! Come in! We've got a lot to discuss, haven't we?"

The long-lost son-in-law was ushered into the parlor and all the family, the young wife included, were quickly summoned. The tone, as set by Reb Mordechai, was of restrained welcome. Many matters had to be straightened out before Shimon might resume his position in the family.

"I think we deserve some explanation, Shimon. What have you got to say for yourself?"

The young man, seated on the sofa, his legs arrogantly crossed, refused to be intimidated. "Look here, Papa, I'm back and that's the main thing, isn't it? Let's just forget the past and continue from where we left off twelve years ago. Right, Freidel?" he flashed her a self-confident smile.

Freidel did not return the smile. She just sat there silent, perplexed.

Reb Muttel, suffused with rage, replied, "What do you mean, forget it! Forget the anguish you caused poor Freidel here? Shrug off the shame you brought upon us, her parents? You mean to step into your old shoes just like that? No regrets? No apologies?" Reb Muttel's crescendoing voice was joined by a raised fist.

"Hold it, Papa," sneered Shimon. "After all, isn't a live husband better than a lost one? I think you should reconsider your attitude. You'll come around and accept me without any fancy apologies and be glad that I returned at all."

This was altogether too much for Mr. Zaltzer's high blood pressure. He grabbed Shimon's collar and dragged him through the hall and, puffing, precipitated him through the front door.

"I'll have no young upstart tell me what to do! If you've got any further business with me, you'll find the channels for it."

"Oh, I'll show you," called Shimon behind his back. "You can't cheat me out of my rightful place. I'll take you to court."

Freidel gently led her overwrought father back to his chair. She sat him down and brought him a drink.

"Papa. Do you know what I think? I think that man isn't Shimon at all. He resembles him physically, and even has all of Shimon's old mannerisms. But Shimon was never coarse and disrespectful like that. He had his own faults, but he never spoke like that."

Malka Zaltzer, a trim woman in her late fifties, spoke up. "Twelve years is a long time, Freidel. People change, you know. I wouldn't make hasty judgment, neither for nor against him. Our cool reception must have upset him."

"Malka," announced Reb Muttel, rising decisively. "We must get to the bottom of this matter, the sooner the better. Son-in-law or not, we've got to settle this. Come, let's go over to the *rav's*. Right now."

And so the case was presented to the *rav* of the city, the illustrious Rav Yechezkel Landau. Shimon was summoned and arrived flanked by several acquaintances — cousin Velvel among them — whom he had recruited to testify as to his true identity.

The Noda B'Yehuda sat and listened, perplexed. He questioned both sides carefully but could find no flaw, no clue. The young man flippantly refused to reveal why he had left his wife so long ago, yet demanded the right to take his place as her rightful husband. Suddenly the Noda B'Yehuda's eyes lit up.

"I'd like all of you to leave the room now, except for Reb Mordechai."

They all left Reb Muttel alone with the *rav*. Reb Muttel soon emerged a much calmer man.

"Come, Shimon. The *rav* says we are to return tomorrow for his final *psak*. Let's go to shul now."

Shimon shrugged his shoulders indifferently and accompanied his father-in-law. The two women looked after them, surprised, and then at one another.

As they walked home, Freidel wondered, "I wonder what the *rav* told Papa to make him change his attitude so suddenly."

They got their answer an hour later when Reb Muttel returned with a satisfied smile on his face.

"You are both dying of curiosity, I can see," he smiled ruefully. "You women are all alike. I just performed an interesting little experiment with gratifying results."

"Tell us, Muttel," exclaimed Malka Zaltzer impatiently. "You know I can't tolerate your joking about such serious matters. What happened?"

"Well, we walked to shul together, as you saw. We caused quite a stir, I must say, both from those who had already heard of Shimon's return and from those who hadn't. Well, just as I reached the door, I stopped to speak to someone, and told Shimon to go on ahead to his place. And guess what?"

"Oh, Papa, how can we guess? Please tell us what happened!"

"That's when my interesting experiment showed results. Shimon gave himself away. He hadn't the faintest notion where his seat was!"

The women gasped in amazement while Reb Muttel chuckled.

"He wandered from corner to corner, from bench to bench, pretending to look for a siddur. But 'our Shimon' finally had to ask someone where I sat. Of course, I had been looking on from the corner of my eye. I went up to him then and accused him in public of being an imposter. He finally admitted it was my money and position that he was after, posing as my absent son-in-law. And thanks to the Noda B'Yehuda's shrewd insight, this plan exposed him."

Reb Muttel paused to let his words sink in. Then he continued, "You see, the Noda B'Yehuda understood that only a lowly man could perpetrate such an insidious hoax. Such a man, prepared to live with a wife not his own, would never have thought to obtain this important piece of information. Someone whose mind lies in *tumah* doesn't think about *kedushah*. You could say, Malka," he turned to his wife with a twinkle in his eye, "that it's all a question of knowing one's place."

SHEINDEL WEINBACH

Payoff in Padua

A Play in Two Acts

ACT ONE

Scene One: *Padua, Italy. The home of wealthy Adon Yechezkel. The curtain rises on the master of the house sitting in his richly furnished library whose every wall is ostentatiously covered with draperies, tapestries, or Florentine paintings. One entire wall, however, boasts (literally) a floor to ceiling bookcase and silver display of Jewish volumes and* tashmishei kedushah *of masterly craftsmanship. Yechezkel is seated in one corner at a huge carved desk, surrounded by bills and account books.*

Yechezkel: Bills, bills, bills! And then more bills! From the looks of things you'd think Padua expects me to go bankrupt tomorrow. The way they hound me! It's absolutely disgusting. What difference does it make how I pay, so long as I do pay in the end? So I pay out slowly, a few *lire* at a time. My credit is good. People just don't have any patience these days. Now me, I'm a patient man, never lose my temper. But this constant badgering — it just wears me out.

Servant: Sir. Shaul, the dry-goods merchant, wishes a few good words with you.

Yechezkel (*shouting*): He can save his breath. I know exactly what he wants. Tell him he's just wasting his time. He wants to squeeze money from me, the rascal. Well, you just go and tell him I haven't any. I'll make a payment next month, in Tevet. I've got too many expenses this month.

(*The servant goes and returns.*)

Servant: But sir, he insists he just wants to say a few words…

Yechezkel: Well, let him make it real snappy. (*Under his breath*) I'll give him a piece of my mind. (*Stands*)

Shaul: Pardon me, sir, but you haven't made a payment on your bill for over two months. You emptied my shop of the most costly materials to make the clothes for you and your family in honor of your son's bar mitzvah. You haven't paid a fraction of it yet, sir. Not even a third. I've got my own family expenses to worry about, you know, shoes for the children, school tuition, a goose for Chanukah, and maybe some gifts for the little ones. And I've got to replenish my depleted stock. I must have some money, sir. Please have some pity.

Yechezkel: Here, take these ten *lire* on account. Now go and leave me alone. I feel a headache coming on.

Shaul: Ten *lire*! Sir, what is ten *lire*? Your bill adds up to 3,750 *lire*. Here, see for yourself. You must be joking with this paltry sum.

Yechezkel (*softening somewhat*): Listen here, I am a very busy man. This is all the cash I can spare right now. Come back next month and I'll give you something a little more substantial. (*He sits down and goes back to his accounts.*)

Servant: Excuse me, sir, but Hillel the *sofer* is here and wishes to see you.

(*An old man with a flowing white beard, elaborate tarbush and worn but impressive long robe enters the room. Yechezkel rises briefly.*)

Yechezkel: I know (*he sighs*). You want the money for the *tefillin* you wrote for my son. Indeed, I never saw such fine writing as in your *parshiyot*, and I appreciate all the work that went into it. I knew what I was getting by ordering the most expensive *tefillin* you ever made. They are well worth it, but I am afraid that you must wait until next month for another payment.

Sofer: But sir, you promised me you would pay on the very day of the bar mitzvah. You don't realize how much time went into those *tefillin*. I dropped all my usual cash business, my *mezuzot* and *ketubot* and *semichah klafim*. I worked a long time on those *parshiyot*, to say nothing of the expense of the *klaf* itself and of the *batim*… It is already two whole months since the bar mitzvah. Do you realize that you have only paid out twenty-five *lire* on a 2000-*lire* item?

Yechezkel: Don't for one instant think, *chas v'chalilah*, that I regard your work and effort lightly. I value those *tefillin* highly as being worth every bit of the price. People can't call me a miser, no sir, especially when it comes to mitzvot. Always the best for me (*he flings his arm out to encompass his luxurious library*). Are you really worrying that I won't pay you? I will pay every last drop, every last coin. It's just that I have had extensive expenses this month. Here, take these twenty-five *lire*, though I can scarcely spare them. Not that I'm going bankrupt, G-d forbid, but you see, I just ordered a solid gold menorah for Chanukah which must be paid up when I take it home with me. I hope to make you another payment by next month.

(*The sofer, too refined to persist, takes the money with a downcast expression and leaves.*)

Yechezkel (*closes his books, stretches and sighs*): I think that'll be it for the day. Time to go to sleep. I can't stand these blasted bills, they give me a headache. Tomorrow I'll hop down to the goldsmith and see how he's progressing. That's sure to lift my spirits. But now, to sleep.

Scene Two: *The next day. Curtain rises on a jewelry shop on a busy market street. Yosef the goldsmith is sitting cross-legged on a mat. The walls are decorated with dangling gold and silver chains and the few shelves contain goblets and household trinkets. A small fire burns in one corner near which stands a low table with jewelers' tools. Yosef is absorbed in carving a huge but shapely urn.*

Yechezkel: Hello, Yosef. How are you this fine morning? And how's our little project progressing? Chanukah is just around the corner. Tomorrow night, in fact.

Yosef: It's coming along fine. But before I show it to you, sir, I must remind you of our agreement —

Yechezkel: Yes, yes. I haven't forgotten. You'll get the full amount on the day I take my menorah home. You can trust me. But that is another matter. What's important now is the menorah itself. Is it living up to my expectations? Bring it. I'm dying to see it already. I've told half the city about it. Just think (*he stares dreamily into the gay market street outside not realizing that Yosef has gone to the back of the shop*), Chanukah night with that treasure brightening up the whole room… Just think of the look on the faces of the passersby as their eyes turn up to see my window ablaze in glory…the candlelight breaking into all colors of the rainbow as it is reflected by the facets on the diamonds and rubies and sapphires. You haven't forgotten to order that two-carat sapphire, have you? Now that's a stone for you. Sapphire. The color of the sunny Italian skies, of the blue waters of the Mediterranean… I'm telling you it will be the talk of the town. That's *pirsumei nisa* like it should be. That's the way to fulfill a mitzvah. Forget about the expenses and concentrate on the mitzvah itself. Oh, there you are (*he turns to see Yosef returning with the menorah*).

Yosef: Here you are, sir. As you can see, there are still some minor details to finish off. This lion here on the right has to be aligned with the rest; it's a fraction of an inch too high. And these oil goblets still need strengthening. The stone settings need a bit of tightening here and there, and the sapphire must be polished before I set it. The whole piece needs a good burnishing to make it gleam. You deserve a perfect job, you're sure paying enough.

Yechezkel: Let's forget about the money, Yosef. Let's just look and enjoy your handicraft. It is truly a work of art. I've heard that you have done work for her majesty the queen, is that correct? You are famous throughout the country. And this masterpiece will yet enhance your reputation. Well, now I must go but I will return tomorrow without fail. You can be sure I won't forget. Tomorrow is Chanukah already.

Yosef: Goodbye, sir. And don't forget to bring the money.

Scene Three: *The same place, twenty-four hours later.*

Yechezkel: And how are we today, Yosef? Fine, I trust. Today's the big day, you know. Me, I feel like a king. Today I am acquiring a treasure fit for a king. Here, let me hold it in my hands for a few moments before you wrap it up. (*He goes to the doorway and makes sure that people are looking.*) Ahhhhh. Look how it sparkles in the sunlight. It actually rivals the sun itself in brilliance. King Solomon himself wouldn't be ashamed of owning such a menorah. But that's enough rapturing. I must hurry. They're waiting for me at home on pins and needles. I promised the bambinos they could help me with the preparations for *hadlakat hanerot*.

(*Yosef wraps the menorah tenderly in silk but holds onto the package.*)

Yechezkel: Well. What are you waiting for? Give it to me already. I told you I'm in a hurry.

Yosef: You forgot one thing.

Yechezkel: Don't talk in riddles. I haven't forgotten anything. How could I if I didn't come with anything?

Yosef: You forgot to pay me like you promised.

Yechezkel: *Mama mia!* You're right! I was in such a hurry to bring back the menorah that I left the house in a rush. Isn't that funny? I forgot to take my purse along. Well, don't worry. I'll drop by sometime during Chanukah.

Yosef: I'm very sorry, but I will not give you the menorah until you pay.

Yechezkel: Come, come now. Don't be stubborn. It doesn't suit a grown man. Don't you believe me? Here, I'll give you a note. (*Writes*) "I, Yechezkel ben Avraham, do hereby promise to pay to Yosef the goldsmith, the sum of five thousand Italian *lire*. Signed, Yechezkel ben Avraham." Okay? Now let's have that package. It's late already.

Yosef: You'll excuse me for talking so bluntly, sir, but you've acquired a name as a man who doesn't pay off his debts. I am not taking any chances.

Yechezkel (raising his voice): Why, that's an outright lie. I always pay my debts. Whoever spread such scandal about me? I'll wring his neck, I will.

Yosef: Maybe you do eventually pay off your debts. After the poor creditor has sweated twice over to get the money that's coming to him. Well, I am going to be the exception. I refuse to give you this menorah until I see you count out every last coin right here before my eyes — in cold cash.

(*Rabbeinu Avraham Ibn Ezra enters the store.*)

Ibn Ezra (good-naturedly): What is this? Jews arguing? I heard you as I was passing by and decided to come in to see if something could be done. Here, here. Tell me your problem and let's see if I can't smooth it over in no time. It doesn't pay to get excited.

Yosef: It is a very simple matter, honored *chacham*. Adon Yechezkel ordered this menorah here. It costs five thousand *lire*. I have as yet received nothing on account for he agreed to pay me in full when he took it home.

Ibn Ezra: I see (*nodding approval*). And now he's probably forgotten his money or some such excuse. I've heard about you, Yechezkel ben Avraham.

Yechezkel: But *k'vod hachacham*, I never said I wouldn't pay. Here, see for yourself. I just wrote out a promissory note. It's got my full signature on it. Can't one Jew trust a fellow Jew?

Ibn Ezra: Let's see this note. Hmmm… No date, no witnesses, no deadline for the payment. Not worth much, is it? I've heard this story before somewhere. In fact, I've had people coming to me asking for advice on how to collect their payments from you. I never had enough evidence to send for you for a *din Torah*. And there is nothing I can do now, either. Of course, you, Yosef, are not to dare let that menorah out of your sight before you see the full sum counted out right into your palm. And as for you,

Yechezkel, all I can say to you is this — I pray that the *malach* of *chibuv mitzvot* will come and teach you a lesson. Do you think you may run up huge accounts at other people's expense? What value can a mitzvah have, even if done in the most lavish style, if you don't pay for it in full? Don't forget one important thing, my friend. Paying back debts is a *mitzvah mid'Orayta* — and that has precedence over *hiddur mitzvot*. Think it over...

Yechezkel (*stalks angrily out of the store muttering under his breath*): Humph! The *chibuv mitzvot malach*. I never heard of such a thing. I bet he invented it on the spot. Just to scare me. Ridiculous, I say. Just a figment of an old man's imagination.

ACT TWO

Scene One: *Same place, twenty-four hours later.*

Yosef: Good day to you, Adon Yechezkel. Let me tell you, it was some experience lighting your...my menorah last night. The labor of my own hands. Truly a work of art if I may say so myself. In fact I'm getting very attached to it. I could hardly keep my eyes off it for the entire three hours that it was burning. Well, have you brought the money today?

Yechezkel: I didn't have a choice, did I? You should have seen what went on in my house. It was almost like Tishah B'Av, I tell you. My kids bawling, my wife screaming at me. It seems she had invited all the neighbors to a catered Chanukah party, intending, of course, to show off our new acquisition. *Oy vey!* Never fear, my friend. I've got it all here. I'll count it out to you in plain daylight. One thousand, two thousand, three, four... Here it is, five thousand Italian *lire*. Are you satisfied now? Let's have that menorah, now. They're waiting for it back home.

Yosef: And here you are, sir. *Titchadesh*.

Yechezkel: Thank you. This is truly a great occasion for me. Goodbye.

Scene Two: *Yechezkel walking into his house. He is greeted by his impatient wife and three sons.*

Yishai: Abba, Abba. Did you bring the menorah?

Shimon: Did you bring it? Let's see. Unwrap it.

Chai: Will we light it tonight? Remember you promised I could light the *shamash*?

Yechezkel: Yes, my sweet ones. I've brought it. Come, let's put it on the windowsill so that everyone can see it. Our menorah is the nicest in the city.

Yishai: In the whole of Italy, Abba.

Chai: In the whole wide world.

Yechezkel: Yes, my children, even in the whole world, as you say. Come now, let's prepare the wicks. Here, you take the cotton and roll it in your palm like this. Then you dip one end in oil and turn it upside down so that it should burn well. Okay. Is everyone here? Miriam?

Baruch atah...shel Chanukah. (*All answer "Amen."*)

Baruch atah...lazman hazeh. (*All answer "Amen." Yechezkel tries to light the menorah but the wicks refuse to ignite. He strikes match after match but the wicks do not catch fire. Even Miriam tries to light the menorah after quickly fitting it with new wicks. Nothing happens. Finally giving up, he signals to his wife to bring the old menorah from its place among the silver. This he succeeds immediately in lighting.*)

That son of a goldsmith! That crook! He makes a menorah that doesn't light! I nearly made two *brachot l'vatalah* thanks to that scoundrel. I'll sue him, I will. I'll call him to a *din Torah* and get my money back. I'm going right now to Chacham Azaryah. I'll take this menorah along and show him. Then he'll call in the goldsmith to render a *din v'cheshbon*. That cheater! I demand justice!

Scene Three: *Chacham Azaryah's home, later that evening.*

Yechezkel (*bursts into the room waving his silk-wrapped package rather violently*): K'vod harav. I demand you summon that dirty crook to a *din Torah*. Such a cheater I never saw in all my born days. He takes five thousand *lire* in cash and shamelessly sells me a lemon. Look at this white elephant! Either it lights or I want a refund!

Rav: Patience, my good man. Start at the beginning. I gather you ordered an expensive menorah which doesn't light. Tell me one thing. Tonight is the *second* night of Chanukah. What happened last night? Why didn't you come to me then?

Yechezkel: Last night? (*abashedly*) Well, yesterday I didn't have it yet. It was still with Yosef. In fact, he told me himself that he lit it in his home and the lights burned for three hours. I bet he sabotaged it.

Rav: Really? Three hours? This requires some investigation. Let me try my luck with your menorah. (*He fails to light the menorah.*) This is interesting. Most interesting. I see nothing faulty with the workmanship. It is most masterful. Tell me, do you think you could have gotten an *ayin hara* on your way home?

Yechezkel: *Ayin hara*? Of course not. Oh, oh, I remember something. Chacham Ibn Ezra was at the goldsmith with me yesterday. He muttered something about a *malach*. I didn't catch what he was saying.

Rav: What are you saying? That Chacham Ibn Ezra "muttered something"? Do you know who you are talking about? The *gadol hador*. He knows more Torah in his little finger than I'll ever know. You must go and ask *mechilah* for talking this way. And I'm coming along. I want to ask him what it was he said at the goldsmith's.

Scene Four: *Chacham Ibn Ezra's home, a poorly furnished one-room cottage, later that evening.*

Ibn Ezra: *Shalom aleichem*, Chacham Azaryah. To what can I attribute the honor of this visit?
Rav: *Aleichem shalom*. We've got a problem that I am sure the *chacham* can solve for us. Adon Yechezkel, here (*Ibn Ezra glances at him and nods knowingly*), purchased a menorah that doesn't seem to work although last night it burned all right at Yosef the goldsmith's. He says you know something about it.
Ibn Ezra: Ahaaa. Yes, I do know something about it. I remember it well. I see that the *malach chibuv mitzvot* did his job well. You see, Chacham Azaryah, this man owes money to half the city. To workers, to merchants, and to craftsmen. He doesn't even think twice about ordering the most expensive *tefillin*, the dearest *etrog*, the fanciest menorah, the costliest *aliyah*. All this at the expense of his fellow citizens. He has not yet been known to pay cash on the spot for any commodity. Except this one time. He still has to learn his lesson for the future. And I hope he is beginning to. For if he wants the *malach* to release his hold over the menorah, he's got to pay back every last *lira* to his every last creditor in this city of Padua. There is nothing I can do. It is up to Yechezkel himself.

Scene Five: *The third night of Chanukah in the large dining room in Adon Yechezkel's home. Yechezkel is seated at the* *head of the table surrounded by all his former creditors. The lovely menorah with its three lights stands on the windowsill and casts a halo about the whole room.*

Hillel the sofer (*seated at Yechezkel's right*): L'chaim to you, Yechezkel.
Yechezkel: L'chaim!
Yosef: L'chaim!
Hillel: May your new menorah continue to delight your eyes and brighten your heart to serve *Hakadosh Baruch Hu*, completely — from within and from without. May you always keep in mind that "*hanerot halalu kodesh hem ve'en lanu reshut l'hishtamesh bahem.*" You may not use the menorah or any mitzvah for your own personal glory. You must glorify Hashem by being a man of your word, by paying your debts on time. By exemplifying all that is good and decent, you yourself will be a *mefarsem hanes*, a true *mekadesh Hashem*.

(Curtain)

RAV NAFTOLI EHRMANN

"Anyone Can Make a Match"

ADAPTED BY SHEINDEL WEINBACH

THE PLACE — Lisbon, Portugal; the year — 1480 or so; the scene — the market square humming with activity.

"Maria," calls out the rosy-cheeked Estella from behind her stall of ripe melons and fresh figs. "Quick, come grab your corner. Geronimo will soon be here. I just heard his donkey bray from the east end of town."

A groan goes up from the other vendors at this announcement. Geronimo, aside from his dashing manner and sparkling black eyes, is famous for the quality of his fruit. His apples are the most delectable, his olives the most mouth-watering. His persimmons are golden perfection; his grapes — clusters of succulence. No wonder then, that when he appears on the scene all housewives and servants rush to buy his wares. But as welcome as he is with the customers, so is he unpopular among the vendors. The only protection they have is to crowd him out of the plaza. If all the corners and stalls are occupied, Geronimo is forced to go elsewhere, for donkey-and-cart traffic does not allow him to remain stationary for very long.

Estella removes the basket from her head, and begins arranging her apples in tempting groups about her on the faded rug which serves as her counter. Then she kneels down beside them to await customers.

"Do you know what I heard just this morning, 'Stella? The king wishes to arrange the betrothal of Prince Fernando to the princess Isabella of Spain. The cook at the palace told me so."

Maria sighs wistfully. "If only I had been of noble birth… why, I could live in the palace, wear expensive gowns and all."

A handsome coach rushes through the plaza at this moment and shakes her from her reveries. When the noise of hoof beats dies down Estella speaks. "It is not only a question of birth, Maria. That was Don Isaac Abarbanel's coach that just passed by. You know, of course, that despite the fact that he is a Jew, he nevertheless holds the influential post of finance minister at the palace."

"That's different, silly. He got there by his brains. Everyone knows that Jews are smart. But for me there is no hope of ever bettering my station in life. Why I could as soon become a princess as…as Lucia the old washerwoman there." This preposterous thought sends the two into convulsions of laughter.

～※～

Don Isaac's coach rolls into the palace courtyard. As it comes to a halt, Don Isaac descends, waving aside the palace footman who attempts to aid him. He has many important things on his mind and gets impatient at gestures that only serve to detain him. He strides purposefully past the guards, nodding briefly, right and left. A Jew, he knows, no matter how high his position, must always be careful not to offend the humblest gentile. He reaches the council room wherein are seated several of the king's cabinet ministers, and his presence is announced. The king acknowledges his bow and motions him to a seat.

"We have just been discussing the journey of the royal delegation to the new pope. As a Catholic country, Portugal is vitally affected by his election. Our delegation is to offer our respects as well as to feel out his position on political matters. You, as finance minister, are to see to it that the expedition is well provided for, suitable gifts and tributes included. I leave those up to your judgment. Expenses are to be taken from the royal treasury from the funds earmarked as religious expenses. I will require, however, an itemized list..."

The king, finished with the business of the day, now dismisses his ministers but signals Don Isaac to remain. He has another matter to discuss with him. King Alfonso enjoys conversations with his Jewish minister, and respects his clarity and perception, his honesty and modesty. The king is aware that since Jews have lived in Portugal they have been treated well and have, in turn, benefited their host country. They have served in the past and present as royal advisers, physicians, and scribes.

The king leans back against the soft cushions on his silken couch and inhales from the long pipe at his side. "What have you, as a disinterested outsider, to say of the political ramifications of the intended match between Prince Fernando and the Princess Isabella of Spain? I wish to do nothing conclusive about this before I consider each aspect of such a move."

"Your majesty. The realm of betrothal is one I do not enter. Marriages are made in heaven. If it is G-d's will that the royal families of Spain and Portugal be united in this match, nothing I say will change things. My opinion is of no significance."

"Don Isaac. Your straightforwardness surprises me no less than your answer displeases me. Do you really believe that marriages are made in heaven? Why, I can marry off my cousin the prince to whomever I so desire. Who will stand in the way of the king?"

"Pardon my brazenness, your gracious majesty, but the Bible, in which you believe as well, testifies to my statement. Did not Lavan, brother of Rebecca, say to Abraham's servant concerning his plight for her hand, 'This thing is from G-d'?"

The king bursts into peals of laughter. "Do you bring the words of the hypocrite Lavan as proof? That is most amusing, ha ha ha."

"Yes, your majesty. *A fortiori*, as they say in Latin. If the wicked Lavan believed that marriages are Heaven-ordained, we must certainly subscribe to that. Let me relate an incident from our Talmud to prove my conviction.

"A Roman matron once approached Rabbi Yosi ben Chalafta and asked of him, 'What has G-d been doing since the end of Creation?' 'The L-d occupies Himself with the arranging of matrimonial matches,' he replied. 'Is that such a difficult thing that He must do it? Why, anyone can make a match.' This wealthy woman summoned immediately one thousand male and one thousand female servants. She lined them up and paired them off arbitrarily. By the very next morning, however, she was faced with the consequences of her foolish experiment. Her servants, battered, bruised, and disheveled, confronted her with loud complaints. Not one of the couples had been compatible."

The king smiles thinly. "That is an amusing story, but it moves me not. In fact, it tempts me to try my hand at such an experiment. Who, wise rabbi, in your opinion, is ordained by Heaven to be the rightful mate of the prince? The princess of Spain or an apple vendor off the market? You refuse to commit yourself? Well, I tell you that this very day Prince Fernando will wed a market maid. We will see whose will prevails. You are dismissed. I've got things to do now." And as Don Isaac leaves the king adds half aloud, "Humph. Providence! Why, anyone can make a match!"

Suddenly enchanted with his own capricious idea, the king takes pen in hand and commences to write.

⊂⊃

In the plaza Maria and Estella are busy serving their customers.

"Look. You've sold almost all your apples, Maria. You can go home soon, lucky thing, while I have to stay here in this dusty marketplace."

"Don't be jealous, Estella. As soon as I return I've got to help in the orchard."

Maria begins gathering the remains of her merchandise. She notices, however, from the corner of her eye, a strange figure dressed in silk and brocade, with the large brim of his incongruous sombrero pulled over his eyes. She watches him curiously, wondering as to his purpose here. He seems to be only interested in apples, for whenever he passes a fruit stall he stops and examines the apples and the vendor as well. Maria, anxious to sell the remainder of her fruit, piles the apples into a small basket, rubbing the uppermost ones quickly on her gay paisley shawl, and walks over to the gentleman.

"Delicious Valencia apples, sire," she offers, curtsying. "Twenty *pesos* the lot for you."

The stranger looks at Maria and thrusts a handful of gold coins into her palm. "Thank you, señorita. I have no need of your fine apples but these twenty *pesos* are yours if you deliver this letter to Prince Fernando at once. You do know where his palace is, don't you?"

Maria looks at the letter and draws her breath in deeply. Although unable to read, she easily recognizes the royal crest on the seal. Looking up, she suddenly recognizes the stranger. Hasn't she seen him often in parades and public ceremonies? It is the king himself! He smiles at her and puts a finger to his lips to signify secrecy. "I want you to deliver this letter personally to the prince and await a reply. It is of the utmost importance. You will receive a handsome reward at the prince's palace." He turns away, chuckling to himself.

Maria rushes back breathlessly to her corner to bid her friend goodbye.

"Please don't go yet," begs Estella. "I hear Geronimo's donkey braying again. He must be coming back for another try at grabbing a place here. If he takes yours, I'm finished! No one will even look at my wares and if I don't sell them I'm in for another beating tonight from my papa. Oh, look! There's Lucia Cardizo the washerwoman. She'll be glad to deliver that letter for half of what you got."

"Lucia — come here a minute!" calls Estella and turns to her friend to take it from there. The old woman stares greedily at the handful of coins offered her, and leaving her heavy basket by the stall, hurries off to deliver the letter.

༒

At the prince's palace, she is told to await a reply. But Lucia insists on delivering the letter herself. Those were her explicit instructions, she adamantly states. Besides, she thinks to herself, when will she ever have another opportunity to see the inside of a palace! And so she is taken to a reception room and told to wait. The page leaves to summon the prince and Lucia seats herself gingerly on a velvet-covered chair of imported mahogany. She stares in awe at the costly furnishings about her, but as soon as footsteps resound from the hall she springs up as fast as her creaky bones permit. She bows deeply and submits her precious missive to the prince himself. He breaks the royal seal and reads its contents. Then he looks strangely at the washerwoman, back at the letter, and then again at the old woman.

"It can't be! There must be some mistake. The king wouldn't do this to me, his own cousin! Manuelo, go ask the padre to be so kind as to come immediately." The prince paces back and forth, oblivious of the puzzled Lucia who awaits her reward. Finally the priest arrives. As he takes the letter from the prince and scans it, it is his turn now to look quizzically from letter to Lucia and back.

"If you please, kind prince," she asks timidly. "I left my wash basket with all its dirty linen in the market. I must hurry back to get it done. Please give me the reward I was promised."

"My dear woman," answers the prince. "If what this letter says is correct, you are to marry me this very day! I am even forbidden by the king to leave my quarters until this has been done!" He looks to the priest to confirm his statement but meanwhile Lucia has let out a shriek and fallen into a faint. She is quickly carried to a couch and revived with smelling salts.

"I'll rush over to the king to see if it is no cruel joke," promises the priest. But he soon returns to confront an impatient prince and an incredulous washerwoman with their fate.

"The king refuses to discuss the matter at all. He merely says that there is no mistake and that you are to obey his letter in detail. Are you both ready then?"

"Do you, Fernando, take this woman… (Hey, he whispers — what is your name?) …er…Lucia, to be your wedded wife?"

Fernando stands tall and stately beside the wrinkled old woman at his side. Determined to behave as befits a nobleman, he is impassive. Only his glossy eyes betray his inner emotions. Lucia, on the other hand, is so confused that she answers automatically. She expects to awaken from this ridiculous situation to find it but a dream.

The ceremony is over; the two are lawfully married in the eyes of the church. Prince Fernando now commands his servants to prepare quarters for the new mistress, to bathe her, and fulfill all her requirements.

Dona Lucia is confined to her quarters for the remainder of the honeymoon. The prince visits her daily, speaks to her courteously, but never appears with her in public. His social life continues as before, attending parties, dinners, performances with the usual court coterie.

Upon one occasion in which the prince describes the lavish ball he has just attended, Lucia bursts into tears. "What is it, my dear?" he asks, half afraid of what the old woman will request. "Do the servants not treat you well?"

"Oh no, it is not that. Your lordship is most kind. I do so enjoy your tales of court life. But I do wish you could bring me sometimes just a little cake from one of the fancy dinners you describe. Some sweet confection iced prettily, for my poor toothless gums. That would make my life here complete."

The prince laughs in relief, and from then on always remembers his wife with the sweets she craves.

∽

The days pass. The prince has accepted his fate. The king, assured that his match has been performed, forgets for the time being the victory he has won over Don Isaac. The new princess must have a decent interval in which to acquire all the court amenities and niceties before she can appear in public. And so, when he invites the prince to a state dinner, he hardly expects the new Dona to accompany him.

This dinner is a grand affair, lavishly served, attended only by the noblest members of the court. The king, fond of fine works of art, has planned an exhibit of his latest acquirements, the most costly of which is a carved ivory snuffbox. Reaching into the pocket of his flowered waistcoat during the course of the evening, the king's face suddenly falls.

"Where is my precious snuffbox!" he cries out in alarm. "It was in my waistcoat earlier this evening. Someone here tonight must have taken it! I demand a thorough search be made among the guests right now." Everyone begins turning pockets inside out, peering under chairs, behind drapes. But the snuffbox is not located.

"I must beg pardon of all my honored guests but due to the value of the snuffbox, I must ask each person present to search his neighbor's pockets."

The company good-naturedly agrees to this invasion of personal privacy. They are surprised, therefore, when Prince Fernando announces his refusal to have his pockets searched. The king is too polite a host to insist and the fruitless search is called to a halt. The guests return to their merrymaking somewhat subdued.

∽

Several days later when the king dons another waistcoat the snuffbox is discovered. This is the attire that he had originally planned to wear to the dinner and had placed the box in that pocket. He now recalls the prince's strange behavior with curiosity and desires an explanation. The prince is summoned.

"Satisfy my inquisitiveness, my dear Fernando," he says to the prince. "But if you did not take my snuffbox, as I was certain that you hadn't, why did you so vehemently refuse to have your pockets searched?"

Fernando blushes. "My pocket contained other things that I did not wish discovered."

"Oh?"

"I had several small iced cakes which I wished to bring home to my wife. There are not many foods that her toothless gums can chew. She loves these goodies so. Just imagine, your majesty, the impeccable Count Cardozo, seated at my right, sticking his jeweled lily hands into the gooey mess." Fernando tried to make light of the incident but a tear glistened in his eye.

"What did you say? Toothless gums? Your wife lacked no teeth in the radiant smile she flashed at me in the marketplace. Please explain."

"Your majesty, please don't jest with me. My burden is hard enough to bear without your poking fun in addition. My wife is old and toothless and probably has been thus for the past decade or two."

"What nonsense, my dear prince! The apple woman I sent to you could not have been over sixteen! As healthy a wench as I ever saw! Please explain yourself."

Prince Fernando stands, head bowed, tears flowing freely now. "Your majesty. My wife is an old ugly washerwoman, seventy years old if she is a day. You should know, it was your majesty who sent her with the letter. I only obeyed your explicit instructions when I married her."

"*Dios mio!* How could this be! Come with me, and we will get to the bottom of this ugly mess."

The king rushes off to the market and angrily confronts the frightened Maria.

"Your majesty," she explains. "I sent the letter you gave me with Lucia the washerwoman. See, here is her basket yet. She never returned to reclaim it. No one knows what has become of her since."

The king now rushes to Don Isaac's villa. He is greeted by a surprised Don Isaac who apologizes for not being prepared for the honor of a royal visit.

"It is I who must apologize. You were right and I was wrong and I've gotten the prince into an ugly mess."

"What is your majesty referring to?" asks the Jew in surprise.

"Do you recall our conversation of a fortnight ago? We held conflicting opinions concerning matrimonial matches. Did I not declare to you then that if I wished, I could marry off the prince to an apple woman off the market. And if I succeeded you would have to concede that there was no Divine guidance in marriages?"

"And how has your majesty failed?" asks Don Isaac with a hint of a smile.

"The prince married according to my written instructions, requiring him to wed the bearer of my letter. It was Providence that brought about the weird turn of events in which my letter passed from the young apple vendor's hands to the possession of an old hag of a washerwoman. You, in your wisdom, foresaw such a possibility but out of courtesy to me did not stop me from carrying out my ill-fated experiment. You are doubtless aware that there is no divorce in our religion. In your sagacity, Don Isaac, can you right what I have wronged? Can you somehow undo my mischief?"

"Your majesty has just sent a delegation to the new pope," replies Don Isaac after several moments of reflection. "He needs your support and recognition. It is in his power alone to annul a marriage that came about by grievous error and was performed against the wishes of all involved. Send a messenger to overtake the delegation and present this petition before the pope. I am confident that he will see fit to declare this marriage null and void. Then, your majesty, Fernando will be free to marry whomever G-d has truly intended for him."

HENDI LETZTER

Rav Eliyahu Chaim Meisel forestalls the plan for

A Pogrom in Lodz

IN THE CITY of Lodz, in the year 5665, a pogrom was brewing. The Jews of Lodz did not sit idle, but created means of self-defense. The house committees did not have real arms, but used their ingenuity to invent homemade weaponry, such as bottles filled with sand, iron bars, hot sand, and stones. Only a few people knew that Lodz was then saved from a horrible pogrom by the *rav* of Lodz, Rav Eliyahu Chaim Meisel.

During the years of political unrest in Russia, the famous Bialystok army unit which was infamous for organizing pogroms was sent to Lodz. It was the arrival of this unit which led to the above-mentioned measures of self-defense. As it turned out later, the leaders of the Bialystok unit had indeed made all the preparations necessary for a devastating pogrom. All the details had been finalized, including the date of the pogrom. Thousands of instruction sheets were printed for distribution on that day.

The pogrom was to begin on Tuesday, which was market day. The first victims were to be the buyers and sellers standing near the Jewish tables in the marketplace.

Fortunately, there was one officer, Sankevitch, who did not approve of the criminal plans of his fellow officers, but he could also not oppose them alone. If he would make known his opposition, he would be considered a "Jew Lover" or perhaps a traitor. He considered many ways of foiling their plan.

Meanwhile time was running short. It was already the Shabbos before the fateful Tuesday. He was contemplating going to the *rav* of Lodz to tell him. He struggled long with this risky idea. In the end, however, his conscience won over his instinct for self-preservation, and he decided to go to the *rav* that morning.

After *davening* on Shabbos morning, the *rav* was told that an officer from the Bialystok army unit had come to see him on an emergency matter. The *rav*, surprised, invited the officer into his study without delay. Sankevitch introduced himself and said that he would reveal the purpose of his visit only on the condition that his visit would never be revealed to anyone. "If they will know that I was here," he said, "it will be my end. But I had to act according to my conscience, and I came to tell you, Rabin Meisel, the sad news of a catastrophe soon to befall the Jews of Lodz. I came to you because I heard of your greatness. Also," Sankevitch added emotionally, "I heard the officers saying that one must beware of the Rabin, lest he hear of their plans and try to foil them." Sankevitch continued, "I am an officer of the Bialystok army unit which was recently sent to Lodz to establish *order* with the socialists. It is my misfortune to be part of this unit. All my efforts to leave it have not yet been fruitful. A decent person can absolutely not bear the wild plundering and murders on which these animals thrive.

"And if you only knew," said Sankevitch in a trembling voice, "how I have suffered and almost gone insane on the days when the wild soldiers, incited by the officers, slaughtered innocent Jews. It is blood-curdling to think of it."

The officer took a long breath. Rav Eliyahu Chaim was no longer as calm as before, and in his mild, kind eyes stood two large tears. He let Sankevitch speak: "But what could I do? I am all by myself. I could not protest the criminal acts in public, lest my own life be in danger. I held everything inside, but I cannot bear it anymore.

"When they sent us to Lodz," Sankevitch said quietly, as if revealing a secret, "my heart foretold a catastrophe. Lodz is a large, prosperous city: among our soldiers the sole topic of conversation was the luscious booty looming in their imaginations. All the plans are now ready, the organization is worked out in detail — the pogrom is to break out this coming Tuesday. The Rabin is probably blaming me for not having come until now. But I struggled with myself until I made myself come. Again, please promise me that no one will learn of our meeting, and now, let the Rabin do whatever he can to prevent this catastrophe."

After promising Sankevitch not to reveal his source to anyone, Rav Eliyahu Chaim thanked him for his information and warmly bade him farewell.

From Sankevitch's words, Rav Eliyahu Chaim derived that it was useless to turn to the army officers. The only one who could help him was the chief of police in Lodz, Choshnovsky, but he had a weak voice in military affairs. The most influential person was the famous general of the Czar, Koshnokov.

But how does one reach Koshnokov? Rav Eliyahu Chaim thought. *I am not allowed to reveal Sankevitch as the source of my information. In such a responsible, important matter, one must give all the exact details as proof.* The *rav* did not have any proof nor could he produce his one witness.

Without a word to anyone, Rav Eliyahu Chaim went to Police Chief Choshnovsky. The *rav's* family sensed there was a very serious matter pending, but no one dared ask him about it.

The *rav* arrived at the home of the chief of police who was very surprised by the *rav's* visit, especially since it was Shabbos.

The *rav* answered his question, "Saving the life of even one person has priority over Shabbos. All the more so when the lives of all the Jews of Lodz are in question, one must take measures to save them even on Shabbos. You, as the guardian of the peace in this city, have the duty of preventing the catastrophe about to hit the Jews of this city. A terrible pogrom is being organized against the Jews," the *rav* said in a hoarse, agitated voice. "I demand that you disrupt these plans."

Choshnovsky was frightened by the *rav's* anger. Rav Elya Chaim's eyes were wide open, he was breathing heavily, and his face was contorted with pain. He waited until the *rav* calmed down, then asked for details.

The *rav* told him all he knew of the organization of the pogrom.

"How do you know all this?"

"I promised not to reveal the source of my information. But I am positive it is all true. Now, do not press me to reveal more. There is no time. The sword is hanging over our heads and you must act quickly."

The earnestness of the *rav's* demand forced Choshnovsky into deep consideration. He could not stall him with conferences and investigations because there was no time. After a while, he said, "But what can I do? I do not even have the power to order an investigation into military affairs. All I can do is notify General Koshnokov. But even that is difficult because I do not know the source of the information."

The *rav* cried hoarsely, "Does that mean we are to wait like sheep before the slaughterer — that we should all say our confessions and give ourselves, our wives, and children cheerfully into the hands of bloodthirsty animals? To whom can we turn if not to the chief of police who is entrusted with the care of the people of Lodz?"

Choshnovsky was completely taken aback by the *rav's* vehemence. Only the heavy breathing of the *rav* could be heard in the silence.

"Tell me what I can do," pleaded Choshnovsky.

"Go immediately to Koshnokov and report everything I told you. Tell him that the *rav* of Lodz is the source of your information."

"Why don't you report it to the general yourself?"

"Because I want you also to take part in this. Later we may need your help," answered the *rav*.

In the *rav's* presence, Choshnovsky telephoned the general who tried to postpone dealing with the issue. However, under the influence of the *rav's* forcefulness, he impressed on the general the emergency nature of the matter. Koshnokov granted the police chief an immediate appointment. Choshnovsky put on his coat and told the *rav* he would send a messenger to inform him of the results of the meeting.

Arriving home pale and fatigued, he found a group of communal leaders waiting for him. They had heard of the visit of any army officer to the *rav* and that of the *rav* to the police chief, and wanted to know what was going on. After greeting them, the *rav* said, "One should not hurry to reveal bad news, even to an enemy. Be patient and you will hear sooner or later. Hopefully, we will talk about it in joy."

Toward nightfall, another Russian officer appeared and summoned the *rav* to the home of General Koshnokov. Choshnovsky was already there. The general's face was red and agitated. It was hard to discern whether he was upset because of his feeling for the Jews' plight or because of the interruption in the plans for the pogrom.

Getting directly to the point, Koshnokov said, "I demand to know the source of your information. Without that I cannot do anything to help you. How do I know this is not just a configuration of someone's imagination?"

"I am the representative of the Jewish people in Lodz and you, General, are the representative of the Czar. It is impossible that between us there should be words of tale-bearing or imagination. In such a serious matter, a responsible person would only base himself on facts. They are planning to rob and murder us in cold blood. I cannot reveal the source of my information and thus hurt an innocent man who tried to help us. I gave my word."

The general paced back and forth.

Rav Eliyahu Chaim spoke. "Call a meeting of the Bialystok army unit and you will have first-hand knowledge of the plans. Will it not be a dishonor for you, General, for a mass slaughter of quiet citizens to take place in the area over which you rule? Can your conscience rest?"

"Good. I will do as you suggest. Tonight I will gather the leaders of the army unit and do whatever I can to disrupt their plans. However, if it turns out that it is not true, you will be forced to reveal the source of your information."

Rav Eliyahu Chaim was not frightened. "I am responsible for my words."

"Go home now," the general said. "We will tell you the results of the meeting."

Upon arriving home, the *rav*, without a word to anyone, started to say Tehillim.

Although it was hard to locate the army officers who were scattered all over the city, the meeting was called to order finally, at one o'clock in the morning at Koshnokov's house. Sankevitch was present.

"Dear officers," began Koshnokov, "everyone knows how loyal you are to the Czar, how you will sacrifice yourselves to keep order in the Russian kingdom and wipe out any revolutionary segments of the population. Therefore, your hatred toward the Jews, enemies of the Czar's dynasty, is very understandable. But we may not allow ourselves to be carried away by our feelings and must carefully consider our plans."

The officers now understood the purpose of the meeting. They looked at one another, wondering who could have revealed their plans.

The general continued, "I have learned from a reliable source that you are planning to disturb the Jews this coming Tuesday. But, did you consider well the effects of this action? Is it worth it? Do you know the influence the Jews have in other countries? A pogrom in an important city like Lodz will raise an outcry from Jews all over the world that will embarrass the Czar's government. I order you to give up your plans."

The officers were not afraid. They were only irritated that someone had revealed their plans.

The colonel of the army unit answered, "It is true that our soldiers were planning to amuse themselves a bit. We officers did not concern ourselves very much with their plans. We neither stirred them up nor did we try to dissuade them. We will meanwhile pass down your order to the soldiers not to carry out their plans."

This brazen answer of the colonel infuriated even the cold-blooded general. He banged on the table and shouted, "What do you mean? Aren't you concerned with what goes on with your soldiers? Now I see that everything Rabbi Meisel told me is absolutely true," he said, involuntarily mentioning the *rav*. He raised his voice, "I will not allow plans to be made and carried out behind my back. The plan is to be abandoned — permanently! Has anyone anything to say?"

The colonel's face had turned white. He could not say a word.

Koshnokov said, "Go back to your barracks and order the entire unit to pack its bags and wait for my further commands."

The next morning Rav Eliyahu Chaim received notice from Koshnokov that the Bialystok army unit was leaving Lodz Monday morning. Sankevitch, dressed in civilian clothing, visited the *rav* on Sunday afternoon and revealed to him the details of the meeting. He thanked him for not having exposed his identity. "But," Sankevitch said, "my joy is not complete. Koshnokov made a slip and said that you were the source of his information, and now the anger of the army officers is focused against you."

"Calm yourself, my dear Sankevitch. I thank G-d for letting me, with your help, foil their plans, and thus save the lives of the Jews in Lodz. Don't worry about me, especially since they did not agree on a plan of action to hurt me. But I will be careful."

"I realize," Sankevitch blurted out, "that your greatness, dear Rabbi, is more than I ever imagined about you. I am leaving Lodz tomorrow morning. I don't know if I will ever be here again, so I would like a blessing from you."

Rav Eliyahu Chaim placed his right hand on Sankevitch's bowed head and said, "You did a very great deed, saving many people from the hands of murderers. Therefore, I wish you success in all your endeavors."

Sankevitch took leave of the *rav*, wiping tears from his eyes.

Soon afterward, the *rav* called together those close to him and a few people of importance in the community and told them the whole story. After a while they resolved to send a delegation to the police chief, demanding his protection for the *rav* against the officers' vengeance. Choshnovsky agreed to do all in his power to ensure the welfare of the *rav*.

Monday morning, the whole city was amazed to see the Bialystok unit, which had just arrived, already leaving Lodz.

Two weeks later, a letter arrived in the name of a colonel of the unit:

Attention, Meisel. Since you have insulted our officers by calling them murderers, we have decided to challenge you to a duel against our colonel. Kindly name your seconds.

The letter was signed by the two officers who were to be the colonel's seconds. The next day a letter came from Sankevitch explaining what had been decided upon by the officers.

Rav Meisel wrote back to the colonel.

I know that according to your laws of conduct one cannot refuse a duel. However, if one never agreed to abide by these rules of conduct, that is, to accept a duel as a means of restoring one's honor, then one can refuse to participate in a duel. I abide by another body of laws, one that is as old as the creation of the universe — the Torah — which forbids a method of restoring one's honor which ends in the shedding of blood. Besides, I did not insult the honor of any particular officer directly, and therefore you cannot challenge me to participate in a duel.

Rav Eliyahu Chaim's family and friends waited anxiously for the officer's response to this letter, meanwhile not leaving him out of their sight for a minute. No one, however, could notice any signs of agitation on Rav Eliyahu Chaim's face.

In a few days, a letter arrived from the would-be seconds:

As of today we have received no mention of the names of your seconds. We assume that you have forfeited the duel.

Another letter followed from the colonel in which he accepted renouncement of the duel, but demanded that the *rav* reveal the source of his information about the would-be pogrom.

The *rav* answered that he would never reveal this, even at the expense of his life. He wrote that he considered the matter ended.

In a few days, another letter arrived from the colonel.

> *We are sorry for disturbing the Jewish population in Lodz. We respect your not revealing the identity of the officer who foiled our plans despite all our threats. We declare that we are withdrawing our demands and our threats and we guarantee that we will not harm you in any way.*

Thus ended the sensational story of the pogrom that the *rav* of Lodz averted.

Adapted from Dos Yiddishe Licht, *Sivan 5723, with permission*

SHEINDEL WEINBACH

A boy's view of the time his mother decided

To Ask the Chafetz Chaim

OY, MY HEAD! It aches so! I'm so hot and sweaty. But I mustn't bother Mama. She's already done everything she can. She's given me cold compresses and hot compresses, back rubs and chest rubs. And so much tea, I'm almost swimming in it. She even spent precious money for oranges to squeeze fresh juice. I tried to tell her not to, but...

I'm so tired. But that soap smell won't let me sleep. Funny how you get used to a thing — when I'm well, I never notice how disgusting the odor really is even though I can smell it from a block away on my way home from *cheder*. When there's a strong wind blowing, the women all the way across the main street nod to each other and say, "That must be the *rebbetzin* at work." But now I feel as if my *kishkes* were being scrubbed and disinfected with the soap. I hope I'm not giving the soap an *ayin hara*, because the soap practically supports the entire yeshivah. I remember how Mama explained it to me that time I got burned by some soap that bubbled over from the vat. As she dressed my hand she told me how important it was. Seems that times were hard during the World War and money was scarce, which meant that people could spare very little for *tzedakah* for the yeshivah. So Mama decided to go into business. The *Ribono shel Olam* put a marvelous idea into her head — since people always need soap, even poor people, she would learn how to make it and support the yeshivah herself. That's when she got those tremendous vats. Hey! I just noticed that the smell hardly bothers me anymore. Maybe thinking about it makes it less of a monster. If I think about getting better, too — real hard like Tatte said — I'll will myself better. Trouble is that flu takes time, and I'm tired. Now that I've overcome the smell I'll be able to sleep. That will surely help.

I do feel better, *baruch Hashem*. But the day is still so long. Tatte says that the day is short, too short for all the learning there still is to be done. Even the night is too short for Tatte. Last night my fever kept me awake a lot and I saw him studying by the lamplight. In the daytime he is so gentle. When he speaks to his *talmidim*, or to anyone, he is so patient. But at night, when no one is watching him, he is fire. It seemed as if his eyes were in a hurry, they seemed to burn through the pages. I could almost feel sparks shooting out, but I guess it was only a reflection of the light. Will I ever be like Tatte? Everyone here in Baranovitch knows him and respects him but Mama told me that he is famous all over the world. Even in America. Even in Eretz Yisrael. Mama told me that when Tatte was only twenty-six — she said that's very young for grownups — he was offered the *rabbanus* in Moscow! But he turned it down because he wouldn't leave his precious yeshivah.

I wish I could at least *chazer* some Chumash while I lie here waiting to get better. But my head hurts so, I just can't think straight. When Simcha comes home I'll *farher* what he learned today. I bet he'll get a kick out of saying over for his older brother. I usually come home when he's asleep already, and anyway I'm already learning Gemara. So what can I think about? I can't see much from this alcove here, but I can hear the sounds around the house. There's the bubbling of the vats. There's the tea kettle that Mama keeps at a boil so that anyone coming here will be sure of a hot drink to warm up his insides. And the soup kettle with its cabbage soup simmering for tonight's supper. And Mama's soft whispering. She must be saying Tehillim now that the baby is sleeping and she has a few free minutes.

I hear footsteps coming up the walk. Sounds like the postman's "Good morning." Mama is bringing in two letters. Those stamps look different. Maybe the letters are from Shavel where the Bubba lives? But how come there are two letters? Poor Bubba, all alone now that Zeida was *niftar*. Mama says old people find it hard to be alone. There I see Mama wiping her eyes on the corner of her apron. But who could the second letter be from? I'd better remember to get those stamps to give Yankel and Chaimke in *cheder*. They've got a whole collection already. But I don't waste my time on useless things like that.

I'll try to get some sleep now, maybe Tatte will be home when I wake up. He'll sit by my side and stroke my hot forehead with his cool, patient hands and I'll feel better.

Oh, good! Tatte is home already. I'll wait till Mama finishes speaking with him. She's showing him the two letters and… what's that? Are those tears in her eyes? Tatte is shaking his head no. What could it mean? I've never seen them disagreeing about anything. If something concerns the yeshivah, Tatte decides, and if it's something that concerns the house or us kids Mama makes the decision. I'll lie still and hear what they're talking about. Who knows, maybe I can do something.

"Shavel...*rabbanus*...the Mama"... Mama is holding out the other letter — what can that mean? What's she saying now? "*Aniyus*...no coal for the furnace...no shoes for the children." Now she's pointing to me. She's probably thinking that I got sick so often this winter because my feet are always getting wet from the holes in my shoes. I tried putting cardboard inside but that just soaked up the snow quicker and kept my feet wetter. Or maybe it's the chill I get after my bath. I don't seem to dry quick enough even if I stand by the stove. One thing, though, at least I get clean with all that soap. It must be clean germs that make me sick.

Now Tatte is speaking, but he talks so softly that I can hardly catch what he's saying. "Can't take more money from yeshivah... have enough to eat..."

"Enough to eat?...soup and bread?" Mama is pointing to the stove. "Children need milk and cheese, eggs and meat." Now she's waving the letter from Bubba. She's crying. *Baruch Hashem*, she's wiping her eyes. Now she's speaking louder.

She's taking off her apron! "...to ask the Chafetz Chaim." Tatte's *Rosh Yeshivah*! The *gadol hador*! I bet Mama is going to ask his advice because she's sure that whatever he says is precious to Tatte.

What can she possibly be going to ask him? If both letters were from Shavel...Mama said something about *rabbanus*. Maybe the *kehillah* in Shavel is offering the *rabbanus* to Tatte? But why is Mama so upset and insistent? Tatte gets offers for positions almost every Monday and Thursday and never pays any attention to them. She knows how important it is for Tatte to continue his learning and teaching here in the yeshivah. He takes care of plenty of *klal inyanim* without the *ol* of *rabbanus*. It must be because of Bubba. She wants to be near her and comfort her in her old age.

Tatte is not saying anything. He's just sitting and watching Mama. She's walking out — without a coat? Oh, she must be going across the street to Zusha the *ba'al agalah*. He'll have to make a special trip to Radin at this time of day. And Tatte is still sitting there, saying Tehillim, or is it Mishnayos, by heart. Mama's back. She's taking her best *tichel* and black dress from the closet. Tatte's still mumbling…Tehillim? Mama's packing some fruit and her siddur for *tefillas haderech* into her handbag. Now she's all set. She's coming over to me…just kissed me goodbye.

Tatte's…crying. Real tears. I never saw him cry except on Tishah B'Av. Is he afraid that the Chafetz Chaim might tell him to leave the yeshivah? Mama, Mama, we children don't really need new clothing. Big patches are warmer than new things. And as far as good food goes — we're growing well, *bli ayin hara*, even without a pint of milk a day. It must be that the *Ribono shel Olam* watches over us specially because Tatte is such a tzaddik who learns Torah all the time. What could be more important than that, anyway? Oh, Mama!

She's hesitating. Zusha is outside already, whoaing the horses to a stop in front of the house. Mama's opening the door and… looking back. At Tatte. She gazes at his silent tears.

"Zusha!" she calls out, "I've changed my mind. I'm not going after all. No, not tomorrow either."

HIYELA HOUSEMAN

Six Magic Words

A fifteen-year-old girl dramatically teaches a priest and a Cossack what it means to be Jewish.

For us seniors at the Birmingham Avenue Bais Yaakov, the middle of June meant one thing: fun. Tests were over, school almost gone. Forever? For some of us, certainly; for others the business of life would be delayed another year, two, or three. The fun was our way of not taking the future seriously — if we were at all capable of taking it seriously.

As I look back now, I am no longer certain Mr. Hanover was the spoilsport we all felt he was on the June day that happened to be the twentieth of Sivan that year. Even then I sympathized with this survivor of the wars and the ghettoes who, like the Ancient Mariner, felt compelled to tell his story. Because he was our history teacher, it wasn't as if he had no right to tell us about the tragedies of contemporary Jewish history. Yet we had difficulty digesting all that he told us. Because it was required learning first of all, and second of all because he was a poor storyteller. Both factors combined to make his lessons a tragedy for us. And for him: his albatross hung all too plainly 'round his neck.

One mid-June morning, Mr. Hanover insisted that we come to attention. He wished to give us a history lesson. He outwaited the groans and half-wails, "I promiz you de lesson will take unly ten minitt." That was so uncharacteristic of him that we repaid him in kind and sat attentively as he told us of the tragedies that had befallen Rabbeinu Tam's contemporaries on the twentieth of Sivan, and of the tragedies that befell Polish Jewry on the same day some five hundred years later. Nine minutes and forty-nine seconds after he had begun (of course, we cruelly timed him), he came to a halt.

After a pause he remarked, "I don't vant to liv such tregedy for a lest lesson, so if you let me, I vill tell you a story about a Jewish *meidel* vot my encestor wrote it down in his history about de *tzaros* of *chuf* Sivan." In recounting the story that I have not in all these years forgotten, I may have rearranged some details or added others. But then I mentioned earlier that Mr. Hanover was a poor storyteller, although he assuredly outdid himself and his "encestor" (whose history book I have since read) that morning.

જાજી

Stefan was enjoying their game with the Jewish boy. Every time the *Zhid* blinked, he would raise his hand as if to strike him again, and the *Zhid* would blink again. Every third or fourth threat had to be turned into a slap, though, to keep the *Zhid* tense. After ten slaps it would be Zoltan's turn. The object of the game was to keep the *Zhid* blinking as long as possible without having to slap him.

Jews hardly ever wandered alone outside the town, and the two Poles had taken instant advantage of the Jewish boy who had walked down to the stream where they were loafing. Sixteen-year-old Shmulik suffered his torment courageously, not deigning to give the *goyim* the pleasure of hearing him scream, also not daring to make things sound too bad to Gittel, his fifteen-year-old sister who was still in the Jewish cemetery up the hill. They had gone to visit their mother's grave on her *yahrtzeit*, and he had come down to the stream to bring up some stones to leave on the tombstone.

What would these grubba goyim *do*, Shmulik thought to himself as Zoltan, who was stronger than Stefan, struck him a wallop, *if they'd* chas v'shalom *get their filthy hands on Gittel?* He shuddered as he blinked again in the familiar pattern, *I'd better remember to keep blinking. But I wonder what gives them more pleasure: watching me blink and thinking that I'm afraid, or actually slapping me?*

As she watched a round of bullying from behind a tree, Gittel pondered a similar question. Intuitively she grasped the psychology of the peasant bullies, and formulated a plan to get her brother out of their hands. She whispered a chapter of Tehillim and a brief prayer to *Hakadosh Baruch Hu*. Then she scooped up a clod of earth and lobbed it ever so surely through the air right into Zoltan's face as he turned away from Shmulik.

"What! Are you trying to be funny, Stefan?!" He swung, but Stefan grabbed his hand.

"Don't accuse me so quickly, my friend."

"Well, who then threw that dirt into my face?"

Their yelling covered any noise Gittel might have made as she ran behind another tree and flung another clod of soil that struck Stefan in his left ear.

"Ouch! Well, I know that wasn't you, Zoltie. Have the Jews in the cemetery risen up to defend their cousin?" Both men crossed themselves as they flung themselves to the ground. They proceeded to crawl slowly toward the cemetery wall, giving both Shmulik and Gittel plenty of time to get around to the city side of the cemetery and safety.

ଓଃଠ

"King Wladislaw is dead!"

"Chmielnicki and his Cossacks made a deal with the Turks and they trapped the Polish army in a vise! Generals Potocki and Kalinowski were both captured!"

"Wiszniwecki is reorganizing the Polish army up north!"

Of the announcements and shouts that reached Nemerov that Shavuos, the above were all true. But to pick just those out of the dozens of variant versions in circulation would have required the gift of prophecy. Yet the Jews of Nemerov were the sons of prophets, and they understood that things were not well. The refugees fleeing all the villages around Nemerov had begun flocking in during Yom Tov, for reports had reached their ears of coming Cossack invasion, plunder, and murder.

Those who had not been fortunate enough to escape were butchered in the most horrible ways imaginable.

As the number of reports increased it grew clearer that Nemerov, too, was to be attacked. Chmielnicki's agents reported that the terror had brought in thousands of "loaded" Jewish refugees, and that Nemerov itself was a "loaded" city. He dispatched a division of swordsmen with a letter to the city fathers recommending his men to their care and assistance. While the Poles did not particularly love the Cossacks, they hated the Jews, and hastened to aid the Cossacks.

The Jews had barricaded themselves in the ghetto until it would become clear to them whether the division marching in was from the royal army or a Cossack division. When the city fathers pointed out to the Jews that the division carried Polish flags, not the unique Cossack colors, the Jews opened up the ghetto and were forthwith put to the pistol and the sword and every conceivable torture. That was Wednesday, the twentieth of Sivan 5408.

Bloodthirsty, armed with cudgels, knives, and makeshift weapons, the Christian citizens of Nemerov joined the slaughter. They knew which houses held the money or the jewelry or the women they were after. Screams, shouts, entreaties fell on deaf ears. Occasionally a sum of money or a precious item of jewelry bought the lives of their owners, even paid for a safe conduct to the outskirts of the city.

ය়ි඼ෆ

Some weeks before, Stefan had run across the boy he had helped beat up earlier that spring. He had been left to loaf alone when Zoltan had joined up with the Cossacks. So he had followed Shmulik to a house whose owners were obviously well-to-do and he had seen Gittel. Zoltan, too, had heard from his second cousin, who worked for the family as a maidservant, about the wealth of the family she worked for. And about their beautiful, clever daughter. As a citizen of Nemerov, he had been assigned to the Cossack division sent to sack the ghetto.

Small wonder then that Stefan and Zoltan and the latter's second cousin's husband all found themselves inside the same Jewish house leading the assault on the room in which the family had barricaded itself.

A voice from inside the room penetrated the door, "How much money do you want?"

"All of it!" the cousin's husband snarled.

"Will you guarantee us safe conduct to the outskirts of the city?"

"Zoltie, that's up to you. I don't need Jewish blood. Just money."

"What's my percentage, though?"

"That depends on how much your friend here wants."

"I don't need much!" Stefan spoke for the first time. "A ruby or two will be enough. And the Jewish girl."

"Okay with me. In that case, what do you say to fifty-fifty, Zoltie?"

"The safe conduct depends on me?"

"I get the message. You want 60 percent for yourself?"

"Only considering that you're a cousin."

The deal was made, the loot divided, and the Cossack on horseback led his charges in safety out of the city.

"We've kept our word. You've come in safety to the outskirts of the city. You may all leave — alive — except for the girl." And he swung Gittel up onto the horse and tied her in place.

"Hey, Zoltan! I only took two rubies. I've still got my share coming!" shouted Stefan.

"I've changed my mind."

"No, you can't!"

"Can't I?" He drew his pistol. With his free hand, he dredged up a bag of gold coins from his saddlebags. "Stefan, take your choice! The gold or a hole in your chest. I'm an honest man, my friend. Be thankful for that." And he tossed the bag at his friend.

Stefan rushed at him in his fury. But he was no match for his friend's pistol: the bullet shattered his forearm and he passed out.

Zoltan kept up a monologue all the way to the next city. He ended it as they rode into town, "So you see, I'm an honest man, and I'm going to marry you properly. That's why I've brought you to this church." He untied her and helped her off the horse.

"And if I refuse, you'll treat me the way you treated your friend." She had recognized them from the incident near the cemetery and had been thinking hard every second of the way.

"Hardly, I wouldn't have to put a bullet through you."

"You wouldn't be able to. You've heard of Jewish magic, haven't you?"

The priest who had been standing in the garden outside the church, commented, "I didn't know Jewish women practiced magic, too."

"With six words I can produce protection even against the bullets in this Cossack's pistol."

"That would be useful to you in your battles, friend Cossack, wouldn't it?"

"Certainly, Father. How?" He turned to her, "What do you do?"

"That's simple. I'll say the magic words and when I nod my head you fire a bullet at me. That ought to satisfy you that my spell works. Then I'll work a spell for you."

"Fair enough."

Gittel stood away from the church and the priest, her back toward both. She smiled up at the sky and said six words. "*Shema Yisrael, Hashem Elokeinu, Hashem Echad.*" Then she nodded.

She had outfoxed Zoltan again.

S.M. LIEDER

Mirel sought mitzvos and Baila the almanah *was willing to be helped. Until it came to a milchig* Shavuos *cake, and Mirel had to decide*

The Price of a Mitzvah

THE TRAINS SIMPLY never ran on time. Inflation was rampant. Flour, good wheat flour, was rare — and precious. His best customers had to pay Refael the flour merchant cash on the spot. Even then he supplied them with less than they wanted or needed.

An exception was Mirel, Bentzion Shuster's wife. As usual, she got as much flour as she needed for her bakery. And she paid Refael for it, as usual, once a week, on Motza'ei Shabbos.

Some of his other customers protested, "That's unfair! You give Mirel her 180-pound sacks of flour and we have to press you hard to get half a sack out of you. And we have to pay in advance!"

Refael took it all in stride. He replied calmly, "Mirel used to buy flour from me regularly when prices were low. She didn't run around from dealer to dealer trying to save a cent on a sack. And then she paid me on time, every Motza'ei Shabbos. She always kept her word. So now I'm repaying her for all her years of loyalty."

Baila, Aharon Nachum's widow, was Mirel's neighbor and also baked for sale. But she could get no flour, not even for cash. In the "good" days, she had never been a good customer, always owing the shopkeepers and the flour dealers; she had always bought where it was cheaper and even then would eat the merchant's heart out before he saw a single cent. Now it was their turn to get even. No matter to whom she turned, there was always someone ahead of her.

Mirel was Baila's personal *nes*. At first she helped her with half a sack a week, then it grew to a whole sack. Soon Mirel was sharing her flour purchases fifty-fifty with the widow. Refael, surprised that Mirel should need so much flour, was curious. "Tell me the truth, you're not baking all that yourself, are you?"

"How can I use five whole sacks in a week?"

"So what do you do with the flour? Did you go into the flour business behind my back?"

Mirel was insulted. "Reb Refael, how can you suspect me of such a thing? Sure, I'm earning a profit on your flour — a mitzvah. And that I share with you."

Refael was all ears. Mirel told him the whole story and added, "You wouldn't want a widow with five grown daughters to starve to death, *chas v'shalom?*"

"Does she pay you, at least?"

"She pays. On time."

"See to it," he warned, "that the mitzvah doesn't cost you too dear. Don't forget that you've got ten mouths of your own to feed. And see to it that none of my other customers gets wind of this, or I'll have my hands full."

Erev Shavuos after breakfast, the widow Baila ran into Mirel's, and burst out breathlessly, "Save me, Mirel!"

"What happened?"

"Woe! Such misfortune," wailed Baila, "you know how I supply rolls for the kiosk at the train station. This morning, at dawn, I go and deliver my two baskets full of rolls, and they tell me they're expecting a whole carload of laborers on the afternoon train and I must supply them with thirty-five pounds of rolls. 'Where on earth will I get thirty-five pounds of rolls?' I ask them. 'That's your business, lady,' they say, 'there'll be a carload of hungry workers and we've got to be prepared for them.'"

"Tell me how I can help you," Mirel asked. "You know that I divided all the flour with you, and that I've already sold out my entire supply. People were just grabbing from all sides today. Reb Refael told me he'd bring in four carfuls of flour right after Yom Tov. Where can I get flour for you now? You tell me."

"Do you think I don't know all this? Promise that you won't get angry, and I'll tell you how you can help me."

Mirel looked at her queerly. "What do you mean 'angry'? You know that if there's any way I can help you, I'll do so."

"We'll see whether you get angry or not."

"Tell me already. Stop stretching my nerves."

Slowly, Baila made her request. "You've got a kneaded dough standing in your mixing pot. It looks like it's nearly forty pounds."

Mirel started at her angrily, "You're out of your mind. What do you mean, 'You've got a kneaded dough'? That's my *milchig* Yom Tov cake!"

"Did I say you'd get angry?" Baila was triumphant.

"So I'm angry!" Mirel shouted. "How did you ever think such a thing? What kind of Yom Tov would it be without the *milchig* cake?"

At this point the widow burst into tears. "And what kind of Yom Tov will I have if I don't supply the rolls? The *goyishe* baker has been on the lookout for an opportunity to supply the kiosk himself. And what do you think my girls and I will be eating this Shavuos? Bread! Cornbread. But you need a cake! And what do I have? Five grown daughters who ought all to have heard wedding music five years ago! To say nothing of *tzaros* and heartache!"

Mirel, pale, stared in astounded silence at the miserable widow. Several minutes elapsed before she waved toward the dough and said, gently, "Take the dough and stop crying. Maybe I'll find myself some substitute. If not, I'll eat cornbread."

Baila rolled up a window, stuck her head out, and hollered, "Rochel! Chava! Perel! Come help me carry over the dough pot."

After they were gone, Mirel realized that she didn't have enough cornbread for two days of Yom Tov. So she went over to Refael the flour merchant. He couldn't contain himself when he heard her story. "*Gevald!* How does a woman make such an absolute fool of herself? How can an intelligent woman like you be such an absolute fool?!"

Mirel reddened. "You're telling me *mussar* now? Is that what I deserve for not being cold-hearted in the face of an *almanah's* tears? Better tell me if you have some flour for me."

Half to himself, Refael mumbled, "The best thing would be to teach you a good lesson and let you and your children go hungry. But that's none of my business. I've got a sack of cheap flour, for black bread. Take as much as you want."

ଓଞ୍ଚ

After the *seudah* on the second day of Shavuos, Baila dropped in at Mirel's. Happy, radiant, she stopped in the middle of the room, spread both her hands across her apron, and asked, "*Nu*, Mirel. How much are you going to charge me for the dough?"

"Charge you? In the middle of Yom Tov?"

"I can't hold it in. I must know how much you're going to charge me, because I'll tell you something that you'd never imagine in your whole life."

"It'll keep till Motza'ei Yom Tov, I'm sure. Besides, what is there to figure up? You know how much flour I used, and you know the price of flour. The price of salt? The bit of yeast? The other little things? That doesn't add up to anything."

"You're wrong," Baila announced festively. "This time you're going to charge me for the flour, the yeast, and even the salt, and then — you'll get an additional ruble and a half."

"Aha! Since when are you giving money away, my rich friend?"

"Ever since I want to show you that Baila, Aharon Nachum's *almanah*, about whom everyone says whatever possible — that she's a poor payer, that she's bankrupt, that she never keeps her word — is also a *mentsch*. Hear a story of crazy Russian kiosk owners. They liked the rolls I baked from your dough. 'Real cake,' they said, so they paid my Sara three rubles extra. 'Here,' they said, 'is a tip for you for bringing us such delicious rolls.'"

"A three-ruble tip?" Mirel was amazed.

"Three rubles," Baila savored every syllable. "And I tell you: this time it goes fifty-fifty, half for you and half for me. If it weren't for your dough, I would have had a fig, certainly no rolls. I may be a penny-pincher, but I possess a sense of justice. Fair is fair."

"Thank you very much, Baila. It really is very nice of you. But I'm not selling my mitzvah. Keep the tip for yourself."

"*Tzaddekes!*" Baila's voice rose. "A ruble and a half will be delivered to you tonight."

Said Mirel feelingly, "I gave you the dough out of my children's mouths. We ate sour bread this Shavuos instead of cake. I did it because I wanted a mitzvah. And my mitzvah is not for sale."

"Oho! The *tzaddekes* is not selling mitzvos!" Baila shouted. "You'll get more mitzvah if you buy shoes for your *cheder yingel* whose toes stick out of his old shoes."

"Not with such money."

Baila caught fire. "What's the matter with my money? Is it *treif*? I didn't earn it in a kosher manner?! I bake and sweat and drag basketloads all over town, and *she*, she treats it like *treifa* money. That's scandalous, pure *rishus*!"

"I tell you again; I'm not selling my mitzvah!" Mirel retorted, angrily this time. "Yell all you want!"

Baila burst into tears. "I made a *neder* to divide it half-and-half; I'm also allowed to do a mitzvah so that your *cheder yingel* can wear whole shoes. The One Above granted you a son, and all you do is stuff yourself with mitzvos for *Olam Haba*. You can let me have a mitzvah sometimes, too."

"Stop picking on me. If you think you'll win your way with me through tears, you're wasting your time. I repeat: I am not selling my mitzvah."

"But I made a *neder* —"

"Go to the *rav*. He'll be *matir* your *neder*."

☙❧

People had begun to gather outside the open windows. Baila let loose in her shrillest tones, "Mirel, you've got the heart of a tyrant. You would deny a person every pleasure!"

Mirel implored, "Don't yell. People will think who knows what I did to you."

"Let them come running. Shame on you for such *rishus*! You —" In midscream, Baila noticed Reb Hirshel the *dayan* on his way to shul. She clapped her hands together and cried to Mirel, "I'll run out and call Reb Hirshel in here to *pasken* who is right."

A minute later, Mirel stood shamefacedly at her door and stammering, greeted the *dayan*, "Sit down, sit down, Rebbi, sit down. I'll bring you, you…I'll, I'll bring you a glass of tea."

Still the hostess, Mirel apologized, "I'm sorry, Rebbi, that I can't offer you anything to eat with the tea, but my cake didn't turn out too well."

Baila stared her down and chuckled, "What nonsense, Mirel. Rebbi, she has bricks of plain, black flour, not cake this Shavuos. And do you know why? Because of me."

"All right, tell me the story," *already!* he added mentally, impatient at having his time wasted by womanish nonsense.

As Baila recounted the above tale, Reb Hirshel's ears perked up. As Baila fumed, he sipped his tea and a placid smile spread across his face. When Baila had finished her story, Reb Hirshel asked Mirel, "Is this all true?"

"Of course," she replied. "Baila is not, *chalilah*, a liar."

Then Reb Hirshel's smile grew into a happy grin. He stroked his beard ever so gently and addressed both women, "Listen carefully, ladies. A case like yours took place once before. The Midrash tells of two men who came before their king for judgment.

ও৪৯

"Your majesty, I bought a field from my neighbor. When I plowed it, I discovered a treasure which I wish to return to him. For I bought only the field. I did not pay for any treasure."

"And I, your majesty," replied the 'defendant,' "refuse to accept this man's treasure. I sold him the field and everything in it."

The king asked the claimant, "Do you have a son or daughter of marriageable age?"

"Yes, your majesty, I have an eligible daughter."

"And you," the king asked the 'defendant,' "do you have an eligible son?"

"Yes, your majesty."

"Then let your son marry his daughter, and give them the treasure as a wedding present."

ଓ୫୦

"So you see," Reb Hirshel sipped some more tea, "that was a case of a whole treasure, where one man had a son and the other a daughter. In your case we're dealing with only a ruble and a half, but by us that is also money. So I *pasken* that you, Mirel, should accept the money and buy flour with it. Bake the flour into loaves of bread, and distribute them to poor people. Baila will be satisfied, and you will have given away the bread to the poor. In that way you won't have taken payment for your mitzvah."

The women nodded in agreement.

Reb Hirshel looked around the room and saw the obvious poverty. He remarked, "Mirel, perhaps it's too much for you to give away all that bread?"

Mirel retorted, "Is it my own that I'm giving away?"

Reb Hirshel rose, went to the door, kissed the *mezuzah*, and turned back to the women. "Baila and Mirel, a good Yom Tov to you. May G-d grant more such *machlokes* among Jews."

SHLOMO BEN-DOVID

No matter how bleak the situation, no matter how depressed you are

Never Despair!

RETOLD BY SHEINDEL WEINBACH

MAZEL TOV! The joyous words — the timeless wish, hope, blessing, and prayer combined — issued from the lips of all the townsfolk assembled in the *beis medrash*. Everyone wished Reb Binyamin luck. Industrious Reb Binyamin had served his community loyally all these years, supplying them and the neighboring towns with wine. He had worked hard and earned his bread honestly, and he surely deserved the fine young man who was shortly to become his son-in-law. Sara, the proud mother of the *kallah*, also received hearty mazel tov wishes. She, too, had toiled and labored all these years to make ends meet, to provide for her family, to maintain a spotless home with its warm, Jewish atmosphere, and to bring up her only daughter, Chana, as a true Yiddish *tochter*. This was her moment of glory, the culmination of all the years of effort. And Chana, at the center of *tena'im* celebration, received the lion's share of mazel tovs. She had caught a real prize, the lion itself, Aryeh, a strapping youth bursting with good looks, energy, and prospects for the future.

It was a perfect *simchah*, attended by friends and family alike. The atmosphere bubbled. There was plenty of good food, stimulating drink, and happy spirits. And if Binyamin felt a momentary shadow cross his face as the *rav* read the terms of the *tena'im* agreement aloud, he banished it quickly before it could mar the completeness of his joy.

But shadow there was. Struggling as he had all these years to eke out an honest living, Binyamin had not managed to put anything aside for his daughter's dowry. At first his good wife, Sara, had refused to discuss any *shidduchim* for Chana when she came of age. When Aryeh had been suggested for their daughter, her mother's pride had fought a heavy inner battle. "Such a fine fellow," she told her husband, "will surely expect a handsome dowry. You know that Chana has nothing besides her own golden qualities."

"And that is a reason to turn down such a superior offer? Other poor people have married off daughters before, haven't they, Sara? There is a way out. We must rely on the good hearts of our fellow Jews. After Pesach I will take up my knapsack and set out to collect the money we will pledge for Chana's dowry. G-d will have pity on an honest man and will surely reward my efforts."

Pesach came and went. It was spring, perfect traveling weather, and Reb Binyamin could put off his trip no longer. Before he set out, he went to offer his respects to the *rav*.

"Let me tell you a short story," the *rav* said as he handed him a golden coin, a donation that would hopefully multiply itself within a short span of time. "A story that will make your future hardships somewhat easier to bear.

"There was once a Jew in the same position as you, who toward his later years was forced to take up his wandering staff. He went from town to village in search of money and of kind souls who would take mercy upon him and share their fare with a poor traveler. It was hard. Very hard, in fact. The traveler grew so full of discouragement that he could contain it no longer. One day, as he entered a strange town, he went to the *beis medrash* and threw himself down before the *aron hakodesh*.

"It was dark and secluded. The last *mispallel* had since left to the comfort of hearth and home. Only the weary traveler remained to pour forth his troubled heart. He sank down on the floor, all spent.

"'How much longer, *Ribono shel Olam*,' he wept aloud, 'how much more must I bear? How much longer must I suffer?'

"'One more year.' The words rang through the empty *beis medrash*. The traveler heard the words as in a dream. Had Heaven heard his plea and actually answered — in human speech? Had his sentence of suffering been determined as precisely a single year? A load removed from his heart, the traveler found heart to raise himself from the floor and seek a bench to spend the first of his last 365 nights of homelessness. As he approached the bench he discovered, to his surprise, that it was occupied. From there, then, must have emanated the 'Heavenly *bas kol*.'

"'One year, you say?' he asked the reclining figure of a fellow homeless traveler. 'How do you know? Do you perhaps have *ruach hakodesh*?' he said wryly. 'And if so, what will happen to me a year hence?'

"'Your *galus* will only be for one year. The first. After that you will be accustomed to your lot and it won't bother you so much,' replied the reclining form, turning over on his other side to end the conversation as much as to find a more comfortable position on the hard, unyielding bench.

"Keep this story in mind," the *rav* told Binyamin kindly. "At first your task may seem almost impossibly difficult. But time will accustom you to the hardships and the degradation of begging. And so, may Hashem be with you. Farewell."

Binyamin did find it difficult, especially after he had visited all the people recommended by the *rav*. Approaching total strangers brought abuse together with the money, but little by little he managed to amass the necessary sum for his daughter's dowry. With a happy heart, he wrote home to his wife to commence the preparations for the wedding. He would return within the month.

The last person he visited was a wealthy merchant. Binyamin told the tale of his travels, and of his eventual success. The merchant took a personal interest in Binyamin and inquired how he intended to transfer the money across the border, an illegal transaction. Binyamin admitted that he had not found a solution to this last problem.

"I can arrange it all for you," the merchant assured his guest. "By the time you will have arrived home, the money will be waiting for you." Of course, he asked for a fee for his services, but it seemed modest enough to the relieved traveler.

With a happy heart, Binyamin returned to his village to find the family in the midst of wedding preparations. No money was lying on his doorstep, but he refused to let that disturb his joyous homecoming. Days went by, and still no sign of the money. The wedding day approached and the bills mounted. Binyamin took pen in hand and wrote to the wealthy merchant across the border.

Once again the mazel tovs rang out, wishing the handsome pair and their parents the best of luck for the future that lay ahead of them. And once again the hint of a shadow passed over Reb Binyamin's face, though he quickly banished it. He refused to think about the missing money during the *chasunah*. Chana was his only child and her *chasunah* must be one to remember. It was. Everyone, everything, sparkled and glowed in the aura of a true *simchah*.

But this, too, had its specified time in the scheme of things — one brief day. And when that was over, and the next six days of *sheva brachos* had passed, Binyamin was forced to face the bitter truth. His money had not arrived and would not arrive; it was still on the other side of the border. He saw no other way but to go and claim it personally. Binyamin retraced the last steps of his journey until he came to the wealthy merchant's home. He grew desperate and forced his way bodily into the merchant's presence. The latter denied ever having performed a transaction and, at Binyamin's hysterical remonstrations, had his servants throw the man out bodily.

Binyamin realized he was a stranger in town. Who would believe his word against that of a wealthy, distinguished citizen? Binyamin returned home empty-handed and poured out his story to his *rav*.

"Do you have any witnesses? A document?"

Binyamin shook his head glumly. How could he have? The whole transaction had been illegal. Besides, in his naiveté, the need for a record hadn't even entered his mind!

The full force of his dilemma struck Binyamin a severe blow. He took to his bed, unable to eat or drink. He developed a high fever which raged for several days. When the initial shock wore off, Binyamin summoned his *mechutanim* to his sick bed and broke the news, promising to resume his travels once again as soon as his health permitted. They took the news as well as could be expected. Not so Aryeh, the young bridegroom. He ranted and raved, claiming that Reb Binyamin had deceived them.

The domestic peace of the young couple grew shaky as its foundations trembled. Matters hardly improved with Chana spending much of her time at her father's bedside. Aryeh spent less and less time at the *beis medrash*, and allowed himself to be sidetracked by a circle of idlers who dragged him, only half unwilling, to a nearby cafe. His bitterness toward his father-in-law and subsequently to his wife, left him bereft of powers of concentration and he felt he needed some diversion to ease his heavy heart. On the surface, he couldn't see anything wrong with relaxing at the kosher cafe and listening to the records of famous *chazzanim*. His friends encouraged him and dragged him there often.

Then Hershele was born.

෴

Hershele's birth seemed to improve the situation, but that improvement was short-lived. Aryeh truly loved his little son, but demonstrated his affection only when his wife was not around. In her presence he would mope and show a morose countenance. Aryeh, golden youth with golden prospects, felt that life had dealt him a raw deal. Instead of a life of comfort, he now had nothing, not even the solace of a comfortable home and a loving wife. Naturally he blamed Chana for spending her time at her father's bedside, disregarding the ever-increasing hours that he spent away from home with his new communist friends.

When a man sees his own world in dusky glasses, that view encompasses the expanse beyond his immediate sphere. Aryeh saw the world in flux; he saw a world of disillusionment, discontent, injustice. And on the horizon blazed the sun of communism, a cure-all for the world's ills, and a solution for his own problems.

Aryeh became a communist. And one fine day he packed his bag, wrapped up his idealism and, leaving his family without a goodbye, crossed the border to Moscow. Aryeh enrolled in the Comintern school for spies. All the enthusiasm, skill, and energy he had put into Torah study in his golden youth, he now devoted to the dialectics of communism. But his prior training, the sharp, keen chiseling of a *Gemara-kup*, did not stand him in good stead for a career that demands total — mental and physical — submission. The once-ideal student began to have ideas of his own, ideas that conflicted with communist doctrine and dogma. Aryeh's instructors watched and waited until the time was ripe. The time came. The inevitable knock on the door that all Russians fear with inbred terror came to usher in a ten-year sentence in Siberia for the unfortunate Aryeh. No trial. No defense. Just the sentence.

No-man's land. The last stop. The end of the world. What words can describe the endless expanse of snow, the intense cold, the lightless day and the dark, dark night, the loneliness, the utter despair that is Siberia? Aryeh was doubly disillusioned. He had abandoned his father's faith and, now, his faith in the communist panacea.

The hard life hardened his personality. Life was brutal and one had to confront it with brutality. In the labor camp, where survival of the fittest was the rule, Aryeh became a leader of his fellow prisoners and he ruled them with an iron hand. When World War II brought an influx of prisoners to the camps, Aryeh was delegated nearly absolute authority over a large number of prisoners. In his barracks, every facet of daily life was strictly regimented. There was a time to eat and a time to sleep. And if anyone disregarded either, he simply did not eat that day or didn't sleep that night; during guard duty he could reflect upon his sins. No one merited mercy from the embittered deputy commander of the barracks, least of all his own brothers, the Jewish prisoners. He harbored a special hatred for them, revealed with a diabolical glee whenever he caught one at some misdemeanor.

He lived to seek them out at prayers, or studying by candlelight. He preyed on them, stalking them by night and by day and ambushing them. And, when he caught a mouse in his trap his whole day brightened up.

One wintry night, Aryeh thought he had bagged a nestful. He gloated as he approached the dimly lit shack from which the singing issued. His heart pounded in expectation, seeing in his mind's eye the terror that would fill the cringing culprits upon his grand entry. He approached stealthily, so as not to give himself away before the time was ripe.

Aryeh did not know at what precise moment he became aware of the melody itself. He had always been sensitive to music, to *chazzanus*. Maybe it was the stillness of night and the dimly lit hut that struck a chord of nostalgia. Maybe it was the pitch of his own intensity in stalking his prey that served as an opportune lever in the hand of *Hashgachah* to turn the tide of his emotions, and of his life. Maybe — no, surely — surely it was nothing other than the *pintele Yid* that burns within the Jewish heart at all times, and which can only be kindled by the torch that is another Jewish soul.

ೞಳಿ

The Jewish soul is not one distinct entity. Each soul is a

fragment of the phenomenon known as the Jewish People. The song that radiated from the tortured, suffering souls within the hut penetrated the tortured soul outside the hut. Aryeh stood transfixed, listening at the window. The prisoners sang a wordless song of eternal Jewish suffering, and Aryeh felt the wellsprings within him releasing the pent-up emotions of his past. Suddenly Aryeh saw clearly that his own suffering had only been the fruit of his selfishness, his obstinacy, his shortsightedness. And Aryeh felt ashamed — for such is the power of *teshuvah* — for what he had been.

The melody stopped and the world was still. No one, nothing moved. The moon shone eerily down on the frozen expanse of snow, freezing those moments into eternity.

"Brothers, do not despair!" The cry broke the stony stillness. The voice of Shneur Zalman, a thin, sickly Jew with unflagging though apologetic optimism, addressed his companions. "Those were the words of Rav Nachman of Breslov. But what do they truly convey? One must never despair, never lose hope, no matter how seemingly perilous the danger. Our saintly rebbe, the Baal HaTanya, whose miraculous release from prison we celebrate this nineteenth night of Kislev, faced far graver danger than we. Over his head hung the death sentence. He was convinced, however, that if his service was required upon earth, some way would open up before him. He would repeat the death-defying cry of Dovid Hamelech, *Although I walk in the valley of death's shadow, I shall not fear!* If our troubles stem from the *galus* of the *Shechinah*, then our release from danger will come from that Source.

"There is another meaning to the cry, 'Brothers, do not despair,'" continued Shneur Zalman in another, softer tone with a far-away lilt to it. "The heavy *galus* threatens to extinguish the flame of the Jewish soul. All the fear and pain and suffering and bitterness have formed layers around the flame which flicker within every Jewish heart. These layers threaten to stifle and extinguish that flame. 'Never despair,'" his words rang out as if to reach all of Jewry. "Do not despair of yourselves, my brothers. You will find the way back to your Source even though you have strayed so far. All you must do is peel off the layers and the flickering light will flare up higher and higher, strong and inexhaustible. The flame will burst into fire, into a blazing torch, a beacon to light the way for all Jewish sons to return to their homeland and their birthright in both the physical and the spiritual senses."

Such resounding words called for happy music. All the assembled burst into joyous singing and though no words escaped their lips, the room seemed to explode with suppressed sound. The small group of men arose, formed a circle and danced 'round and 'round, their feet barely touching the ground, scarcely making a sound. Their bodies seemed ethereally elevated by the *niggun* itself.

The Siberian prisoners whirled around and around, whisking away the worries of their everyday lives in a fervent hope and trust that somewhere in the future a measure of happiness was still stored away for them.

Meanwhile a flickering flame strengthened and burned away layers of hate and disillusionment. The flame ate away at charred peels, revealing healthy tissue beyond the cancerous growths. How Aryeh ached to join the dancers, identifying with them, to be at peace with his inner self! But not yet. The conflict was still too great. First he must be certain that there was a place for him, too, in a specific sense. He must first be certain that they would accept him, black wolf that he was. And now was not the time.

Aryeh turned back uncertainly, and went to his quarters. He

spent a sleepless night. Childhood figures returned to fill nightmarish visions. His mind buzzed with *pesukim* about *teshuvah*. "Do not despair!" The words seemed to have been intended specifically for him.

When morning came, Aryeh's resolve had congealed into a firm decision. Return he must. But he needed help. Shneur Zalman, the leader of the small group, would surely help him "never to despair." It wasn't too late. It couldn't be.

When Shneur Zalman received the summons to appear before the deputy commander of the barracks, his knees shook. But not for long. He faced life philosophically, the good with the bad. He didn't let life touch him too deeply — that way he was immune to hurt. But wonder of wonders, when he stood before the fearsome deputy commander, the latter seemed actually sheepish. No one had ever before seen a smile on Aryeh's face that was not sardonic. Today Aryeh's smile put Shneur Zalman at ease.

"Tell me," he began gently, "what was the celebration about last night?"

Aha, he thought, *the calm before the storm.* But the thunder never broke and the lightning never struck. After a moment of silence, the prisoner summoned up his courage and told the story as it had happened, beginning with the Baal HaTanya and his miraculous rescue from death, developing the thread with ensuing flourishing of the Chabad movement and summing up hundreds of gatherings that had taken place all over the globe.

Aryeh asked questions and Shneur Zalman answered, concisely though comprehensively, convinced that the deputy commander was sincere in his interest.

And indeed he was. Aryeh was an eager and willing student.

That nineteenth day of Kislev proved to be a turning point in the lives of the Siberian prisoners. From then on their lives changed for the better. All the cunning and scheming that Aryeh had once put into making their lives a hell, he now turned to making their conditions livable. He tried to procure better food, he loosened the regulations, and gave his fellow Jews more freedom. Everyone breathed more freely, above all Aryeh himself.

◈

The hand of *Hashgachah* brought Chana and little Hershele to Siberia as well. Chana had suffered much during World War II and had brought with her little hope for the future. But her ties with the past, unlike Aryeh's, were still firm. Chana's parents had not survived the German invasion and the subsequent *selektzia* at the concentration camp. She had been fortunate enough to escape across the Russian border and, after a long and arduous journey, had ended up a prisoner in Siberia, unaware that her husband was nearby, or that he was even alive. Her tribulations robbed her of her strength and, had it not been for her child, she would have despaired of life altogether.

Large groups of prisoners were often transported from place to place and so it happened that Chana found herself, together with many other widows and orphans, in a Teheran camp for displaced persons. From there it was only a short step to Eretz Yisrael, for the British Mandate allowed Jewish Agency *shlichim* to recruit children for Youth Aliyah. The *shaliach*, wearing a yarmulke, assured Chana that Hershele would be placed in a religious institution or kibbutz. Chana really had no choice. What could she, in her forlorn state, offer her child? And so she tearfully bade Hershele goodbye as he was whisked away on eagle's wings.

For his part, Hershele was all joyous expectation. True, he

would have preferred to have his mother along, but the magic of the words "Eretz Yisrael," etched into his young consciousness through the *tefillos* he knew so well, drew him like a magnet. Besides, he was not alone; he had scores of little companions who were also going to the Promised Land.

When Hershele arrived at his destination he was brought before a Youth Aliyah panel who were to decide his fate. Among the several men behind the desks Hershel saw a few men with yarmulkes, but the majority were bareheaded. Something should have warned him but he was still so small and naive…

Hershele was asked all kinds of questions — whether he knew the *brachos*, if his mother lit candles on Friday eve, if he could read the *aleph-beis*. To all these he proudly answered affirmatively. Chana had taught him well, tender of age though he was. Her parting words to him had been not to forget that he was a *frum* boy, a soldier in Mashiach's army. Hershele addressed his questioners firmly, unwaveringly. It was their last question, however, that threw him off.

"Where is your father?" one man thought to ask. Hershele had heard this question before; he had seen how deeply it had affected his mother. And he, too, wondered often, "Where is my father?" He blurted the only answer, the reply that his mother tersely gave, "My father is a communist, somewhere in Russia."

"Aha! That changes the picture completely. If this boy is the son of a communist, then justice demands that he be brought up as one." So argued the bareheaded men.

"But what about his religious upbringing?" countered the religious representatives. But they argued in vain; they were outnumbered. Hershele had sealed his own fate and was assigned to a Shomer Hatza'ir kibbutz.

ೋನ

Home at last. Poor homeless waif, cast from one shore to the next, from one camp to another. The warmth, the friendly atmosphere, the carefree laughter, the bountiful food — all these served to make the *galus* boy breathe free. Life was always busy on the kibbutz; he was always involved in some group activity. There were the *chalutz* songs and dances glorifying the love of the land and of labor. The lonely boy lapped it up hungrily. Of course he noticed that everyone went around bareheaded. Surely he remarked that no one found time for *davening*. And to give him credit, it bothered him deeply. But in the kibbutz there was very little time for introspection. And what could a little boy do, after all, one against so many, against the establishment?

The biggest blow came on his first Shabbos. All the frustration of the preceding day struck the boy with stunning finality when he vainly sought the familiar Shabbos candles and, on the following day, when he was told that Shabbos was like any other weekday.

He couldn't believe his ears. "You don't understand," his *madrich* explained with a casual shrug of his shoulders. "Those old-fashioned religious practices are fine for a *galut*. Here we've got different responsibilities. We must build the land."

Hershele reeled with the impact of those words. He couldn't fight them, he realized, but he could run away. It was his only alternative. That very day, Shabbos, he slipped away from his group, and left the kibbutz grounds. He ran along the country road to escape the evil place. His pace slowed down to a walk and then to an automatic trudge until, exhausted, he lay down at the foot of a tree and fell asleep.

That's how the searching party found him later. They picked up the sleeping boy and carried him back to the kibbutz. He was so exhausted, emotionally as well as physically, that he never awoke until the next morning — when he found himself in his own bed.

It was not his last mark of defiance. He tried on several other occasions to run away. But he never succeeded in escaping altogether. His indoctrination process was a slow and difficult one, but Hershele proved too young, weak, and alone to withstand the relentless pressure. Within half a year, Hershele was indistinguishable from his other kibbutz peers.

Chana tried to keep contact with her son through letters but noted, to her dismay, that her son was changing. He slowly forgot his Yiddish; his ways were foreign to her. And, when she finally came to Eretz Yisrael two years later, her worst fears were confirmed. Chana haunted the offices of Youth Aliyah, begging to have her son transferred to a religious institution. The authorities were understanding — she could have her son back if she undertook to house him and care for him. As for a transfer, this was an impossibility, since the initial decision of the Youth Aliyah board was, for all purposes, immutable law.

Homeless herself and penniless, Chana could not hope to take her child under her wing. And so she decided to join Hershele's kibbutz hoping that somehow in the course of time a miracle would occur to return her child's heart to his tradition.

ᛊᛊ

The war finally reached its bitter end, bringing hope of a better life for Aryeh and his new circle of friends. They wended their long way from Siberia to Eretz Yisrael where they settled in Kfar Chabad, a small village near Tel Aviv. Aryeh's leadership once again asserted itself in a whirlwind of activity as he and his companions founded *yeshivos* and Talmud Torahs and recruited students for them from among the newly arrived immigrants. Aryeh personally participated in all the work, never satisfied until the voice of Torah could be heard from within the four walls of every new building. His energy and enthusiasm, and above all, his resonant singing, gave everyone added impetus to strive harder and work faster.

The weeks flew by and Lag B'Omer approached. It was to be Aryeh's first visit to Meron and he looked forward to it eagerly. Most of the Kfar Chabad populace made the journey, for the impressive event was a highlight for children and adults alike. It began on the evening of the thirty-third day of *sefiras ha'omer* when candles were lit ceremoniously inside the *kever* of Rabbi Shimon bar Yochai. This moment lent an aura of sanctity and solemnity to the evening's celebration that remained throughout the joyous dancing that took place inside as well as outside around a raging bonfire. But to Aryeh the burning candles seemed to portend something deeper and longer lasting than one day's festivities. He recalled the deeper meaning that Shneur Zalman had given the words, "Brothers, never despair," assuring him and all of Jewry that the tiny flame that was the Jewish soul would not die out. And somehow he felt that the roaring bonfire was the very embodiment of that flame that had been fanned and fed to its present potency.

Aryeh left his companions and went for a solitary walk on the hillside. The keen mountain air prickled his nostrils, the sound of singing filled his ears, and he felt strangely detached, as if he were partly back with his friends, losing himself in the magic of a whirling circle, while yet alone, apart, unfulfilled somehow. His past drifted slowly but poignantly through his mind's eye. The central figure was his wife Chana and, beside her, his infant son Hershele as he remembered him. And he knew why he felt alone.

He ached for the injustice he had done to two innocent souls and for his powerlessness to make amends. True, he had dedicated his life to helping homeless war orphans by giving them a Torah education. But what could he do for his own flesh and blood? What, after all, had become of them, poor souls?

Aryeh returned to the cave, wending his way past the circles of flying feet. Tonight he felt he could not join them. His heart was too heavy. Instead he went inside and by the light of the hundreds of candles, said Tehillim for many hours.

The day that dawned was to be a busy one for Aryeh. His group had organized a full program of activities to attract all the children celebrating in Meron. They specifically wanted to reach children whose knowledge of *Yiddishkeit* was meager, attracting them through stories and songs to the rich heritage of which they knew so little. They had prepared sweets to distribute among them, accompanied by a fervent appeal that they seek to enroll in religious schools in their areas. Loudspeakers would blare forth gay chassidic tunes and small circles would be formed all over the hilltop, where the young men could appeal to youthful imaginations through moving stories of Rabbi Shimon bar Yochai and the giants of his generation.

The sun had barely made its way up from behind the mountain and the air was still cool and refreshing. The smell of new grass and spring flowers floated hazily in the air, and colored butterflies flitted brightly about. Aryeh wandered down Mount Meron, past the *kever* of Hillel, down to a small lake where he intended to *tovel*.

As he neared he noticed a small group of kibbutz children with their leader. The latter was briefing them on the history and geography of the area in a detached manner.

"Why do you tell them only half the story?" Aryeh asked, half jestingly but with significant overtones. "Why don't you tell them who Rabbi Shimon was, why he ran away, and what he dedicated his life to? Why don't you tell them about the *kedushah* of this place? Why do you only tell the facts that make the pretty picture of your preconceived notions? Tell them the truth. Tell them who they are and what it means to be a Jew…"

Fearing that he might get carried away with himself, Aryeh continued to the lake and, when he had emerged from its waters, saw that the group had already left.

After Shacharis Aryeh returned to the courtyard outside the grave where hundreds of Jews milled around, distributed schnapps, cookies, and mazel tovs. With his resonant voice, Aryeh began the traditional "*Bar Yochai*" chant, singing the verse while the people roared the refrain in response. And suddenly, spontaneously, they all found themselves part of a huge circle. Hands interlocked and feet kicked away mundane cares as everyone began dancing. Meah Shearim grocers found themselves side by side with factory workers from Migdal Ha'emek; Haifa stevedores grasped kibbutzniks' hands; children stretched to meet work-worn hands from all parts of the country. Iraqi Jews joined with Americans, Germans with Moroccans, Russians with Egyptians. Their voices blended together and, if you closed your eyes, you could imagine how it would be when Mashiach came. This uniting of hearts must be what at least one *navi* had meant. Amid the crescendoing sound a cry escaped Aryeh's lips, "Brothers, never despair!"

It had to end. Drained of all energy, Aryeh went to rest under a shady tree. Soon he found himself surrounded by a group of the kibbutz youths he had spoken to so forcefully earlier that morning. They had many questions to ask him and he was glad to see their genuine interest.

He got up somewhat refreshed, a little excited, and made his way through the crowds to the microphone. Then he began to sing. At first he sang slow, moving *niggunim*. Then he quickened the pace with marches. Between the songs he would address the crowd with brief messages about the importance of religious *chinuch* for children, about the emptiness of modern life as compared with the richness of Torah tradition. He made brief appeals for Shabbos, for *tefillin*, for *davening*, breaking off into song when he felt his audience growing restless.

There was one woman who was particularly restless. Chana had accompanied her son on this kibbutz outgoing to Meron, intending to spend the major part of the day in prayer for herself and for her son's *neshamah*. She had spent most of her time during the Lag B'Omer outing inside the tomb. But the air there was stuffy with the breath of scores of other praying Jews. So she ventured out occasionally to inhale the fresh spring air into her lungs. Upon one such excursion, she became aware of a man's voice singing.

Chana felt a strange stirring; the voice was one she should know. *It is a voice I have heard before.* She turned to the nearest person she could find. "Is that a phonograph record?" she asked agitatedly.

"Why, no," she was told. "That's someone singing on the microphone."

It can't be. That's Aryeh's voice. She couldn't mistake it. Suddenly the music stopped. Aryeh had been singing for a good hour and had gone to keep his appointment with the kibbutz youths.

"Where is the singer?" she cried out, her knees melting under her. "Who is he?" she asked again, fearfully.

"That's Aryeh the Chabadnik," came the casual reply. "There he is, down by the lake, resting."

Chana made her way weakly toward the shady tree by the

lake. There sat Aryeh surrounded by a group of boys, among them her Hershele.

"Hershele! Aryeh!" she called out. But the excitement was too much. She fainted on the grass.

When she awoke, she saw the two dearest faces in her life looking down at her, on the one side Aryeh and on the other, Hershele.

"*A sheinem dank*," she smiled beatifically. "*A sheinem dank, Ribono shel Olam.*"

SAMUEL COHEN

The Angel

---

*Two angels accompany a man home from shul
every Shabbos eve. One seeks good; the other — bad.
If the man comes home to find his table set and his candles lit...*

THE GROUND FLOOR of one of the houses that opened into the courtyard belonged entirely to the Gantzfeins. Reb Shmuel — whom G-d had blessed with wealth — was a G-d-fearing perpetual student of Torah and one of Vilna's leading *ba'alei batim*. His pious wife, Sarah, was scrupulous in her observance of every mitzvah. When she covered her hair not a single hair showed out. When she *davened*, three times a day, she filled the Gantzfein living room with her fervid whispers: she did not dare raise her voice to G-d. Friendly with all the women who shared the large courtyard, she shared their sorrows and joys but never their gossip nor even the small talk that remotely resembled *lashon hara*.

Sarah's Shabbos was special. To be more exact: Sarah's Erev Shabbos. Of course, everything she needed for Shabbos was prepared Erev Shabbos. What made Sarah unique was that her Shabbos was all ready by noon — not just on summer Fridays, but in the winter as well. Admittedly, the maid the Gantzfeins had in the house all week long made it easier for Sarah to bake her own challos, and to cook the fish and the soup and the chicken and the kugel and the cholent all by herself. By noon all the food was cooked and replaced in the oven to stay warm. To say nothing of the sumptuous dining room where a shimmering white tablecloth graced the table; an embroidered silk napkin hid the challos, its sheen surpassed only by the highly polished gloss of the delicate silver candlesticks; a crystal decanter filled with homemade raisin wine twisted the sun's rays into rainbows through its prisms; and the golden Kiddush goblet waited for the wine with its mouth wide open. The Shabbos sparkle throughout the apartment delighted the eye, and the fragrance of sacred cleanliness delighted the nose.

Sarah, at noon, dressed in her Shabbos best, began her spiritual preparations to receive *Shabbos Hamalkah*. She read through her *Tzenah Ur'enah* on the *sedrah* of the week. If there was time, she read some *Kav Hayashar* or *Shevet Mussar*. That's how she made herself worthy to receive the Queen. As soon as you're properly allowed to welcome Shabbos — at the *plag haMinchah*, one and one-quarter sun hours before sunset — Sarah would light the candles that turned as much of Friday as possible into holy Shabbos. Sarah's desire to include herself among those we sing about every Shabbos eve, the *memaharim lavo*, brought the pleasurable restfulness of Shabbos and its holy purity into the Gantzfein home long before the men set out for shul.

> *...If the man comes home to find his table set and his candles lit, the good angel says, "May it be this way next week,*

too." And the bad angel must reply, "Amen." If the situation, however...

When the neighbor women looked out into the courtyard during their Shabbos preparations and saw Sarah's lit candles through the window — especially in the winter — their anxiety grew great and their tempers short for fear they might, *chas v'shalom*, desecrate the sacred Shabbos.

One of the cellar apartments off the big courtyard belonged to Velvel the water carrier. His wife, Charna, peddled fruit because Velvel's labors earned him only a subsistence income. Winters especially, when snow had blanketed the orchards and ice had frosted the trees, Charna hawked the frozen winter apples everyone called "wine goblets." The best day in Charna's week was Friday. What Jew didn't buy some fruit in honor of Shabbos? And some of the trade, thank G-d, always came Charna's way. But the frosty winter Fridays were the best of all, for then the "wine goblet" apples were grabbed up as special Shabbos treats.

Those all-important Friday earnings meant that Charna arrived home only about two hours before Shabbos. The candles she saw a few minutes later as she looked out of her window across the courtyard rent her poor heart, and a sigh that was also a sob would salt the open wound. She would rush, rush, rush. And then Velvel would come home. His backbreaking work turned good-natured-in-the-morning Velvel into a temperamental-in-the-evening tyrant. The Shabbos so plainly visible through Sarah Gantzfein's window greeted him as he walked through the courtyard. When he descended into his dreary apartment, his spirits would sink at the confusion: Charna at the oven, Charna sweeping, Charna diapering a child, feeding another; the children on the table, under the table, under Charna's feet, under his feet… It was too much for Velvel. Exhausted, disappointed, he'd shout. Charna, in frustrated tears, would retort. So it was every Erev Shabbos.

Erev Shabbos?! What Shabbos? The noise and the rancor of the "Battle in the Cellar" carried weekday Friday well into what should have been hallowed Shabbos, past the time the men walked through the courtyard on their way back from shul.

> *…If the situation, however, is otherwise, the bad angel says, "May it be this way next week, too." And the good angel must reply, "Amen."*

Week after week, year in, year out, the situation remained the same. Shabbos reigned in Sarah's home from *plag haMinchah* on, almost from noon. In the cellar, Friday sunsets found Charna wishing she had never been born. If Shabbos did not have to arrive at sunset by G-d's decree — it would never voluntarily pick its way between the clouds of verbal abuse or through the mist of Charna's tears into that unsanctified cellar.

☙❧

Reb Elya Leizer, the new tenant, was all ready to go to shul when the shouting from the cellar reached his ears that first Erev Shabbos in his new apartment. When the battle raged on and on, he realized it was more than a one-time flare-up. The son-in-law of Rav Yisrael of Salant and the father-in-law of Rav Chaim Ozer Grodzenski, Reb Elya Leizer was one of Vilna's rabbis — for Vilna had a Rabbinic Council instead of a single *rav*. He proceeded to analyze the situation from every angle. He made a few inquiries in the course of the next week, and by Friday he had a plan.

Friday that week began as frostily as the other midwinter days had. By midafternoon, the wind had convinced whoever was on the street that coats were useless. The few who still braved the cold were performing vital services (Velvel, for one), or were desperate for the money they might earn (Charna, for one), or were in need of some commodity ("wine goblets," for instance). The wind altered only part of Reb Elya Leizer's plan: he had to light his pipe indoors. He pulled his rabbinic fur-lined coat on over his Shabbos garb, donned his rabbinic hat, and calmly sat himself down on his balcony to smoke his pipe. Ignoring the cold and the wind, his mind on the solution of a halachah problem, he calmly "enjoyed" his smoke until a minute before candle-lighting time.

While he was sitting there, the neighbor women paused as usual in midwork and looked out into the courtyard. As usual, they saw Sarah's lit candles through the window, and their anxiety grew great. One of them groaned, "She's lucky. If she had to work for a living — G-d forgive me — I wish her no ill."

Ready to rush back to her labors, each of them noticed the same phenomenon. "That's funny. It's Shabbos at Sarah's, but Reb Elya Leizer is sitting out there…smoking. *Nu?* If the *rav* can smoke, it's surely not Shabbos yet."

Unflustered, each of the housewives completed her Shabbos preparations in good spirits. Some of the husbands were mildly surprised to hear their wives humming to themselves as they worked. When Velvel the water carrier entered the courtyard he tensed up at the sight of Sarah's candles. And then he saw Reb Elya Leizer's pipe.

Certain that Shabbos was further away than Sarah Gantzfein's window, Velvel good-naturedly helped Charna usher in the Shabbos, much to his wife's delighted surprise. By candle-lighting time, the apartment was clean and everything in perfect order.

When the men returned from shul that Shabbos eve, they heard Velvel and his children singing "*Shalom Aleichem*" in greeting to the angels who had escorted him home.

The good angel said, "May it be this way next week, too." And the bad angel had to agree, "Amen. So be it." And so it was.

TZIVIA TABAK

The Benefit and the Doubt

In these two mildly edited letters written to a friend, Mrs. Tabak relates a unique personal experience that heightened her own awareness of human doubt and Divine benefit.

A TRUE STORY

MARCH 17

Dear Sheindel,

The war in Eretz Yisrael really shook us up a lot and that sort of changed our plans temporarily. You take it in stride and make the best of the situation. But to consider uprooting and resettling from the safe, secure (?) ghetto of Boro Park is another matter.

Until now I was rather neck high with a large open-house benefit for a mutual friend who was left alone with the responsibility of a large family. It was very successful — we netted almost 4Gs.

I never really was at the party even though it was in my own house. At about one o'clock in the afternoon, the first three guests knocked on the front door. I rushed into the back bedroom to get dressed while they let themselves in. Halfway through, I noticed my small bottle of red low-blood-sugar pills spilled on my bed (I have hypoglycemia). All of a sudden everything fitted in... My head was whirling... I didn't believe it... Little three-year-old Goldie.

She was the only one of my children home that morning. Earlier in the day she had come into the kitchen and asked for water. Nothing unusual about that — she's a big drinker. Now I remembered that I had noticed her mouth being a little red around the lips but the thought had only lasted a fleeting second. She could have gotten to anything. With such a huge party in preparation, there were so many women in the kitchen that I just didn't think long enough about it to realize that there was nothing red being served, as it was a natural and health food and dietetic menu — no nosh, no cake, no candy or soda at all!

And then she had announced that she was going to sleep in Esty's bed — also quite natural. She hadn't quite made it, though.

I had found her slouched up against a kitchen wall, fast asleep. I still hadn't realized anything, and had picked her up and carried her to the bed, covering her up nicely. She very often sleeps on my long bench in the kitchen while I do my work, so falling asleep on the floor was not the least bit odd.

With my heart pounding, I rushed into the back room where I had put her down. I tried to wake her. I called — shouted — shook her. She was unconscious. Her face was red but she was still breathing. I knew I mustn't panic but I foolishly ran into the kitchen. The women got wind of it. We called poison control. I called the doctor who had prescribed my medicine. He was hysterical, it's surely toxic. I must RUSH her to the emergency room of the nearest hospital and have her pumped.

All along I was mentally counting the pills in the bottle. There had been one hundred in the bottle to begin with. I found twenty-three on the bed. None on the floor. I had only taken about twenty myself because I didn't care for it. It made me sleepy and drowsy. Me! According to my count, Goldie had swallowed around fifty! It was unbelievable! How could this happen to me?

We rushed to my sister-in-law's car with the child. I ran to the car, taking my shoes with me. In the car Goldie had a terrible convulsion. I was helpless. We hit Thirteenth Avenue — a very busy thoroughfare for Sunday afternoon at 1:00 p.m. We couldn't get through. We kept beeping so loudly I nearly went deaf. Nothing doing.

I ran out of the car with my unconscious child in my arms, screaming for people to get out of the way. A yeshivah guy saw me. Leaving his car stranded, he jumped into mine and started driving without looking, beeping the whole way down.

We finally arrived. I ran in without the usual preliminaries, surprised that they let me through. They pumped her immediately but found nothing. It was too late. Too many hours had elapsed and the poison was already coursing through her bloodstream. They kept asking me how many, how many did the kid swallow? How was I to know? We kept doing math. We called the pharmacy to determine the original amount. It was useless.

Two more doctors arrived from someplace. They looked gray, grim, dismal, and angry. I was feeling very guilty. More guilty than sad. They announced that there was no known antidote. I was falling into a stupor. Was all this real?

My husband! He knew nothing about this. I ran to the phone. He was in yeshivah in Manhattan. Why scare him — he had to travel an hour. I told him to come to the hospital, that Goldie wasn't feeling too well. Nothing major, but I'd rather he be there. I was unusually calm. We called Rabbi Twersky for more recommendations. The doctor said she was critical. My own doctor was in Florida on vacation. Second best was in New Jersey, but it was Sunday and the going was rough. Meanwhile we called a few *yeshivos* to say Tehillim.

After about an hour or so, the house doctor approached and said in a low voice that he had done all he could. All we could do now was stand by and watch her. And pray. He said that any amount over eight or ten pills was fatal… We should be ready for the worst. The last child that had come in on this stuff never went home.

My knees began to shake. My stomach felt weak. I hadn't realized it was that bad. They had removed Goldie from the emergency room and sent her up to Pediatrics where they connected an intravenous tube to give her some energy. They put a monitor machine on her and told me to watch it; if the numbers went below 80 I should quickly call a nurse. I was petrified. Meanwhile the numbers were running 85–88. Anywhere between 80 and 120 beats per second was normal. When my husband came I saw that there wasn't much to say. I could see by his expression that he had found out the details downstairs. My parents came. My in-laws came. Some people from the party. We all stood around the crib saying Tehillim out loud. I *davened* hard but no tears came. Why was all this happening? Again I felt guilt. Terrible, weakening, threatening guilt. Poor Goldie! What had she done? Children die young as an *onesh* for the *aveiros* of parents… I had just taught that myself last Sunday in *kallah* class.

Her breaths came heavily now, panting in and out as if each one would be her last. It was getting harder and harder for me to watch. Goldie, please fight. Goldie, come on. You're such a tough, stubborn kid. Now fight for real! Oh, Goldie, please don't go under.

Goldie was tall and thin with blue eyes. She weighed only twenty-six pounds. But she was a strong child. Lying there in that hospital crib she looked like a scarecrow, her little chest heaving in and out with every breath. You could count every rib. Goldie was clever and rather spoiled; the baby. Very quick and agile, long and lanky, the week before she had climbed up on a chair and with wet hands rolled thirty meatballs for supper. And she had kept remembering to dip her hands in water every few minutes.

Just that Shabbos Goldie had stood up on the bench and told the *complete* story of Hillel Hanasi on the roof in the snow. The family had beamed with *nachas*. My mother had told her that story on the phone. I never knew she could repeat so many sentences without any prompting.

It was easy to keep thinking so many nice thoughts about her. But *why* hadn't I brought her earlier? *Why* didn't I suspect the red mouth? The water? Why? WHY? What was the use of backtracking? Here she was now, almost dead.

Thoughts of *teshuvah* filled my heart. Maybe it was all a warning. I started bargaining with Hashem. I'll improve in the hard things. *Tzedakah* was too easy at this point. *Lashon hara* — that's hard. *Machshavah*. Other intimate areas of my life. I had to think of some more things that were hard. I felt pretty hopeless, pretty weak. My *bitachon* was fading. I won't run after *kavod*. That's a hard one for me. After all, wasn't that one of my motivations when I planned the benefit? Would I have put in that much effort, originality, strength, initiative if someone else were making this affair in her house? I was getting dizzy and sweaty. I really didn't know what to offer Hashem.

All of a sudden the green light went out on the monitor. The numbers disappeared. No more 80.

My heart sank. Big, fat hot tears rolled down my face. I ran out quickly into the hall to call the nurse. She came in, looked at the machine and then at Goldie and then at me. She quickly lifted an arm. One of the four connections had come loose and the whole machine had been disconnected. Goldie was still alive. The nurse reconnected the monitor and I saw the precious 80 again. What a narrow escape! But there still wasn't much hope.

The women from the party kept insisting that I not lose hope, that the *zechus* of the great mitzvah of *tzedakah* that was going on in my own home right at that very minute would make Goldie live. *Tzedakah tatzil mimaves*. Simple. How could I be so dumb to think otherwise? But the doctor's harsh words drumming in my ears made it hard to believe.

The doctor returned from downstairs and called me to the desk. I left the machine and walked slowly to the desk. No news was good news at this point. He said that the chances were that Goldie might remain in her present coma from forty-eight hours to three weeks. She might wake up, she might not, he explained pessimistically. It was already 6:00 p.m. He asked if we wanted any more doctors in. Yes, anyone, anything. He called up the Chief of Pediatrics who promised to come over immediately. We stood around and *davened*. We could see the sun setting from the window. We were pale and weak, and things did not look too good.

As the hours ticked by I kept picturing the funeral. The *shivah*. I kept thinking about friends who had lost children, *Rachmana litzlan*. My neighbor's boy of ten, another neighbor's three-month-old baby. And now it would be us. It was so unlike me, such an unrealistic optimist in real life, to be such a prophet of doom.

At 8:30 p.m. the Big Chief arrived, washed his hands, went to

The Benefit and the Doubt

the desk for a consultation with the other doctors. At 8:45 he came into the room. There were eight of us around the crib. Sixteen eyes watching. Some of us stepped aside to let him lower the crib railing. *Goldie opened one eye. And then another. And he hadn't even touched her!*

"Ma," she said, "I don't sleep in a cribby. Take me home."

And then she sat up, pulled out the intravenous tube, and disconnected the monitor. The Big Chief put on his hat and said, "You don't need me, lady. Your G-d helped you!"

Goldie! Goldie! Goldie! To think that I doubted Hashem's strength. Everyone was buzzing around. All the nurses came running in. They were all knocked for a loop!

We stayed with Goldie all that night to observe any residual side effects. At 10:00 p.m. I went home to personally reassure my six other fretting children that Goldie was really all right. When I arrived home every light was on. The party was over and the box was full of money for my poor, lonely friend. I found three children in my bed, three in my husband's. Boy, were they scared. Levi, eight, had said all of Tehillim twice and was on his third round. The girls were crying. I tried to pacify them. I hadn't seen them all day — for when I had left they had all been in school, but they seemed to have heard all sorts of conflicting stories from everyone. My oldest, Chaya, hadn't even gone into the dining room all day. She said she had locked herself in the bedroom and *davened* to Hashem. Chaya is twelve.

Four days later Goldie came home. All was well, *baruch Hashem*; there were no side effects. But it had been a tremendous emotional strain on me which I only began to feel a week later. I now carried new guilt feelings for not having felt the proper *bitachon* at the crucial hours. And for having apparently not had pure motivation in organizing the party. I was grateful for the results, of course, and I also felt that removing me from the scene of the party at that moment of climax was perhaps to purify me of *redifas kavod*. I hadn't got to wear that new *sheitel* or outfit but I was somewhat cleansed and a little glad.

I called up Rav Avigdor Miller (whose *shiur* I attend religiously and tape) to discuss some of my mixed-up feelings. He left me with a number of important thoughts: to be more responsible toward the children and aware of them; to verbally thank Hashem for the kindness He bestowed upon us, repeating our thanks over and over until we really believed it; *not* to reduce my involvement in *kehillah* work; who knows if something worse was not in store for us which was mitigated by the *zechus* of the mitzvah; and finally, to forget my guilt about my lack of *bitachon*. People can fall through at crucial times. The *ikar* is the merchandise that one carries along. Better to do a few sins along the way that will be cleansed in Gehinnom than be overcautious about getting involved and coming out clean. When a person is asked what *sechorah* he brought along with him and shows nothing, he won't get much of a seat.

I guess I got carried away with this story. Anyway, best regards and wishes.

Yours,
Tzivie

೦৪௧

MAY 1

Dear Sheindel,

About publishing my other letter…I really had intended to send it to *LIGHT* but I misplaced the original. The only thing I would conceal is whom the party was for. Every human being I know knows this story.

There was really much more to the story and what went into the benefit which I feel makes the climax more meaningful. The idea was born when I was asked to collect some money and line up people to give on a monthly basis. I wasn't in the mood to go knocking on doors and so the party came to mind. It was eight weeks in the making.

I was told pessimistically that there had been dozens of parties in Boro Park and no one would come. But others said, "You do it. We'll come and bring some food." So I picked a date and dashed off a rough copy of the invitation. Then I tried to get lists. Organizations were not willing to give them out. But I did find one large local organization that agreed. They had three thousand names. That was eighty pages, and I was expected to give back the list the same day. I marched to the library with eighty dimes and Xeroxed for two hours straight.

Against my friends' better judgment, I photo-offset the invitation rather than printing it even though I was warned that no one would respond to a *shmatte* invitation.

Then came the addressing. I dragged 1,500 to school the next day and instead of cooking (I teach home economics), we did a mitzvah. Each girl got a sheet of addresses instead of a recipe and we polished them all off that very day. I dragged home the envelopes and we started on the stuffing. For days the house was rolling in stamps, envelopes, return cards. Goldie and Avrum pasted a complete window pane with stamps! Kids of all ages came to stuff. Boys one night, girls the next. Ladies all day.

Finally, to the post office. Lo and behold the postmaster proclaimed that one more stamp was due on each envelope. Me and my big fat invitations! That cost $250 more! Well, we started pasting. That took about three hours, but we weren't going to shlep these six heavy, giant cartons home again.

I got a phone call the next day. Had I checked the date? A monument maker wanted to know. I had written "5733" and "Teves" instead of Shevat. Both were long gone. We had postponed the party along the way but none of us geniuses had noticed it. It took a *matzeivah macher*! We even forgot the word "Sunday." It was the "January 27" that (literally) saved the day. And everybody came.

Then came refreshment planning. I had decided to make it more interesting with health and dietetic foods. No cake, soda, or nosh. I needed twenty-five pounds of diced fried onions, lots of hardboiled eggs and boiled mixed vegetables. I planned vegetable roast with mushroom sauce for about three hundred people. My friends were hysterical. Fried onions! But again they rallied to the tune of six women at four pounds each. I was able to sell them on the fresh-fruit-and-honey salad, and herb-and-mint tea. But they insisted on coffee, too. They weren't getting the point. But we compromised on Sanka. Then came the setting! Candles, of course, and small round tables. They wanted electricity. And paper goods. I wanted fancy china. Again we compromised.

The night before the party ten women came over to help grind vegetables and cut fruit. They were half hysterical. I don't own an electric grinder; mine is a hand model #2 and we should have been using an electric model #8 at least. After two hours, someone finally went home to bring her electric one. The onions arrived in three shifts and the roast got larger and larger as time went by. We were somewhat done by 2:00 a.m. But I wasn't. The recipes still had to be typed and run off, because I knew that everyone would really want them once they had tasted the food.

And the first question they threw at me when I called home the next day was, where in heaven did I hide those recipes. They had unearthed my *kesubah*, old canceled checks, wedding album, but no recipes — when they had been sitting on the most obvious place — the shelf.

This benefit was pretty much "my baby" as far as financial decisions and responsibility, even though many women gave me a hand throughout, and I was prepared to foot the bill if not a dime came in. So now you can realize the shock and disappointment I actually experienced when I was hauled out so unexpectedly at exactly the time of the party.

But as Rav Miller says, as long as we come through with the merchandise…

Yours,
Tzivie

SHEINDEL WEINBACH

Rain

"If one who is only flesh and blood can take pity on his ex-wife, cannot You, Who are not of flesh and blood, have mercy on us?"

THERE WASN'T A cloud in the sky. Perfect picnic weather. Great for doing that heavy wash or airing out mattresses. Just right for drying the wheat in the fields, ripening the pomegranates, or giving the apples that extra turn of rosy maturity. Real lazy fishing weather.

Only no one had his mind on pastimes. Not even the children.

Not a cloud in the sky. Not even the fleecy white ones that make a lazy summer day even lazier, the kind that give you the urge to drop whatever you're doing and go lie down in some daisy field and watch them float by.

That kind of day would have been perfect for spring or summer. But for the last week in Cheshvan it just wasn't right. People's inner clocks presaged brisk winds and falling leaves even though in Eretz Yisrael many trees keep their dress all winter long only to exchange it for greener garb in spring. But there was no breeze.

The air hung heavy. Hearts were heavy, brows beclouded, backs bowed. The rains should have begun to fall already. During Sukkos everyone had rejoiced with the hot weather and had taken refuge under the cool branches of the *s'chach*. But the hot spell was no longer welcome.

Day after day farmers had looked heavenward to place their hopes upon the tiniest bit of fluff, but even a wisp of cloud had been denied them. Day after day the sun had shone down upon the land, drying up grass, wheat stalks, brooks and creeks, fields and roads. It was futile to think of plowing, for the land was as thoroughly baked as an earthenware vessel. So what was there to do?

❧

"Rabbeinu," the people came pleading. "What are we to do? There is no hint of rain. How can we plow and plant? Our sustenance for the entire year depends upon these winter rains. Pray for us, Rabbeinu."

Rabbi Tanchuma had been expecting the farmers. "The *chachamim* have fasted both Mondays and Thursdays since the seventeenth of Mar Cheshvan. You see we have not been answered. Now you, my good people, must turn to the Sustainer of life and entreat Him. We must proclaim a public fast. That is not an easy thing to do, you understand, for it is so hot and dry. The responsibility rests upon the entire community. In such circumstances *beis din* usually waits until Rosh Chodesh Kislev to declare the Monday, Thursday, and Monday after Rosh Chodesh as fast days."

"Yes, yes, Rabbeinu," came voices from all sides. "We are ready. We must ask for *rachamim*. For we must have rain. May the *zechus* of our acceptance now be added to our merit." Thus, though it was still Cheshvan, the first Monday in Kislev and the succeeding Thursday and Monday were proclaimed as fast days, days of *tefillah* to Hashem, Keeper of the rains. Monday passed. Thursday came and went, and the last Monday came. Still the same untroubled azure skies mocked the beclouded faces of the populace convened in shul.

"What more can we do, Rabbeinu? We have poured out our very hearts. We are drained, our tear wells have dried up. Our throats are parched from prayer. What must we do? What can we do?"

"My dear people," began Rabbi Tanchuma. "Today, Monday, is the last of the public fasts. Cast aside your personal problems for the while and listen with open hearts to what I have to say."

He paused and looked from face to face, and all seemed to be listening with their hearts. Satisfied, he continued, "Today is the third in a series of fasts. We must make this last effort a meaningful one. We cannot continue fasting indefinitely; our bodies are in no condition to do so. This physical burden cannot be imposed upon an entire *tzibbur*. And who knows if while we torture our bodies, we are not neglecting our souls?"

Intelligent faces nodded back at him, imploring him to continue. "We must concentrate upon today, upon this last fast still ahead with more than the physical effort of fasting and the spiritual effort of praying. Both are essential for they focus Hashem's attention upon us. But we must make this opportunity of *einei Hashem* at a time of mercy, a *sha'as rachamim*. How? By ourselves performing deeds of *rachamim*! Let us approach Hashem today with *ma'asei rachamim* in our hands! With Hashem's eyes upon us at such a crucial time, let us show ourselves as His sons, emulators of His ways. *Mah Hu rachum, af atah rachum.* I will not detain you, my dear people. Time is too precious. Let us all return home and fulfill at least one significant act of *rachamim* for a fellow Jew, be it with money or in any other way. I need not tell the children of Avraham Avinu how to go about doing *rachamim* and *chessed*. So go, my children. And let us pray that our *tefillos* and *ma'asim* will be favorably accepted today. May G-d be with us."

The crowd dispersed, each to his own destination.

ଓଛ୭

Chanan the moneychanger hurried home. He, thank G-d, did not have to rack his brain for a way to show *rachamim*. A wealthy man, he merely had to fill a moneybag and distribute it among the poor. Chanan's wealth was a bittersweet blessing, for he had no children to help consume his wealth. As for his wife, Chanan had divorced her and made the *kesubah* settlement with her which was to provide her needs for at least a year, as the *din* required. So he was not concerned for her. Filling a large pouch with heavy coins, he hurried to the poor section of town to bestow his bounty upon the needy. Unfamiliar with the narrow streets of the poorer section of town, he walked slowly. He rarely bothered with distributing *tzedakah* personally. To a wealthy man, opportunity for *tzedakah* came knocking often enough, in shul, at home, and at work. As a busy man, Chanan was happy that he need not seek legitimate beneficiaries for his money; he gave as the right cause presented itself. And as a divorced man, he was relieved not to have to visit the poorer sections of town to avoid the awkwardness of meeting his former wife. But since Rabbi Tanchuma had made it clear that the act of *rachamim* be performed personally, Chanan now found himself in unknown territory.

Ah, here comes someone poor, dressed as she is in cast-off sandals and a tattered shawl. Poor thing, she's carrying a basket of wash. Probably not even her own. I hope she won't be too proud to accept money from a stranger, though I would prefer to give it to her husband...

"Ahem. *Giveret*...er...I have some money here which I'd..."

His position was ticklish enough, stopping a strange woman on the street. But when he caught sight of the woman's face he blushed and faltered and knew not whether to advance or to retreat. For the woman he had addressed was none other than his divorcée. He was shocked to find her in such desperate straits, even more so when she filled in the details of her dire poverty.

"Here," he thrust the entire pouch into her trembling hands. "You surely need this."

༺༻

Monday. Blue skies. Sun at its brilliant zenith. But not even a wisp of smoke to be desperately, hopefully, mistaken for a cloud. Yet no one has time to look heavenward now. People are too busy scurrying about trying to fill the day with as much *chessed* as they can before Minchah. They intend to approach their Maker with confident hearts. Women laden with baskets of aromatic foods are hurrying to distribute their bounty among those more needy than they — among the old, the ill, and the infirm of the community. Little boys lead tottering old men to their destinations. Young girls tend neighbors' babies. Horses kick up wagon dust as their masters hurry about their business with an expectant air. Stomachs grumble for their usual midday fare and go unheeded. Today is different. Something is in the air. Everyone feels it, yet also feels very much part of it.

꘎꘎꘎

A Jew stood in front of Rabbi Tanchuma's *beis medrash*. In contrast to all the hustle and bustle about him, he was motionless, debating whether to retreat while there was still time or advance in the direction his conscience pointed.

Rabbi Tanchuma told us to perform chessed. *What I am about to do is* mesirah — *tale-bearing. On the other hand, today we stand as a* tzibbur *being judged by Hashem. If there is a sinner among us it is our aggregate responsibility. Should I enter the* beis medrash *and tell the* rav *what I saw today? Or should I remain silent?*

He stood a long while before he heaved a sigh and took the first step into the courtyard that led to the *beis medrash*.

It's not easy to speak against a fellow Jew, but today is no day for taking the easy way out.

"Rabbeinu," he said, entering the room where Rabbi Tanchuma sat surrounded by *sefarim*, "I must speak with you.

"I — I think I know what has been holding up the rains. Or rather *who*. Shortly after you spoke to us this morning I noticed Chanan the moneychanger heading straight for the home of his divorcée. I happen to know where she lives, and I followed him. He met her on the way and gave her a bagful of money. What purpose could this money have served other than payment? He is probably sinning with her — I can think of no other explanation. It's not his wash that she takes in, and I don't suppose she has foreign coins to trade. Since our present trouble is a collective one, for which any of us may be the cause of his fellows' suffering, we are each responsible for the actions of his brother. I felt I just had to come to you." Relief flooded his face now that he had transferred his burden to more responsible shoulders.

It was Rabbi Tanchuma's turn to look worried. "This is truly a serious matter. A fellow Jew suspected of such a sin! We must send for him without delay."

Before long a puzzled Chanan stood before Rabbi Tanchuma. "Could it be, my son, that at a time when all of Israel is seeking to perform acts of *rachamim* to be worthy of Hashem's blessing, you pay your debts for forbidden acts?"

"Whatever does Rabbeinu mean?" It was strange enough to have been called to appear before the *rav*, but this enigmatic accusation was beyond him. Rabbi Tanchuma saw that he must be more explicit. "You were seen this morning giving a huge sum of money to your *grushah*. Since you are not obligated to support her, I wonder at the purpose of the payment?" Rabbi Tanchuma gazed directly into the moneychanger's face to catch every nuance of expression — whether the surprised guilt he feared, or the shocked repudiation he hoped for. To his relief, Chanan's face expressed the latter. He waited as Chanan explained.

"Our meeting this morning was purely unintentional, Rabbeinu. I went where my feet led me, for I am totally unfamiliar with the poorer quarter. But when my *grushah* crossed my path and I saw for myself her plight, I was glad to be of assistance. Doesn't the *navi* warn us not to ignore the needs of our own flesh, which, our *chachamim* have taught us, includes even a wife no longer tied to her husband by matrimonial bonds? I only did what was right, Rabbeinu. I did not harbor any wrong intentions, *chas v'shalom*."

Rabbi Tanchuma's shoulders straightened. A light suffused his face as he rose and looked heavenward. "*Ribono shel Olam!* If one who is only flesh and blood, and subject to anger and hate, can take pity on his *grushah* to give her sufficient means to support herself, cannot You, Who are not flesh and blood, have mercy on us, the children of Avraham, Yitzchak, and Yaakov, Your servants, who look to You for food, and give us rain for our crops?"

❧

The courtyard around the *beis medrash* is filled with people. The last syllable of Kaddish after Minchah has faded into the heavy stillness of the air. Rabbi Tanchuma looks toward the sky, and hundreds of eyes follow his. An ominous gray cloud looms in the north. Ominous? No one seems to be hurrying to find shelter. It soon fills the horizon, looms overhead and hovers over the multitude. No one moves. Breaths are bated. Slowly the raindrops fall. Faces lift to greet them, mouths open to catch them. They're falling faster now, drenching the populace, but still no one moves to go home. People cup their hands to drink the pure rainwater, to bathe their dusty faces in it. What are they still waiting for?

"Our prayers have been answered, our *ma'asim* have been accepted. Let us go home and rejoice in a *seudas hoda'ah*."

"Then we shall return to raise our voices in '*Hodu laShem ki tov*'…

"…*Ki l'olam chasdo*," came the thunderous reply joined by the very thunder itself.

S.M. LIEDER

What makes one doctor more expert than another? In this fictionalized case history, a doctor tells what made him a

Specialist

"SHALOM. DR. LEVIN? This is Arzovsky speaking from the Swedish Hospital."

Arzovsky is a skilled surgeon who often operates at my hospital in Tzfas. For him to ring from Teveria was a bit unusual. "Shalom, Dr. Arzovsky, what can I do for you?"

"Reiner, Guttmann, and I have been pumping blood into a *moshavnik* from Yuta here, but we haven't been able to locate the source of his hemorrhage. We figure it may be the lungs and we want you to have a look."

"I'll be done with my rounds in about forty minutes. Figure I'll be over in about an hour."

"I'll be waiting. Shalom."

Lungs are my specialty. I had studied them under Guttmann.

If he couldn't puzzle out the source of the bleeding, why should I be able to? Well, there's a point where even the proudest doctor's pride won't interfere with a patient's life. Consultation, at least in the hospital, is where we admit we don't know everything. Even a student may come up with a point a department head has overlooked.

The twenty minutes it takes to drive to Teveria, if you don't want to overheat your engine, I spent mulling over the points Guttmann might have missed — if it were a lung problem. Tuberculosis was obviously out: no one in that *moshav* had ever had TB, nor did the man's history indicate it. The hot-air draft that was drying my face reminded me how parched my throat was. I raised my canteen to my lips. As I said "*Shehakol*" on the water, a new possibility dawned on me, one that none of the other doctors would have thought of. Only a few days ago the *Daf Yomi* had been *Avodah Zarah* 12, otherwise I might never have thought of it myself. *Let Guttmann laugh that one off if I've guessed correctly*, I thought.

Guttmann had come as a child from Minsk with his soil-minded father to colonize one of the Baron's settlements. His father, an old-time semi-*maskil*, taught his son next to nothing about *Yiddishkeit*; "next to" only being a pretext for poking fun. Then he sent the boy off for *tachlis* to Boston where an uncle put him through medical school and internship.

Old Reiner was from Leipzig, and remembered going to shul with his father. Respectful he was, of course, but not at all knowledgeable about *Yiddishkeit*.

Arzovsky, like me, was a *Yerushalmi*. That was the entire resemblance. His father, under Pines's influence, had sent him to the first "school" founded before Rav Yehoshua Leib's *issur*. He had kept him there even after the *cherem*. When the father — still a young man — dropped dead one day, the widow tried to place the boy in a *cheder*, any *cheder*. At fourteen, though, he was not wanted. She took him with her to her parents' home in Poland where he attended university and completed medical school.

Their love for things Jewish — I often wonder if that is enough to explain it — had drawn them all to Eretz Yisrael. They serve the little Galil cities and the *moshav* and *kibbutz* dots around them through the local hospitals.

My basic medical knowledge came from Reb Feivel Apteik, my uncle. A *cheder yingel* tantalized by the aroma of the powders and elixirs in his medicine closet, I had been mystified by his ability to help others more with his presence, it seemed, than with his medicines. As childless Uncle Feivel grew older, he came to rely on me more and more. I helped him mix his compounds when his aging hands trembled too much. And I guided him to and from his *bikur cholim* calls. Soon I knew the "trade." At seventeen, I had *cheishek* for formal medical study to organize the array of pragmatic knowledge Uncle Feivel had provided me. Because I was a *kovei'a ittim laTorah* and had no inclination to become a *lamdan*, my father consented to send me to his brother in London to study medicine.

The Gemara in *Avodah Zarah* I was sure they didn't know: *No person should drink from a river or from still water with his mouth or with one hand. If he does drink, his blood is on his own head, because of the danger…of leeches.* Rashi comments that the use of one hand indicates the haste of the drinker; someone scooping up water in both hands is more careful.

Besides, I was familiar with the water supply available to each *moshav* and *kibbutz* and they weren't. I knew that this patient's *moshav* had a spring in the fields where he might easily have taken a dangerously hasty drink in midwork. A leech in the man's throat or stomach was a possibility the others would have missed. If it were in his lungs, Guttmann and I would look for some way to save him; if in the stomach, Reiner could. But the real problem was diagnosis: How do you locate a leech? No x-ray machine can spot one.

At the Swedish Hospital, the head nurse and Arzovsky accompanied me to the patient's bedside. I asked for, and was handed, a tongue depressor and tweezers. The first touch on his tongue must have hurt the man intensely, for he resisted my further efforts. He was weak, though, and I was more concerned for his life than for his comfort. I forced his mouth wide open. A small dark blue mound rose near his right tonsil. Was it a distended vein or a leech?

Ever so gently, I prodded the little blue mound with my tweezers. Pulling on it — if it were a distended vein — might cause it to burst. Its jelly-like consistency, though, gave me hope. I wrapped the tweezers around it and tugged, gently of course. Off it came, out of his mouth and onto the table. I released the pressure of the tweezers and the little blue mound began to crawl.

ILYA DAVIDOVICH MOROZOV
AS TOLD TO L.M. BERKOWITZ

The true story of a Jew in the Soviet Union who gave his comrades

A Political Lecture

Now, don't overestimate me. I'm not one of your dissident "refuseniks" or human rights fighters. I'm just a plain Jew who always tried to stay out of trouble by keeping my mouth shut. But to take sides with the Russians against my own brothers in Israel — that's something I would never, never do!

In '73, during the Yom Kippur War, I was a soldier in the Army, the all-glorious Red Army of the U.S.S.R., against which the pipsqueak legions of the Israel Defense Forces didn't even stand a chance. I was in a unit of engineers stationed outside Moscow, and what we did was carry out maneuvers, setting up portable bridges and driving tanks over them. These same portable bridges were being used by the Egyptians to storm the Suez! These same

Soviet tanks were being used by the Syrians to crush Jewish bodies! Nevertheless I kept quiet and nobody knew that within me my heart was aching for those who were being stormed and crushed.

It can get pretty dull in the engineering unit, and we used to fight off boredom in one of two ways: by getting plastered on vodka or listening to the radio. I don't care much for vodka, so I brought along a Nippon shortwave radio. In this way I could listen to the foreign transmissions. Out in the boondocks, the jamming is weak and most of the soldiers tried to tune in the Voice of America or the Scandinavian broadcasts to catch the latest rock 'n' roll.

Once, while I was twisting the dial in an effort to locate the VOA, I came across a transmission in my favorite language — Yiddish! Where was it coming from? I turned up the volume all the way and through the static I managed to hear, "*Kol Yisrael lagolah.*" The Voice of Israel! This was, to me, even better than the VOA. I could keep up with all the news of the war. From that time on, I only listened to *Kol Yisrael*.

In every Red Army unit, there is a *politruk* — this is a professional lecturer who is appointed by the Party to give indoctrination lectures in Marxism-Leninism and keep the unit up to date on current events, naturally all along the Party Line. And it is his job to see that everyone is imbued with an attitude that is ideologically correct.

One day this *politruk* sought me out and, throwing his arm around me like we were the best of comrades, he said in a big, loud voice, "Ilya Davidovich! You are an educated fellow! How about giving a lecture for our unit on the Mideast situation? Give us some background history, and show how the Zionist aggressors started the whole thing."

I stared at him, and the blood in my veins turned into crushed ice. The first thought that entered my mind was: *Somebody heard me listening to Kol Yisrael and squealed to the* politruk *that my mind was being poisoned by rabid and unrestrained Zionist propaganda. But in that case he wouldn't be asking me to give a lecture, he'd have ordered me hauled off for court-martial! No, this is a test of my loyalty. I am the only Jew in the whole unit and he wants to find out if I am really Red or if I am White and Blue.*

The funny thing is, I'm not really a political Zionist at all — just a plain Jew, like I already told you. I learned about Judaism from my grandfather, and he was a deeply religious man, not a Zionist. But anyhow, just try explaining that to a Russian *politruk*, I dare you! Nevertheless, I couldn't bring myself to stand up there and slander the Israelis in front of *goyim*. My grandfather taught me: "*Chaveirim kol Yisrael* — All Jews are comrades" and we ought to stick together.

But I couldn't refuse to give the lecture either. That would really spell Trouble with a capital T. And meanwhile the *politruk* stood there grinning at my predicament, waiting to devour me with his stainless steel teeth.

"Okay," I managed to blurt out. I'll give the lecture, but I'll need some time to prepare."

"Sure, Ilya Davidovich. Take all the time you want. Just be ready a week from tomorrow night."

I prepared, all right. I asked the *politruk* to provide me with a big map of the Middle East, and I tried to remember everything my grandfather ever taught me about the history of the Jewish People. I was going to give my unit a political lecture that they wouldn't soon forget, and now that I look back on it, I am really amazed at my own chutzpah.

The *politruk* assembled all the soldiers and placed me up in front with a big wall map and pointer. And then he nodded for me to go ahead and begin the lecture. I don't know whether he realized that I could barely force myself to stand on my feet — but maybe he thought it was because I wasn't used to public speaking.

I located Eretz Yisrael on the map. "Here is Israel," I announced. "A population of two and a half million Jews. You can see for yourself how tiny it is. And now, surrounding Israel on three sides are Egypt, Jordan, Lebanon, and Syria, with a population of one hundred million Arabs all ready to push Israel from its present position, to here..." (And on the map I indicated the middle of the Mediterranean.)

"Now," I continued, "you may be asking yourself, how can such a tiny scrap of a country dominate and terrorize countries so much bigger and more populous? So here is the historical background of the People of Israel..."

And I began to tell them the whole story of the Jewish exile, beginning with *churban Bayis Sheini* when Rabban Yochanan ben Zakkai had himself hauled out of Yerushalayim playing "possum" in order to set up the yeshivah at Yavneh. I told them how the Jews have taken the *galus-shteken* to practically every country on the face of the earth and I traced our tragic wanderings through the Crusades, the Inquisition, the pogroms, and the ultimate Holocaust which destroyed six million Jews. I must admit that I really got carried away. And my comrades were absolutely astounded. They had never heard of such a thing before! After all, the Soviet history books say only that the Fascists killed ten million Russians. This was the first time they had ever heard that Jews had been murdered, too.

Yes, indeed, I really laid it on thick. I even thought that I saw a tear or two steal into some of those glassy eyes. Maybe I really moved them, or maybe they were soused on vodka, but I was inspired to go on.

To be brief, I confused the living daylights out of them.

Without deviating one iota from the Party Line, I managed to instill in their muddled minds a kernel of doubt as to who the real Mideast aggressors were. Could such a tiny country, with such a small population, really be aggressive in the face of such overwhelming opposition? Why, the other countries would crush her like a worm!

I finished speaking and asked if anyone had any questions. Instantly, every hand in the room shot up. They wanted to know one thing. The Jewish People have been through Crusades, Inquisition, pogroms, and Holocaust. How come they haven't been wiped off the face of the earth? How come they are still around? What's their secret of survival?

How do you talk about G-d before a gathering of communists? How do you tell a bunch of Reds about Hashem's promise to Avraham Avinu? I wasn't exactly anxious to slit my own throat.

"I've told you all the facts, Comrades," I said with a smile. "Draw your own conclusions."

After the lecture, the *politruk* came over to me.

"Ilya Davidovich!" he said to me. "Why didn't you tell me that you know so much about Israel? Where did you learn all this?"

"What do you mean, where did I learn it? This is my own history! This is my tradition! I learned about it from my grandfather!"

And here is the punch line. The *politruk* hadn't even known that I was a Jew! It hadn't ever entered his *goyishe kup* that a Jew in Russia could have anything in common with a Jew in Israel, any more than *he* had in common with a communist in, say, Cambodia.

Like I said, I'm just a plain Jew, not an activist. I'm just telling you about this to let you know that we Jews from behind the Iron Curtain haven't forgotten who we are.

MIRIAM SHAPIRO

One can acquire a world, one can lose a world, all in

One Moment

A NOVELETTE
RETOLD BY SHEINDEL WEINBACH

OBSCURITY IS HARD to come by in a Jewish *shtetl* where half the town has known the other half for generations. Even newcomers find it impossible to escape wagging tongues that slip into the hidden corners of the past. How was it, then, that no one knew Chaim Leib?

No one knew Chaim Leib, not for what he appeared to be, not for what he was. Outside of his name and his father's name to which he answered when called up for an occasional *aliyah* on a Shabbos or Yom Tov, he did not exist. It is an art to remain a "nobody" — not a somebody who does not count, but rather a faceless, unknown entity. Chaim Leib had mastered this art; for he was a somebody, a tzaddik, yet a *nistar* by preference. His days were spent in the study of the *Torah hakedoshah*; his nights were no different. He occasionally left the sanctuary of the shoemakers' *beis medrash* to visit his wife and children. How, then, did he escape everyone's attention if he did indeed spend all his time in the *beis medrash*? Was it maybe that there were no shoemakers in that town? The fact of the matter was that this house of study was the smallest of the seven *batei medrash* in the town, and situated as it was on a distant slope, it was rarely frequented by any of the townspeople, most of whom preferred the central *beis medrash*. Of course, that was precisely why Chaim Leib had chosen it as his headquarters. Another reason was the view. The magnificent expanse of rolling fields which seemed to burst through the windowpanes made Chaim Leib's heart expand when he looked upon them. And his expanding heart in turn expanded his mind to encompass Hashem's world through its blueprint, the Torah.

There were times, many times, when the four chambers of his heart could not contain his ecstasy. Then his soul would explode into music, the ineffable expression of sublime spheres.

The Gemara would come alive with his chanting, sometimes sweet and dulcet, sometimes sorrowful and dolorous, at times majestic, at others apologetic. Always beautiful. And as stirring as his notes were by day, they were doubly moving at night when there was no sunshine to deflect their impact and they reverberated throughout the somnolent fields with the totality of a thunderclap.

The fields that provided such inspiration to Chaim Leib belonged to a certain Count Poznanski, a wealthy gentile landowner who had built his home not far from the shoemakers' *beis medrash*. In the course of events, he came to hear the haunting melody of the Jew at study. And the count was never the same again.

Fully captivated by the music, he resolved to trace it to its source. Just as a foxhound follows a scent with his nose, the count followed his ears to where they led him, to the little *beis medrash* he hadn't even known existed. He was about to skirt the building and confront the chanter in his hideaway when the music suddenly stopped. A figure emerged and left the building from the other side. It was not that Chaim Leib had sensed an impending intruder. He had become involved in an intricate Talmudic *sugya* that defied clarification. What does one do when faced with an impasse? Seek some opening, of course. A whiff of fresh country air, an eyeful of shimmering sunshine, an earful of whispering willows are all calculated to open the heart and expand the mind. So Chaim Leib took a brief stroll to clear his mind and let it come to terms with the problem on its own. If this stratagem would work, as it usually did, fine. But if, after a few turns, he'd find his problem still not clarified, he would return to take his Talmudic bull by its horns. He would be the victor in either case.

The count found the door open. His "nightingale" had flown its cage, leaving its "songsheet" behind. Poznanski removed a five-ruble note from his pocket and laid it upon the open Gemara; a connoisseur pays well for his pleasures. Then he left as unobtrusively as he had come.

On this occasion Chaim Leib's bull still had plenty of fight in it. The spirited beast lunged forward at Chaim Leib from the pages of the Gemara, sidestepping each piercing thrust of his genius mind and returning to confound the fighter with its massive bulk and tenacity. But Chaim Leib was no neophyte matador. He approached his *shtender* courageously with determination. Small wonder that, in his total absorption, his fingers forgot to report to his mind their finding a note among the pages of the Gemara. In Chaim Leib's fingers, the note became an object to twist and turn, a cape to wave before the bull to render him blind with fury and frustration. The faster his fingers furled the paper cape, the clearer the problem became. The animal fought back furiously, but Chaim Leib parried to the right and parried to the left. The problematic bull grew weaker with each attack, the cape grew more ragged with each counterattack. Bull and cape finally both dropped to the ground, the one devoid of life, the other devoid of form and substance. And Chaim Leib emerged the victor. Not a shred remained of the five-ruble note, not a remnant of resistance to the problem. Chaim Leib now closed his Gemara and went home to recover from the terrific effort and to renew his strength for future battles.

ଔଚ

Few words are needed to describe Chaim Leib's dwelling. There was actually very little to describe: four peeling plaster walls, one table in the center of the room which seemingly remained erect by Heavenly decree, three chairs that could actually support a sitter, another table propped against a wall to serve as kitchen cupboard, two metal bed frames upon which many lumpy straw mattresses were piled high and, finally, a long wooden shelf that generously accommodated the other household items Chaim Leib owned. The blessing of the little cottage was its small front yard which served as playpen, laundry room, and general room for overflow of activities.

Heart overflowing with a victorious song of Torah, Chaim Leib entered the small room. He greeted his spouse, Kreindel, with a merry lilt to his voice. But she answered with a different tune.

"You're singing, are you?" she shrilled. "Here your children are wasting away before your very eyes and you are as cheerful as a skylark!"

"*Pekudei Hashem yesharim*," he sang back. "Hashem's commandments are righteous; they gladden the heart."

"Heart?" Kreindel croaked. "And where is your heart, Leib?"

How is she to know, poor woman? What use is it for me to explain? She'd only have another retort. If I hold my peace now she'll be happy at least with her last word. I'll leave it at that instead of incurring further wrath and having her throw pots and pans at me.

Chaim Leib's silence did prevent her throwing any dishes at him: why waste anything that still had form or shape? But it did not prevent further words. She continued ranting until the little ones set up such a wail that the four walls could not contain all the noise.

What will the neighbors say? she worried and tried to calm her little ones. In the process her own temper cooled as well and she reflected: *What do I want from him, after all? Such a tzaddik he is, studying all day, and I have to greet him like that the minute he sets foot into his own home? What kind of a wicked woman am I?* Before she had time to indulge in remorse, the pot of barley overflowed and she had to run and douse the fire. She set the table for supper and they all sat down to eat.

It was during *bentching* that Kreindel's first thoughts reawakened. "*Na'ar hayisi*," she heard herself say, "*v'lo ra'isi tzaddik ne'ezav.*" *Why are we, then, forsaken?* she asked herself. *It must be because Hashem's blessing has nothing to fall upon. My Leib doesn't even make the effort of seeking some way to bring in* parnassah. *Can money fall into a purse that does not exist?*

She turned to her husband with a gentle plea. "Leibel, I know that you don't need money. You have no use for it and can hardly recognize it. But we, your wife and children, do need it and know well enough what to do with it. Go and seek some for your wife.

And if not for me, at least for your own children's sake."

"Why are we any better than Rabbi Chanina ben Dosa?" answered Chaim Leib. "The whole world was sustained in his merit while he was satisfied with a measure of carobs from Friday to Friday. Anyway, I'm leaving. Hashem will prepare my portion."

As soon as Chaim Leib stepped out of the house the clouds dispersed and his original *simchah* returned to him. He left his problems behind and returned to the haven of his little *beis medrash* and his big Gemara. And in a flash it hit him — the answer to a difficult *sugya* that had troubled him time and again. It hit him with the impact of a fist shattering a window. Now he felt completely untrammeled. He hadn't even been thinking about this particular problem when its solution catapulted him into the joy of Talmud. As usual, his joy expressed itself in song. A song of triumph.

A feeling of supreme well-being suffused his 248 organs and limbs and 365 sinews as they joined his mouth in song. Impossible to believe that this was a man whose household lacked the bare essentials of survival!

The notes danced around the *beis medrash* that night, sweeping with them the satin folds of the *paroches*, the stiff wooden expanses of the benches, the curved iron legs of the stove, the curling plaster of the neglected walls, the swinging doors. Imbued with a life all of their own, the swirling words joined the pulsing music to escape the confining cube of a man-made room. The notes tumbled into the open and made partners with the wind, the wheat, and the night owls, and gradually faded out into the night. The pre-morning dew laved the dying notes and the breeze carried the sparkling gems to the count's window.

Accustomed to awakening to the twittering birds for an early morning constitutional in his fields, the count welcomed this new sound by leaping out of bed. *I will surely catch the marvelous musician today*, he thought. He neared the *beis medrash*, soaking up the Gemara chant into the very fiber of his being. He tiptoed up to the window and saw what he had never dreamed to see upon this world. There, in the center of the room, stood a man whose face beamed like an angel's.

The count felt sunstruck by the glory of that radiance. It was Chaim Leib who unwittingly broke the spell by going into an adjoining room to prepare for Shacharis. The count shot forward into the *beis medrash* and once again placed a new five-ruble note on the *shtender*. Then he stole out and disappeared.

Chaim Leib began his *tefillah* with total involvement, with more fervor than usual. Keeping his wife's rancorous complaint in mind, he reacted in the only way a tzaddik can. When one is in need, whom does he approach but the One Who can provide his want! *My wife*, he reflected, *claims that I fail in* hishtadlus. *Well, then, I will try in the only way I know how.* And he proceeded to pour out his heart for his wife's sake and for his children's sake.

Shacharis was important, but it had its allotted time. *Tefillah* over, Chaim Leib removed his *tallis* and *tefillin*, drank a glassful of water, and proceeded to his learning. His head felt clear and was ready for the plunge. The night's vigil had rejuvenated him. Apparently the food for his soul was sufficient to nourish his body as well. Not only was food unnecessary after the ecstasy of the past night's study, it was actually irrelevant and irreverent. As he now approached the wooden *shtender* with a clear head, Chaim Leib immediately noticed the anomaly — the legal tender note atop the Gemara. He fingered the strange paper, turned it over to find some clue as to how it had arrived at that spot. Looking about at the empty room he simply could not imagine where the money had come from. He drew the natural conclusion that

Hashem had answered the plea of a Jew in distress.

I surely owe it to my wife to bring this at once, he decided, closing his Gemara. *Her cries and complaints are only the natural outcome of her situation. She is not a bad sort, really. It is only the poverty that twists her basic good nature to make a shrew out of her.* He kissed the Gemara and went home.

His wife saw him approaching and resolved this time to keep her peace. She patted her kerchief in place, retied her apron snugly, and smiled to him in greeting. And he answered her with his contented smile. He entered the house and sat down.

"Is there anything the matter? I mean, is everything all right?" Kreindel asked.

"Why do you ask?" he answered with a smile.

"I don't know," she admitted, confused, "it's just that you never come home this early."

He didn't have the heart to tease her or keep her in suspense. He pulled out the fiver. "Here, Kreindel, this is yours."

With shaking fingers she touched the note and almost pulled back, afraid it would burn or bite. Tentatively, she touched it again and then dared to hold it. She turned it over gingerly, then snapped it taut with both hands to make sure it was real. It was real, she concluded.

For once she had nothing to say. So she turned to her husband, exclaiming superfluously, "This is five rubles, Chaim Leib, and you have nothing to say?"

She didn't wait for an answer. She clutched the note tightly and ran out of the little cottage, down the road, where her feet slowed down somewhat to a more decent pace. She bought and bought and then bought some more. Fish, meat, fruit, vegetables, goodies for the children. What didn't she buy! When she reached the limit of what she could carry home, she ended the spree and rushed home. She whirled through the peeling, preparing, and cooking, and soon had a banquet spread on a groaning table. But such a banquet! She could not recall having ever eaten as well since her own *chasunah* seventeen years before. And the children — they had nothing at all to compare this feast to in their deprived experience. They ate and stuffed themselves until they threatened to burst. But how to stop when the food still stared them in the face? At last merciful sleep overcame them. Their eyes closed and mouths opened in contented smiles, as they relived this feast in the privacy of their dreams.

Kreindel, as her husband had justly determined, was not a bad sort. It was the constant worrying where the next meal would come from that had turned her into a nag. That worry gone, she reverted to her natural, complacent self. More than that, she now made a special effort to please her husband. She cooked for him and scrubbed for him, served him, and spoiled him. The five-ruble incident repeated itself often and they were all too involved in spending it to really wonder how this heaven-sent welfare check was actually delivered. The children thrived on the good food, the adequate clothing, and the attention they received. Kreindel watched them with a new love and warmed to their happy noises where she had once answered wail with slap and whine with sharp retort.

Chaim Leib found it increasingly more pleasant to spend his time at home. In his humble castle, he was treated royally. He began coming home early in the afternoon, leaving late in the morning, and eating his fill instead of the glassful of water that had once sufficed for breakfast. He slept the sleep of one well sated. Though the quantity of his Torah study decreased, the quality remained the same. Chaim Leib's patron had nothing to complain about. The Gemara *niggun* still came forth vigorously, resonantly, and wove a charm about his gentile heart.

Who can assess the worth of an inspiring piece of music? Can you weigh it? Measure it? Count it? Poznanski began leaving ten-ruble notes at frequent intervals. And Chaim Leib dutifully brought his paychecks home to his treasurer. He enjoyed the new bounty in the house, noting how his children filled out. And as their bodies were relieved of the crying need for food, their minds were freed to learn with total involvement. Chaim Leib would take his sons on his knee and review their lessons with them, tease their brains with questions and riddles, and rejoice in their mental dexterity.

The days passed happily. Not so the nights. The more time Chaim Leib devoted to sleep in his new regimen, the more time he had for dreams. It was these dreams that disturbed his equanimity by returning to haunt him in the daytime.

Does not our omniscient Torah have a solution for every problem? Didn't Chaim Leib know what to do to dispel bad dreams? There was fasting, for one. There were the *yehi ratzons* at *Birkas Kohanim*. And then, there was *hatavas chalom* performed by three friends who heard the dream and gave it their blessing of positivity. Why did he not follow any of these possibilities to rid himself of bad dreams?

Actually, the dreams were not evil, frightening ones from which one awakens in a cold sweat with a pounding heart. Recurrent, the dreams were strange and unsettling, but not nightmares.

There was one particular recurrent dream that disturbed him. In it he was studying at his *shtender*, but the *shtender* was in his house. As he stood and studied, a huge jar descended from the caves and danced before him. He paid no attention to it in his dream, but the more engrossed he became in his study, the larger this jar grew until it reached from floor to ceiling. He could not help staring at the jar. His children entered the room one by one, each one dipped into the jar, ate, and walked out satisfied. After every member of the family had eaten his fill, he saw clearly that the jar was not diminished by one drop. There it still stood, full height, brimful. His lips still mouthing the words of the Gemara, he reached out to grasp the jar. But it eluded him and disappeared through the ceiling.

Each time he dreamed this dream, Chaim Leib would awaken and see the jar just fading before his vision. He almost felt as if he could grasp it now before it vanished from sight. *What does it all mean?* he wondered. *What in heaven or earth does this container have to do with me?* So caught up was he in making some sense out of the dream that he didn't even think of seeking a favorable interpretation through *hatavas chalom* before three men.

The count meanwhile had become deeply involved with Chaim Leib's captivating learning *niggun*. So much so that he desired to possess it. To have it for his own. To buy it and thereby acquire the rights to it. He felt that the Gemara *niggun* possessed eternal worth. In the World to Come which the sensitive count knew must exist, the melody would somehow acquire substance, some golden or silvery substance. He wanted that ethereal loveliness to be all his. He began showering Chaim Leib with twenty-five-ruble notes so that he could purchase a stake, a claim. But the more money Chaim Leib received, the less time he found for study. It finally came to the point where he only came to the *beis medrash* to take his rubles.

The inevitable showdown took place. One day as Chaim Leib was leaving the *beis medrash* confidently with his twenty-five-ruble note safely in his hand, the count stood before him. Chaim Leib eyed the gentile in surprise, too polite to ask what business he had in the *beis medrash*. But business it was.

"You don't know who I am?" the count asked, likewise somewhat surprised that Chaim Leib didn't recognize the owner of the adjacent estate, at least by sight.

Seeing his hesitation, the count introduced himself, "I am Count Poznanski, owner of these fields. It is I who have been putting the ruble notes into your Talmud book all this while."

Chaim Leib felt an icicle pierce his heart. A gentile had been subsidizing his learning? Why? What for?

And what significance did that have? He waited for the count to continue.

"I have a business deal to offer you."

"Business? Me? Here?" he asked stupidly.

"I want to buy your share in the World to Come. I want to make up a bill of sale, legally airtight, in which you sign over your share in the hereafter."

It was a blow, but a clean one. There had been no beating around the bush. The count held his bid in his hand and would not release him until he had what he wanted.

What an impossible decision to make! On the one hand, Chaim Leib could not bear to see his children grow thin, deprived of the nourishment they had lately been getting. It hurt to think how Kreindel would take lean days after having been accustomed to recent plenty. As for himself, it was not easy either, after months of rich breakfasts, hearty lunches, and satisfying dinners to go back to the pot of barley as the culinary climax of a hungry day.

But on the other hand, his *Olam Haba* was considerable, for even the most humble man does not sell a mitzvah short. Torah study is Torah study. The time alone: the days, nights, weeks, months, and years added up to a sea of Torah. Who in this world can reckon the worth of one hour spent in Torah study, let alone years and years? Chaim Leib contemplated all this and felt weak with indecision. The conflict tore at his very *kishkes*.

"I must go home and ask my wife," Chaim Leib faltered.

He went home to share the immense responsibility with his helpmate. Kreindel immediately took the practical side of the problem. "True, your share in *Olam Haba* is indeed considerable. But all the mitzvos you have accomplished, all the Torah you have learned, these are in the past. Tomorrow is another day and you have all your life ahead of you. We are young. There are still many days to be filled with Torah and *ma'asim tovim*. Just think of worriless days — days which will follow one another like sunset succeeds sunrise and sunrise sunset, days on which you can spend all your time in the *beis medrash* without care. Think of the mitzvos you can perform with *hiddur*, of the *tzedakah* you can give. Think of the children you can marry off without having to borrow or beg. You still have your whole life ahead of you, Chaim Leib. I tell you to go and accept the deal and be glad of the opportunity."

I won't be the first one to split his Olam Haba, thought Chaim Leib in desperate justification. *Shimon, brother of Azaryah, did it before me by splitting his share in return for his brother's financial support. Let my first half, then, be for the count, while I work to create for myself a bigger, better half by studying with the breadth of mind one gets from being freed from financial responsibility.*

But a little voice that Chaim Leib could not still nagged on. *That's a comparison, Chaim Leib?* it buzzed. *Look who you are driving your bargain with!* But Chaim Leib just drowned out the buzzing with the comfortable self-assurance that he had more than half of his life-years ahead of him. He was determined to sign on the dotted line.

He went to the count's house at the appointed time on the appointed day. Poznanski strode forward and greeted him like an old respected friend. "So you have come to do business with me?"

Chaim Leib could not bear to look at the happy man. He lowered his eyes and nodded affirmatively. His head pounded and his thoughts whirled around with his emotions. The little voice within made one last attempt.

Chaim Leib, whatever are you doing! How can you accept a woman's decision in dinei nefashos — *a question of life and death? Does G-d's arm not extend enough to provide for you? Turn back! Before it is too late!*

Chaim Leib saw the mysterious jar of his dreams take shape before his confused mind. Its dimensions were larger than ever and somehow threatening. A hand stretched out from it to grasp his own hot, trembling one. Chaim Leib quickly drew his hand back. Meanwhile the count had prepared paper and placed a pen in Chaim Leib's hand. The latter nearly dropped it, but the count stood over him, encouraging, wheedling him. Chaim Leib saw the huge container dance up to his very face and shatter into millions of razor-thin slivers. The pen fell from his hand. The count placed it again into the lifeless fingers and urged him to sign.

Chaim Leib summoned his failing strength and wrote his name. The count took the paper with a happy heart, leaving Chaim Leib with a heavy, broken heart, and a check for an incredible sum.

That moment seemed to Chaim Leib as if he had poured all his flesh and blood into the sheet of paper. And once spilled thereon, all his future years seemed to curl and shrivel up before his eyes. His life-force flowed through his fingers into the pen, onto the letters that wrote themselves on the paper.

With his last ounces of strength, Chaim Leib began to walk toward home.

A numbing lassitude overcame the shell of what had once

been a man. Originating in the culprit hand, the heaviness spread through the arm, coursed through the body, until it gripped his heart. That organ ceased to function, and Chaim Leib fell down lifeless.

There he lay on the ground, on the outskirts of the village where no one passed by to pity him, to bring him to decent burial. As lonely and isolated as he had been in life, so was he alone in death. Ashes and dust returned to ashes and dust.

Chaim Leib lay thus for one hour, two hours. Eventually, some Jewish laborers, returning in the twilight from the fields, spied his form by the wayside. They immediately recognized Chaim Leib. His pulseless arms and cold forehead revealed immediately that he was beyond their help. They began beating their breasts with a "*Baruch Dayan ha'emes*," blaming themselves, the community, for his death. "Who knows if he didn't die of starvation," they wailed, "in which case we are at fault. Who of us ever inquired about his family?"

Amid all the confusion and consternation, another group of Jewish peasants passed by with a wagon. They took the corpse to the *chevra kaddisha* while the first group rushed immediately to tell the *rav* what had happened.

଼ଽ଼

The *rav* held his daily between-Minchah-and-Ma'ariv *shiur* in *Ein Yaakov* in the central *beis medrash*. All the tradesmen of the village attended and sat, oblivious of the lack of space, just drinking in the palatable words of Torah. The *rav's* children, at home, were hungry as usual and clamored for food. At her wits' end, the *rebbetzin* told them to go to their father and pester him for a change. They did not hesitate to do so and ran all the way to the *beis medrash* and burst in with their hungry cries.

The *rav* was in the midst of his *shiur* when they ran right up to him. He blushed deeply and tousled their heads. "Thank G-d, they've got healthy appetites," he said sheepishly. Seeing their father brush them aside, they began to cry. The *rav* got up, took them by the hands, and led them home. The people were amazed at his presence of mind. While they waited, they convinced each other that their *rav* was a truly great man, comparing his acts to those of the tzaddikim of bygone eras.

In the midst of this talk, the *beis medrash* was again invaded, this time by the excited people who had discovered the corpse on the road. This was no commonplace event, especially among peaceful village folk. They were immediately surrounded by concentric circles of curious laymen. The newcomers undoubtedly wished to discuss the matter with their *rav*, but in his absence who could remain silent on such a subject? They had got the main points across over the babel of many voices when the *rav* returned. Immediately all were silent. The circles disintegrated as the *rav* passed through.

The *rav* listened quietly. Overcome with emotion, his body began to tremble uncontrollably. When the bearers of the ill tidings had finished, he exclaimed aloud, "Who knows if we are not directly to blame for this unfortunate man's untimely death?"

He then ordered the messengers to go and inform the widow, and to proclaim all over the village that tomorrow would be a general day of mourning. All shops were to be closed during the funeral, which everyone was to attend, to pay the community's last respects to the tzaddik, Reb Chaim Leib.

The congregation dispersed, each going his separate way, whether to *daven* Ma'ariv, tend to the *taharah*, or comfort the widow. On the following day, the whole village turned out for the *levayah*.

Most moving were the poignant words of the *rav* in his *hesped*:

"Fortunate are those departed ones who leave all their wealth for their children. Reb Chaim Leib did not benefit from this world or enjoy it one iota. He took the treasures of the world and passed on to his resting place, leaving us, who were not concerned with his welfare during his lifetime, to sigh and worry."

The people heard his words and burst into wails. The sons now came forward to say Kaddish and the *rav* once again took his place at the foot of the open grave. He publicly begged the departed man's forgiveness for not having looked after his needs in his lifetime. Then an earthen blanket was dropped to cover his body.

☙❧

Chaim Leib's soul soared heavenward. It was accosted by hordes of angels who pulled him in opposite directions.

"He is ours," claimed the good angels. "He will come with us to Gan Eden." But the evil angels pulled him downward toward Gehinnom.

"No, no!" protested the good angels. "It is only fitting that this man who knew only the four cubits of Torah all his life should find a place beneath the throne of the Almighty Who also has for Himself only the four cubits of Torah in His world. This man, who rejoiced with the Torah all his days on the nether world, will now rejoice with it in the celestial realms and reap the reward that is his due!"

The evil angels prevailed, however. "He has already reaped his reward," they announced. "He has renounced all of his Torah. Can one who shamed the Torah claim reward for honoring it?"

The good angels bowed their heads in shamefaced acquiescence.

"If that is true, then he surely does not belong in heaven. Woe to the man who must account for shaming the Torah. Woe unto him who comes here with empty hands."

※

A person dies, is buried, and his memory slowly fades from the minds of those who knew him. Such was not the simple fate of Chaim Leib. His burial did not take. The good earth of the weary Jewish cemetery of the village rejected his corpse.

On the day following the funeral, the townspeople learned that something was amiss when the day-old corpse was found outside upon its grave. The word flew from tongue to tongue and reached the *rav* faster than a hummingbird's wingbeat.

The *rav* understood this strange event as a matter of moment involving the community at large. He immediately assembled his flock and spoke to them. A deathly hush gripped them all as they heard his words:

"We don't know the reason for the body having been found outside its final resting place. Clearly, one of us here has committed some wrong and owes an apology to the *niftar*. There is only one way to make amends. We will all proceed now to the grave. Each of us will pass by the grave and personally beg *mechilah*."

One by one they followed the *rav* to the lonely place outside the village limits. In sepulchral tones they intoned one by one, "I have sinned to Hashem, the G-d of Israel, and to this man Chaim Leib," to which the bystanders replied as one, "*Machul lach* — you have been absolved," and twice again, "*Machul lach*." When every last person had been proclaimed "absolved," the gravediggers took up the tools of their trade and, for the second time in twenty-four hours, cast cold, loose earthen clumps into a hole which gaped all the way into the cold interiors of petrified hearts. Chaim Leib was, hopefully, laid to rest at last and the townspeople moved slowly away and back to the comforting forgetfulness of their day-to-day lives.

But the comfort was shortlived. Chaim Leib's body could not remain at rest among those who awaited their final awakening. On the morrow the townspeople were again rudely shaken out of their daily routine with the news that Chaim Leib's body had again been found above the little plot that had already twice been designated as his "final" resting place. The elders sped to their spiritual leader for explanation, for a solution to the mystery. This time the *rav's* reaction was different. "There must be some other reason behind this occurrence. If we are not at fault, then it must be the *niftar* himself who committed some grave transgression that is keeping the earth from assimilating his remains, some serious sin that is barring his way to the World of Truth. There must be some way that we can help this unfortunate man who is beyond helping himself now. I must find out from his wife what irreparable sin keeps this tzaddik from entering the kingdom of heaven. There may be something that we on earth can do to atone for him." He arose and set forth for the house of mourning.

Kreindel and the children were seated on the earthen floor of the tiny room. The *rav* began with gentle words, but saw at once that an introduction was unnecessary. Kreindel seemed to know very well why he had come and what he wished to know. But she sat silent and very, very ashamed. The *rav* tried a direct approach.

"Your husband is dead, Kreindel. He is being prevented by Heaven from standing before his final judgment. His soul has no place to go and therefore his body comes back to us again and again so that we may right whatever wrong he has done. If I do not know what that wrong is I cannot possibly help him. Is that not so? Poor soul! Tell me what you know, Kreindel. For his sake and for our sake."

Suddenly Kreindel could not contain herself anymore. She broke down and told the *rav* the entire story from the second time Chaim Leib discovered a five-ruble note until the episode with the count in which he had signed over his share in *Olam Haba*, on the very day that he died. Her story was interspersed with vehement self-recriminations and desperate handwringing. The *rav's* hair stood on end as the story unfolded before him. Shudders raced up and down his spine when Kreindel handed him the count's check.

"It was my foolishness that drove him to such an end," she went on. "What a good, righteous man he was, and what a mess I made of things by nagging him and giving him such evil advice. What a naive soul he was and what a conniving person I am! How undeserving and unfortunate is his lot, not to have anything of either world — to have suffered deprivation here, to have lived the life of an ascetic, and to now be cheated of his portion in the *Olam Ha'emes* in the bargain! How cruel and thoughtless I was to make him listen to my foolishness!"

She wrung her hands helplessly, desperately, as if that action could help. "Rebbi, I have told everything. I have not denied anything. Now that you know my story, do you think there is any hope for him? Is there a *tikkun* for his *neshamah* so that his body may rest in eternal peace? Oh! If only his shame could atone for him!" She then buried her face in her hands and wept bitterly.

Besides unearthing the reason for the strange happenings at the cemetery, it was also the *rav's* duty to comfort the widow. He did his best. He promised her that he would do all he could for the poor departed man.

When he reached home the *rav* called the elders of the community together.

"My friends, we are to blame for the disturbing incidents in the cemetery. At first I had thought we might be to blame directly. Now I know that we are at fault for not having shown any interest in a destitute family in our midst. In our obliviousness to Reb Chaim Leib's needs, we caused his downfall and perhaps even his death. It is our duty, then, at least to see that his soul is released from its present horrible state." And he told them the story he had just heard from the widow.

They sat around for hours, the *rav*, the *dayanim*, the community trustees, and discussed the matter back and forth. They finally came to the conclusion that they would approach the count and explain the matter to him, asking him for a release from the deadly contract. If he consented, all would be wonderful. If not, they would make a sit-in strike and refuse to move until he agreed to annul the sale.

They walked and talked, preparing their arguments for a gentile ear. The "gentile ear" meanwhile was in the midst of nostalgic contemplation.

"Those were good days, when I would awaken to the song of the Jew's study, relax after midday dinner to the soul-stirring notes of his learning, drift off to sleep at night to the clear chords of his voice. His music made me feel as clean as a freshly-bathed infant, pure and unblemished inside as well as out. But now, those hours are gone, gone until forever comes. Then they will be mine again."

In this mood, the count noticed a group of people walking toward his front gate. He recognized them as the *rav* accompanied by the notables of the Jewish community. Unaware of their difficult mission, he went to greet them personally and warmly welcomed them in. It happened to be Sunday, the day when the house servants went to squander their weekly wages at the local tavern. And so the count himself opened the door.

"Welcome, welcome," he greeted them heartily, in genuine respect. After he had settled them in the parlor, he inquired politely, "To what may I attribute this honor?"

The *rav* came to the point. "There lived of late, a pious Jew in our midst, a certain Chaim Leib. He spent his days and nights alike in the sacred study of the Torah. This particular Jew sold you his share in the World to Come. He intended to acquire another portion for himself but Heaven intervened. He died that very day, bereft of a place in the World to Come and ejected from his very grave. There is nowhere for him to go — neither body nor soul — no place that will contain or accept him. Can you actually deny this tzaddik what is rightfully his, lost in a moment of despair?"

The count's face darkened. A compassionate man, he felt for the unfortunate Chaim Leib and the fate that was his. But if his compassion meant that he must break the contract, he explained, then they must forget it.

"Our bargain," he argued, "was made in good faith. There was no coercion whatsoever on my part. I even gave him a chance to go home and reflect, to consult with his family and think things over. I have his signature on my contract, in his own handwriting, written of his own free will. What you ask of me is unfair and I refuse to comply."

He then drew out the contract and exhibited it clearly before their eyes. It shook them all up considerably. To hear of such a "devil's bargain" is one matter. To see a man's signature, a man whom they had assumed to be faultless, affixed in black and white, that is altogether another matter. A very shaking, shocking matter.

The *rav* addressed the count in a calm, confident tone. "True, you did not coerce Chaim Leib into signing the agreement. But he was nevertheless forced. He was forced by circumstances, forced by poverty, forced by his wife. Surely, had he known that he would not live long enough to acquire another claim, he would never have signed. Try to understand the situation. Have pity on the poor soul and release him from his bond. In the merit of this kind deed, the Almighty will surely bestow upon you another portion in the World to Come, a richly-deserved share."

"It is just impossible for me to agree. There cannot possibly be another portion to compare with that of Chaim Leib's — earned through the power of his Torah study. And since I am fortunate enough to own it — it is all mine. I will not forfeit it."

They tried in vain to convince him otherwise. They tried with soft words and with harsh words. They pleaded, they demanded, they begged, they threatened. But the count would have none of it. He raised his voice angrily and said, "Without that portion, my life has less value than an onion skin. What you are telling me is to virtually commit spiritual suicide! Be silent! You will never sway me."

Finally convinced that he would indeed not be swayed by any further words, they got up and bade him a weak goodbye.

The *rav* sent the *shamash* back to the village while he waited at the edge of the count's property with the remaining elders who had accompanied him there. The *shamash* was to assemble every last living soul in the village to come and join them. Then, as a group, they would descend upon the count's mansion.

Within the half hour, everybody, but everybody, was standing staunchly by the side of their *rav*. The mob-in-the-making advanced, their voices rising with every step. Inside, the count heard the threatening sound and stepped onto his second-floor balcony to see the cause of it. As soon as he appeared, the townspeople hurled threats at him, demanding that the precious slip of paper be handed over to them. Who knows to what extent the count actually feared the mob? He could easily have set his dogs on them. But he respected the Jews highly, and wished them no harm.

"Wouldn't that be defeating my very purpose?" he asked himself. "Here I am fighting for my right to the World to Come. Do I battle with the Jews at the same time? It is inconsistent. I will surely lose the very portion I mean to have if I harm any of the people outside. And if they succeed in storming my mansion and taking my contract away from me, I am equally lost."

The count disappeared into the mansion. He reappeared on the balcony several minutes later, to the steady chant of the mob, "The paper!" "The contract!" "We want the bill of sale!" He raised the precious paper, which the people glimpsed for one brief moment. Then it vanished into his mouth.

This triggered off the hotheads in the crowd. "We'll tear him apart," they shouted. "We'll get that paper back at any price." Empty threats, no doubt, but the count took them seriously. He panicked and disappeared into the house once more.

He reappeared a few minutes later, on the same balcony. He held a small can in his hand. The crowd was silent for a few breathless moments. What did he intend to do now? The count reached up and poured the can's contents — kerosene — over his head. When he was well doused he struck a match and put it to his clothing. He was a living torch within seconds, wrapped up in a *tallis* of fire. All of his last strength poured into a declaration that must have reached the very throne of the Almighty.

"G-d of Israel!" he screamed proudly, "You are true and Your Torah is true! Give me my portion in the World of Truth for I have purchased the Torah of Truth!"

The living torch slowly burned itself out. The spark of life within it was extinguished. Only a heap of charred flesh remained on the balcony, the remains of a man with an indomitable will. Outside the house there stood a group of Jews, stunned, speechless, motionless. And in the air there lingered the piercing echo, "Truth," the deceased man's last word and testament.

Why? the Jews asked themselves, as they slowly shook themselves out of shock. There was no doubt that this man had had pure intentions. *Where,* they asked themselves, *had he gotten the idea to make such a sacrifice for his convictions? And the courage?* Everyone admired the gentile's act and found his simple prayer before leaving the world the poignant climax of the stirring episode.

It was the talk of the day and continued to be the main subject of discussion on village tongues for many days to follow. The count's stature grew with each retelling of the incident, each time embellished and expanded. People began to recall prior incidents that had showed glimpses of his greatness. All sorts of stories were unearthed from the dusty past to prove the immortality of the count's soul with the wisdom that hindsight provided. With everyone adding on a detail here and there, a story finally emerged that the count's grandfather had been a Jew who in his childhood had been forced to convert.

The *rav* was busy with other, down-to-earth things. He was still concerned with what was to become of Chaim Leib. The count's death did not solve the problem; it stalemated it. But the *rav* sought some roundabout way to get Chaim Leib into Gan Eden now that his ticket had been consumed.

Again the *rav* called together all the elders of the community. It was decided that the best, if not the only, way to secure a place in heaven for the lost soul would be through Torah study in the deceased's name. The entire *Shas* was divided and subdivided, and apportioned to every man and boy who could learn Gemara. It was unanimously decided to credit Chaim Leib's "account" with the merit of everybody's study during the coming year. It was further decided to appoint round-the-clock watches in the very *beis medrash* that had heard the sweet Torah *niggun* of the departed, the shoemakers' *beis medrash*. Every group and its assignment was duly recorded in the community annals, and one *gabbai* was appointed to see that all went smoothly. Then Chaim Leib was reinterred.

It was a community project. Everyone who could open a *sefer* was involved. The sound of Torah never ceased in the shoemakers' *beis medrash*. And those who used the *Gemaros* that had been loved by and learned in by Chaim Leib discovered many comments, explanations, insights, and interpretations written in the margins. These were collected and printed and studied. Benevolent eyes and minds guided Chaim Leib's sons so that their study, above all the others', should stand their father in good stead in the world where Torah study is valued at its true worth.

Many *Kiddush Levanos* were heard in the little village. Many Rosh Chodesh blessings came and went. Chaim Leib did not leave the comfort of his earthen bed again. His slumber was final.

On the day of his *yahrtzeit*, all the learning groups were assembled in the central *beis medrash* at the request of the *rav*, every group with its study program fulfilled, each commitment complied with. The Kaddish was recited aloud for Chaim Leib. The worthy women had prepared challos and fish and honey cake for the occasion. Liquor was also not lacking. Everyone washed and partook of this communal *seudah shel mitzvah*. Chaim Leib's Torah was repeated so that, as our Sages have taught, the deceased's lips might whisper the Torah words after them. And a fund was established in his name to help needy *talmidei chachamim* persist in their study.

That night Chaim Leib appeared to the *rav* in a dream.

"You may finally rest assured, worthy *rav*, that your efforts bore fruit. Today I was allowed into Gan Eden."

"What have you been doing until now?" asked the *rav*.

"When I died, my soul rose to the portals of Gan Eden. I was denied entry to the Heavenly Court. They refused to consider my case altogether. In the words of King Shlomo they said, 'If one were to exchange a fortune for the Torah, he is to be ostracized. 'This man,' they said, 'who has shamed the Torah and its mitzvos by exchanging it for wealth is to be severely condemned. Where has such a one a place among us? To relegate him to Gehinnom is impossible out of respect for the Torah that he did study. To make a place for him in Gan Eden is equally unthinkable,' they argued. It was only after the good people of this community took it upon themselves to study in my name, and after my body had twice suffered expulsion from its grave, that the case was reviewed. It was decided to let me experience a thorough cleansing in Gehinnom.

"And so," continued Chaim Leib. "I spent this year in the cleansing of suffering and mourning. Today I was granted admission to Gan Eden through all the Torah learned in my name."

"What about the count? What happened to him?"

"When he reached the Heavenly Court he created a great stir. To his credit was his unflinching desire to be among the worthy souls in Gan Eden as well as the charity he had bestowed upon me and my family. He was duly appointed a place among the other worthy souls in the *Olam Ha'emes*."

"And where is his place?"

"I cannot even glance at his place for the brilliance it emits."

Having said all he had to say, Chaim Leib disappeared.

The *rav* awoke very excited. He said a "*Modeh Ani*" like he had never said before, washed his hands, and sighed.

"One can acquire a world. One can lose a world. All in one moment."

SYLVIE LAMM

A Little Bird Told Me

> *Too much knowledge is a dangerous thing if you hear too much and understand too little.*

CONFRONTING HIS REFLECTION in the privacy of his carpeted, sunken-bathtubbed dressing room, Bernard — (as his business associates knew him) — Berel (as his friends and neighbors knew him) Shapiro reviewed his program for the day.

Well, first there's davening, he ticked off mentally as his hand automatically guided the electric toothbrush in its inexorable fight against tooth decay. He dashed some before-shave lotion on his cheeks and put his shaver to the right one. *Then there's my daily hour of* blatt shiur, he reviewed mentally and slapped on some after-shave cologne. Running through the various business appointments and obligations he had scheduled for the day, he gave a finishing pat to his silk tie and rushed downstairs to the welcome purr of his waiting Lincoln (all warmed up and driven by Shmerel the butler).

Berel made no effort to deny it; he enjoyed the good life. And why shouldn't he reap the rewards of success that he could so well afford, as long as he did not forget the duties of the soul. To the *yeshivah bachur*-turned *balabos*, this meant punctiliousness in *davening*, Torah study, and mitzvos identical to that which had led him up the ladder of financial success.

In six and a half minutes flat, Berel reached the shul, just in time to don his *tefillin* before answering to *brachos*. As he looked around at the familiar faces before settling down, he couldn't help noticing that his *chavrusa* for the daily morning *blatt* was not in his regular place.

"That's unusual," he mused, "Yankel is always here at least ten minutes before *davening*. He's probably come down with a bad cold or something. I guess he won't come at all today. And if I know Yankel, he'll probably shlep out of bed to make the *minyan* across from him so as not to miss *tefillah b'tzibbur*." Berel verified his prediction later that day when he called his friend and found him bedridden with a case of flu.

Davening over, Berel found himself with the more demanding but less stimulating prospect of learning alone that morning. His mind and eyes couldn't help wandering as he sat by the open Gemara. And each time they would come to rest upon the old man staring out of the window. Reb Alter was reputed to have been a *talmid chacham* of stature, an *ilui*, in Russia. But the War had robbed him of family, fortune, and fame. He now spent the greater part of the day in the *beis medrash* looking out of the window. It wasn't as if he had lost command of his faculties. On the contrary, he would occasionally express perceptive, even prophetic observations about world politics or current topics of the day. But people rarely asked Reb Alter's opinion. They just did not dare penetrate the mysterious shell that enclosed him. There were even whispers that Reb Alter was one of the *lamed vav...*

Time and again Berel felt his eyes magnetically drawn to the lonely figure at the window. Then suddenly they grew round with amazement. The clouded expression on Reb Alter's face had turned to one of concentration as two little sparrows hopped onto the ledge outside. *There's no mistake about it*, thought Berel as he watched transfixed, *the man is listening to their chatter. And look! He is even nodding from time to time!*

A practical Wall-Street broker has no use for the unexplainable, and Berel felt relieved when the birds flew away and he could immerse himself in his Gemara. He dismissed the strange incident from his mind during the remainder of the day. The next day Yankel again failed to show up and Berel once more found himself in the still *beis medrash*, alone with Reb Alter and his own disturbing thoughts.

Funny, he reflected, *that I never noticed it before, but come to think of it, he always sits there by the window. And that window is always open at least a crack, even on the bitterest winter day. I remember what a tirade he let loose once when someone merely suggested he might catch cold. Oh, there they are again, the pair of sparrows from yesterday, chattering away while Reb Alter sits and listens.* Berel's curiosity got the better of him and he got up and walked purposefully over to the seated figure. But before he could summon the courage to address him, the old man lashed out.

"Look what you've done! You chased them away!"

"Who? What?!" asked Berel in feigned innocence. Reb Alter opened his mouth to reply but had second thoughts. He remained silent. Berel tried a direct approach.

"You were listening to the birds, weren't you?" he asked gently.

A stony silence.

"You always sit here by the window, waiting for the birds, don't you? What do they speak about, Reb Alter?"

Reb Alter shrugged his shoulders.

"You understand their language, Reb Alter. What strange and wonderful things do they tell you?"

"Yes, I understand the language of the birds," the old man sighed after a pause. "They tell me of things past and future, of places near and far, of people's joys and sorrows."

The wistful note in Reb Alter's voice struck a chord in Berel's heart. "Teach me, too, to understand the language of the birds," he begged softly.

"No, my son. Leave well enough alone. Too much knowledge is a dangerous thing. Now leave me be." A shadow crossed the old man's face and settled in his eyes. Berel felt he had been dismissed.

This scene haunted Bernard all day at the office. He became obsessed with the desire to understand the language of the birds. It was a yearning for the mystic shared by all mankind, the desire to dominate the unknown, to explain the inexplicable. Such knowledge, offered in addition — though Bernard did not realize it — potential power.

Berel began an intensive campaign on Reb Alter. Twice daily he approached the old man, beseeching him to teach him the language of the birds. And twice a day Reb Alter would put him off with one excuse or another. "You are too young," or "You have no use for such knowledge."

As a last resort he would argue that one must fast many days and weed the mind of extraneous matter before approaching such a study. It was unthinkable for a businessman so steeped in worldly affairs to even begin! His recurrent themes, however, were "Too much knowledge is a dangerous thing," and "You will hear too much and understand too little."

An old man cannot hold out indefinitely against the tireless efforts of an offensive campaign. There came a day when, in a moment of weakness, the old man capitulated. "All right," Reb Alter agreed. "Meet my requirements and I will teach you."

On the pretext of a business trip, Berel went off to spend a few weeks in solitude and contemplation to fulfill Reb Alter's prescription of fasts, prayer, and abstinence. Then he returned to his unwilling teacher who proceeded to keep his end of the bargain, much against his will and better judgment.

It was not long before Berel could stroll down the street and overhear conversations on all sides.

"My little one has indigestion," one mother would complain. "The birdbrain swallowed his worm whole before I had a chance to cut it up for him."

"Serves him right," came the answering chirp. "If he insists on being greedy let him suffer the consequences!"

Berel hid a smile. *Mothers are the same everywhere!*

"To think we flew thousands of miles just to find our favorite trees plagued by pests this year," came a blue jay's shrill complaint.

"It's still better than being poisoned by DDT-contaminated trees," the soft voice of a sparrow answered back.

Berel's ears were assailed from all sides. He found it difficult to walk with someone and maintain intelligent conversation without his thoughts being pervaded by tiny voices from above. But he soon learned to relegate these to the back of his mind for fear of his secret being discovered.

For a while, Berel's new awareness was merely a source of entertainment and pleasure. Only after several weeks was he given the opportunity to put his knowledge to use. Waiting by a rather long traffic light near his downtown office he heard a low-pitched voice that he had come to recognize as the cry of the seagull.

"I wouldn't go down to the Forty-Second Street pier if I were you," one called out to his friend. "My cousin told me that the new tanker that just pulled in is going to explode one of these days."

"Where does your cousin get his information?"

"Oh, he's got the most sensitive sonar between here and Tokyo. He's detected a loose screw in the hum of the engines. Remember the explosion back in '28? He predicted it a week in advance. You mark my words. Me, I'm going to do my fishing up the Hudson."

The light turned green, but Bernard had changed his mind about going to the office. Instead he told Shmerel to rush to the pier. He had too much money invested in that particular tanker…

On the wharf he flashed a small card and was allowed on board. Bernard hurried to the engine room. "Look here, Bill," he said breathlessly. "I want your men to give all the engines a thorough going over. Now! Don't ask me why; I just want it done. I'll be waiting up on deck for a report, okay?"

Bill pulled the main switch and the engines were silent. Then he began issuing orders. Bernard went upstairs to escape the unbearable heat and await the results. Within half an hour, he got a reaction.

"It's uncanny! How did you guess there was something wrong?" Bill confronted him. "If not for you this whole ship would have been blown to bits!"

"And my investment, too," Bernard muttered with relief.

Berel's next lucky break came that summer. Having shipped the kids off to camp, the Shapiros were headed for Kennedy Airport to catch the evening flight to Israel. Berel suddenly became aware of a flock of birds flying in the opposite direction. Amid the flutter of wings and flurry of voices, he could distinguish sounds of alarm.

"What's this mad rush inland? The weather looks fine to me."

"There's a hurricane brewing."

"Hurricane? Don't be a goose. The weather report at the observation tower predicted clear skies."

"And since when is the weatherman always right? My bones tell me storm, and they've never been wrong yet. You'll see."

Berel pulled up at the side of the road. "Listen, Rivka. I forgot something important at the office. I know we've been planning this trip for a long time, but it'll just have to wait another day."

The flash report that interrupted Berel's favorite symphony that evening justified his move. "Residents of Long Island are warned to fasten doors and windows and remain indoors. A hurricane is expected sometime tonight. All flights have been canceled." In succeeding reports Berel learned that his scheduled flight had made an emergency landing in Puerto Rico; the passengers had suffered various minor injuries.

By the next evening, the winds had abated, and the Shapiros went on their vacation as planned. Life went on as usual, with Berel applying his knowledge in ways that saved him time and money.

Then one day Berel fell ill. Sharp pains shot through his entire body, leaving him weak and exhausted. "Your case is too far gone, Mr. Shapiro," the doctor announced gravely. "I will do all I possibly can to relieve your pain," and he paused to prepare his patient for his prognosis, "but I fear you have only several more weeks to live."

The news stunned Berel. He could no longer eat or sleep, but tossed restlessly in bed, unable to find consolation even in the Tehillim that lay by his bedside. Only Reb Alter, the one visitor he did not refuse to see, was able to shed light upon his sudden illness.

Berel smiled wanly and struggled to sit up. "You came to see me, Reb Alter. How did you know I was ill?"

"How did I know, Berel?" Reb Alter echoed sadly. "A little bird told me… I had to come because I felt you deserved an explanation. A man must prepare himself to meet his Creator."

"So that is the final verdict, the decree from Heaven?" Berel sank back weakly on his pillows. "Reb Alter, tell me what you know."

Reb Alter gazed out the window. "It's an old story.

"Adam Harishon made the choice for us… He could have served Hashem in Gan Eden without conflicts, as do the angels, to offer daily praise to the Creator, basking in the light of *Sheishes Yemei Bereishis*. Adam chose otherwise. When he ate of the *eitz hada'as*, he acquired a heightened perception as well as a *yetzer hara* to equalize his *da'as*. And with this began the eternal conflict of man seeking knowledge. Yet knowledge is not an end in itself, Berel, as you now see. There is only one purpose in all knowledge and that is to come closer to Hashem and to serve Him more fully. If knowledge does not bring you closer to the *Ribono shel Olam*, it can only drive you further away. You chose to amuse yourself with bird language by making life easier. You could instead have risen at sunrise to hear the birds fill the universe with praise for their Creator, learning how He provides each one with his daily portion. There are countless examples, Berel…

"Don't you recall what *Chazal* said, '*Ein Ba'al Harachamim pogei'a b'nefashos techilah*'? When *Hakadosh Baruch Hu* wishes to punish a person, He attacks his property first. If the person does not react by doing *teshuvah*, he is given a poke in the ribs, that is, Hashem brings physical suffering upon him. If neither misfortune nor suffering serve the purpose, He must then strike at the person's life. That was your mistake! You thought you were very clever when you saved your investment in the ship. But you failed to see a finger of G-d in it. You saved yourself some broken bones — by postponing your flight — at the expense of the broken hearts that you will leave behind. You may be the captain of your soul, but you're not the master of your fate. Did I not warn you over and over, that too much knowledge is a dangerous thing?"

Reb Alter got up and shuffled to the door, palms upturned in despair, "…that one should hear so much, yet understand so little."

Berel's tear-filled eyes rested on the worn Tehillim by his bedside. As he picked it up, it fell open to the familiar *passuk*, *They didn't know, and they won't understand; they walk in the dark.* He sighed.

AHUVA COHEN

Forgery

An industrialist learns an expensive lesson.

As Yitzchak Levenstein sat at his desk looking over the daily mail, he felt happy. In fact, Yitzchak usually felt at ease with the world. His housewares business prospered continuously, and the wealth it brought him, invested as it was in real estate and savings, had more than doubled itself in the last years. His wife and children, if not overly affectionate, were easygoing and considerate of his wishes, and contrived to make his home his palace.

Wealth, obedient children, and a good wife. What more could a man want?

Yes, Yitzchak Levenstein considered himself a happy man. He supposed himself an object of envy and admiration on the part of his townsmen. This supposition was only partially correct, however. The envy was there, along with a type of grudging admiration and respect. But for the most part, Lodz's Jews regarded Yitzchak Levenstein with hatred mingled with fear. For Yitzchak Levenstein held the unenviable and uncontested reputation as the worst employer in Lodz. His warehouse boasted the highest turnover rate of employees in the city. Yitzchak's employees could and did expect anything from their ill-humored employer, ranging from a blow across the face to sudden and unwarranted dismissal for some slight slip-up.

And yet, Levenstein, like any man, had his redeeming qualities. He gave generously to charity and was gentle toward his family. Paradoxically, he paid his workers well and granted them liberal holidays. These qualities, together with the hard work which had brought him his fortune, earned for Yitzchak Levenstein, alongside deep dislike, a grudging respect.

But as Yitzchak Levenstein sat at his desk that March afternoon, he was conscious only of the good feeling that comes with prosperity. He reached for an envelope, slit it open and quickly scanned the contents, a letter from his bank requesting him to redeem a promissory note for 900 rubles which he had issued. Routine enough. Yitzchak laid the letter aside, determined to attend to it that very day, and continued on through the pile of mail. When he had finished, Yitzchak put on his hat and coat, meanwhile quickly glancing around to make sure that everything was in order. Then, stuffing the bank letter into his coat pocket, he quickly left the office.

The next two days passed much like the first. In fact, all of Yitzchak Levenstein's days varied little. But on the fourth day, Yitzchak received another letter from his bank, requesting him to redeem a second promissory note, this time for the sum of 1,600 rubles. Yitzchak was startled. No one could accuse him of miserliness, but Yitzchak prided himself on keeping his finances in order; he did not have to consult his ledger to know that he had not issued a promissory note for 1,600 rubles to fall due only four days after one for 900 rubles. Nevertheless, Yitzchak opened his ledger for a quick look. Yes, it was just as he thought; he had not issued the note.

But what was this?! With a slight shock, Yitzchak noted the blank space next to the date of March 8th. Then he had not issued the first note either!

Well, it must be the bank's mistake, Yitzchak decided, although it was certainly unlike them to be so careless. Be that as it may, he would soon have it rectified.

But when Yitzchak emerged from the bank less than an hour later, the worry line between his brows had deepened and his shoulders sagged. Resolutely, he turned the corner and headed toward the police station.

ଔଓ

"Now, let's go over this once more," the burly chief of police said. "You say that someone is forging your signature on these promissory notes?"

"Yes," Yitzchak replied. "The bank manager showed me the notes. I saw at once that the signature was forged, but I doubt that anyone besides myself could have detected it. It was very cleverly done."

"Well," the Lodz chief of police said. "You have nothing to worry about. We've had cases like this before and we always found our man within the week. Go home and get a good night's sleep. I promise to keep you informed."

But either the chief of police had spoken too glibly, or this forger was cleverer than most, for the weeks turned into months and still he was not found. In the meantime the forged promissory notes continued to appear with ever-increasing frequency until the sums that Levenstein was called upon to pay ran into the thousands. The police multiplied their efforts but to no avail.

It was without much hope, therefore, that Yitzchak stopped in at the police station one day to ask if there was any news.

"Yes, there is," the chief of police replied unexpectedly. He immediately added, "No, we haven't caught the fellow, but we have finally gotten a clue. A merchant from Warsaw informed us that a young man appeared in his warehouse last Sunday and identified himself as the chief housewares merchant from Lodz. He ordered a large quantity of merchandise and paid for it with some forged notes. He is obviously our man."

Levenstein digested this information in silence.

"The police in Warsaw are making every effort to track him down, using the description given to us by the local merchant. They stand a very good chance of success."

Yitzchak left the station, hopeful for the first time in weeks. But when another three weeks had passed and the forger still had not been found, Yitzchak decided on the advice of a friend to seek the assistance of Rav Eliyahu Chaim Meisel.

"If anyone can track down the forger, he can," the friend had said confidently. "He's succeeded in scores of cases where the police failed."

But Yitzchak was skeptical. A detective rabbi! What a combination. Yitzchak knew and respected Rav Elya Chaim as a great *talmid chacham*, and he had witnessed his untiring efforts on behalf of the Jews of Lodz during his years as *rav* of that city. Those things befitted a *rav*. But tracking down criminals, Yitzchak personally felt, was best left to the police. Nevertheless, he conceded that anything was worth a try, and so one sunny May morning found him on the steps of Rav Elya Chaim's house.

Rav Elya Chaim listened intently as Yitzchak related his story.

"You must understand," he said finally, "that if the police could find no trace of the forger, then I certainly would not know how to locate him."

Yitzchak's face fell, but he fought to cover his disappointment. Pretending not to notice, Rav Elya Chaim continued to chat about other matters for a short while, and then suddenly he said, "However, if you go to 17 Petorska Street you might just find the forger there."

Yitzchak was astonished.

Rav Elya Chaim continued unperturbed, "Since you don't know what he looks like, you had better ask the Warsaw merchant to accompany you so that he can identify the man. Oh, and one more thing. If you do find him at this address, don't speak to him. Just come back here and report to me."

Yitzchak left the house in a daze. An hour later he was on his way to Warsaw.

Once in Warsaw, Yitzchak lost no time in finding his fellow merchant and explaining what had brought him to Warsaw. The merchant readily agreed to accompany him and together they hurried back to Lodz.

It was drizzling when the two men set out the next day for 17 Petorska Street. They soon found the narrow alleyway, hardly deserving of the title "street," among a maze of narrow paths and filthy alleys. As they prepared to enter number 17, a dingy two-story building in the middle of the block, they spotted through the half-open window on the ground floor a young man aimlessly pacing about the room.

"I know that man," Yitzchak whispered excitedly. "He once

worked for me as a clerk in my warehouse." But his companion, staring intently through the window, appeared not to hear.

"Reb Yitzchak," he said finally in a hoarse voice, gripping the other man's arm tightly. "That is the man who appeared in my warehouse in Warsaw and offered me the forged notes. We have found the forger."

The two men hurried away.

An hour later, the former clerk appeared in Rav Elya Chaim's study in response to a summons which had been brought by the *rav's shamash*.

Rav Elya Chaim did not mince words.

"The game is up," he said. "Return the stolen money immediately, and I will see to it that the police do not find you out."

The young man turned white. Wordlessly, he reached into his breast pocket and drew out a thick sheaf of bills which he laid on the table. Still without a word, he turned and left.

Taking the bills in his hand, the *rav* went into the next room where Yitzchak was waiting for him.

"Here is your money," he said, extending it to the dumbfounded merchant. "There will be no more forged notes."

"I can never thank you enough," Yitzchak said earnestly as he pocketed the bills. "But there is one thing that troubles me. How did you know that this man who lives at 17 Petorska Street is the forger?"

"A few years ago, a young man stormed into my study, demanding justice. He was employed then as a clerk in a wholesale housewares establishment, and he complained that his employer had struck him, and then fired him, also without reason. I told him that if he would tell me his name and address, I might be able to find him another job. He complied, but left vowing revenge on the employer who had so ill-treated him. When you came to me, I thought of him immediately and I recalled that he had given his address then as 17 Petorska Street."

Yitzchak, who had turned pale and then red during the *rav's* recital, was silent.

And no one except Yitzchak and the *rav* ever knew why from that day on Yitzchak Levenstein treated his employees with respect and kindness.

SHMUEL STOCKHAMMER

The Blind Fiddler

Rav Pinchas of Koritz watches a dying man open his eyes for the last time.

THE BLIND FIDDLER. That's what everyone in Koritz called him. And when he drew his bow across the strings of his fiddle, and his gentle fingers made the strings tremble, out came melodies so sweet that they touched your heart and brought tears flooding from your eyes.

One day the town heard, "The blind fiddler is sick, he's dying." Everyone was pained, and everyone wished him a *refuah sheleimah*. And when the tzaddik Rav Pinchas heard that the blind fiddler was sick, he donned his hat, took up his walking stick, and went to visit the *choleh*.

The whole town was nonplussed. "In what way is this sick man different from all other sick men?"

"If Rav Pinchas is going to visit the *choleh*, the blind fiddler must be a *lamed-vavnik* or something!" For the rebbe, the great man of truth who could not tolerate the slightest false movement, whose ears grated at the sound of a false *krechtz*, never went to visit the sick. How often does a sick man groan not because he is sick but because someone is present! So the rebbe avoided visiting the sick for fear he might be angered by a false *krechtz*, and…

"Granted the fiddler's music is fabulous," argued the more reasonable, "he is still a Jew like all of us. So how come the rebbe is going to visit him?"

⊂₰⊃

The blind fiddler lay on his deathbed, breathing heavily. His family stood around his bed, the rebbe with them, in fearsome expectation. The rebbe did not take his eyes off the dying man for even a moment.

Time passed slowly. They heard the sick, dying man whisper to himself. They leaned forward and heard, much to their amazement, "*Nu!* Let me have another look at the world before I leave it." Suddenly the blind fiddler opened his eyes wide and looked around at all the people standing near him. A shaft of sunlight smiled on him and he smiled back.

With that smile on his face, the blind fiddler closed his eyes once more, forever.

⊂₰⊃

After the funeral, the rebbe explained what had happened.

"This simple Jew, who was, apparently, a Jew like all other Jews, was not as simple as people thought. The man had a great *neshamah*. No wonder his music was so appealing and inspiring: It came from a pure source.

"Since he sensed that his purpose in life was to make Jews happy, he decided to make his *parnassah* from being a *klezemer*. As he thought the matter through, he realized that, despite the pleasure he would give other Jews with his music, there was a drawback. His mitzvah would often be derived from an *aveirah*. By appearing at all kinds of Jewish *simchos,* he would necessarily see things he ought not to see; things that would harm his eyes and his soul. Yet his very soul bound him to this kind of work.

"How did he solve his problem? He finally concluded that the only possible solution was not to see. In other words, to go blind.

"How does one go blind? To put out your eyes with your own hands is *assur*. So one fine day the word went out in the town of Koritz that the fiddler was blind. From the moment he closed his eyes so determinedly, he simply did not open them again until the final moment of his life."

Translated from Mesilah, Kislev 5732, *with permission*

SHLOMO BEN-DOVID

Genuine leadership implies readiness to pay

The Price

*I*F EVER THERE was a golden boy, Benzion was the one. Everything he touched turned to gold. Everyone he smiled upon was bathed in sunlight. A modern observer would have labeled Benzion's magic "charisma"; his generation might have called it "magnetism." But to those who knew Benzion, such superficial terms fell far short of defining the myriad qualities so deeply ingrained in him.

Benzion did everything seemingly without effort, whether it was his weekly night-long stand of *mishmar* learning, his intuitive grasp of a difficult *sugya*, or his assuming center-stage in any situation. And he maintained his focal position not only through some intangible charisma-magnetism but through sheer innate goodness. Elders and peers alike gravitated toward him, glad for the warmth he radiated.

It seemed natural, for instance, when Benzion suggested a sing-out, and it was hailed by students and *rebbi* alike. The tightly-knit group of yeshivah *bachurim* who devoted their whole week to intensive study felt a need to release pent-up emotions, and his friends quickly agreed to Benzion's suggestion to spend a midnight hour singing under the stars. They found themselves a grassy knoll just outside their village and under the friendly, starry, midsummer sky sang songs close to their hearts. They sang *niggunim* in *Lashon Hakodesh* and in Yiddish. The villagers slept peacefully on while the youthful voices spun their melodies into a cloak of togetherness and love. The magic never flagged with Benzion at the center of the circle, as the night became a series of pleasant hours stolen from sleep rather than from study. Only dawn itself dissolved the spell, reminding the boys that the Creator Whose praises they had been singing all night had other plans for their day.

Summer nights have a way of spinning themselves away into gossamer nothingness and, before one knows it, autumn has come. And that idyllic summer, more than others, dissolved into mist and was no more. Many things changed. Benzion stopped attending yeshivah. As the son of a successful lumber dealer, Benzion was expected to help out in the business. But by no means did he neglect his learning. Mornings he would study by himself while during the evenings he would join his friends in group study.

But as winter drew on, people noticed a change in Benzion. His manner was the same; his parents still took pride in the friendly, engaging salesmanship that boosted their business volume. It was his actions, rather, that puzzled people. On Sundays, when the lumberyard was closed and Benzion had the day to himself, he would take his skis and disappear.

Without a Gemara under his arm, without even a Tehillim in

his pocket, he would be gone the entire day, and when he finally did return, late in the evening, he managed to evade questions with his usual charm. No one could begin to understand a where, what, or why for his actions.

In normal times, people might have paid more attention to Benzion. But these were troublesome times. The whole of Europe was in upheaval as Hitler's death machine trampled relentlessly on, striking terror in human hearts everywhere.

A Jew's first refuge is his *tefillah*, whereby he fortifies himself for whatever bitterness lies ahead. And since it is sinful to sit and wait for miracles, the village Jews tried to find refuge in the neighboring farms, among kindly gentiles. It wasn't easy. There were also the typical few who deluded themselves into thinking that the storm would pass without touching them.

And so it was that the actual attack caught the little village not quite by surprise. The long-feared dawn knock on the door that foretold doom was not the Gestapo yet, thank G-d. But the accompanying voice warned the occupants of house after house that in an hour's time the Germans would indeed be upon them.

Good heavens! Was it too late to do anything now? Where could one go? In what direction did one escape the ubiquitous German monsters? On the border of panic, the village Jews heard a familiar, reassuring voice from the outside: "Whoever has not prepared a hiding place is to meet in the woods behind the village."

A sigh of relief — momentary reprieve. Some last minute packing of absolute essentials was followed by a mad rush to the woods outside the village to see if the voice in the dawn had not been a figment of tortured imaginations.

It was a silent group that met in the woods. Without a word, without a question, they boarded the two trucks that whisked them silently into the mountains beyond. No one had words to thank Benzion, their benefactor. Death was still just a cannonshot away. Besides, they knew Benzion. Doing good was inherent in his nature; he always shrugged off thanks like a duck water. If he had now assumed leadership of his fellow townsmen, it was because the cloak suited him.

The secret hideout that was their destination was a single acre of land, hidden deep within a ring of mountains, accessible only to those who knew where to look. When the travelers arrived at their destination, two large huts were waiting for them, erected by Benzion himself during the past Sundays of his disappearances. But he had not worked single-handedly. His friends had helped Benzion gather the materials which they had transported themselves on those Sundays.

A home away from home awaited the refugees, complete with straw mattresses, tables, and chairs — all handmade — and even toys for the children. And of course Benzion was not the one to forget a *sefer Torah* and other *sefarim* — the Tree of Life to those who cling to it.

The group of fugitives, like bewildered sheep rescued from slaughter, did not even realize the extent of Benzion's efforts. Not till a day or two had passed and they had grown accustomed to their new surroundings, did they learn the full story of the pre-dawn warning that had saved their lives. Benzion had at considerable risk established a link to an S.S. officer who promised to forewarn him of a German invasion — for a price. But the price was a small one considering that not one of the Jews had fallen into German hands.

It was not long before a daily schedule was established for the fifty souls in the hideout. Benzion himself was excluded since the burden of leadership required that he spend days on end away from his charges. Rumor had it that he would dress up in German uniform and scout around neighboring villages to pick up necessary information. As the months passed, Benzion's reports on military affairs grew more favorable. The Russians were advancing, the Germans were retreating, and the end of the war was imminent.

The snows melted. Pesach approached with all the preparations that preceded it. A lot of energies that might have gone into housecleaning were now diverted into matzah baking. The group had planted its own wheat, harvested it, threshed and milled it, and finally climaxed their labors by baking matzos. The Seder would, of course, be a communal one. Most activities were done together since the group felt itself a unit, an extended family.

The Seder was conducted in family spirit. The men led the Haggadah-telling while the children responded eagerly. The women were content to sit back and survey the fruit of many hard days of labor — the snowy white tables laden with the traditional food that even their exile had not denied them. It was a lively Seder that lasted long into the night with Benzion in a muted limelight. He tried to escape the glory that was due him as provider and benefactor. Finally all the gratitude swelled up and crescendoed into a demand for a speech.

Benzion's words were simple but explicit. "There is a time to speak," he quoted the words of *Koheles*, "and a time to be silent. When the Jews were on the brink of Yam Suf with disaster facing them from all sides, that was the time for action rather than words. And it was their subsequent action that made Hashem come to their aid. Our case is similar to theirs for our lives are in imminent danger, too. Let us, in this moment of dedication, make a decision in terms of action. Let us, here and now, consecrate our lives to *Hakadosh Baruch Hu*, and if necessary sacrifice our lives for His Name. Who knows what will become of us — of the Jewish nation, for that matter? Who will survive? Who will, G-d forbid, perish? We must be Hashem's soldiers; we must pave the way for Mashiach for these are surely times that precede his coming."

Thunderous applause hailed the end of his brief speech, and was suddenly cut short when the door flew open. Some hearts stopped beating while others thumped wildly. What outsider could be visiting them now? Their worst fears were realized as they saw the dreaded uniforms of the S.S. officers.

"Well, well. So we have finally caught you in your neat little hideout. Isn't it cozy here all together?" their commander sneered. No one dared move. Not with machine guns pointed right into their midst. The sneer turned into a nasty bark. "Who's the leader here?"

No answer. Only the fearless stepping forward of Benzion.

"Let's see your kingdom!" the officer barked, not unaffected by the majesty of Benzion's stance. Benzion strode forward, slowly, deliberately, out of the first building, past the second structure, and past the storehouse, to a fourth little building. He was followed by the group of soldiers. This hut was usually locked, and no one but Benzion ever used it. Within minutes there was a huge blast that knocked over the terror-stricken group in the first cabin. The explosion that had blown the shack to bits had killed all the German soldiers — along with Benzion.

This, too, Benzion had anticipated in his phenomenal sense of preparedness. The secret explosive device that had brought death to the Germans and granted life to his townspeople had claimed Benzion as the price.

Adapted by Sheindel Weinbach from Yehudim — Al Yei'ush, *with permission*

TZVI ZOBIN

How would you fare if you were woken in the middle of the night to submit to an immediate

Audit

BANG! BANG!

Judah turned over and looked at his bedside clock — one o'clock! Who could be knocking at a time like this? He slipped on his housecoat and padded softly to the front door.

Looking through the peephole, Judah could hardly believe his eyes. A figure out of Meah Shearim was standing there — long *peyos* and beard, long black coat and wide-brimmed hat. The main worries in Purple Heights were the Toussainters and the Swahili; this man's face was too kindly looking to be at all homicidal. So Judah pulled off the chains and opened the door.

"Good evening, Yehuda. I'm so sorry to disturb you at such a late hour, but I have some very important business to discuss with you and I couldn't come at any other time. May I come in?"

Openmouthed, Judah stepped dumbly to one side. With a quick kiss of the *mezuzah*, the stranger was in and sitting by the lounge table.

"No doubt you are wondering who I am. Well, my name is Elya, and I am an accountant. I have been sent to do an audit of your business. I have so much to do, I've only now been able to fit you in."

Reb Elya was busy emptying out his attaché case — files, papers, and a calculating machine were soon spread all over the table.

Judah began to recover from the initial shock — and was surprised at his own acceptance of the situation. It suddenly seemed perfectly normal for someone to walk into his home at 1:00 a.m. and start an audit.

"But I already have a very good accountant," he managed at last to blurt out.

"Oh, I know," replied Reb Elya, "but you don't use him as you ought to. No, indeed!" Reb Elya ruffled through some files. "From our records it appears that you have been severely over-earning and not devoting enough time to *avodas hakodesh*. In fact, so far as I can see, you are totally bankrupt!"

"What does that mean?" asked Judah uneasily.

"Well, it means you have been misusing your time and spending too much of your energies on unimportant matters. If you are declared bankrupt and don't make a suitable settlement offer, a Notice of Seizure is issued." Reb Elya looked grim.

"I don't understand," said Judah.

"It means, my dear Yehuda, that your material being is liquidated and your *neshamah* returned in disgrace to where it came from."

As the full implications of Reb Elya's words dawned on him, Judah's face turned red, then a ghastly white.

"But! But! But!..."

Reb Elya's face softened a little. "Don't worry too much, Yehuda, the Court is very fair and will normally accept any reasonable offer — as long as it is a genuine one."

"This is terrible, I just can't think straight! You mean that..."

"It will be easier if we take this step by step. Get comfortable because we've got a few hours of hard work in front of us. Now," Reb Elya took out a largish red folder. "Your name is Yehuda ben Chaim Toglieb, correct?"

Judah nodded.

"You are now thirty-two years old and left yeshivah ten years ago. You entered your father's law practice, married soon after, went through law school with flying colors, and now have your own practice."

Judah nodded his assent.

"Now, when you left yeshivah, you understood that a Jew is only allowed to work in order to learn without having to rely on others."

"But I do learn — I have a *kevius* of two hours a day in the evening when I come home from work," blurted Judah.

"I know," replied Reb Elya, "but at the rate you earn, you could work far less and learn far more! What I have to do now is to make an inventory of all your expenditures and see how much you have overspent and therefore under-learned. What I do is as follows. First, I note each item. Next to each item I list the price you paid for it. Then I list the amount you could have spent and still gotten by. Then the excess I convert into the amount of time you spent earning that money, and that is the time that you underspent in learning in respect of that article. Follow?"

Judah shook his head. "No!"

"For example, the necktie you are wearing —"

Judah looked down and was surprised to see that he was fully dressed.

"How much did you pay for it?"

Judah thought for a moment. "It's a very good one — I think about eighty-five dollars."

"Right. Now, at that time were there cheaper neckties available?"

"Yes, of course," replied Judah.

"Okay. How much could you have paid for a cheaper necktie and still looked decent?"

"Oh, I suppose around fifteen dollars."

"So you overspent on that necktie seventy dollars." Reb Elya got busy on his calculating machine. "Now, you earn about three hundred dollars an hour before taxes. It takes you about five minutes to earn twenty-five dollars. So to overspend seventy dollars on your necktie, you gave up fourteen minutes which should have been spent learning — almost a quarter of an hour of *bitul zman* for a fancy necktie! Was it worth it?"

Judah looked very glum. "Of course not," he admitted, "but I didn't look at it that way."

"Well, you've got the idea now; let's get down to work."

"I'd better have a cigarette," said Judah. "I think I'm going to need it."

❦

Two hours and twenty-four cigarettes later, Judah and Reb Elya leaned back in their chairs.

Judah's face was ashen gray and drawn. "What's the total?" he asked hoarsely.

Reb Elya pushed a button and the calculator chattered for a few moments. Reb Elya tore off the paper ribbon. "Whew! Twenty-one thousand, seven hundred and forty-two hours, twenty-five minutes and thirty seconds."

Judah's face sunk down even further. "I'm finished!"

"Wait a minute. This calculator is special. It is computerized and programmed with a profile of your abilities. So let's see what you could have learned in that time." Reb Elya pushed another button and the calculator chattered again.

"*Oy yoy yoy!* You could have gone through *Shas* twice with *Rashi* and *Tosafos* and had *semichah* in *Orach Chaim* and *Yoreh De'ah* from your *rosh yeshivah.*"

Judah gasped.

"But that is not all," Reb Elya continued. "That is at the simple rate assuming that you had kept up at the same rate as when you left yeshivah. In fact, however, you could have improved with each *blatt*, so a compound rate would be more realistic."

A third button went down, and the result came chattering out.

"With your abilities, you could have been a *baki* in the whole of *Shas*, had *semichah* in the whole of *Shulchan Aruch* and have gone through *Yerushalmi, Tosefta, Mechilta, Sifri, Sifra,* and more. *Oy!* What a waste of time! Ten years!"

Judah looked up, despair in his eyes. "What should I do? I'm finished!"

"No! No! Yehuda, *chas v'shalom*! Don't give up hope. Just have a deep think and then make a reasonable offer, and I'm sure it will be favorably received. Meanwhile I'll clear up my odds and ends and let myself out. You are exhausted, *nebach*. Go straight to bed and leave the thinking until morning."

"Thank you very much, Reb Elya, thank you very much!"

Judah tottered back to his bedroom and flopped into bed. Rachel, his wife, looked up. "Have you been sleepwalking again, Judah?"

"No, dear. I've just been through an audit with Reb Elya and I'm bankrupt. I'm sure I'm bankrupt."

By the time Rachel had recovered from the answer, Judah was fast asleep and she had to wait for morning.

⊙₴⊙

Before getting out of bed, Judah had a long think. He didn't want to tell Rachel the whole story because she'd never believe it. She would assume it was another one of his dreams. Her hand would reach for the telephone and she'd have Dr. Minsky 'round for another of his "frank chats." Usually he didn't mind — it kept Rachel happy and it amused him to listen to the doctor's *meshugassen* but now he was in no mood for that sort of lark. He had some very serious thinking to do. So he decided to play it down as much as possible and make his own arrangements. His plan failed.

"Judah!"

"Yes, dear."

"What is this pile of cigarette butts doing all over the lounge table? What were you doing last night?"

"Wow, I'm late for *davening* — we'll talk later." Judah ran.

Over the breakfast table, Rachel changed her tactics. "Look, Judah, I'm your wife and I can tell when you're trying to avoid an issue. What is the matter? Please tell me."

Judah gave in and told her the whole story.

"Well, it could still be just a dream. You could have sleepwalked to the lounge, and smoked your way through two packs of cigarettes." Rachel's hand crept toward the telephone.

"No, dear, I insist! No Dr. Minsky! Even if it was just a dream, the *cheshbon* is a good one — I am working too much and not learning enough. I was the best *bachur* in yeshivah, remember? I imagine I could have been a *baki b'Shas* by now."

"But how can you cut back work now? We have our vacation

in Miami Beach in two months' time. The house is filthy. Look — it needs a good redecoration, or I'll go mad."

That's why we have no children; she is so tense and gets so excited so easily. A few children are what she needs. A few children running 'round the place and she'd be okay.

"My dear," he said aloud, "it could be you'd get your vacation in Miami Beach, but as a widow, *chas v'shalom*. This is no light matter."

That silenced her, and Judah left for the office.

At the office, Judah went through all his files, throwing out all the bothersome and unprofitable ones, and all those that didn't seem too promising. The throwaway pile didn't seem very big, so Judah did another search and threw away a few bigger, more time-consuming clients. Then he dictated a standard letter to be sent to all of them, telling his ex-clients that due to the pressure of work he was no longer able to act on their behalf.

Then he got on the phone to some of his ex-yeshivah *chaveirim* and arranged *sedarim* for another two hours a day.

That seems like a reasonable settlement offer — two extra hours of learning every day, Judah thought. And he was quite pleased with the new arrangement.

In the evening he told Rachel who, naturally, blew her top. "Why two hours?! Isn't an extra hour enough? Which of your friends learns four hours a day? You're a professional man, not a *kollelnik*! Is your Reb Elya going to send you a check each month to pay for all our expenses?"

Judah was adamant. As he told Rachel, it was worth economizing for the extra two hours of learning a day. So they economized, and Judah kept to his *sedarim* rigorously.

○○○

BANG! BANG!

Judah turned over and looked at the clock — *one o'clock — just like two weeks ago, perhaps it's Reb Elya again!*

Judah dashed out of bed and ran to open the door.

There, to his surprise, was Joe the postman.

"Sorry to trouble you, Boss. Special Delivery. G'night!"

Judah closed the door and opened the long manila envelope.

SUPREME COURT OF JUSTICE
Notice of Seizure
It is regretfully necessary to inform you that your settlement offer has been rejected as being insufficient…

"There is still hope, Yehuda!"

Judah spun around and saw Reb Elya seated at the lounge table.

"But what was wrong with my new schedule?" Judah was too shocked to wonder how Reb Elya had gotten there.

"Tut! Tut! I can see we need a good chat. Sit down in one of your armchairs and make yourself comfortable."

"I gave up two hours of work! I admitted I had been over-earning and not learning enough. I even had a fight with my wife about it. Did you expect me to give up work completely and join a *kollel*?" Judah gave a laugh.

Reb Elya looked up sharply. "It wasn't your offer that the Court objected to, it was your whole attitude to Torah! Do you think that Torah is just a hobby, *chas v'shalom*, to be indulged in when you can spare the time? Don't you realize that you were created for Torah and mitzvos; everything else is insignificant?"

"But four hours a day and *davening* three times a day…"

"You're still missing the point, my friend. Tell me, when you go to work or go to a meeting of your club, why do you wear a $500 suit?" Reb Elya asked.

"Well, I've got to look decent and respectable; after all, I meet important people," Judah replied.

"So tell me, Yehuda, why on Sunday afternoon, after you've finished washing the car, do you go to shul in your old *shmattes* and *daven* Minchah before the Most Important Ruler of rulers without changing your clothes?"

Judah opened his eyes wide in amazement — he was dumbstruck. Reb Elya continued, "And how does the concentration you put into work compare with the concentration you put into your learning? Do you learn when you are fresh and leave the work until you are tired, or the opposite?" Reb Elya rifled through one of his files. "Out of the 11,792 times you have *davened* the Amidah since you left yeshivah, you concentrated on only four of them; your work and law studies interrupted most of the others. Similarly, of the 36,973 *brachos* you have made, only fifty-three conformed to the requirements of minimal forethought laid down by Section Five of *Orach Chaim*. Under that same section, all but eighty-three of the 4,214,973 *Sheimos* you have said were disqualified. You have made no attempt to go deeper into your learning or your *davening*. Whereas in your work, every word you say is weighed and chosen carefully and you are continually delving deeper and deeper into your law studies." Reb Elya leaned back in his chair. "In short, your *avodas hakodesh* has been pushed back to second place, and you have forgotten your real *tachlis*."

"And for that crime I must pay with my life?"

"Well, it's not so much a punishment as a preventive measure to keep you from harming yourself even more. You have been endowed with the abilities to become a *talmid chacham* and a tzaddik. If you squander such rare abilities on *goyishe* laws and their *fardreite sevaros* you are doing yourself immeasurable harm and it is better for you if you are removed from this world."

"But Reb Elya, you said before that there is still hope for me," pleaded Judah.

"Correct, Yehuda," replied Reb Elya. "At the moment, the Court decree has been issued on a Red-for-*Din* Seizure Form, effective immediately. However, if you feel that you can now look at things differently and you can see where you have gone wrong, we can apply for a Writ of *Rachamim* to stay the Notice of Seizure. This means that the Notice isn't put into effect straightaway but is held in abeyance. Then, of course, if your subsequent actions convince the Court, the Notice can be revoked."

"Oh, I'm sure I can! Please let me have another chance!"

Reb Elya took a form out of his case and began filling it in.

"It is a very wise decision, Yehuda. After all, I think your children will stand a better chance of growing up as really *frum* Jews if their father is a great *talmid chacham* than if he were just a lawyer."

"But we can't have children, Reb Elya. The doctors told us so."

Reb Elya looked up, a twinkle in his eyes. "Are you telling me that as a lawyer or as a Jew?"

Judah didn't understand clearly what Reb Elya meant. After he had read through the form, signed it, and bade Reb Elya farewell, one thing was very clear: he had to change his whole way of life and he had to face Rachel. *Which will be harder?*

Slowly he walked back into the bedroom and got into bed. Rachel looked up. "Another dream, Judah?"

"Yes, my dear — and I've only just woken up."

"What do you mean?"

"I'm giving up work and joining a *kollel*. I'm going back to Torah." Yehuda was amazed at the way it slipped out of his mouth. "And we're not going to discuss it now. It will have to wait until morning. Good night!"

ଓଃ୪ଠ

Rachel tossed and turned. *Crazy! He must be dreaming. Fancy Judah going back to yeshivah! Huh! Will he grow a beard like my grandfather had? He'd look fine in one. What a* talmid chacham *Zeida was! People always used to come to him for advice and to answer* she'eilos. *And the way people used to stand up for him when he came into the room! But for us it's impossible. How could we manage? What about Judah's practice?* So the thoughts went racing back and forth through her mind for what seemed like ages and ages. Then, suddenly, knocking on the front door disturbed Rachel's reveries.

ଓଃ୪ଠ

Rochel slipped on her robe and slippers and hurried out.
"Who is there?"
"Mr. Goldberg and Mr. Korley. We have an important she'eilah *for your husband. It's urgent."*
Rochel was surprised to hear the voice of the president of the kehillah. Quickly, she unlocked the door.
"Please make yourselves comfortable. I'll go and tell my husband you're here." Rochel hurried to the study door, knocked gently and went in.
"Yes, Rochel?" Yehuda looked up from his sefer.
"Mr. Goldberg and Mr. Korley have an urgent she'eilah *for you, dear. They're waiting for you in the dining room."*
Rochel took Yehuda's long black coat from the hanger and brushed off some fluff.

"Okay, I'll be out in a moment. You must go back to bed."
"I'll just check on the children. Try not to go to bed too late."
Rochel popped her head into the children's room.
"Who is it, Mommy?"
"Why aren't you asleep, Eliyahu? Two people came to ask Daddy a *she'eilah* about an important matter. Now I'll tuck you in and you go right off to sleep."

༺༻

Rachel found herself back in bed. She smiled. *My husband the great* talmid chacham. She felt herself relaxing. Muscles she never knew were tensed gently relaxed and she drifted off into a deep, calm sleep.

AHUVA COHEN

Who could know what evil lurked in the heart of

The Stranger

THE CANDLE CAST its dim light on the page, illuminating the figure bent earnestly over the heavy green ledger.

He was of medium height, with mousy brown hair, deeply sunken eyes and a stubble of beard. His face wore a habitual expression of cynicism. The fingers that held the short stub of a pencil were long and slender, the fingers of an artist.

At the moment, however, Binyamin Katz was engaged in an activity that bore no relation to art. He was going over the monthly accounts. "*Oy yoy, oy yoy,*" he hummed tonelessly to himself as he worked, rapidly adding up figures.

He snapped the ledger shut angrily and jumped up, nearly upsetting the candle.

"Losses, losses!" he muttered sullenly. "At this rate I'll have to close up soon and go into the poorhouse. And all because of that miserable rival of mine, Shmuel. And whose fault is it that he opened an inn only three blocks away from mine? Rav Elya Chaim Meisel! I took the scoundrel to *beis din*, but the high and mighty *rav* of Lodz gave his *psak* permitting it. 'There's no problem of *hasagas gevul* here.'" Binyamin imitated the *rav* in a mincing tone. "'There's more than enough business for both.'

"Sure, sure," Binyamin continued bitterly, "that's why my account books are so dismal."

Although Binyamin didn't realize it, his voice had grown louder and louder until he was almost shouting. The noise awakened his wife, Freida, who was asleep in the next room.

Freida was the image of her husband but their personalities were markedly different. The fifteen years of a childless marriage that had turned the once good-natured Binyamin into a bitter and cynical man, had had no such effect on Freida. She remained a cheerful and loving woman with a strong sense of right: as generous of heart and hand as her husband was miserly, as strong of will and spirit as her husband was weak.

Now she hastened into the room on slippered feet, her wrapper clutched tightly around her.

"Binyamin, what is the matter?" she asked, a worried frown on her face. "Don't you feel well?"

"I'm all right," muttered Binyamin.

"You've been working too hard lately," Freida went on. "You'll have a breakdown if you go on like this. I'll call Dr. Brenner tomorrow."

Binyamin had been clenching his teeth together to keep from talking. He did not want to tell Freida that he was upset over the inn's accounts. 'Cheapskate,' she would tease him, as she always did. *What do women know about these things anyway*, he thought angrily.

But at her last words, unable to control himself any longer, he exploded.

"Doctor?! You will not call a doctor, do you hear? I won't hear of it. You must think I'm a millionaire the way you carry on. *They* can afford to pay doctors' fees, but I can't. I'm a poor man."

Binyamin glanced up suddenly and met Freida's eyes. She gazed steadily into his face for a full minute until he was forced to drop his eyes in embarrassment.

"I must be tired," he said uneasily.

But Freida acted as if she hadn't heard. When she spoke, the sadness in her voice was unmistakable.

"I see. I see now," she said slowly. "You've been going over the account books, Binyamin, haven't you?" It was more a statement than a question and without waiting for her husband to confirm her words, Freida went on.

"I suppose you're going to tell me about all the losses that we've suffered in the last five months. You know as well as I do that there haven't been any losses. True, our profits are less than they were, but so what? What do we need so much money for? To take with us to the grave?" Freida's voice broke as she thought of those happy first years of their marriage when they had made plans... Oh, so many plans! How they had scrimped and saved to move into a larger house so that when there would be children... How they had once laughingly calculated how much they would have to save every year, so that in eighteen or so years they could stand their as yet unborn eldest child under the *chuppah*... And then had come the long years of waiting and praying and hoping against hope that a miracle would happen...

"But none did," Freida unconsciously continued her thoughts aloud. But at a startled glance from her husband, she stopped abruptly.

"What are you talking about?" he inquired uneasily. Freida sighed. "About your so-called losses," she replied. "They aren't losses at all, they're only a slight decrease in profit. Only you're such a pessimist that to you it seems like the last step before bankruptcy. Why do you begrudge Shmuel half of your customers? Don't you think he has to earn a living, too? There are more than enough Jewish travelers coming to Lodz on business, or passing through the city, to fill both inns and an extra one besides. Besides, Binyamin," Freida continued quietly, "no one is really to blame but yourself. If you were a little more pleasant to the lodgers, and didn't give them inferior service, and lowered your prices like I've told you a million times, business would pick up. Is it any wonder that people choose Shmuel's inn over ours?"

Binyamin felt ashamed. *She's always right and she knows me like a book.* He could never hide his faults from her. His shame gave way to anger, and he turned upon her furiously.

"Will you stop nagging me already?"

To his amazement, Freida's eyes filled with tears. "I feel sorry for you, Binyamin," she sobbed, "very sorry." And sobbing, she ran from the room.

Binyamin started to follow her, but his legs felt like lead. Rarely in their marriage had Freida given way to tears.

Self-reproach flooded Binyamin, pushing all his other emotions aside. *How can I have done this to Freida*, he wondered, *how could I hurt her, make her cry? I'll make it up to her,* Binyamin vowed. He would do something to earn her respect.

"I feel sorry for you," Freida had cried, but Binyamin was determined to change all that. He would make his wife proud of him, he would show her. He would show them all; his dissatisfied patrons, Shmuel, and Rav Elya Chaim...

Like the pointed blade of a knife piercing his flesh came the recollection of Rav Elya Chaim. Never would he forget that sticky summer day when he had stood eagerly in the *rav's* study, wondering why he had been summoned. Perhaps a delegation of *rabbanim* was coming to Lodz and Rav Elya Chaim wanted him to put them up. Perhaps the *rav* needed Binyamin's help in some important community affair. Perhaps...

But Rav Elya Chaim's first words had deflated those happy thoughts and indeed had deflated Binyamin himself as neatly as a pinprick deflates a balloon. The *rav's mussar* was short but powerful, and he spared no words as he laced into the innkeeper, reproaching him for his greediness, his shoddy business practices, and his refusal to give *tzedakah*.

Binyamin had stood silent and shamefaced, not daring to open his mouth in his own defense. Promising to do *teshuvah* and to donate a large sum of money to *tzedakah* that very day, he had slunk out of Rav Elya Chaim's house. But by the time Binyamin had reached the inn and had crept upstairs to the attic rooms in which he and his wife lived, he had worked himself into an indignant fury.

How dare he! How dare he speak to me like that! Why, if word of the scene in the rav's *study ever leaks out I'll never be able to hold my head up in Lodz again.*

On the spot, Binyamin had decided that he would never forgive Rav Elya Chaim, and he had been true to his word, nursing the spark of his anger tenderly until it was a brightly glowing ember.

Now, thinking of the *rav*, Binyamin gnashed his teeth in hatred. He hated Rav Elya Chaim only a particle less than he hated his rival innkeeper, Shmuel.

And as Binyamin stood thinking these thoughts, a new

thought seeped its way into his consciousness until it had become a word. REVENGE. A terrifying word. Binyamin struggled with the word, trying to push it away, but the more he struggled the more appealing the idea seemed to him, until finally he gave up resisting altogether. *Revenge.* How good it sounded! He would wreak revenge on Shmuel and on Rav Elya Chaim, his two enemies, in one blow.

But how? A worried frown puckered up Binyamin's forehead, and then it was gone, replaced by a cunning grin.

He had a plan.

ርא%ס

The large, square dining room of the little inn was bustling with activity. People were everywhere — eating, laughing, and talking, while the help scurried about with platters and dishrags in hand, shooing the playing children from under their feet as they ran.

Shmuel stood to one side, surveying the bustling scene with a happy smile.

Baruch Hashem. Hashem has been good to me, he thought. *After that fire that wiped out my business...*

But Shmuel abruptly cut short his musings and jumped to his feet. *Here I am sitting and daydreaming like a big oaf and I've forgotten all about my boarders.* He laughed at himself as he dashed off. Soon he was running about as hard and as fast as the wildest little boy present, flashing the lodgers the warm boyish smile that made him so likable. And as he dodged his way between the tables, stopping to ask if one had enough sugar and the other enough salt — running himself to fetch the missing item — he emanated such cheerfulness that the dourest patron couldn't help being caught up in the happy spirit that pervaded the little inn.

Suddenly, Shmuel spied the stranger. Of course, almost all of the inn's lodgers were strangers to Shmuel, but this one stood out. For one thing, he was shabbily dressed, and he hardly looked the sort of person who could afford to put up at any but the most inferior inn for the night.

For another thing, he did not go right up to Shmuel. Instead he skulked in the doorway, casting uneasy glances in all directions.

Feeling Shmuel's eyes upon him, the stranger shot the innkeeper a guilty look, but to his surprise and dismay, Shmuel's eyes shone and he gave an involuntary little jump of pleasure.

He must be someone whom Rav Elya Chaim has sent, he thought happily.

Several years previously when Shmuel and his family had arrived destitute and bewildered in Lodz, and he had opened the new inn with the material assistance and the encouragement of Rav Elya Chaim, Shmuel had made a *neder*. "If Hashem helps me succeed in this new venture so that I have enough *parnassah* for my family, I will give free room and board to any person who comes to Lodz and is in need of lodging but cannot afford to pay."

And Shmuel had indeed done well.

In order to facilitate the observance of his *neder*, Shmuel had approached Rav Elya Chaim and confided his secret to him.

"I'll try to do what I can," Rav Elya Chaim assured him, a twinkle in his eyes. "There are enough poor people in and around Lodz."

But Rav Elya Chaim had sent only a trickle of needy people to Shmuel's door. The others were put up in the *rav's* own home. When Shmuel came to protest, Rav Elya Chaim apologized. But Rav Elya Chaim just couldn't let go of a guest, especially a needy one, to send him elsewhere for food and lodging. So no matter how full the house — and it was always full — another place was laid at the table and another bed dug up from somewhere. As the *rav* had finally brought himself to explain to the woebegone innkeeper, he couldn't possibly do otherwise. So Shmuel had resigned himself to fulfilling his *neder* as best he could by giving a lot of money to *tzedakah* and by showing the most royal hospitality to the few and infrequent needy lodgers Rav Elya Chaim sent his way.

So, at long last, Rav Elya Chaim had sent him another one! Shmuel was thrilled. Not wishing to embarrass the stranger, Shmuel rushed up to him, took his arm and began to propel him rapidly toward a small room off the kitchen. Once there, he closed the door and turned to look searchingly into the other man's face.

"Rav Elya Chaim?" Shmuel asked urgently, his voice barely rising above a whisper.

"What do you mean by dragging me in here? What's going on here?" the stranger demanded.

Shmuel continued to stare at the other man stupidly.

"Rav Elya Chaim?" he repeated patiently. "Didn't he send you here?"

"What kind of nonsense is this?" the stranger barked, his face red with suppressed anger. "Where is the innkeeper? Lead me to him quickly, idiot. I'll have you sacked for this impertinence!"

"I am the innkeeper," Shmuel replied quietly.

"Well, then," the stranger retorted shortly, without the slightest indication that he was embarrassed by his mistake, "I want a room for three nights."

"It can be arranged," Shmuel replied in the same low tone as he led the stranger away. Disappointment was etched in every line of the innkeeper's face, and his figure drooped.

They reached the room the stranger was to occupy, and Shmuel's train of thought was lost in the bustle of seeing to his new lodger.

But, as he gently closed the door behind him and made his way back to the crowded dining room, he could not still the sense of foreboding that swelled inside him.

ଔଯ

Shmuel advanced rapidly into the dark room and pulled up the window shade to let in a flood of sunlight. He looked carefully around the room, feeling the bedcovers for any bulky objects that might lie underneath, opening the doors of the narrow closet, and searching the shelves. He was just about to go out when he remembered that there was a drawer in the round, carved bedside table that he had neglected to open.

But the drawer did not seem amenable to Shmuel's plans, for it stuck hard: the more Shmuel pulled, the harder it stuck. Finally, Shmuel gave a tremendous tug, and with an ominous creaking, the drawer flew out and hit Shmuel, who had been holding on to its handle with all his might, squarely in the chest.

So stunned was he for a moment that he did not notice that someone else had entered the room, and that the newcomer was regarding him with a look of gleeful cunning.

"So," the voice was icy. "I see that you are in the habit of going through your lodgers' rooms after they sign out. Just in case one of them left a little something behind, eh?" The sarcasm was unmistakable but Shmuel was still too flustered to detect it.

Turning now in the direction of the speaker, he recognized him for the former occupant of the room they were in — the stranger he had mistakenly thought Rav Elya Chaim had sent.

"Oh, hello," the innkeeper exclaimed a bit breathlessly, at the same time flashing the other man a warm smile. "Did you perhaps forget something? You see, I always go through the rooms just in case someone has accidentally left something. That way I can return a lost item to its rightful owner when he comes to claim it, and I don't have to worry that anything might have been stolen from the room after the lodger has left it."

"I'll bet," the stranger muttered under his breath. "But," he addressed himself to Shmuel, "if you've been through the room, you must have found my wallet. That's why I came back, because I accidentally forgot it."

Shmuel turned first red and then white. "N-no," he stammered. "I didn't see it. Are you sure you left it here?"

"Am I sure?" the man asked in angry disbelief. "Of course I'm sure! Do you mean to tell me that it's not here? There was quite a sum of money in it and if you don't find it for me quickly —" He paused menacingly and Shmuel shuddered.

"Now, now," he said, "calm down. Let's go through the room again together. Perhaps I overlooked it the first time."

But a second and then a third search revealed nothing.

"Perhaps you lost it on the way. Perhaps you have it among your possessions," Shmuel persisted, but there was a hopeless note in his voice. "Calm yourself," he added, "you are overwrought."

The stranger, however, paid no heed. He threatened to take his case to the police unless the wallet with the stolen money was returned to him immediately.

CR ෨ට

"So you see, Rebbi," the man was saying, "I originally planned to go to the police, but then I thought better of it. After all, I haven't got any witnesses and without witnesses I haven't a leg to stand on in a court of law. That's why I came to you instead. The innkeeper himself admitted that he was the only one to enter my room after I left. It's clear that he's guilty; all the evidence points in his direction. Rebbi, I've come to you for justice!" He slammed his fist down hard on the table in Rav Elya Chaim's study, where the two of them were sitting.

Rav Elya Chaim somehow didn't trust this man. Shmuel was innocent. Rav Elya Chaim knew the innkeeper too well to harbor any reservations on that point.

"I'm sure we'll be able to find your stolen wallet," Rav Elya Chaim encouraged him. "In any event, I'll certainly do my best. Come back here tomorrow afternoon. Perhaps by then I'll have made some progress in the matter."

The stranger had just left the *rav's* house when Shmuel came running in.

"Rebbi," he panted, "forgive me for bursting in on you like this but a terrible thing has happened. I've been accused…"

"I know the whole story," Rav Elya Chaim interrupted him calmly. "Your accuser was just here. But let's have your version."

Shmuel complied and ended by saying, "Rebbi, please believe me when I say that I am innocent. After the fire that destroyed my home and business in Russia, I came here destitute, but Hashem helped me. And you helped me, Rebbi. Now if the scoundrel succeeds in casting suspicion on my inn, I am finished. You must help me, Rebbi. Help me again!"

Shmuel's words affected Rav Elya Chaim deeply.

"I believe you, Shmuel, and I'll do whatever I can," he assured him. "I hope *b'ezras Hashem* that by tomorrow evening something may be accomplished. Now go home and get some sleep."

Obediently, Shmuel went, and the *rav's* house settled into silence as one by one its members went to sleep. Only Rav Elya Chaim sat up, learning Gemara and thinking about Shmuel and the stranger — late into the night.

༺༻

There was a loud knock on the study door.

"Come in, come in," the *rav* called cheerfully. The stranger entered and Rav Elya Chaim greeted him warmly.

"I'm glad to see you. Didn't I tell you that your wallet wasn't stolen? Shmuel was here yesterday after you had left and he brought me the wallet. It seems it had fallen under the bed and he didn't notice it the first few times he looked."

Rav Elya Chaim peered at the man closely to note his reaction to the news. And a strange reaction it was! For he showed no signs of happiness at the recovery of his money. He looked startled, and his face fell.

Rav Elya Chaim had been prepared for this strange reaction. Before his listener had a chance to collect his thoughts, he hurried on.

"Of course you must describe the wallet to me, so that we can be certain that it's yours, you know. The color, the size, the amount of money it contained…"

But here the stranger broke down completely, and fell moaning at the *rav's* feet.

"Rebbi," he cried in anguish. "I never lost my wallet. It is here in my pocket."

"But why did you lie?" asked Rav Elya Chaim.

"For twenty rubles," the man answered. "Rebbi, Binyamin Katz put me up to it."

"Binyamin!"

"Yes, you know, Binyamin the innkeeper. He has always held a grudge against Shmuel for taking away part of his business, and against you, Rebbi, for, well, I guess you know the reasons yourself."

Rav Elya Chaim did know.

"Anyway, Rebbi, he wanted revenge on you both. So he thought up this plan to slander Shmuel's reputation and to stop people from frequenting his inn. Eventually he would have been forced out of business."

"But me?" Rav Elya Chaim asked sharply. "Why?"

"That's why he took his accusation to you instead of to the police. He knew that as *rav* you had to dispense justice, and of course in this case you couldn't return the money, since none was stolen. But if he claimed that his money *was* stolen, and the evidence pointed to it, yet you did nothing to rectify matters, it would be easy enough to use that as a means of blackening your reputation. And once that was accomplished, your downfall would have been imminent. Forgive me, Rebbi!"

Rav Elya Chaim retorted, "Do you think that a *rav* can be deposed like a monarch? Do you think that popularity is the determining factor? That you tried to slander me personally — that I could forgive in a second. But that you tried to slander me as a *rav*, as a leader of a *kehillah*! That I can never forgive, for it is not only I who am being slandered, but every *rav* from Russia to Eretz Yisrael. Nor can I forgive you for trying to ruin an innocent and good man. Forgiveness you want? Never! Never!"

And with these words, Rav Elya Chaim left the room, leaving the stranger to his own bitter reflections.

A. I. LAZOVIK

As the joyous Purim shpielers *make the rounds, let us remove the masks from*

Two Disguises

EARLY EVERY MORNING, Aharon the porter finds himself in the village marketplace. His eyes seek out, in every single corner, the remotest possibility that someone might give him some work: to take a package or to load merchandise onto a cart so that he might thereby earn a few coins. To his great sorrow, no such work is available for days, sometimes for weeks on end. Money is in such circumstances an obviously infrequent guest in his pocket.

"So what?" Aharon smiles to himself. "Life isn't so bad. Things could be a lot worse. After all, I've got a Father in Heaven."

Aharon spends his day going from one end of the marketplace to the other, up one street and down another. But mostly in vain. As the sun sets, he runs into the *beis medrash*, *davens* Minchah, takes it easy a bit, regains strength, and says some Tehillim till Ma'ariv.

"*Nu*, Aharon, did you make anything today?"

"Thank G-d, I really took in a lot today."

"Really, how much did you take in?"

Aharon chants peacefully, "Let's see now… *Tefillah b'tzibbur* at dawn. *Barchu* here. *Kedushah* there. Amen here and amen there… Um, how many? I really didn't count. You know it's better when you don't count. Much more *brachah*."

"And parcels? Did you get any of those today?"

"What do you mean? Of course. I dragged quite a load today. I had to carry it around with me all day."

"And what might that have been?"

"Naturally, my load of worries and troubles."

"Is it such a heavy load?"

"Ridiculous. Not at all heavy. It just gets a bit heavy toward evening when I've got to come home with empty hands, and my wife and the kids don't understand the joke."

⋄

There was one day of the year when no one was as happy as Aharon the porter. It was as if the day had been created especially for him. Or perhaps it was the other way around — that he had been created especially for this day. That was Purim; Aharon felt himself a born king. His joy would begin in the morning, right after Shacharis. On his table he had laid out his royal outfit: an old army coat with bright copper buttons, a gold-colored crown and a shiny scepter, plus a number of medals which he pinned onto his army coat and a few other little trimmings without which a king wouldn't be a king.

Amid the joyous Purim *shpielers* who went around from

house to house, Aharon the porter played a major role: he was Achashveirosh. For him it was simple pleasure, fun and joy. When Aharon was dressed in all this kingly glory, his face covered with the mask of a nobleman, it was very difficult to recognize the real Aharon the porter.

Directly across the street from the porter, in a well-constructed, well-heated home, lived Mr. Osip Grasimovitch. In the old days, the village had known him as Yoshke Knocker. Years had passed, and he had amassed a fortune, so that no one called him anything other than Mr. Grasimovitch.

Osip was busy with himself, and only himself. He ate well and he drank well. No poor man ever crossed his threshold. He had all the time in the world to devote to himself, and he did this with full fervor. He always wore the latest fashions, and ate and drank until he was perfectly satisfied. He did not neglect a single opportunity to enjoy himself.

Naturally, Mr. Grasimovitch was not the kind of man to miss an opportunity. When it came to participating in the Purim masquerade he had no intention of being left out.

Nu, exactly what costume will I choose? He chose to disguise himself as an impoverished beggar. Imagine wealthy, respected Grasimovitch joining the Purim *shpielers* dressed in rags with a faded knapsack on his back. *Ah, fantastic! My costume will be the most original of all.*

He didn't think much or long about it. He put on an old faded coat full of holes and covered with stains. He put on a stained hat that he had found in a bundle of old rags. He found himself a pair of torn shoes and an unusual mask with fallen cheeks and large black pouches under the eyes and a few straggly hairs attached to its sharp chin.

A quick look in the mirror and Grasimovitch was overjoyed.

"Beautiful! Beautiful! Such genius! I never thought I had it in me!"

And so the two neighbors, Aharon the porter and Osip Grasimovitch, celebrate Purim — each in his own way with his own disguise.

Yet I wonder. I wonder whether it might not be that on Purim of all days neither of them is disguised at all.

Translated by S.M. Leider from Bais Yaakov Monthly, *with permission*

FAYGIE BORCHARDT

Some people's lives are one long

Rush Hour

"EXCUSE ME, SIR. Would you happen to know where the home of Bartholomew Hoffenmeyer is?"

"What? Bart Hoffenmeyer of Hoffenmeyer Industries? Friend of yours?"

"Well — I wouldn't say that. I've heard a lot about him, though. They say he's practically tops on the financial ladder in this city."

"Practically? Friend, let me tell you! Did you ever hear of someone who was up before six every morning to run for the first train and be at his office early enough to do advance work on his accounts; then come home at seven, gulp down a five-minute supper and work until midnight, planning, speaking to clients, checking records… Do you know any executives who make a clean six hundred thousand during a recession? How many people did you come across whose brains are constantly ticking away, their blood tingling with business schemes — and whose hands are constantly picking up the golden fruits of their toil?"

"Remarkable! But how does a man like that have time for his family and friends?"

"Hoffenmeyer? Ha! He always looked at socializing as the lazy man's copping-out security blanket. As for his family — well, who can complain when the breadwinner always brings home the baker's finest?

"Getting ahead and not letting precious time slip away was his goal. And he pursued it as the young pursue dreams. Despite terrible migraines and extreme nervous tension — constantly going on..."

"Incredible. Well, I wish we could talk some more, but I have to take the subway back and I'd like to avoid the rush hour. So would you show me where this Mr. Hoffenmeyer lives? I'd like to present him with a proposition and —"

"I beg your pardon! Did you mean you were thinking of visiting him personally? I thought you intended to pay your respects to his family, or to see where the great man had lived..."

"What do you mean?"

"I don't see how you possibly could not have heard. Bart Hoffenmeyer died last night. Some say it was a case of severe migraine. In the marketplace, we call it a heart attack."

"I — I can't believe it! He died in the hospital?"

"No, at home. Almost immediately after the attack. Strange, within an instant a human being like that should cease to exist. But do you know what's even stranger?"

"What?"

"The last words he said while he lay dying. I don't understand it.

"Mr. Bartholomew Hoffenmeyer of Hoffenmeyer Industries looked around him, as the newspapers tell it, and whispered, 'I wish I had, just once, seen a flower.'"

"Why is that so hard to understand?"

"There were a dozen roses on his table every day."